Transformed by Evil

She expected him to scream as her fangs
punctured his soft flesh again and again,
driving venom into his body.

He did not.

He continued fighting her, shouting the words
of a prayer of dismissal.

It might have worked, had Halisstra been a demon,
but she was much more than that.

She was the Lady Penitent, higher in stature than
any of Lolth's demonic handmaidens,
battle captive and left hand of the dark elf
who had become

Lolth.

The New York Times
Best-selling Author

THE
LADY PENITENT

Book I
Sacrifice of the Widow

Book II
Storm of the Dead
September 2007

Book III
Ascendancy of the Last
June 2008

FORGOTTEN REALMS®

LISA SMEDMAN

SACRIFICE OF THE WIDOW

THE LADY PENITENT

BOOK I

The Lady Penitent, Book I

SACRIFICE OF THE WIDOW

©2007 Wizards of the Coast, Inc.

Cover art by Wes Benscoter

First Printing: February 2007

9 8 7 6 5 4 3 2 1

ISBN: 978-0-7869-4250-3
620-95916740-001-EN

U.S., CANADA,
ASIA, PACIFIC, & LATIN AMERICA
Wizards of the Coast, Inc.
P.O. Box 707
Renton, WA 98057-0707
+1-800-324-6496

EUROPEAN HEADQUARTERS
Hasbro UK Ltd
Caswell Way
Newport, Gwent NP9 0YH
GREAT BRITAIN
Save this address for your records.

Visit our web site at www.wizards.com

Also by Lisa Smedman

HOUSE OF SERPENTS

Book I
Venom's Taste

Book II
Viper's Kiss

Book III
Vanity's Brood

R.A. SALVATORE'S
WAR OF THE SPIDER QUEEN

Book IV
Extinction

SEMBIA:
GATEWAY TO THE REALMS

The Halls of Stormweather

Heirs of Prophecy
October 2007

PRELUDE

Two deities stared at each other across an immense gulf: a gate, forged between two domains. Lolth and Eilistraee, mother and daughter. Goddess of darkness and cruelty, goddess of kindness and light.

Eilistraee stood in a forest, bathed in moonlight. Branches heavy with blue-white moonstones the size of apples twined in a bower above her head. The goddess was naked, her silvery white, ankle-length hair flowing over velvet-black skin like streams of liquid moonlight. Twin swords floated in the air, one at each hip. Their silver blades vibrated softly, their blended music like women's voices raised in wordless song. Eilistraee's face was proud and perfectly formed. Those few priestesses who had gazed directly upon it were only able to recall, in tear-choked voices, that it was beautiful beyond description. Her eyes were what these mortal women remembered best: irises that held a shifting hint of blue, the elusive glint found in moonstone.

Lolth, goddess of spiders, sat on a black iron throne, its bulbous seat as bloated as an egg-filled abdomen and supported by eight segmented legs. Above her, shrieks of tortured souls filled a boiling black-and-purple sky. Lolth wore her drow form—just one of the eight aspects the goddess had fragmented into after ending her Silence. Her ebon skin was clothed in strand upon strand of spider silk that wove itself, at her shoulders, into her bone-white hair. Tiny red spiders spilled from her mouth as she spoke and dangled from her lower lip on hair-thin strands of webbing, swaying in the foul breeze. Her eyes blazed red with the reflected fires of the Demonweb Pits, but they were the only points of light on her body. Darkness seemed to fold itself about her like a cloak.

Between the two goddesses, straddling the gate, was a *sava* board. Shaped like a web and formed from a living slab of wood that was both part of the World Tree and separate from it, the board floated at waist height, suspended by its own magic. The game being played upon it had been going on for as long as mortals drew breath. Hundreds of thousands of playing pieces covered the circular board, the vast majority of them Slaves. A few thousand were of higher merit: the Priestess, Wizard, and Warrior pieces.

The usual arrangement of white pieces and black pieces did not hold in this game. All of Lolth's pieces were black as the ebon skin of a drow, as were the vast majority of Eilistraee's, yet the goddesses knew their pieces by feel. Each held a mortal soul.

Lolth had been sitting in stillness for several turns, the result of her self-imposed Silence. During that time, Eilistraee had made tremendous gains. For the first time in many, many ages, she felt confident of victory, so when Lolth stirred and proposed the addition of an additional playing piece on each side, Eilistraee's interest was piqued.

"What sort of piece?" she asked cautiously. Her mother was, above all else, treacherous.

"The Mother."

Eilistraee gave a sharp intake of breath. "We enter the game ourselves?"

Lolth nodded. "A battle to the death. Winner take all, with Ao as witness to our wager." She gave her daughter a taunting smile. "Do you agree to those terms?"

Eilistraee hesitated. She stared across the board, her face drawn with lines of pity, deep sorrow, and hope. This might end it, she thought. Once and for all time.

"I agree."

Lolth smiled. "Then let us begin." Her hands gave darkness and malice shape, creating a midnight-black spider—another of her eight aspects. She placed it on the board at the center of her House.

Eilistraee shaped moonlight into a glowing likeness of herself and placed it at the center of her House. That done, she looked up—and saw something that startled her. Lolth was no longer alone. A familiar figure crouched to the right of her throne: an enormous spider with the head of a drow male—Lolth's champion, the demigod Selvetarm. He laid his sword and mace down and spun a likeness of himself. He placed it on the board beside Lolth's Mother piece.

"Unfair!" Eilistraee cried.

"Scared?" Lolth taunted. "Do you wish to capitulate?" She leaned forward, as if to gather up the pieces on the board.

"Never," Eilistraee said. "I should have expected this of you. Play."

Lolth reclined on her throne. She glanced at the board then casually moved a piece forward. A Slave, the hood of his *piwafwi* shadowing his face, a dagger held behind his back. Strands of webbing from Lolth's hand clung to the piece then tore free as she set it down, causing it to rock gently.

Lolth sat lazily back on her throne, and said, "Your move."

A furtive movement behind Lolth drew Eilistraee's eye. A figure lurked in the shadow of her throne. An exquisitely beautiful drow male, the lower half of his face hidden by a soft black mask: Eilistraee's brother Vhaeraun. Had he slipped a piece onto the board as well—and if so, on which side? He was as much Lolth's enemy as Eilistraee's.

Perhaps he was just trying to distract her.

Ignoring him, Eilistraee studied the *sava* board. She could see now why her brother might have wanted to pull her attention away from the game. Lolth had just made a foolish a move, one that left her Slave piece completely exposed. It could easily be taken by one of Eilistraee's Wizard pieces—a piece that had entered the game only recently. She lifted the Wizard from the board, weighing its strength and will in her hand. Then she moved it forward. She set it down, nudging Lolth's piece aside.

"Wizard takes Slave," Eilistraee announced. With slender fingers, she removed Lolth's piece from the board. Her eyes widened as she took its measure and realized what it was. Not a Slave piece at all.

Lolth sat forward, her eyes blazing. "What?" Her fists gripped the knobbed legs of her throne. "That's not where I placed . . ."

She glanced behind her throne, but Vhaeraun was no longer there.

Eilistraee hid her smile as Lolth turned back to the board, a deep frown creasing her forehead. Then, abruptly, the frown vanished. The Spider Queen laughed, a fresh gout of spiders cascading from her lips.

"Poorly done, daughter," she said. "Your impulsive counter move has opened a path straight to the heart of your House."

Lolth leaned forward, reaching for the Warrior piece Selvetarm had placed on the board. She moved it along the line that led to Eilistraee's Mother. Beside her, Selvetarm watched intently, eyes gloating above the weapons he held crossed against his spider body.

"You lose," Lolth gloated. "Your life is forfeit and the drow are mine." Eyes blazing with triumph, she lowered the piece to the board. "Warrior takes—"

"Wait!" Eilistraee cried.

She scooped up a pair of dice that sat at one edge of the *sava* board. Two perfect octahedrons of blackest obsidian, each with a glint of moonlight trapped within: a spark of Eilistraee's light within Lolth's dark heart. The dice were marked with a different number on each side. The one was the round dot of a spider, legs splayed.

The dice rattled in Eilistraee's cupped hands like bones clattering together in a chilling wind. "One throw per game," she said. "I claim it now."

Lolth paused, the drider-shaped Warrior piece nearly hidden by the webbing that laced her fingers. A look of unease flickered in her red eyes then disappeared.

"An impossible throw," she smirked. "The odds against double spiders are as long as the Abyss is deep. Corellon is as likely to forgive our betrayal and call us home to Arvandor as you are to make that throw."

Anger swirled in Eilistraee's blue eyes. "*Our* betrayal?" she spat. "It was your dark magic that twisted my arrow in mid-flight."

Lolth arched an eyebrow. "Yet you accepted exile without protest. Why?"

"I knew there would be some among the drow, despite your corruption, who could be drawn into my dance."

Lolth sank back into her throne, still holding the

Warrior piece. She waved a disdainful hand, and strands of web fluttered in its wake.

"Pretty words," she said with infinite scorn, "but it's time for the dance to end. Make your throw."

Eilistraee held her cupped hands before her like a supplicant, gently rattling the dice inside them. She closed her eyes, extended her hands over the *sava* board, and let the dice fall.

CHAPTER ONE

The Year of Wild Magic (1372 DR)

Qilué leaned over the scrying font, waiting for images to coalesce in its depths. The font was of polished alabaster, its yellow-orange stone the color of a harvest moon. An inscription ran around the rim, carved in ancient Elvish characters reminiscent of the slashes left by swords. The water inside the font was pure, made holy through dance and song by the six drow priestesses who stood in a loose circle around Qilué, waiting. At the moment, however, all the water held was Qilué's own reflection, haloed by the full moon above.

Her face was beautiful still, its ebon-black skin unwrinkled, though her world-weary eyes betrayed her age. Six centuries of life weighed heavily upon her shoulders, as did the responsibilities of attending to the goddess's many shrines. Qilué's hair had been silver since birth and glowed with the same sparkling radiance as her robe. A strand of it fell across her face, and she tucked it behind one delicately pointed ear.

The other priestesses knew better than to interrupt her, despite their tense anticipation. They stood, still breathing heavily from their dance, naked bodies glistening with sweat. Waiting. Silent as the snow-dappled trees that hemmed this glade in the Ardeep Forest. It was winter, and late at night, yet the women were still too warm to shiver. The footprints left by their dance were a dark ring in the snow.

Something stirred in the water within the font, something that broke the moon's reflection into swirling ripples.

"It comes," Qilué breathed. "The vision rises."

The priestesses tensed. One touched a hand to the holy symbol that hung at her throat while another whispered a prayer. Still another raised on tiptoe in an attempt to see into the font. This vision would be a rare thing. Only the combined powers of Eilistraee and Mystra could draw aside the dark veil that had shrouded the Demonweb Pits for the last few months.

Within the font, an image formed: the face of a drow female, not beautiful, but of noble bearing. Her nose was slightly snubbed, her eyes a burning-coal red. She was dressed for battle in a chain mail tunic and a silver breastplate embossed with the sword-and-moon symbol of Eilistraee. A shield hung from one arm and she held a curved sword in her other hand: the Crescent Blade. With it, she hoped to kill a goddess.

Halisstra hacked at something with the sword— something that didn't show up in the scrying. For a moment, Qilué thought that the font's water had been stirred by the breeze that sighed through the treetops. Then she realized that those were not ripples that obscured Halisstra's face, but shimmers of light on frozen water.

Halisstra Melarn, Eilistraee's champion, was trapped under a bowl-shaped wall of ice.

The tip of the Crescent Blade poked through the ice. Halisstra stared with horrified eyes at something just beyond the range of the scrying.

"No!" she shouted.

Five streaks of magical energy shot through the hole, slamming into her. She staggered back, gasping. After a moment, she recovered. With a look of resolve on her face, she began chopping at the ice, trying to free herself.

Tension stiffened Qilué's body. If she did not find a way to intervene, all would be lost. Scrying magic was normally passive. It would channel simple detections or messages, but only imperfectly. She was one of the Chosen of Mystra, though, and the silver fire was hers to command. She let it build within her until it sparked from her hair and crackled the chill air around her, then she directed it downward with a finger. It streaked into the water, hissing toward its target. The hemisphere of ice enclosing Halisstra sparkled briefly, as if each crystal was a glinting mote.

Halisstra's next sword blow shattered it.

Halisstra burst from the collapsing ice, already running. She passed the body of a drow female whose throat had been slit. It was the priestess Uluyara. Dead.

Qilué fought down the lump in her throat. Uluyara's part was done. She was with Eilistraee.

Halisstra ran, shouting, toward a drow female who held a dripping adamantine knife in her right hand and a whip with five writhing serpent heads in her left. That would be Quenthel, leader of the expedition from Menzoberranzan, a high priestess of Lolth. She had turned her back on Halisstra and was walking disdainfully away. A male drow walked beside Quenthel, his once elegant clothes torn and travel-stained. He must be, Qilué decided, the wizard Pharaun.

Halisstra had described for Uluyara each of the

members of the expedition that had gone to Ched Nasad, and Uluyàra had passed those descriptions on to Qilué. Quenthel and Pharaun had been mere names when Uluyara had come to the Promenade to discuss with Qilué what must be done, but they had become a threat that seemed very close at hand, despite the vast distance that lay between them and Qilué.

"Stop, Baenre!" Halisstra shouted at their backs. "Face us and let's see which goddess is the stronger."

The priestess and her male ignored Halisstra. They strode to a fissure in a high stone wall: the entrance to a tunnel. Translucent shapes—the moaning souls of the dead—flowed past them into the tunnel. As the souls entered it, their moans rose to howling shrieks. Quenthel spoke briefly with Pharaun, then stepped forward into the passage and was swallowed by the darkness.

"Face us, coward," Halisstra shouted at the male.

Pharaun spared her a brief, undecided glance. Then he too stepped forward into darkness and disappeared.

Halisstra faltered to a halt at the mouth of the tunnel. The hand that gripped the Crescent Blade shook with anger.

Qilué touched a finger to the water, above Halisstra's image. "Follow them, priestess," she instructed. "At the other end lies Lolth. Remember your quest."

Halisstra didn't answer—if indeed she had heard. Something more immediate had captured her attention: a drow female with striking pale gray eyes who moved toward Halisstra, a morningstar held loosely in one hand. The female—it could only be Danifae, Halisstra's battle-captive—apologized to her mistress, an apology that was patently insincere to Qilué's ears. Yet Halisstra made no move to raise her weapon. Did she think that Danifae might yet be brought into the light?

Qilué touched the water. "Do not trust her, Halisstra. Be wary."

Halisstra made no reply.

A third figure ambled into range of the scrying: a draegloth. Half demon and half drow, it had four arms, a snarling, bestial face and blood-matted mane of tangled off-white hair. It paid Danifae no attention; it clearly trusted her.

Qilué's apprehension grew.

Halisstra stood her ground as the draegloth loomed over her. Staring defiantly up into its eyes, she told it that its mistress had abandoned it.

She raised the Crescent Blade and vowed, "I'll have your heart for killing Ryld Argith."

Qilué watched, concerned that Halisstra was no longer paying attention to Danifae, despite the fact that the battle-captive was easing behind her. The spiked ball of Danifae's morningstar swung slightly as she lifted it.

"Halisstra!" Qilué shouted, but the priestess didn't turn.

Ordinary mortals could employ only two senses through a scrying, those of sight and hearing, but Qilué was no ordinary mortal. Gripping the edges of the font with both hands, she sank her awareness deep into its holy water then into the mind of Halisstra herself. It was a desperate gamble—so linked, Qilué might suffer whatever wounds Halisstra took—but the priestess had to be warned of the impending treachery. Somehow.

Qilué gasped as her awareness blossomed inside Halisstra's body. All of Halisstra's senses were hers. Qilué could smell the harsh, hot wind that howled through the chasm behind her, could feel the aching chill of the souls that streamed past overhead, and she could smell the foul breath of the draegloth as it sneered down at her.

"My mistress has not abandoned me, heretic," the draegloth spat.

From inside Halisstra's awareness, Qilué could see that the priestess was not alone. Some distance behind the draegloth stood a moon elf with pale skin and dark brown hair: Feliane, the other priestess who had accompanied Halisstra on her quest. Feliane panted, as if she'd just been in battle, but the thin-bladed sword in her hand was unbloodied. She moved toward the draegloth with faltering steps, hugging her ribs with her free arm, and wincing with each inhalation of breath.

Danifae was fully behind Halisstra, and the priestess could no longer see her. Qilué fought to turn Halisstra's head in that direction, but Halisstra's attention remained wholly fixed on the draegloth. She trusted the woman—saw her not as a battle-captive seething with a thirst for revenge, but as an ally. A friend.

Qilué shouted from inside Halisstra's head. "Halisstra! Behind you! Watch Danifae!"

Too late. Qilué's awareness exploded into pain as Danifae's morningstar slammed into Halisstra's back, smashing the priestess to her hands and knees.

Halisstra understood it all then. The pain of betrayal was even greater than the sharp ache of her shattered ribs.

You could have warned me, Halisstra thought.

The bitter rebuke was directed at Eilistraee, but it was Qilué who answered, *I tried.*

Halisstra, at last hearing her, nodded weakly.

Danifae's morningstar slammed into her back a second time, knocking her to the ground. She dimly heard Danifae give an order to the draegloth, then its bestial roar.

Feliane answered with a battle song.

Danifae's fingers twined in Halisstra's hair and yanked her head up.

"Watch," Danifae said, her voice a harsh gloat.

Qilué did, through Halisstra's eyes. Feliane wounded the draegloth, but the monster didn't even slow. He slammed Feliane to the ground and began tearing at the priestess's body with his fangs.

Feliane screamed as her stomach was torn open.

Halisstra's vision blurred with tears.

Another gone to Eilistraee. Only Halisstra was left, and her mind was filled with despair and doubt.

"Have faith, Halisstra!" Qilué cried. "Eilistraee will—"

Danifae slammed a fist into Halisstra's temple. Sparks of pain exploded inside Qilué's mind as well, disrupting her awareness. She fought to cling to it as Halisstra coughed, weakly, blood dribbling from her lips. Halisstra turned her head slightly, looking up at Danifae. The other drow swung her morningstar in a lazy arc, her face ugly with cruel mirth.

Halisstra's despair brimmed over. *I am not worthy*, she thought. *I have failed*.

"No!" Qilué shouted. "You—"

Too late. She lost the connection. Her awareness was back in her own body, and she stared into the font. Perhaps it was not too late. She summoned silver fire and stabbed a finger into the water, unleashing a beam of pure white flame. Instead of blasting Danifae, however, the magical flame skipped off the surface of the holy water like a stone and ricocheted into the night.

The water in the font rippled, obscuring the scrying. Qilué could see movement—fragmentary glimpses of what was going on. A flash of silver: the Crescent Blade, picked up by Danifae and tossed contemptuously aside. The head of a morningstar, swinging in a deadly arc. Halisstra's eyes, brimming with tears. Danifae's face, twisted with hatred as she spat. Sound was likewise garbled. Halisstra's voice, faintly whispering, "Why?" Danifae's voice, haughty and triumphant: ". . . weak."

Qilué thrust a hand at the moon, clutching desperately for some other magic that could be channeled through the scrying.

"Eilistraee!" she cried. "Hear me! Your Chosen needs your aid!"

Behind her, the six lesser priestesses shot uneasy glances

at one another. They crowded closer, prayers tumbling from their lips. "Eilistraee," they crooned. Swaying, they placed their hands on Qilué's shoulders, lending power to her prayer. Silver fire built once more around Qilué, brighter than before, but slowly. Too slowly.

The ripples in the font cleared. Words bubbled up from its depths. Danifae's voice, gloating.

"Good-bye, Halisstra."

Then the whistle of a descending morningstar.

Qilué heard a dull *crunch*, a sound like wet wood splintering. She looked down and saw collapsed bone and blood where Halisstra's face had been.

"No!" she cried as the image slowly faded from the font.

She plunged a hand into the water as if trying to pluck Halisstra from it. Holy water slopped over the edges of the font, trickling down its smooth stone sides like a flood of tears. Qilué channeled everything she had into one last spell and felt the water grow as warm as blood. Eilistraee had granted her the power to heal the most grievous of wounds with a touch. Even if Halisstra had slipped beyond life's door, Qilué could resurrect her with a word, but could the spell reach her? Would it have any effect in the domain of Eilistraee's greatest enemy?

It might. Lolth was silent, after all, her priestesses bereft of their power. That was why Halisstra had been sent on this quest, except that *something* had turned Qilué's last spell, and the souls streaming into the darkened tunnel had been moving towards . . . something.

The font was quiet and still. Images no longer filled it. Qilué lifted her dripping hand from the water.

One of the priestesses leaned closer, stared down into the font's blank depths. "Mistress Qilué," she whispered—mistakenly addressing her, in a moment of extreme tension, as a drow of the Underdark would address her matron. "Is she . . . dead? Is all lost?"

The other priestesses held their breath, waiting for Qilué's reply.

Qilué glanced up at the moon. Eilistraee's moon. Selûne shone brightly, not yet diminished, the Tears of Selûne twinkling in its wake.

"There is still hope," she told them. "There is always hope."

She needed to believe that, yet deep in her heart was a sliver of doubt.

Qilué stood beside the font for the rest of the night. The other priestesses crowded around her for a time, and she answered their nervous questions as soothingly as she could. When at last they fell silent, she sought to touch the mind of Eilistraee.

In a moonlit glade, deep in a forest that needed only the moon's light to thrive and grow, she found her goddess. Eilistraee was a drow-shaped glimmer of unspeakably beautiful radiance. Qilué touched that with her mind. She needed no lips to frame her question. The goddess poured moonlight into her heart, throwing the words that were scribed upon it into sharp relief. She answered in a voice that flowed like liquid silver.

"House Melarn will aid me yet."

Qilué sighed her relief. All was not lost. Not yet. If Eilistraee had indeed heard Qilué's prayer and revived Halisstra, there was still a chance that the Melarn priestess would slay Lolth.

"And House Melarn will betray me."

The glow that was the goddess flickered and grew dim.

Qilué started. Her awareness was back in her body again. She stood in the forest beside the font, the connection with her goddess at an end. The priestesses who had aided in her scrying were seated on the ground, clothed. Snow dusted their hair and shoulders. More snow fell and the sun was rising, a blood-red smudge against the clouds to the east. Much time had passed since Qilué had slipped into communion with Eilistraee, and the hand that gripped the edge of the font was covered in snow. She shook it off and shivered.

Something was wrong. She could feel it in the sick hollow that had opened in her stomach. Turning to the font, she cast a second scrying. Far easier than the first had been, its target was on Toril, at least, not in some deep hollow of the Abyss. The target was the matron mother of one of the noble Houses of Menzoberranzan—a priestess of Lolth. Qilué leaned closer and saw that the drow was wielding magic.

Sensing Qilué scrying her, Lolth's priestess stared a challenge at her observer. Wild laughter, joyous and cruel, bubbled from the font as she began a magical attack.

Qilué had seen enough. She ended the scrying.

One of the priestesses of Eilistraee who had waited with Qilué rose to her feet. "Lady Qilué?" she asked. She sounded nervous, uncertain. "Is something wrong?"

The other priestesses also rose, some whispering tense prayers, others silent with dread anticipation.

Qilué closed her eyes. Her shoulders slumped in defeat. "Halisstra has failed," she told them. "Lolth lives. Her Silence is broken."

CHAPTER TWO

The Month of Uktar,
the Year of Risen Elfkin (1375 DR)

Q'arlynd stood, hands laced together behind his back, at the broken lip of what had once been a broad street of calcified webbing. Across the wide chasm he could see a jagged protrusion, the spot where the street had anchored to the far wall. Similar protrusions dotted the walls above and below him. The city that had filled the vast cavern had been more than a hundred layers deep. This once-intricate stone web lay in a shattered heap far below, together with fragments of the noble Houses, temples, and academies that had hung from it like glowing pendants. The magical glow that had suffused the stone was all but extinguished, hidden under the scab of mold and fungi that had grown in the three years since the city's fall.

He shivered. The air was cool and moist, humidified by the constant trickle of water that dampened the cavern walls. He'd grown up in Ched Nasad, but a century of life there still hadn't inured him to the climate. He could feel the chill deep in his bones.

Ched Nasad had once been home to nearly thirty thousand drow. Perhaps one-tenth of that number remained, scrabbling out an existence in the ruins while trying to salvage whatever the duergar stonefire bombs hadn't burned. And fighting. Always fighting. Only a handful of the hundred or so noble Houses had survived the fall of the city—Houses of no consequence whose strongholds had been at the less desirable, outer edges of the web, against the damp cavern walls. They squabbled amongst themselves still, unable to come together in an alliance that might rid what remained of the city of its Jaezred Chaulssin masters.

Somewhere under that dark jumble of stone lay the ruins of House Melarn. It had been the first of the noble Houses to fall, and it had taken a good chunk of the city down with it, which was fitting, since House Melarn's matron—Q'arlynd's mother—had been murdered by those below her. That murder had set the other eleven noble Houses squabbling with one another, rendering them unable to meet the duergar threat.

"Divided we fall," Q'arlynd murmured.

He lifted his left arm and stared at the House insignia he wore on a wide leather band around his wrist. Carved into the adamantine oval was House Melarn's symbol, a glyph vaguely reminiscent of a stick-figure person, arms bent and one leg raised as if dancing. The insignia counted for little now. Q'arlynd was the only one of his House to survive, and he was male. Since inheritance and title passed through the female line, he could make no claim on any of the property that had been salvaged from the ruins of his former home. He'd had to watch, powerless, as it was looted by others.

Lowering his hand, he leaned forward to stare down at the bulge, low on the opposite wall, that was the domicile of House Teh'Kinrellz—the House he had reluctantly offered his services to after the city's fall. Below it was a depression in the rubble: the salvage excavation. The uncovered stones glowed faintly with faerie fire, a jumble of lavender, indigo, and crimson that looked like an iridescent puddle from above. A platform slowly rose over the hole as it was winched up from a high ledge. The dozen dark shapes slumped on it would be the slaves, exhausted from a cycle of digging.

The effort seemed futile. Though some magical treasures must have survived the fall, so deeply did they lie buried that excavating them would have taken an army of dwarves and the better part of a century. The efforts of House Teh'Kinrellz offered one thing, however—a semblance of organization. Under the leadership of that once-insignificant House, the drow of Ched Nasad might yet reclaim their cavern.

Q'arlynd snorted with bitter laughter. Who was he fooling? The city was as likely to be reclaimed as rothé were to suddenly sprout wings and fly.

Stone shifted under his left foot. It gave him the instant's warning he needed to pull his foot away. A chunk of stone tumbled from the edge, smaller fragments falling in its wake. Q'arlynd listened but couldn't hear them land. The bottom of the cavern was too far below.

Enough of this.

He closed his eyes, inhaled deeply, and took a step back from the edge, then another. He ran forward, flinging himself into space.

The air snatched at his *piwafwi* as he fell, yanking its hood back from his head. It pressed his shirt and trousers against his body and plucked at his shoulder-length white hair, turning it into a ragged streamer. He opened his eyes, feeling the wind squeeze tears from them. He flung out his arms to let air whistle through his splayed fingers. His heart hammered wildly in his chest, and it felt as though his stomach flattened against his spine. Grinning, he watched in morbid fascination as the floor of the cavern rushed up to meet him. That jumble of stone below—that was death.

Closer, closer . . .

Now!

Q'arlynd mentally shouted a command, activating the magic of his House insignia. His body jerked to a halt so close to the ground that his neck purse bounced off an up-thrust slab of stone. In the instant that he went from falling to levitating, his vitals felt as if they were being pulled from his body by an invisible hand. Bright sparkles of light crackled across his vision. Blackness roaring with blood nearly claimed him, but he shook it off and fought down the urge to vomit.

He floated, dizzy but exultant. A laugh burst from his lips, wild as that of the victim of a hideous mirth spell. Then he got hold of himself. It wasn't the first time he'd free-fallen from a great height. As a student at the Conservatory, he'd competed with the other novice mages to see who had the most nerve, but that had been years ago.

Never had he come so close to hitting the ground.

Twisting his body upright, he gave a second mental command, one that would summon a driftdisc to carry him back to House Teh'Kinrellz. As he waited for it, something caught his eye. The body of a drow female lay on the rubble. A corpse in the fallen city was unremarkable in itself, but he hadn't heard of any recent quarrels, and the body looked fresh.

Very fresh.

He sank to the ground, landing gracefully. The back of the female's head looked like a hollow, broken cup.

Something had smashed it in. The patch of red that stained her hair and the rubble she lay on was still spreading.

Q'arlynd looked around warily, certain he'd just interrupted something, but he didn't see anyone nearby. Even a glance through his crystal revealed no invisible enemies lurking nearby. Tucking the magical quartz back into his pocket, he cast an incantation that revealed obvious magical items on the dead female—the sword in her scabbard, her boots, two rings on an outflung hand. Mediocre dweomers all.

As Q'arlynd stepped closer on shifting rubble, part of the mystery resolved itself. A chunk of calcified web, also bright with blood, lay near the corpse's feet.

"By the Dark Mother," he whispered. He looked up, trying to calculate the odds of the stone that had been dislodged by his foot falling in precisely the right spot to strike the female on the head. Lolth's work, surely.

He shook his head.

Kneeling on the unstable rubble, he rolled the body over to see if she wore a House insignia. She did not, but there was a silver chain around her neck that held a sword-shaped pendant with blunted edges. On the blade was engraved a circle on which a sword was superimposed—the holy symbol of Eilistraee.

The pendant emitted an aura of magic. Q'arlynd nearly left it where it was, but the mystery of what a priestess of a forbidden faith was doing in Ched Nasad intrigued him. He broke the chain and slipped the pendant into a pocket. It would prove useful, should he ever need to cast doubt on someone's loyalties.

The priestess looked young, perhaps still in her first century of life. Her forehead didn't yet have frown lines. Q'arlynd didn't recognize her. Perhaps she was a scavenger, come to Ched Nasad in search of plunder.

His lips twitched at the irony of it. All she'd harvested from the ruin was death.

He eased the rings from her fingers and pocketed them. Then he slid her sword half out of its scabbard. The blade gritted against something. Sand had found its way into the scabbard. The blade was steel, rather than adamantine, and filigreed with gold. It looked like something the surface elves had made. It wasn't something Q'arlynd wanted to keep. He preferred fighting from a distance, with spells. He slid it back into its sheath and continued to search the body.

A dozen tiny swords hung from a metal loop attached to the priestess's belt. They reminded Q'arlynd of keys on a ring, though their edges had no notches. They were silver and shaped like the pendant but not magical. On an impulse, he unfastened them from her belt and pocketed them, too. He felt around inside her pockets but found nothing of interest. The insides of her pockets were also gritty—more sand. Her clothes, however, were dry, so it wasn't river sand.

He yanked the boots from her feet. They were too large for him at the moment, but their magic would shape them to his feet, assuming he decided to keep them and not barter them away. One of the boots had several tiny spines embedded in its sole, and at the end of each of the spines was a moist chunk of green plant flesh. She must have stepped on a spiny plant. Q'arlynd sniffed them, but the scent wasn't one he recognized.

He plucked the spines out and tossed them aside, then stroked his chin with a forefinger. "A surface plant?" he mused aloud.

He stood, contemplating the mystery the priestess presented. That she'd used magic to reach Ched Nasad was clear. The vegetable matter on the spines was still fresh, which it wouldn't be if she'd walked to the ruined city through the Underdark. She couldn't have teleported there. The *Faerzress* that surrounded the ruined city would have made the odds of arriving on target about as unlikely as . . .

Well, as unlikely as winding up in the precise spot for a rock, dislodged by a foot above, to strike her dead.

A portal, perhaps?

If there was a portal, it was something Q'arlynd wanted to keep to himself.

Knowing that others might see the body and draw the same conclusions he had, he touched it and spoke the words of a spell. The body vanished from sight. A second spell ensured that the invisibility would remain in place. Straightening, he reached into a pocket for a tiny length of forked twig, and spoke a divination. He closed his eyes and slowly turned, the twig in his hand.

There. A faint tug at his consciousness caused him to lean forward.

Opening his eyes, he set out across the shifting rubble. He'd only gone the equivalent of a dozen paces when he saw a horizontal crevice between two slabs of rock—an opening just large enough for a drow to worm through on her belly. The mental tug came strongly from within.

He kneeled and peered inside. At the back of the crevice, something glowed with an eerie purple light: magical script, arranged in a semi-circle along the curved top of a half-buried arch. He'd been right! The dead priestess *had* arrived through a portal. The top half of the arch was clear. The rubble that had previously hidden it from view must have tumbled through the portal after it was activated. The lower half of the arch was still hidden by an enormous slab of fallen stone. Still, enough of the portal was clear for it to be useful.

And—here was the truly amazing thing—he'd seen that portal before. It was the one he'd led his sister and her companions to, three years ago, as they fled the collapsing city.

He rocked back on his heels, amazed at the coincidence.

Remembering.

The portal had been inside the Dangling Tower. Q'arlynd had led Halisstra and her companions to it, only to be confronted by the portal's protector, an iron golem. The golem had attacked the group, driving them back from the portal and seizing Q'arlynd. When a fissure opened in the floor beneath the golem, it had fallen through, dragging Q'arlynd along as well. Q'arlynd had been in the clutches of the golem, falling, as the stalactite that housed the Dangling Tower tore free of the cavern's ceiling and plunged down through the city, careening off the streets and buildings below. He'd escaped the golem by teleporting away in mid-fall.

He'd assumed that his sister and her companions had been killed when the tower smashed to pieces on the cavern floor far below. He hadn't even bothered to search for Halisstra's body, thinking it would lie buried deep in the rubble, but the survival of the portal presented a new possibility. Perhaps Halisstra had managed to escape through it as the tower was falling. If so, she might still be wherever it led. She, too, would have assumed her sibling was dead. The last she'd seen of Q'arlynd he was in the grip of a golem dragging him to a certain-death fall. She likely would have heard of the city's complete destruction—which would explain why, if she was still alive, she hadn't returned to Ched Nasad.

If Halisstra *was* alive and Q'arlynd could locate her, he might be able to improve his lot. Instead of being a vassal to another House—little better than a slave, really—he would once again be part of a noble House. It would, of course, be a House of two, but time would remedy that. House Melarn would rise again.

He took a deep breath, forcing himself to slow down. Halisstra may not have even made it through the portal, he reminded himself. Her skeleton might very well be somewhere under the heap of rubble on which he squatted. He would not allow himself to hope. Not yet.

A sighing noise behind him made him whirl, his free hand reaching for the wand sheathed at his hip, but it was only the driftdisc he'd summoned earlier. It could just as easily, however, have been one of his enemies. He chastised himself for letting his guard down. It was a stupid thing to do, if one wanted to keep on living.

And Q'arlynd wanted very much to do just that.

He glanced back at the arch. The script no longer glowed. It should be a simple enough matter to re-activate the portal—the inscription was in Draconic, which Q'arlynd could read—but he wasn't about to step blindly into unknown territory, not without learning all he could about the dead priestess. She had, after all, come from wherever the portal led to.

He took a careful look around, noting landmarks in the rubble. Then he settled himself cross-legged on the driftdisc and sped away.

Nearly three hundred leagues to the east, in a little-visited section of the sprawling underground labyrinth known as Undermountain, a Darksong Knight and a novice priestess of Eilistraee patrolled a dark cavern that wound its way past several natural columns of stone. Nearly a thousand years ago, the cavern had been one arm of a sprawling Underdark city. The drow who built that city were long gone—consumed by the slimes and oozes they had venerated—but traces of what they built could be seen still. The columns and walls, for example, were carved with notches that had once served as hand-holds and footholds. Holes in the cavern ceiling were the entrances to buildings that had been hollowed by magic out of native stone. Still more holes, arranged in intricate, lacelike patterns, had served as windows in the floors of these buildings. Some of the clearstone in these windows was still intact, but centuries of accumulated bat guano had obliterated any view inside.

The Darksong Knight pointed out those details as they walked along. "We only recently claimed this area. We hope to incorporate it into the Promenade, one day," Cavatina told the novice. "For now, though, it's home only to dire bats, cloakers, crawlers—and the occasional adventurer who blunders in and manages not to get eaten by the first three."

The novice obliged Cavatina by smiling. Her posture, however, was tense. Her eyes kept straying to the dark holes in the cavern ceiling above. Understandable, Cavatina thought. It was Thaleste's first patrol south of the Sargauth River. The novice had trained for two years but had yet to blood her sword. She'd spent all that time within the safe confines of the Promenade—the name Eilistraee's faithful had given the temple that lay on the other side of the river. Cavatina could hear the low gurgle of the Sargauth still, but the comforting sounds of the Cavern of Song lay far behind.

She pointed to a spot on the floor. "You see this smooth patch?" she asked.

The novice nodded.

"A slime passed this way, long ago, but it, along with the rest of the minions of the god of oozes and slimes, was driven into the Pit of Ghaunadaur. Which is . . . ?" she prompted.

The novice spoke solemnly. "The pit in which the Ancient One was imprisoned by Eilistraee's Chosen, Qilué, First Lady of the Dance. She built Eilistraee's Mound to mark the spot where Ghaunadaur was defeated."

"Where his *avatar* was defeated, Thaleste," Cavatina corrected. "Ghaunadaur himself still lurks in his domain. That is why we patrol these dark halls—why we have built our temple here. We must ensure that his avatar never rises again."

Thaleste nodded nervously.

Cavatina smiled. "It's been a long time since anything oozed through these halls," she reassured the novice. "About six hundred years."

Another nervous nod.

Cavatina sighed to herself. Novices were not, as a rule, allowed to venture into truly dangerous areas, even with a seasoned Darksong Knight accompanying them. There was little there for Thaleste to fret about. The purpose of the patrol was simply to check the defensive glyphs and symbols that had recently been set there and report any that needed to be restored.

They continued on through the cavern, a novice in simple leather armor, and a warrior-priestess in a mithral chain mail shirt, her steel breastplate embossed with her goddess's symbols. Each female had a sword sheathed at her hip, next to a dagger. The Darksong Knight carried a hunting horn as well, slung from a strap that crossed one shoulder. Both priestesses were drow, their ebon skin blending with the darkness, their white hair and eyebrows standing out in stark contrast.

Cavatina, despite her vastly higher station, was still in her first century of life. Barely adult, by drow standards. The daughter of a Sword Dancer, she had her mother's lean, wiry build. She was tall, even for a drow female. Most of the other priestesses came only to her shoulder. Only Qilué herself was taller. During Cavatina's youth, there had been innumerable teasing about her being long and narrow as a sword blade but blunt as a maul when it came to speaking her mind.

Thaleste, on the other hand, was well into middle age, her body soft after decades of sloth. She had come to Eilistraee's faith only recently after a life of pampered luxury in one of the noble Houses of Menzoberranzan. Her motive for leaving that city had been far from holy. She'd angered her matron and barely survived the poison that had been slipped into her wine. She had been headed for

Skullport for some poison of her own when she'd taken a wrong turn and blundered into the Promenade—a fork in life's path she later understood to be the unseen hand of Eilistraee.

Thaleste had gone from being a lazy, self-indulgent viper to a fervent worshiper who had embraced the goddess wholeheartedly, once she understood what the worship of Eilistraee truly meant. When that enlightenment had come, she'd wept openly, something a drow of the Underdark never did. She later confided in Cavatina that it had been the first time in two and a half centuries that she'd allowed herself to *feel*.

Cavatina had heard it many times before. She'd been born into Eilistraee's worship, seen many conversions. She envied each and every one. She herself would never know the moment of rapture redemption could bring. Though she had—and she smiled—experienced the intense exhilaration of skewering one of Lolth's demonic minions on her sword. More than one, in fact.

She sighed. Compared to a demon hunt, patrolling was dull work. She almost hoped that a cloaker *would* swoop down from the ceiling. She patted the bastard sword at her hip. Demonbane would make short work of it. The sword might not hum as prettily as the temple's singing swords, but it had seen Cavatina through more battles than she could count.

They continued through the cavern, checking to make sure that none of the magical symbols had been dispelled. Each symbol was as large as a breastplate, painted prominently on a wall, floor, or column where those passing through the cavern couldn't help but glance at it. The symbols had been painted using a paste made from a blend of liquid mercury and red phosphorus, sprinkled with powdered diamond and opal. Attuned to Eilistraee's faithful, the symbols could be safely stared at by her priestesses and lay worshipers, but anyone with evil intentions who so much as glanced at a symbol would trigger it, as would any cleric who served Eilistraee's enemies. Cavatina pointed out for Thaleste the difference between those symbols that caused wracking pain, and those that sapped strength.

"None that kill?" the novice asked. "Why not slay our enemies outright?"

"Because for all drow, there is a chance of redemption," Cavatina answered. Then she smiled grimly. "Though for some, the chance is much slimmer than for others. That's what our swords are for. Once an intruder is debilitated, we give her one chance. She can live by the song—or die by the sword."

Thaleste nodded, her eyes bright with tears. She'd made that very choice, just two years ago.

They moved on, softly singing the hymn that disabled the cavern's other magical protections. Tiny bells, hanging from silver threads, had been secreted here and there among the columns. Capable of detecting anything that moved in the cavern without singing the proper wards, the bells were ensorcelled to sound a clamorous alarm that could be heard dozens of paces away. A silence spell could muffle the sound, but the spell would have to be cast several times over—once per bell—and each bell's hiding place would have to be found first.

All of the bells Cavatina randomly selected to inspect were in place; none had been disturbed. Each rang with a clear *ping* when Cavatina flicked it with a fingernail.

Just like the Promenade itself, the caverns were protected not only by visible defenses but also by less tangible magic. Forbiddance spells had been put in place with sprinkles of holy water and wafts of incense, invisible to any who did not have the magic to detect them. They were a potent barrier, one that prevented enemies from teleporting or shifting there—even in astral or ethereal form. The forbiddance spells were permanent, and only the most powerful of spellcasters could remove them. The only way to bypass them was with one of Eilistraee's holy songs, and even that held no guarantee of safety. Those who used the song to slip past the magical barrier would, if of evil intent, arrive with grievous wounds—possibly even fatal ones.

The cavern narrowed, and the floor rose and fell. The priestesses clambered over half-formed stalagmites that looked like sagging lumps of dough. Several times, Thaleste's scabbard scraped against the soft limestone, tracing a faint line. The novice had a lot to learn about moving silently.

"The cloakers are going to have ample time to spring an ambush, with all that noise you're making," Cavatina warned her.

Thaleste was breathing hard from her exertions. Her face darkened in a blush. "My apologies, Mistress."

"Dark Lady," Cavatina corrected. "There are no matron mothers here."

"Dark Lady. My apologies."

Cavatina accepted the apology with a nod.

Eventually, they reached the spot where the cavern ended. The ceiling was low enough that Cavatina could have touched it. A faint breeze issued from a crack above her head. A narrow chimney, barely as wide as her shoulders, twisted up to the surface. She watched as Thaleste peered up into the opening.

There was movement inside the chimney—a flutter of wings. Thaleste shrieked as something small and black burst out of it. Cavatina, who had started to draw her sword even as Thaleste flinched, slid it back into its sheath. She stared at the creature as it flew away, squeaking.

"A bat." She sighed. "The next time something comes hurtling at you, Thaleste, try drawing your sword or casting a spell." She nodded at the chimney. "Now check the glyph."

Thaleste, blushing, murmured a prayer, casting a detection spell. Just inside the chimney, a glyph sprang into luminescence, sparkling like the light scattered by a diamond. Frowning in concentration, Thaleste studied its outlines, her finger tracing through the air in front of it.

"A songblast glyph," she announced at last, letting the glow fade. "Untriggered. Nothing evil has passed this way." Her shoulders relaxed a little as she said this.

"Unless it was ethereal," Cavatina reminded her.

The shoulders tensed again.

"Fortunately, the ability to assume ethereal form is something that few creatures—and only the most powerful spellcasters—are capable of," Cavatina continued. "And those that are capable of ethereal travel have no need for entrances like this one. They can pass through solid stone."

Thaleste swallowed nervously and glanced at the wall next to her out of the corner of her eye.

"The walls here are thick," Cavatina assured her. "Any spellcaster out on an ethereal jaunt would materialize inside solid stone long before reaching this spot."

Thaleste nodded.

"We're done here," Cavatina said. "Let's go back."

As they made their way back along the winding corridor they'd just traveled, Cavatina once again saw Thaleste startle. "Have you spotted something, Novice?"

Thaleste pointed at the ceiling. "A movement. Behind that broken window." She gave her mentor an apologetic smile. "Probably just another bat."

Cavatina chastised herself for having missed whatever Thaleste had just spotted. She should have been paying more attention. Then again, Thaleste was a nervous one. She'd only occasionally ventured outside the walls of her residence in Menzoberranzan. Her trip to Skullport had been an act of desperation. Eilistraee only knew how Thaleste had managed to survive as many decades as she had inside the City of Spiders. She was prone to seeing monsters in every shadow.

Even so, Cavatina drew her sword. The temple's battle-mistress had given specific orders to those on patrol. Any monster, no matter how small a threat it posed, was to be killed. The caverns the Promenade had recently claimed must be kept clean of vermin, and there were protocols to be followed. The use of silent speech during alerts, for example.

Stay here, Cavatina signed to Thaleste. *I'll investigate. Cast a protection upon yourself, just in case.*

Shouldn't I come with you?

No. The last thing Cavatina needed was a novice getting in the way of a hunt, and even if it turned out to be a cloaker up above, it would all be over in a few moments.

As Thaleste hurriedly whispered a protective prayer, Cavatina spoke the word that activated her magical boots. They lifted her into the air toward the window the novice had pointed at. The ceiling was perhaps a hundred paces high, and the window was one of those that had fallen away. Only a few jagged shards of clearstone hung from a hole that gaped a dozen paces wide. As Cavatina levitated toward it, a palm-sized fragment of clearstone dislodged from the remains of the window frame and fell, shattering to pieces on the stone floor below. Thaleste flinched away from it, her sword shaking in her hand.

Cavatina smiled as she rose toward the hole in the ceiling. *Something* was inside the room above. She gripped Demonbane in both hands, adjusting her grip on the worn leather of its hilt. Whatever it was, she was ready for it.

The window opened onto what had once been a grand hall. Pedestals along each wall held stone busts of those who had once inhabited the noble manor. Several of the busts had fallen and lay in pieces on the floor, but others had survived. A dais at one end of the room had probably once supported a throne. Behind the dais were the remains of a mosaic, most of its tiles long since fallen out. Enough remained, however, to show drow kneeling in submission before an altar, though the object of their veneration was indistinguishable. Side passages led off from the left and right.

All this, Cavatina took in at a glance. To all appearances, the room was as empty as any other in this area, but appearances could be deceiving. She twisted as she rose through the window, pushing off from what remained of the sill. Another piece of clearstone fell—something else for Thaleste to flinch at. As Cavatina drifted toward a more solid piece of floor, she sang a prayer. Divine magic surged out from her in a rippling circle, filling the room. If whatever was in here with her was invisible, the magic that cloaked it from sight was about to be purged.

The creature was revealed in mid-leap: a spider the size of a large dog, its spindly legs twice as long as Cavatina was tall. It came at her with its fang-tipped jaws distended, its mouth trailing drops of saliva that sparkled like golden faerie fire.

Cavatina slashed at the creature as it hurtled toward her, but the spider twisted in mid-leap, avoiding the blade. A slash that should have cleaved its body in two instead merely sliced off a couple of the bristles protruding from its cheek. Odd, that the spider had twisted its head toward the sword—it almost seemed to be trying to bite the weapon.

The spider landed on a wall and immediately flexed its abdomen toward her. As its spinnerets opened, Cavatina flung out her left hand and shouted Eilistraee's name. A shimmering, crescent-shaped shield sprang into being in front of Cavatina just in time to block the web the spider shot at her. The magical shield shuddered as the webs struck, then slowly sagged to the floor, weighed down by a mass of glowing golden webbing. Cavatina dispelled the shield, letting the sticky tangle fall.

She attacked. Releasing Demonbane, she sang a prayer

that sent the sword dancing through the air toward the monster—a feint that would allow her to mount a second attack. She expected the spider to shy away from the blade, but instead the monster watched, unmoving, as the sword, directed by Cavatina's outstretched hand, wove through the air toward it. The spider sprang from the wall, directly at the sword. Twin fangs scissored against the metal. The spider sailed past Cavatina to land upside down on the ceiling, the sword between its fangs. Then it began to chew, as if savoring the taste of the blade.

Belatedly, Cavatina realized what she must be facing. "A spellgaunt!" she cried. She yanked her hand back, trying to wrench Demonbane from its jaws, but they were locked around the sword. The spellgaunt stood utterly still for a heartbeat, a dribble of sparkling drool sliding out of the corners of its mouth. Then it spat the weapon to the ground. The sword hit the floor with a dull clank. It landed next to Cavatina's foot, its midpoint dented with a neat row of tooth marks.

That gave Cavatina an idea. She sang a prayer that called a curtain of whirling blades into being between her and the monster.

"Come on," she taunted, holding them steady over her head. "Take a bite of these, why don't you?"

The spellgaunt hungrily eyed the whirling blades—each composed entirely of magical energy—then dropped from the ceiling. With a sweep of her hand, Cavatina sent the blades into its gaping mouth, even as she dodged aside. The spider stretched its mouth wide and gulped them down as it fell, heedless of the chunks of flesh being slashed from its face. Palps were severed, multifaceted eyes imploded as blades stabbed into them, and blood dribbled from the gaping wound its mouth had become, but still the frenzied spellgaunt, standing on the floor, gulped the blades down, whipping its head this way and that to pluck them from the air. As it ate, its abdomen distended and began to quiver.

Cavatina watched, holding her breath. The spellgaunt's body burst with a loud *crack*. Bloody chunks of chitin skittered across the floor, leaving smears of pale blue blood. The spider wavered on its spindly legs, then collapsed. It lay on the floor, its jaws weakly gnashing.

Cavatina picked up her sword. The spellgaunt raised its head groggily, empty eye sockets staring sightlessly in Cavatina's direction as it strained to reach the magical items she still carried. A ragged tongue slimed her boot with blood. Cavatina drew her foot away and turned Demonbane point downward. Then she thrust. Chitin crunched as the point pierced the spellgaunt's skull and scraped against the blade as she shoved it home. The monstrous spider quivered then collapsed, dead.

Cavatina put a foot on the monster's head and yanked her sword free. She held her palm over the blade, and a quick prayer confirmed what she already knew. The weapon had been completely drained of its magic. Demonbane had slain its last foe.

She wiped the sword clean on the hem of her tunic then thrust it back into its scabbard. It stuck, momentarily, as the teeth-dented section caught on the edge of the scabbard. Cavatina forced it down. She wouldn't be drawing it again.

She stared down at the dead spellgaunt. "Abyss take you," she growled. "That was my *mother's* sword." She gave the lifeless body a kick.

Only then did she stop to wonder what a spellgaunt was doing there. She knew little about the creatures, but she didn't think they were normally capable of turning themselves invisible.

Even so, it shouldn't have been able to enter the area undetected. It was a mere animal—albeit a magical one—bereft of either a good or evil aura, but it should have triggered the alarms. Most disturbing of all, it was one of Lolth's creatures.

That alone was cause for disturbing the temple's battle-mistress.

Cavatina sang a prayer that ended with Iljrene's name. When she had the battle-mistress's attention, she sent her silent message.

I found a spellgaunt in the caverns south of the river and west of the bridge. It triggered no alarms. I killed it.

Iljrene's voice came back at once. It sounded high and squeaky, just as it did in person. *A spellgaunt couldn't bypass the alarms on its own; someone helped it get there. Begin a search. I'll send other patrols.*

Cavatina immediately bent and inspected the spellgaunt's corpse. Something on its back sparkled: diamond dust. Iljrene was right. Someone had helped the spellgaunt to bypass the alarms, someone capable of casting a nondetection spell. Those abjurations lasted only so long. Whoever had worked their magic on the spellgaunt would be close by.

Cavatina remembered Thaleste, waiting below.

She strode over to the broken window and peered down, but there was no sign of Thaleste. Cavatina hoped the novice was hiding behind a pillar somewhere. She cast a sending to Thaleste.

Where are you? What do you see?

The answer was a moment in coming. *There's another priestess down here. A dancer. I'm going over to talk to her.*

Cavatina frowned. It wasn't yet time for the evening devotions, and even if it had been, a dancer shouldn't be there. Eilistraee's faithful danced naked, save for their holy symbols. While the area was well patrolled, it still had its dangers. Venturing into it unarmored would be a foolish thing to do. Losing oneself in a dance of devotion there would be more foolish, still.

A chill slid down Cavatina's spine as she realized what Thaleste might have just spotted. She sent a second, more urgent message.

Thaleste! That may be a yochlol in drow form! They have powerful enchantments. Get away from it!

No reply came.

Cursing, Cavatina leaped through the gap in the floor. Descending swiftly, she looked around for Thaleste. She spotted movement: Thaleste's legs, disappearing behind a column. Someone—or some*thing*—was dragging her away.

Cavatina cursed. She should never have left the novice on her own. She crossed the cavern floor in great bounding leaps, levitating slightly with each step. As she ran, she cast a protection on herself. She no longer had Demonbane, a weapon that would have sliced neatly through a yochlol, even were it to shift to gaseous form, but she did have her magical horn. She raised it and blew a blast, aiming it at the column ahead. A blare of noise crashed through the cavern, rattling the loose stones on the floor and shattering the fragments of clearstone that lay there. The sound wouldn't harm Thaleste—the magical horn had been attuned to do no damage to Eilistraee's faithful—but it would stun and deafen everything else in its path, leaving larger creatures bleeding from the ears and killing lesser creatures outright. A yochlol would probably just teleport out of the blast, but at least that would drive it away from Thaleste.

Releasing the horn, Cavatina wrenched her holy symbol from around her neck. Holding it aloft, she sang a prayer. A beam of light formed around the pendant then grew until it was the length of a bastard sword. The blade-shaped moonbeam crackled with magical energy as Cavatina held it aloft.

"Come out from behind there," she shouted. "I know what you are."

A naked drow female staggered out from behind the column, hands clapped over her ears and an anguished expression on her face. For a heartbeat, Cavatina still believed it to be a yochlol—a weak one that had been damaged by the blast. Then she saw the sword-shaped pendant hanging between the female's breasts. No servant of Lolth's would wear Eilistraee's holy symbol, even a false one. When the priestess stumbled and fell to her knees, but the rubble she landed on neither shifted nor made a sound, Cavatina realized the whole thing was an illusion. She glanced up to see a mass of web hurtling down at her.

"Eilistraee shield me!" she shouted.

The magical shield appeared above her just in time to send the web sloughing off to one side. Heaving the sticky mass behind her, Cavatina sprang into the air. She could finally see what she was dealing with: an aranea, a shape-shifting spider capable of assuming humanoid form. The aranea was in hybrid form, a drow female at first glance but with a strangely articulated jaw and black bristles growing out of her head in place of hair. She wore a blood-red robe that hung heavily due to its chain mail lining, but her legs were bare. Strands of webbing dangled from the bottom of the robe that was just long enough to cover the rounded bulge of her spiderlike hindquarters. She clung to the column of stone with bare feet and her bare right hand. Her left hand was encased in a gauntlet that had a dagger blade protruding from between the knuckles. A platinum disk hung around her neck on a chain. Cavatina knew what the medallion's symbol would be by the vestments the aranea wore. She was one of Selvetarm's faithful—a Selvetargtlin.

The blast from Cavatina's horn didn't seem to have hurt her at all. The aranea had probably already been out of range above it before it sounded.

All that flashed through Cavatina's mind in an instant, followed by cold rage that the enemy had penetrated the caverns surrounding Eilistraee's temple. The aranea shouted. A pleasant humming filled Cavatina's head, but it was gone an instant later. Whatever spell the aranea had cast was too weak to affect the Darksong Knight.

Cavatina countered with one of her own, a song of smiting. The aranea reeled as it struck her, eyes rolling back in her head, but she recovered in time to leap away from the column as Cavatina came at her with the moonblade.

The aranea landed on the floor of the cavern, and Cavatina followed. She feinted with the moonblade, thrust, but the Selvetargtlin was too skilled to fall for such tactics. Suddenly she was inside Cavatina's guard, the stench of her spider musk filling the Darksong Knight's nostrils. Cavatina twisted to the side, anticipating a slash from the gauntlet blade as she shoved the enemy to arm's length once more, but the aranea instead thrust her fingers out stiffly.

"Selvetarm!" she screamed.

Blades erupted from the aranea's hands, legs, face, and scalp—even her clothing. Hundreds of them, slender and deadly. Still screaming Selvetarm's name, she flung herself at Cavatina.

It was a suicidal move. Cavatina thrust her moonblade at the aranea's chest. Any other sword might have been turned or at least slowed by the chain mail lining of the cleric's blood-red robe, but the moonblade was a thing of pure magic, like the blade barrier Cavatina had summoned earlier. It slid through the chain mail like a hot knife through soft wax, and Cavatina's hand and arm were wet with blood. Even though the thrust was to the heart, the aranea had enough fight left in her to slam her arms together, driving the spike-thin blades in through the holes in Cavatina's chain mail. Cavatina gasped in agony as they pierced her sides.

The aranea sagged against Cavatina but still did not die. Hot purple blood sprayed Cavatina's chest and face as the Selvetargtlin, her eyes rolling wildly, twisted her left arm, trying to bring her gauntlet blade to bear. The blade only managed to graze Cavatina's right cheek, but the wound throbbed as if boiling oil had been poured into it. A foul smell rose from the cut, and Cavatina could feel herself weakening with each pulse of her heart. The periapt around her neck absorbed the initial injury—the cut itself—but there was something more.

The aranea had used magic to envenom her.

Furious, she thrust the aranea away from her, screaming out as the blades tore free of her flesh. The moonblade in Cavatina's hand flared silver-white as the aranea's blood sloughed off it.

Selvetarm's priestess fell to the ground and lay there, blood bubbling from her lips. "You're too late," she said in a voice choked with blood and insane laughter. "It's already done."

A bloody hand trembled toward the holy symbol that hung at the aranea's neck. Cavatina, in agony from her many wounds and with blood running down her sides in rivulets, realized that the Selvetargtlin was trying to cast one last spell. She slashed down with her moonblade at the aranea's wrist, severing its hand. Blood rushed from the stump like water from a broken pipe. The aranea trembled then lay still.

Cavatina had just started to turn away when the body exploded, pelting her with a rain of bloody flesh and slivers of bone. She ducked then glanced at the spot where the aranea had fallen. All that lay there was a blood-soaked robe, empty and loose on the cavern floor. The largest piece of the body was the size of a fingernail.

There was no time to contemplate what had just happened. Blood loss had made Cavatina weak, and her legs felt ready to collapse at any moment. Calling upon her goddess, she sang a healing spell. Eilistraee's moonlight illuminated her body, knitting flesh and replenishing the blood she'd lost. The shallow cut on Cavatina's cheek, however, remained. It would close in time, but for a while the Selvetargtlin's dark magic would deny it the benefits of magical healing.

There was no time to worry about that, though. Cavatina hurried around the column, looking for Thaleste.

The novice lay face-down on the cavern floor, buried under a thick tangle of spiderweb. Tearing the sticky mass away, Cavatina saw a bloody puncture in the back of Cavatina's neck: a bite. The aranea's venom wasn't usually fatal—it typically sapped the strength, rather than killing outright—but in some instances it could kill. Dropping to her knees, Cavatina laid her palm across the wound and sang a prayer of healing. Under her touch, the wound closed. A second prayer drove the remaining toxins from the novice's body.

Groaning, Thaleste sat up. Cavatina placed a hand on her shoulder, steadying her. It was only then that she noticed the novice's sword lying beside her. Its tip was blooded, but just barely—whatever wound the weapon had inflicted had been slight indeed.

Thaleste touched the back of her neck with a shaking hand then stared at her fingers, obviously surprised to see no blood. She was still inexperienced enough to be astonished by the fact that another drow had come to her aid.

"Did we kill her?"

Cavatina hung her holy symbol around her neck. "We did. Your sword thrust weakened her, and I finished the job."

Thaleste smiled. A seed of confidence was in her eye, and over time, it would grow.

Cavatina whispered a prayer and sent, *Iljrene, it was a Selvetargtlin. I killed her. We were wounded but have healed.*

Iljrene's reply came at once: *Well done, but keep alert. Where there's one Selvetargtlin, there's usually more.*

Cavatina nodded, still troubled by the aranea's final words. The Selvetargtlin hadn't just been talking about the spellgaunt she'd somehow smuggled into the caverns surrounding the Promenade but about something else, something that had put an evil gleam of pleasure in her eyes even as she died.

She'd gone to her death secure in the knowledge that Selvetarm would reward her for whatever dark service she'd performed.

CHAPTER THREE

Q'arlynd pointed a finger at the jagged slab of rubble and whispered an incantation. The slab—a piece of calcified webbing that had once been part of the wall of House Ysh'nil—rose into the air, revealing a gap in the rubble beneath it.

He nodded at the svirfneblin who stood next to him. "In you go."

The deep gnome cocked his bald head to the side. His eyes, black as pebbles, studied the gap in the rubble. "Looks unstable," Flinderspeld said in a low, raspy voice.

Q'arlynd's nostrils flared in irritation. "Of course it's unstable," he snapped. "The city didn't land in neat rows, like stacked blocks. It *collapsed.*"

"I'd feel better if it was shored up first."

Q'arlynd moved his finger slightly, levitating the slab of rubble over the spot where Flinderspeld stood. He nodded meaningfully at it. "You'll feel worse if I drop this on your head."

The deep gnome shrugged. "If you do, you'll have no one to go in after whatever radiated that magical aura you saw."

Q'arlynd's eyes narrowed. He levitated the slab to one side and set it down, gently enough that the only noise it made was a slight grating of stone against stone. Then he held up his left hand and waggled his index finger—the one with the dull black ring on it, the ring whose only surviving counterpart was on Flinderspeld's own hand. "Don't make me use this."

The deep gnome glared. "All right, all right. I'm going." He clambered toward the hole, muttering under his breath.

Q'arlynd narrowed his eyes. He should discipline Flinderspeld, he knew, flay him and leave him staked out for lizards to feed on, but the deep gnome did have his uses. Like all those of his race, he showed up as little more than a blur—if at all—to anyone trying to scry him or otherwise locate him by magical means. It made Flinderspeld the perfect vehicle for carrying objects Q'arlynd didn't want found—the rings Q'arlynd had recently lifted from the body of the dead priestess, for example.

The deep gnome didn't realize he was being utilized in such a way, and he had no idea that the new clothing Q'arlynd kept bestowing upon him had items sewn inside it. He regarded these "gifts" as kindness. He'd concluded that Q'arlynd must have purchased him out of some sense of compassion, after seeing the sorry state the slavers had reduced the deep gnome to. A notion that was laughable, really. Q'arlynd's heart was as dark as that of any drow.

"I see something!" Flinderspeld called out. "It's a . . . dagger of some sort. It's silver with a thin blade, shaped more like a sword than a dagger really. It's strung on a chain like a pendant."

Q'arlynd knew this, of course. He'd placed the priestess's pendant there himself for the detection spell to reveal.

"There's a much smaller sword next to it," Flinderspeld continued. "It's no longer than my finger. Another piece of jewelry, I think."

"Bring both to me."

As Flinderspeld began crawling back through the crevice, Q'arlynd heard rubble shift behind him. That would be Prellyn, the velvet-gloved fist of Matron Teh'Kinrellz. As he'd arranged, she'd "spotted" him sneaking out of the Teh'Kinrellz stronghold earlier and had followed him here. Q'arlynd pretended to be startled by her approach.

"You've set up your own excavation, I see," she said in a voice silky with menace. "Find anything interesting?"

"Nothing." He waved a hand dismissively. "Just an empty hole."

"Liar."

Prellyn seized his chin and jerked his head up, forcing him to meet her eyes. Like most drow females, she stood head and shoulders taller than he. Red eyes smoldered under brows that pinched together in a perpetual frown. Her arms were more muscular than his own, her hands roughly calloused. The wrist-crossbow strapped to her forearm was loaded, its barbed point uncomfortably close to Q'arlynd's cheek. If he turned his head, it would gouge his eye.

"Still," Prellyn whispered, "I like a boy with some fire in his eye. A fire . . ." Her free hand drifted down between his legs, "that kindles at my command."

She kissed him. Hard. Q'arlynd felt himself responding to her touch. Her air of menace was as exhilarating as a freefall. She was going to take him. Now. And when she was done, she'd punish him for daring to scavenge on his own. Not with a whipping, like those doled out to common

House boys, but with something far more subtle. A wounding spell, perhaps, one that would burn a thousand tiny spider bites into his flesh.

He hoped it was going to be worth it.

Prellyn forced Q'arlynd onto his back atop the rubble and straddled him. She ran a finger down his nose, lingering over the spot where it had been broken decades ago. Then she yanked open his shirt.

Aroused though he was, Q'arlynd had a more pressing need. Information.

Flinderspeld was hiding in the hole, unwilling to come out. He'd blurred himself and was all but invisible, though the ring he wore allowed Q'arlynd to overhear his every thought whenever his master wished. At the moment, Flinderspeld was mentally shaking his head at Q'arlynd's infatuation for Prellyn—a drow female he knew his master feared as much as he himself did. Flinderspeld also watched for a chance to slip away and hide the magical booty his master had just found.

Sometimes, Flinderspeld could be a little too efficient.

Q'arlynd seized control of his slave's body and forced Flinderspeld to drop his magical camouflage, crawl out of hiding, and attempt to sneak away.

Prellyn's attention was drawn to the deep gnome. She stood, leaving Q'arlynd forgotten on the rubble. Her eyes locked on the pendant.

"Give me that," she ordered.

Q'arlynd made Flinderspeld hesitate. "You heard her, slave," Q'arlynd said in a harsh voice as he sat up. "Give it to her!"

Flinderspeld looked at his master, confused. What was Q'arlynd up to? Normally the wizard expected him to lie low so he could keep whatever booty he'd found to himself.

Q'arlynd, growing impatient, gave a mental jerk. The deep gnome's hand shot forward. The pendant, which

Flinderspeld held by its chain, swung back and forth like a pendulum.

Prellyn reached out to grab it then suddenly recoiled as if she'd been about to touch something smeared with contact poison.

Q'arlynd climbed to his feet. Through the rings, he could sense Flinderspeld's dawning understanding. His master *wanted* Prellyn to see the silver pendant. The deep gnome also wondered why she was so afraid of it.

Q'arlynd feigned ignorance. "What's wrong?" he asked Prellyn. He moved toward Flinderspeld and bent for a closer look at the pendant, pretending to be observing it for the first time. "Interesting emblem on the blade," he said, reaching out to touch it. "A circle and sword. If I'm not mistaken, those are the symbols of—"

The hiss of steel—a weapon being drawn from a scabbard—was his only warning. He jerked his hand back just as Prellyn's sword cut through the chain Flinderspeld was holding. Had Q'arlynd not moved, the blade might have sliced open his hand. The pendant clattered to the ground.

Flinderspeld still held the tiny sword. Q'arlynd made the deep gnome place it on a flat chunk of rock then released his mental hold on Flinderspeld, letting him ease away. He didn't want the deep gnome to wind up on the receiving end of Prellyn's wrath. If he did, Q'arlynd would be without a slave, and without a coin to his name, he couldn't buy another.

"That pendant is Eilistraee's holy symbol," Prellyn spat, her mouth twisting as if at a foul taste. "Be thankful I was here to keep you from touching it."

"I am," Q'arlynd said smoothly. He pointed. "And that tiny sword? Is it connected with Eilistraee's worship, too?"

Prellyn used the tip of her sword to flick the tiny blade into a deep crevice in the rubble. "That's not something you want to touch, either."

"I won't," Q'arlynd said, "but what is a holy symbol of Eilistraee doing here, in Ched Nasad?"

"It must have been carried here by one of her priestesses before the city's fall. They do that sometimes—come below to try to subvert Lolth's children and seduce them up to the surface realms."

"Where the simpletons who fall for it are immediately killed, no doubt."

Prellyn laughed. "How little you know, male. Eilistraee's followers actually welcome strangers into their midst."

"Any stranger?" Q'arlynd asked, thinking of his sister. "Even one of Lolth's faithful?"

Prellyn gave him a sharp look. For a moment, Q'arlynd thought she might not answer. "If the drow professes a willingness to turn to Eilistraee's worship, yes."

"But . . ." Q'arlynd furrowed his brow, pretending to work the thought out aloud. "How do they know who is lying and who is a genuine petitioner?"

"They rely on . . . *trust*," she said, switching to a word in the language of the surface elves. There was no true equivalent in either Drowic or High Drow. "They hand those tiny swords out to whoever asks for them. It is their greatest weakness, and it shows how low they have fallen. Trust among drow is like a shard of ice in lava, except that ice lasts longer."

Q'arlynd dutifully laughed at her joke, though he knew full well that no drow would ever be as stupid as Prellyn had just made Eilistraee's priestesses out to be. Assuming Prellyn was right, he'd just learned what those tiny swords were for.

"Those who are duped into turning away from Lolth are fools, of course," Prellyn continued. "Not only do they face the Spider Queen's wrath but the ravages of the surface realms as well. The sunlight blinds them, and they fall victim to strange diseases. Their armor and weapons crumble to dust, leaving them defenseless. Drow aren't meant to live on the surface. We're creatures of the Underdark—Lolth's children."

Q'arlynd nodded dutifully. Prellyn was merely repeating what the priestesses at the temple taught. His instructors at the Conservatory had provided other even more dire warnings, back when Q'arlynd had been a novice wizard, teaching that all magical items crafted by the drow lost their powers when removed from the energies of the Underdark and exposed to the light of the sun. Though that as no longer the case, they continued to admonish against journeys to the World Above.

Q'arlynd, however, didn't believe the stories of sickness and misery. He knew exaggeration when he heard it. He'd once met a drow who lived on the surface and survived there quite nicely, thank you very much, but that had been long ago.

He wondered whether Eilistraee's worship was prevalent in whatever surface realm the portal led to and whether Halisstra, if she had survived, had embraced that heretical faith. If so, it would explain why she'd never returned to Ched Nasad. Halisstra's professed worship of Lolth had always seemed, to Q'arlynd, a touch insincere.

He stroked his chin, pretending to stare thoughtfully at the rubble. "This ruin bears the glyphs of House Ysh'nil," he said, naming the minor House whose surviving members were currently a thorn in House Teh'Kinrellz's side. "Do you suppose someone in that House secretly worshiped Eilistraee?" He dropped his voice to a whisper. "That wouldn't bode well for the survivors, especially if the Jaezred Chaulssin knew of it."

Prellyn, taller than Q'arlynd by a head, stared down at him. "You're entirely too smart for a male." She touched the end of his nose almost affectionately. "This is female business. Keep your nose out of it."

Q'arlynd met her eye briefly. "I will," he promised.

Prellyn's hand fell away. She speared the point of her

sword into the soft metal of the pendant then lifted it like a trophy head. "And keep your hands off the rubble. Any salvage belongs to House Teh'Kinrellz. Find some other way to get up to mischief."

Q'arlynd bowed. "As you command, Mistress."

Prellyn snapped her fingers, summoning her driftdisc. She mounted it and whispered away, presumably to report House Ysh'nil's ancient blasphemy. So hurried was her departure, she'd forgotten to punish Q'arlynd. He was almost disappointed.

Flinderspeld peeked out from behind a slab of stone. He glanced at the departing Prellyn then at Q'arlynd, who fished the tiny sword out of the crevice that Prellyn had flicked it into and pocketed it.

Are you planning a trip to the surface, Master? he asked in the silent hand-speech of the drow.

Q'arlynd frowned. *You're entirely too smart for a svirfneblin.*

Qilué listened as the Darksong Knight made her report. Cavatina's battle with the Selvetargtlin and spellgaunt had occurred three days ago, but a breach of this nature warranted hearing the report firsthand. Thankfully, there had been no other incidents since then. Iljrene had reported that every room in the ceilings of the caverns south of the Sargauth had been inspected and found empty, save for the usual vermin, which the patrols swiftly dispatched. The magical wards in the Promenade itself had also been checked, found intact, and the seals on the Pit had not been disturbed.

The aranea's robes and equipment had been recovered, and in them was the answer to how she had broached the magical defenses. It was a ring, a gold band with three empty spaces where gems should have been. When the ring had been examined and found to be non-magical, it was very nearly dismissed as nothing noteworthy, but to Qilué's trained eye, it spoke volumes. The "trinket" had once been one of the most powerful magical items of all: a ring of wishes, with the faintest hint of an aura clinging to the setting where the third gem had been.

The aranea had been able to teleport into a heavily warded area using the ring's third and final wish. Once inside, the Selvetargtlin had used her clerical magic to render herself undetectable by the alarms. She'd brought the spellgaunt along to consume the magical energy of any symbols as they were triggered. That was why Cavatina's spell had the effect that it did. The spellgaunt was already gorged when the Darksong Knight discovered it. Consuming the magical blades conjured by Cavatina's spell had caused it to rupture, its body torn to pieces from within by the strains it had placed on the Weave.

There was no way of knowing how long the aranea had been within the area claimed by the Promenade before Cavatina discovered her. Had the symbols in the southern caverns not been permanent ones, the path the Selvetargtlin had followed might have been traced, but being permanent, they refreshed themselves soon after they were triggered.

Thus the Selvetargtlin's goal in penetrating the area remained a mystery. An inventory of the temple had found nothing missing. Nothing had been desecrated, and nothing was disturbed, yet the aranea's mission had been of great import, judging by her final words and the way she chose to die. She had deliberately destroyed her body, leaving nothing behind that could be questioned by a necromancer.

The spellgaunt's carcass was intact, but questioning it would do little good. Spellgaunts couldn't tell the difference between a lowly light pellet and an artifact. Magical items were all the same to them—raw energy, waiting to be consumed.

Qilué had hoped to find clues in the reports of either the Darksong Knight or the novice Thaleste, but none had presented themselves in either priestess's account.

The whole episode was deeply troubling, and it wasn't the only bad news Qilué had received lately. Another of Eilistraee's enemies, it seemed, had also become active.

Four nights ago, one of Vhaeraun's assassins had infiltrated the shrine at Lake Sember. One priestess and two lay worshipers had been killed before the assassin had been driven off. This came at a time when the drow Houses of Cormanthor should have been fully engaged in their war against the levees of the newly reclaimed Myth Drannor. Why, in the midst of their battle with a powerful adversary, would the Masked Lord's priests have turned their attention to Eilistraee's shrine? Hopefully, Iljrene's spy would be able to turn up some answers, but for the moment, Qilué was baffled.

There were other murmurs of trouble. In the north, an evil that had been laid to rest three years ago had seemingly resurfaced. In the Year of Wild Magic, when Kiaransalee's followers had taken over Maerimydra, they'd torn a terrible hole in the Weave. The corruption had spread from that city to the surface realms before they had been defeated. Pockets of corrupted magic still dotted the Dales. Though the priestess responsible for it had been defeated, there were indications that at least one of the high-ranking Crones who served her might have survived. The handful of Eilistraee's priestesses who ministered to the drow of the distant north had heard tales from the survivors of undead rallying around a ghostly Crone whose wailing keen was capable of slaying scores of drow at one go. Once slain they were added to her ghastly ranks. The tales were obviously an exaggeration, but the region would have to be watched carefully. If further disruptions in the Weave arose, Qilué would be forced to respond.

Finally, from far to the south came troubling news that the cult of Ghaunadaur in Lurth Drier was becoming increasingly active. No longer content to prey upon each other, the drow of that Underdark city had burst onto the surface like an ugly boil, not far from Eilistraee's temples in the Shaar and the Chondalwood. Something had caused them to set aside their relentless feuding and act as a cohesive force. Qilué prayed that an avatar of Ghaunadaur had not arisen there. If so, she would be forced to lead a contingent of priestesses south to drive it back below—a crusade that would seriously deplete the resources of the Promenade.

The only one of Eilistraee's enemies *not* currently active, it seemed, was Lolth. Indeed, the Spider Queen's worshipers had not shown themselves in some time. That in itself was suspicious. Lolth, still and silent, was probably waiting patiently for the best moment to strike, while others did the work of tangling Eilistraee's faithful in a web of conflict.

The Darksong Knight had concluded her report and was standing in silence, waiting for Qilué's response.

"Walk with me," Qilué told her.

They had just returned from an inspection of the caverns where the aranea's attack took place, and stood on the southern bank of the underground river that flowed past the Promenade at a spot where a recently constructed bridge arched high above the river. The original bridge had fallen into the river more than a century ago, but Qilué could still remember how it had looked when she fought her way across it with the companions who had helped her defeat Ghaunadaur's avatar. The oozes and slimes had reduced its stone steps to rounded humps, making the footing treacherous. Ch'arla, one of Qilué's childhood companions, had died, songsword in hand, at the very spot Qilué and Cavatina approached. The death had been a terrible blow, but Ch'arla's soul danced with

Eilistraee. All pain was behind her.

Pride welled in Qilué as she walked across the rebuilt bridge and considered the fruits that two decades of labor had produced. The Promenade was a place of beauty and tranquility, hewn from the depths of the Underdark. A place that had once held nothing but madness and despair had been made sacred and filled with folk made whole through Eilistraee's grace. Every time she visited the Promenade, it brought a fierce ache to her heart and the sting of tears to the corners of her eyes. The sacrifices of so many centuries ago had been worth it, every last one of them.

Below the bridge, the temple's lay worshipers worked the river, hauling in fine-meshed nets filled with white, wriggling blindfish no longer than a finger. Others, baskets slung at their hips, collected lizard eggs and ripplebark fungus from the fissures that lined the cavern walls. Most were drow, converts from cities scattered throughout the Underdark, but there were also many who had been rescued from Skullport's slave ships: surface elves, dwarves, humans—even the occasional halfling—who had turned to the goddess as a result. One of them, a stocky half-drow with bristly hair and protruding fangs that betrayed his orc father's parentage, paused in his labors and made the sign of Eilistraee as Qilué and Cavatina passed him, touching forefinger to forefinger and thumb to thumb to form a circle representing the full moon.

Qilué acknowledged Jub with a nod and murmured blessing. His eyes lingered on her, a fawning expression on his face. Qilué secretly smiled. Even the most unlikely of worshipers were welcome there.

The Promenade comprised five main caverns that had once been part of the Sargauth Enclave, an outpost of fallen Netheril. The ancient buildings within the caverns had been reclaimed and put to use. One of the caverns housed the priestesses, another was home to the Promenade's lay worshipers, and a third contained storehouses and the barracks of the Protectors of the Song—the soldiers who guarded the Promenade. The fourth cavern, once a temple to a foul god, had been turned into the Hall of Healing.

The fifth cavern was the holiest of all: the Cavern of Song. Even over the rush of the river behind them, Qilué could hear the sound of singing—Eilistraee's priestesses continuing the psalm that had not faltered since the temple had been established twenty years past in the Year of the Harp.

As they made their way along one of the winding corridors that led to the Cavern of Song, Qilué spoke to the Darksong Knight. "Cavatina, you're familiar with the Velarswood, are you not?"

Cavatina nodded. "My mother was born there. I've visited it frequently."

"I would like you to go there now."

Cavatina's nostrils flared. "Lady Qilué, if this is about the aranea—"

"It is not."

"I realize that I should have been more vigilant. If I had, perhaps I might have spotted the Selvetargtlin on my first pass through the cavern."

"What is done is done. You danced well. The battle was won. It's just unfortunate that . . ."

Qilué didn't complete the sentence. She wasn't there to chastise the Darksong Knight. Cavatina had been trained to kill, and the thought of capturing an enemy alive would never have entered her head.

"You enjoy the hunt," Qilué said.

Cavatina halted. "I guard the Promenade as diligently as any other priestess."

"I'm sure you do."

"I do not, as some believe, think myself above indoctrinating a novice."

"I suggested nothing of the sort."

"I followed the procedures Iljrene laid down. When Thaleste spotted a movement above us, I—"

Qilué silenced Cavatina with a stern look. She could see that nearly losing the novice had pricked the warrior-priestess's pride. Darksong Knights didn't bear mistakes easily—in themselves or in others.

When Cavatina was at last ready to listen, Qilué continued. "A strange creature has been sighted in the Velarswood in recent months. It has the general appearance of a drow female, yet it is far larger and stronger. It appears to be preying upon the drow of House Jaelre. Last night, a survivor of one of its attacks staggered into our shrine, begging for healing. He described the creature as having skin hard as obsidian—no blade can pierce it—and eight tiny legs that emerge from the torso, below the arms, like protruding ribs."

Cavatina's head came up like a hound on the scent. "Some new form of drider?" she guessed. "Or . . . demon?"

"Nobody knows. What we do know is that the survivor drew the creature's attention to our shrine. It followed him there last night then scuttled away before the priestesses could assemble for a hunt. I'm worried it's going to attack one of our people next. That's why I'm sending you to the Velarswood. I want you to remove the threat."

Cavatina nodded, her eyes gleaming. "Do you see Lolth's hand in this?"

Qilué paused. "It's hard to say, but the creature—whatever it is—has a venomous bite and is capable of spinning webs. The survivor said that those it took were found dangling from tree branches, inside cocoons. Dead." Her expression hardened. "Innocents who might have been brought into Eilistraee's light, but now their souls are lost to us."

"May those souls find mercy," Cavatina intoned.

Both females stood in silence a moment. Then Cavatina spoke again. "Lady, I lost my sword, Demonbane, to the spellgaunt."

Qilué nodded. She glanced off into the distance and spoke in a low voice, as if to herself. "Quartermaster, a sword if you please." She held up a hand, and a moment later one of the temple's singing swords appeared out of thin air. Qilué caught it deftly by the hilt and passed it to Cavatina. "You may use this."

Cavatina's eyes widened. She stepped away from Qilué and swung the weapon back and forth in sweeping arcs, alternating between a one-handed and a two-handed grip. A note flowed from it, pure as holy water. The sword glowed faintly, tracing a line of moonfire through the darkness.

Qilué watched, admiring the other priestess's skill. "Only twenty-five of these weapons remain. See to it that you use it well."

Cavatina bowed and promised, "I will keep it safe, Lady."

"If it does turn out to be a demon you are hunting, the singing sword will render you immune to any attacks it might make against your mind. It can also be used to counter certain baleful songs and cries—those of harpies and shriekers, for example—and to entrance lesser creatures."

"A most potent weapon," Cavatina said. Then she looked up at Qilué. "I thought the singing swords were never to leave the Promenade."

Qilué's expression grew grim. "The coming hunt, according to my divinations, will be of great consequence." She nodded down at the weapon. "It will be worthy of that blade."

Cavatina bowed again. "By Eilistraee's grace, may I also prove worthy of it."

"I'm sure you shall," Qilué said with a smile. "Now that you're armed, let's get you on your way. Come."

They entered the Cavern of Song. It had been cleared of its buildings and returned to its natural state two decades ago during the temple's construction. It was flooded with Eilistraee's moonfire, which illuminated a statue of Qilué that the Protectors had insisted on erecting over the hidden staircase that led to the Pit of Ghaunadaur. Shimmering waves of light danced across the ceiling in constantly changing hues: blue-white, pale green, moon-white and silver.

Three priestesses sang there, their voices blended in complex harmonies that waxed and waned. Two of the singers were drow, the third, a surface elf whose pale skin was bathed in shifting colors by the moonfire above. Each was naked, save for the holy symbol that hung from a mithral chain around her neck. Each singer sat on a different outcropping of stone, holding a sword above her head, its point directed at the moon. They pointed overhead, but the swords were slowly descending, their tips moving almost imperceptibly downward as the moon sank toward an unseen horizon. The priestesses would hold these positions until others came to join the song. Sometimes a single priestess sang there, but during Evensong, two dozen or more would lend their voices to the sacred hymn.

Qilué joined in the singing as they walked through the cavern. "Climb out of the darkness, rise into the light . . ." It had always been one of her favorite lines.

Her own climb into the light had happened centuries ago. She barely remembered the tiny town in the Underdark where she had been born. It had been a long and difficult struggle to reawaken Eilistraee's worship among the drow, but a worthwhile one. The young Darksong Knight beside her was proof of that. Cavatina was a fourth-generation devotee of the Lady of the Dance, born on the surface. The drow were reclaiming their birthright.

Qilué and Cavatina turned in to a side cavern that led to a pool of water. One of the Protectors of the Song stood guard there whenever the moon was risen, even though it was unlikely that enemies would pass that way. She bowed as they approached.

"Is the portal active?" Qilué asked.

The priestess nodded. She pointed out a spot on the surface of the pool—a circle that shimmered like a reflection of the full moon.

"I'd like you to leave at once for the Velarswood via the Moonspring," Qilué said. "Take all the time you need to find out what's going on there. Be thorough, and use the resources that Eilistraee places in your hands. Do whatever you need to in order to protect our shrines in Cormanthor."

Cavatina's eyes glittered with anticipation. She looked delighted to be off on the hunt again, and Qilué knew that the patrols of the temple had bored the Darksong Knight to tears. She saluted Qilué with the singing sword.

"They will be safe under my blade," she promised. Then she paused. "Any other instructions, Lady?"

"Only one," Qilué said, hiding her smile. "If you're carrying any scrolls or other equipment that can be damaged by water, I'd suggest you remove them.

Q'arlynd winced as the arcane eye he'd just conjured passed through the portal. He'd done a similar reconnaissance twice already, waiting for the fall of night in the surface world, but even under the light of that realm's lesser disc—the moon—everything was painfully bright. It took him several moments to make sense of what he was seeing: pale stone walls, a floor dusted with sand, and a black sky dotted with points of white—the stars. They reminded him, a little, of the magical, twinkling faerie fire that had covered Ched Nasad's buildings, but not nearly as beautiful.

The portal was affixed to a wall in a ruined building whose roof was open to the sky. A second arch, non-magical, opened onto a street paved with large slabs of stone. The building had probably been built by humans or surface elves, judging by the height of the arch. The frescoes on its walls might have given more clues, but they were faded to the point where only faint smudges of pigment could still be seen.

Q'arlynd sent the eye roving through the arch and out into the street. There didn't seem to be anyone around.

His view dissolved into static as the spell ended. He turned to Flinderspeld, who lay on his belly beside him in the gap in the rubble. His slave was fidgeting, tugging at the tight leather gloves Q'arlynd had ordered him to wear. Q'arlynd rapped him on the head with a knuckle.

"Gnomes first," he said, gesturing at the arch with its glowing runes.

"Where does it lead to?" Flinderspeld asked.

Q'arlynd's ring gave him a glimpse into the deep gnome's thoughts. Flinderspeld was weighing the possibilities. If the portal led to another plane, he was thinking, he might at last be free of the ring's binding.

"Crawl through it and find out if you're right," Q'arlynd suggested aloud. Inwardly, he chuckled.

Flinderspeld hesitated then realized that refusal to enter the portal would only cause his master to force him through. Muttering under his breath, he crawled forward, his head, shoulders, and chest gradually disappearing into the arch.

When the deep gnome was about halfway through, his legs and feet jerked forward abruptly, as if he'd been yanked the rest of the way. This gave Q'arlynd a moment's pause, then he realized that the floor level on the other side of the portal was well below the uppermost part of the arch—the only part of the portal not hidden by rubble. Flinderspeld had simply fallen. Q'arlynd concentrated, but he could no longer hear Flinderspeld's thoughts. That was to be expected, since the range of the rings was limited and the deep gnome was leagues away.

He conjured a second arcane eye and sent it through the gate. Flinderspeld stood next to the gate, rubbing one cheek and wincing. He must have scuffed it during his fall, but nothing was attacking him.

So far, so good, but before using the portal himself, Q'arlynd cast a spell that would encase him in a layer of force like magical armor. Then he eased his way through the arch feet first. He felt a brief, mildly disorienting lurch before landing on the floor beyond, next to Flinderspeld. The deep gnome shivered, even though he wore a warm cloak.

Q'arlynd was immediately aware of the dryness of the air. It was as cold here as it had been underground, but the air he drew into his lungs tasted of dust. His feet scuffed sand as he turned to survey the roofless room. After the constant trickle of water that had filled Ched Nasad, the World Above was eerily silent. He could even hear Flinderspeld breathing.

"Where are we?" the deep gnome asked in a whisper.

A shadow swept across the room, swift as the blink of an eye, as something leaped across the open ceiling and landed on the far wall. Q'arlynd caught a glimpse of a creature the size of a riding lizard but covered in tawny, golden fur. The upper torso was humanoid and golden-skinned, and at the end of its animal rump was a lashing tail.

The creature didn't seem to have spotted them. Even as Q'arlynd raised his hands to cast a spell, it tensed in a crouch, still facing away from them, then sprang away.

Any idea what that was? Q'arlynd signed.

Flinderspeld's mind was a blank parchment. He'd never seen anything like it. Mutely, he shook his head.

Q'arlynd listened, but he couldn't hear the creature. As a precaution, he rendered himself invisible. A second whisper and a touch rendered Flinderspeld invisible as well.

Q'arlynd felt Flinderspeld grab the hem of his *piwafwi*. They started for the arch that led to the street.

Before they reached it, a drow slipped in from outside, a male with long white hair, wearing a *piwafwi* and lizard-skin gloves similar to Q'arlynd's own. His eyes were an unusual pale blue rather than red.

"Quickly," he whispered in High Drowic that had the distinctive accent of someone from Ched Nasad. "Before the monster returns. Follow me."

Q'arlynd was instantly suspicious. Why wasn't the drow using the silent speech, if a hostile creature was nearby? And why, if he could penetrate Q'arlynd's invisibility spell, was he staring so intently at the portal?

Flinderspeld's own suspicions supplied the missing piece of the puzzle. Where Q'arlynd saw a drow, Flinderspeld saw another deep gnome—one who spoke to him in svirfneblin. The newcomer was an illusion.

That didn't necessarily mean whoever had created the illusion was an enemy, of course. Perhaps she was just cautious.

Q'arlynd fished out of his pocket one of the tiny silver swords the dead priestess had been carrying, found Flinderspeld's hand, and pressed the trinket into it. Then he rendered the deep gnome visible again and stepped swiftly aside.

The drow-illusion turned toward Flinderspeld—whoever had cast it was watching the room—and repeated the exhortation to follow.

Q'arlynd forced Flinderspeld to hold up the trinket. The illusion barely glanced at the tiny sword.

Q'arlynd levitated while forcing Flinderspeld to walk toward the drow-illusion. As soon as Q'arlynd was high enough to see over the ruined walls, he spotted the tawny-furred creature hiding in an alley just up the street. As Q'arlynd turned the silently protesting Flinderspeld to follow the drow-illusion in that direction, the creature crouched, tail whisking in anticipation. Claws flexed from its furred feet.

Definitely an enemy, but one who could, perhaps, tell Q'arlynd more about this place.

He cast a spell. The slab of paving stone on which the creature crouched became soft as mud and the creature's feet sank into it. A second, equally quick whisper, and the paving stone was solid once more. The creature, realizing its feet were trapped, thrashed about, trying to free itself. Realizing it could not, it snarled.

The drow-illusion disappeared. As it did, Q'arlynd released his hold on Flinderspeld's body. The deep gnome had served his purpose as a distraction, and Q'arlynd didn't want him getting within range of whatever other magic the tawny-furred creature might have at its disposal.

Instead of retreating, the deep gnome collapsed in the middle of the street, the tiny silver sword falling from his hand.

Q'arlynd probed his slave's mind. Flinderspeld was still alive. His thoughts were sluggish and dreamlike, but there.

The tawny-furred creature let out a loud roar. An answering roar came from elsewhere in the ruined city.

Realizing it had just called another of its kind, Q'arlynd immediately sank to the floor of the ruined building. Still invisible, he hurried out into the street, toward Flinderspeld.

He wasn't the only one. A drow came running out of a doorway on the opposite side of the street—a female with waist-length white hair, wearing a chain mail tunic over trousers and a padded shirt. She reached Flinderspeld a heartbeat ahead of Q'arlynd and slapped a hand onto the deep gnome's chest.

"Sanctuary!" she cried.

Both the drow female and Flinderspeld disappeared.

Q'arlynd skidded to a stop on the sand-dusted flagstones and swore softly under his breath. His only slave, gone. Before he had time for regret, however, he felt a tickling sensation, deep within his mind.

I know you're there, somewhere. Free me. I can help you.

Q'arlynd glanced toward the trapped creature. It held its arms out imploringly, its eyes fixed on the dust that slowly settled around Q'arlynd's boots.

Q'arlynd laughed. The creature's magical suggestion might have worked on someone less suspicious than a drow. He drew his wand from its sheath, pointed it, then spoke its command word. Jagged balls of ice erupted from it. They streaked across the street and slammed into the creature's chest with harsh, meaty thuds. Q'arlynd corrected his aim and shot again, and the ice smashed into the creature's face, knocking its head back. The creature collapsed, either unconscious or dead, its feet still encased in stone. Q'arlynd heard a bone snap as one of its ankles twisted and broke.

His direct attack had rendered him visible once more. He could sense eyes on him. He whirled and saw another drow female standing in the street staring at him. She was armored as the first had been, in a chain mail tunic, and she carried a sword. Her hair was whiter than the other female's and was twisted in a knot at the back of her head. The tiny sword that was Eilistraee's pendant hung against her chest. She glanced past Q'arlynd at the collapsed creature, then nodded and moved forward.

"Nicely done. Lamias can be challenging opponents."

Q'arlynd lowered his wand but did not sheathe it. Under his breath, he whispered a simple cantrip. When he pinched his fingers together, the tiny silver sword that had been lying on the ground at his feet—the one Flinderspeld had dropped—rose to his hand. He held it out with a flourish and bowed. When he straightened, the female had visibly relaxed.

"Where did the other female take the deep gnome?" Q'arlynd asked.

"Your friend is safe. Rowaan will take care of him."

Q'arlynd nearly laughed aloud. Friend? Anyone with half a cup of cunning would have realized Flinderspeld was Q'arlynd's slave.

As the priestess walked toward Q'arlynd, her eyes lingered on his face. He suppressed a sigh. Despite his broken nose, he seemed to have that effect on females, but still she frowned when she asked, "What House are you?"

Q'arlynd almost lied—deceit was a reflex—then decided against it. "House Melarn."

The priestess's eyes widened.

Q'arlynd's heartbeat quickened. He took a risk—something he would normally not have done. "You know my sister," he said. A statement, rather than a question. "Halisstra Melarn."

She started to nod then checked herself. "I knew her."

"Knew?" Q'arlynd asked. "Is she—"

From another part of the ruined city, a roar sounded. The second tawny-furred creature, calling out. Or perhaps a third.

"We must go." The female raised a hand, her palm toward Q'arlynd's chest. "Are you willing?"

Q'arlynd met her eyes briefly then lowered his gaze submissively. "Yes. Take me."

The female's eyebrows rose in surprise. Then she laughed. The laughter had a pure sound, devoid of the sharpness Q'arlynd was used to. "You've got a lot to learn, petitioner," she said. "That's not how it's done here."

She touched his chest, spoke a word, and the ruined city disappeared.

CHAPTER FOUR

Q'arlynd glanced around at the place the priestess had teleported him to. The ground was a flat, rocky expanse that stretched as far as the eye could see. The place was vast, bigger than any cavern he'd had ever been in. Above was a black dome, studded with twinkling points of light—the night sky.

"Where are we?" he asked.

"The High Moor," the priestess who had teleported him answered.

The other priestess kneeled beside Flinderspeld and shook him awake. The gnome groaned, then groggily rose to his feet, the priestess helping him.

Q'arlynd gave the deep gnome a cursory glance, assuring himself his slave was undamaged. Then he returned his attention to the priestesses.

The two females were very similar in appearance. Both had lean, muscular bodies and red eyes, and they walked with light, precise footsteps, as if moving through the steps of a dance. They were dressed alike and shared several of the same gestures and expressions. The major difference that Q'arlynd could see was that the one who had teleported him was older, with ice-white hair, whereas the younger one, Rowaan, had hair that was shaded with hints of yellow.

Each, he noted, wore a ring on the index finger of her right hand: a plain band of platinum. A discreetly whispered divination revealed that the rings were magical. Q'arlynd wondered if they were the equivalent of his own master-and-slave rings. Rowaan deferred to the older priestess, but Q'arlynd could see no overt signs that the other priestess was controlling her.

"Mistress," he said, bowing before the one in charge.

"It's 'Lady,' " she answered, "not 'Mistress.' "

Q'arlynd bowed still deeper. "Lady."

"I'd prefer you called me by name: Leliana."

"Leliana," Q'arlynd dutifully murmured.

A testy note crept into Leliana's voice. "And look me in the eye, will you? I told you before, we do things differently here. You don't have to grovel, just because you're male."

Q'arlynd straightened. "As you—" He'd been about to say "command" but quickly amended that. "As you wish." He grinned. "Old habits. . . ." he added with a shrug. Then he turned his expression serious again. "You said you knew my sister Halisstra. *Knew,*" he repeated. He braced himself for bad news. "Is she dead?"

Rowaan's eyes widened. "This is Halisstra's *brother?*"

Q'arlynd noted her tone. Halisstra had achieved some status up on the surface, it seemed.

Leliana glanced away. She seemed to be carefully

composing her reply. "There's a slim chance your sister is alive," she said at last.

"But you don't think so," Q'arlynd finished for her.

"No."

"There's always hope," Rowaan insisted. "Slim as the new moon, maybe, but . . ." her voice trailed off.

Leliana made no comment.

"What happened to her?" Q'arlynd asked.

"You weren't told?"

Q'arlynd realized that Leliana must have been wondering why the priestess who "gave" him the sword-token hadn't already answered any questions he might have about Halisstra.

He shrugged and said, "Things were . . . a bit rushed in Ched Nasad. There wasn't much time for talk."

Flinderspeld, thankfully, kept his expression neutral. The deep gnome had been schooled well. He carefully noted—but didn't react to—his master's odd remarks.

Q'arlynd gave the priestesses his best mournful look and continued, "It's been three years since I've seen Halisstra. She disappeared when our city fell, during Lolth's Silence. All this time, I've been wondering if my sister still lived, or . . ." He made a small, choked sound, as if struggling to contain his emotions.

Leliana's expression at last softened.

"Tell me what happened to her," Q'arlynd begged the two priestesses. "Don't hold anything back—tell me everything."

They did.

Halisstra, it seemed, had indeed converted to Eilistraee's faith. Not only that, but she'd made quite a name for herself. Shortly after her "redemption," as the priestesses called it, Halisstra had undertaken a pilgrimage to recover an artifact sacred to Eilistraee—a sword known as the Crescent Blade. That weapon in hand, she'd set out for the Abyss during Lolth's Silence with two other priestesses to—and Q'arlynd reflexively shivered—try to *kill* the Queen of the Demonweb Pits with that magical sword.

What hubris! A mortal slaying a god! Even so, Leliana and Rowaan assured him that not only was it possible, but that it had almost come to pass. Halisstra, however, had been slain on the very doorstep of the Demonweb Pits by one of Lolth's faithful. Shortly afterward, Lolth's Silence had ended. Halisstra had failed in her quest.

Q'arlynd recognized his sister's killer at once from her description. "Danifae," he said.

Leliana paused. "You knew her?"

Q'arlynd nodded. "She was my sister's battle-captive. What you've just told me doesn't surprise me. Danifae was . . . treacherous."

An understatement, that. Treachery was something all drow expected of one another, especially of their battle-captives. Danifae, however, took the word to new levels. A seductress whose talents in that regard were near legendary, Danifae combined her exquisite beauty with utter ruthlessness. For years, Q'arlynd had observed the resentment that smoldered in Danifae's eyes each time his sister's back was turned, yet the battle-captive had actually succeeded in convincing Halisstra that she was a friend. All the while, Danifae had been working her way through the males—and females—of House Melarn, trying to seduce one of them into killing Halisstra. Danifae had eventually turned her lascivious attentions to Q'arlynd, hoping to enlist his aid in removing the magical Binding that compelled her loyalty to Halisstra, so she could kill her mistress herself.

Thinking back to that time, Q'arlynd shook his head. Of all of the children of Drisinil Melarn, he would have been the last one to slide a dagger into Halisstra's back. Not because he cared for her, but because of what she'd done.

He resisted the urge to touch a finger to his nose, to hide the smile that threatened. As a boy, he'd been injured in a riding accident. He'd tumbled from his lizard and fallen only a short distance to the street below—no more than a dozen paces—but it had happened so quickly there hadn't been time to activate his House insignia. He'd landed face-first, smashing his face against stone. He'd been only a novice wizard then—a clumsy oaf who wasn't worth wasting magical healing on, in the opinion of Matron Melarn, but Halisstra had secretly healed him. She'd had to do it without leaving any evidence, so she'd cast her spell selectively, leaving his black eyes and broken nose untouched. Afterward, Q'arlynd had expected his sister to demand something of him in return. He'd prepared himself for a lifetime spent in thrall to her, but Halisstra had demanded nothing.

She'd healed him, he later realized, out of simple pity and something more. Affection. Something that was as rare among drow siblings as a spider that didn't bite.

It had been a startling revelation. Q'arlynd had never realized that a female could be soft, especially one sworn to serve Lolth.

From that point on, he'd done everything he could to ensure that Halisstra would survive long enough to become House Melarn's next matron mother. He'd arranged for her introduction to the bard who had taught her *bae'qeshel* magic, and he had eliminated her rivals. Through his careful planning, he had all but ensured that Halisstra would be the next in succession to House Melarn's highest post—thus ensuring himself a position as her House wizard, the power behind that throne.

Then the Silence came, and it had all fallen apart. —literally—when the city fell.

With a mental wrench, he brought himself back to the present. "Were you the two who accompanied my sister into the Abyss?" he asked. "Did you see her die?"

Leliana shook her head. "She was accompanied by

Feliane and Uluyara—two priestesses who also died on that quest. I did see your sister's death. I aided Lady Qilué with her scrying. I could see, over her shoulder, the events as they unfolded in the font."

Q'arlynd carefully noted the name and title, Lady Qilué—probably a high priestess, if she was capable of getting clear images out of a scrying into the Abyss.

"Describe Halisstra's death for me," Q'arlynd said.

Leliana did, in hushed tones, as if Q'arlynd were a stranger to violent death. Halisstra had been felled by a blow to the head—a blow from Danifae's morningstar. There was little hope that Halisstra had survived the blow, she added.

Unless . . .

Hearing her hesitation, Q'arlynd pressed Leliana for more. She told him their high priestess had been attempting to resurrect Halisstra at the moment that the scrying was lost. Shortly afterward, Qilué had communed with their goddess. The high priestess had not divulged Eilistraee's words to anyone, but she had let one fact slip out. The goddess, it seemed, had spoken of Halisstra in the present tense, as one would refer to someone who was still alive.

Q'arlynd took it all in without betraying any emotion. He was too much of a realist to expect that Halisstra had benefited from the last-minute spell—or even if she had, that she'd been able to escape the Demonweb Pits, which meant that his quest to find his sister was probably a futile one.

He sighed. It seemed he would have to return to the drudgery of rooting through the ruins of Ched Nasad, and tedious years of servitude to House Teh'Kinrellz.

Unless . . .

"Qilué," he mused aloud. "I think I've heard the name, but I can't quite place her House."

Rowaan supplied the name. "Veladorn."

Veladorn. It was not a House Q'arlynd recognized.

Leliana cocked her head. "Lady Qilué Veladorn, High Protector of the Song, and Right Hand of Eilistraee." She paused. "Sounding familiar yet?"

Q'arlynd spread his hands. "I'm new to all this; I'm afraid. Just a petitioner." He favored her with a boyish smile. "I'm sure I'll learn all of your honorifics and titles, in time." In fact, he had no intentions of any kind. He'd done what he'd intended by coming to the surface—gleaned everything he could from the priestesses. His sister was dead. That was the end of it. There was nothing further to be gained by pretending to be a petitioner.

He opened his mouth, intending to bid them farewell, grab Flinderspeld, and teleport back to the portal, when Rowaan picked up where Leliana left off. "Qilué is not only a high priestess of Eilistraee," she continued in an annoyingly helpful tone. "She's also one of the Seven Sisters."

Q'arlynd stared at her blankly. That title was obviously supposed to impress him, but he had no idea what Rowaan was talking about.

"She's one of the Chosen of Mystra," Rowaan continued. She had his attention.

"Is that so?" he said in a soft voice. Most of the surface peoples' gods were of little interest—especially those worshiped by humans—but that was one name he recognized. "Mystra, goddess of magic? The one who tends the Weave and makes magic possible for all mortals?"

"I see you're familiar with her," Leliana said.

Q'arlynd gave an apologetic smile. "I'm a wizard," he told her. "My instructors at the Conservatory mentioned the goddess of magic, once or twice." He touched the pocket where he'd placed his sword-token. "But it's *Eilistraee* I'm petitioning."

"Well then," Leliana said, "in that case, we'd better get moving. The moor can be a dangerous place, home to marauding orcs and hobgoblins—even trolls. The sooner we get to the shrine, the better."

Q'arlynd bowed—it helped hide the gleam in his eyes. This Qilué person sounded powerful—a priestess and a mage both, and not just any mage but one of Mystra's "Chosen."

Now *that* was a matron mother Q'arlynd wouldn't mind serving.

"Will I . . ." He feigned boyish hesitation and tried to call a blush to his cheeks. "Will I *meet* Qilué once we get to the shrine?"

Leliana and Rowaan glanced at each other.

He molded his face into a pleading expression. "If I could hear from her own lips what happened to Halisstra—what she saw in her scrying—then perhaps . . ."

Rowaan nodded in sympathy. It was Leliana, however, who spoke. "I'll see if it can be arranged."

Q'arlynd bowed. "Thank you, Lady."

He smiled. Prellyn had been right. Eilistraee's faithful were entirely too trusting.

Deep in a little-frequented section of the forest of Cormanthor, the cleric Malvag cast his eye over the drow who had assembled inside the enormous hollow tree: nine males, all but one with faces hidden by black masks that left only their restless eyes visible. Most wore leather armor, dark as the cloaks that protected them from the winter chill. Their breath fogged below their masks as they eyed one another warily, wrist-crossbows and bracer-sheathed daggers prominently visible. Crowding into such a small space had made them uneasy, as Malvag had intended. The smell of nervous sweat blended with the earthy smell of long-since fallen leaves and the faint, slightly sweet scent of the poison that coated the heads of their crossbow bolts.

"Men of Jaelre," he said, greeting the five who had come from that House. All wore masks except their leader, a cripple with a brace of leather and iron encasing his left leg.

Malvag turned to the other four and inclined his head slightly. "And men of Auzkovyn. Dark deeds."

"Dark deeds," they murmured.

"You sent a shadow summons," the crippled male said. "Why?"

"Ah, Jezz. Always the first to come to the point," Malvag said. He looked at each man in turn, nodding as if silently counting them, then shrugged. "I sent the summons to several more of the faithful, but only you nine answered. Just as well—that's fewer to reap the rewards."

"What rewards?" one asked.

"Power," Malvag said. "Beyond anything you might ever have imagined. The ability to work *arselu'tel'quess*—high magic."

There was silence for several moments. Jezz broke it with a snort of barely contained laughter. "Everyone knows drow aren't capable of touching the Weave in that way, and even if we were, only wizards can work high magic. Clerics merely assist in their spells."

"Wrong!" Malvag said firmly. "On both counts. There are high magic spells designed for clerics—or rather, there were in ancient times. I have discovered a scroll, written by a priest of ancient Ilythiir, that bears one such prayer. If high magic was possible for our *ssri Tel'Quessir* ancestors, it can be possible for us."

"But we're *drow*," another of the males said.

"Indeed we are," Malvag said. He held up his hands and turned them back and forth, as if examining them. "But what is it that prevents us from working high magic? Our black skin? Our white hair?" He chuckled softly and lowered his hands. "Neither. It is simply that we lack the will." He glanced at each male in turn. "Who among you would not stab a fellow Nightshadow in the back, if there was something to be gained by it? We form alliances, but they are as tenuous and fleeting as faerie fire. In order to work high magic, we must forge something more lasting, a permanent bond between ourselves. We must set aside our suspicions and learn to work as one."

Again, Jezz gave a snort of derisive laughter. "Pretty words," he said, "but this is hardly the time for impossible alliances and grand schemes. In case you've forgotten, both House Jaelre and House Auzkovyn are fighting for our very survival. The army of Myth Drannor won't be happy until they've driven every last one of us below or into the arms of those dancing bitches—we've lost more than one of the faithful to Eilistraee in recent months. Then there's that *thing* that's been hunting us." He shook his head. "Lolth herself has taken an interest in both our Houses for some reason."

Malvag smiled beneath his mask. He'd counted on comments like that from the battle-scarred sorcerer, which was why he'd included Jezz in the summons. Jezz helped remind the others that things had come to a desperate pass. Those with their backs already against the wall, Malvag knew, were more easily persuaded to grasp at the "impossible."

"These are troubled times," Malvag agreed, his voice smooth as assassin's strangle silk, "but what better time to strike our enemies than when they least expect it? Instead of continuing to just skirmish, we'll hit back. Hard. With high magic. Vhaeraun himself will be our weapon."

Several of the men frowned. Jezz voiced the question that was no doubt foremost in their minds. "You hope to summon an avatar of the Masked Lord's to do battle for us?"

Malvag shook his head. "I wasn't speaking of his avatar. I was speaking of Vhaeraun himself."

Jezz laughed openly. "Let me guess. You're going to

replicate the Time of Troubles and force Vhaeraun to walk Toril in physical form by using 'high magic.'" He rolled his eyes. "You're mad. You must think yourself the equal of Ao."

Malvag locked eyes with the cripple. "When did I ever mention a summoning—or Toril, for that matter?" he asked in a steely voice. He shook his head. "I have something entirely different in mind. The scroll I possess will enable us to open a gate between Vhaeraun's domain and that of another god. A back door, if you will, that the Masked Lord can use to sneak out of Ellaniath undetected."

"To what end?" one of the others asked.

"The assassination," Malvag said slowly, "of another god."

All eyes were locked on him. "Which one?" one of the Nightshadows asked.

"Corellon Larethian." Malvag let his smile crinkle the corners of his eyes. "The death of the lord of the Seldarine should give the army of Myth Drannor pause, don't you agree?"

The Nightshadows exchanged excited glances. Jezz, however, slowly shook his head. "Let me get this straight," he said. "You want to open a gate between Vhaeraun's domain and Arvandor?"

Malvag nodded.

"A gate that might very well work in the reverse direction to the one you describe, allowing the Seldarine to invade Vhaeraun's domain, instead of the other way around." He shifted his weight, favoring his crippled leg. One hand drifted near the hilt of his kukri. "This makes me wonder which god you really do serve."

Eyes darted back and forth between Jezz and Malvag. The other males drew slightly apart from the sorcerer, giving him room for whatever treachery he planned.

Malvag made no move. "What do you mean?"

"You're neither Jaelre nor Auzkovyn. You appeared among us a year ago from out of nowhere, claiming to be from the south, around the same time that the demon-thing started slaughtering our people. Now you propose something which, assuming it is possible, may very well be the death of the Masked Lord. I ask again, which god do you really serve?"

Malvag stood utterly still, not making any threatening moves. "They should have called you Jezz the Suspicious," he drawled, "not Jezz the Lame."

One of the males from House Auzkovyn chuckled softly.

Jezz's eyes narrowed still further. "I think you're a spider kisser."

Eyes widened. Malvag heard several sharp intakes of breath.

"You call me a traitor?" he whispered. "You think me a servant of Lolth?" He curled the fingers of his right hand then suddenly flipped it palm-up. The sign for a dead spider. "*This*, for the spider bitch. If I worship her, may she strike me dead for blaspheming."

As nervous chuckles filled the air, Malvag added, "I'm a loyal servant of Vhaeraun—a shadow in the Night Above—as are all of you." He paused. "Well . . . almost all of you," he added, his glance lingering on Jezz's naked face.

He held it for several moments then tore his gaze away. "Some of us, it seems, think Corellon Larethian too high a mark for the Masked Lord to aim for," he told the others, giving Jezz the kind of disdainful glance one would reserve for a coward, "so let me propose an alternative. Instead of Arvandor, we'll use the scroll to open a gate to Eilistraee's domain." He chuckled. "Wouldn't it be a wonderful turnabout if the Masked Lord took Eilistraee down? Her priestesses have stolen enough of our people in recent years. I think it's Vhaeraun's turn to take the lead in that dance. Permanently."

Low laughter greeted his joke.

Jezz glared. "This is not a laughing matter. You're talking about tampering with the domains of the gods."

"True," Malvag said, his expression serious once more, "which is why I came prepared to show how serious I am about this. Realizing that some might be . . . *reluctant* to tackle Arvandor, I began my preparations for opening a gate to Eilistraee's domain instead."

He reached behind his head and untied his mask. Lifting it from his face, he held it high. Then he gave it a savage twist, as if wringing water from it. A faint but sharp sound filled the hollow tree: a female voice, screaming.

He relaxed the twist in the fabric. "A soul," he explained, "trapped by soultheft and held there still."

The other clerics' eyes widened. Malvag could tell they were impressed. Most Nightshadows could hold a soul within their masks for only a moment or two. "You may have heard of the attack on the shrine at Lake Sember five nights ago?"

Heads nodded.

Jezz looked impressed. Fleetingly.

"You mean to tell us you've got the soul of a priestess of *Eilistraee* trapped in there?" asked one of the Auzkovyn—a thin man whose protruding nose creased the fabric of his mask into a tent shape. His breathing was light and fast, his eyes wide.

"What better tool for opening a gate to her domain?" Malvag asked. "As some of you may already know, the working of high magic demands a price. Better we fuel it with this—" he fluttered the mask gently—"than with our own souls, wouldn't you agree?"

Smiles crinkled the eyes of the other Nightshadows as they laughed at his wry joke.

"I can teach you to do the same, to hold a soul in your mask until you are ready to spend its energy," Malvag told them. "When each of us has gathered this necessary focus, we will meet again to work the spell." He retied the mask around his face. "Through soultheft, each of you will have the fuel needed to work high magic." He met the eyes of each male in turn. "The only question remaining is, do you have the faith?"

The Nightshadows were silent for several moments. The eyes behind the masks were thoughtful.

All but those of the House Jaelre leader. "Assuming this scroll of yours really exists, there's a flaw in your plan," Jezz said. "In order to create a gate, the caster has to enter the plane that is the gate's destination. As soon as one of you enters the domain of another god—be it Eilistraee's domain or Arvandor—the element of surprise is lost."

"That would be true," Malvag admitted, "except that this spell will allow us to open a gate between two domains from a distance—from a location on Toril."

"Nonsense," Jezz scoffed. "That would require more power than you possess. The combined efforts of a hundred clerics. A thousand."

"What if I told you I know of something that will augment the magic of each cleric participating in the spell a hundredfold?" he asked. "Perhaps even a thousandfold." He paused. "There is a cavern, deep in the Underdark," he told the Nightshadows, "a cavern lined with darkstone crystals, and thus a perfect vehicle for the Masked Lord's magic. It lies at the center of an earth node of incredible power—something that will boost our magic to the levels we need to work the spell."

"And this cavern?" Jezz demanded. "Where is it, exactly? Or is that something you're not prepared to share with us?" He glanced at the others, then back at Malvag. "Perhaps because it, like the 'ancient scroll' you've told us about, doesn't exist."

Malvag carefully hid his delight. He could not have scripted Jezz's comments better himself. "On the contrary," he countered. "Those who choose to join me will be

shown both the cavern—and the scroll—this very night.
I'll teleport them there."

The word hung in the air. "Them." Not "you."

Jezz glared at Malvag, then stared around at the others,
slowly shaking his head. "You *trust* him?" A scornful word,
in the mouth of a drow.

Eyes shifted from Jezz to Malvag and back again.

"Then you're fools," Jezz said. "Anyone with eyes can
see that this is a ploy to thin the ranks of the faithful, so
this newcomer can rise to a more prominent position. He'll
teleport you into a cavern filled with sickstone, or somewhere equally unhealthy, and abandon you there."

His words hung in the air for several moments.

The Nightshadows shuffled, glancing at one another.
One of the House Jaelre males, a large fellow with close-
cropped hair and an old burn scar on his right hand, at
last broke the silence. "I'm in," he grunted from behind his
mask. He moved to Malvag's side.

Jezz merely snorted. Without further comment he
turned on his heel and strode out into the night. Two of
the males from House Jaelre immediately followed. The
remaining male from that House who had not yet declared
himself glanced sidelong at the Auzkovyn, as if waiting to
see what they would do.

One of the Auzkovyn glanced at his fellows, shook his
head, then also left.

Malvag waited, holding his breath, as the four males
who had not yet declared themselves—one from House
Jaelre and three from House Auzkovyn—shifted slightly
on their feet, hesitating. One of the Auzkovyn males muttered something under his breath at his companions then
departed. The hatchet-nosed Auzkovyn also turned to
leave, then hesitated, glancing back over his shoulder.
Even from where he stood, Malvag could smell the reek
of nervous sweat clinging to the male. A moment more of
hesitation then that Auzkovyn abruptly left.

That left only two in addition to Malvag and the male from House Auzkovyn who had been so quick to declare himself. If both of them stayed, that would give Malvag only the slightest of margins. The spell Malvag hoped to use required at least two other clerics, besides himself, to cast.

"May the Masked Lord forgive them for their lack of faith," he whispered under his breath—but loud enough for the remaining two to hear. He stared out through the crack in the tree trunk, sadly shaking his head. "They've given up a chance to stand at Vhaeraun's side. They'll never know what true power is."

Out of the corner of his eye, he saw the remaining two square their shoulders and turn slightly toward him. They had made their decision. They would stay.

He turned to the three clerics who remained and spread his arms. He could see, by the wary glint in their eyes, that they didn't quite trust him. Yet. But they would.

They would have to trust him by the night of the winter solstice, if his plan was to succeed.

He smiled behind his mask. "Now then," he said, readying his teleportation spell. "Let me show you that scroll."

Halisstra waited, high in the treetop. The wind plucked at her hair, tangling its sticky white strands. A fallen leaf fluttered by and became stuck in the tangle. She ignored it, her attention wholly focused on the hollow tree below. Inside it was her prey.

Three male drow emerged from it. The one in the lead was limping. His aura betrayed the fact that he had powerful arcane magic, but he did not wear a mask. He was not one of those Lolth wanted dead.

She watched them go.

Two more males emerged from the hollow tree, one after

another. Each was a cleric, but neither was very powerful, so their deaths would be of little consequence. Halisstra let them go, too, listening as their footsteps faded into the darkened forest.

A few moments passed, then another male emerged, alone, and with a strong aura of divine magic about him. He paused to lean against a tree, as if feeling ill, but after a moment straightened again, a determined look on his sweat-sheeted face.

Halisstra hissed. Curved fangs emerged from the bulges in her cheeks, one under each eye. The fangs scissored together in anticipation, their hollow tips dripping venom. *That* one.

Halisstra followed him, moving through the treetops above, ignoring the pain that creaked through her body with each pulse of her blood. Her bare hands and feet clung to the branches like the sticky feet of a spider, so there was no need to grip. Just scuttle and spring. Once the male halted and glanced up, his wrist-crossbow raised. Halisstra froze in place, not because she feared his feeble weapon, but to draw out his growing unease.

After a moment, the male lowered his weapon. He made a pass with his hand, evoking magic, then formed forefinger and thumb into a circle. Lifting his mask, he spoke into the circle he'd formed. Halisstra's keen ears picked up every word.

"Lady, I report as commanded," he said in a tense voice. "Your priestesses are in danger. A Nightshadow named Malvag plans to open a—"

As he spoke, Halisstra flicked her fingers, releasing a fluttering strand of web. It landed on the cleric's shoulder and arm, startling him. He looked up, saw her—and immediately abandoned his message, firing a crossbow bolt at her instead. The missile glanced off her hardened skin, ricocheting away into the night.

The cleric's eyes widened. He spoke a prayer, and a

square of darkness formed atop his mask, darkening it.

"Die!" he shouted, pointing at her.

The square of darkness lifted from his mask and flew toward Halisstra, turning edge-on just before it struck. It slashed across her chest, opening a wound from shoulder to shoulder. A little higher, and it would have severed her neck. She grunted, felt thick blood begin a sticky slide down her body. It dripped from her bare breasts and the eight tiny spider legs that drummed against her lower torso like restless fingers. The pain was intense. Exquisite. Nearly enough to overwhelm the lesser, constant pain of the eight pairs of never-healing punctures in her neck, arms, torso, and legs. She drank it in for a moment, letting it dampen the turmoil of emotion that boiled through her mind.

Then she sprang.

She landed on the cleric, knocking him to the ground and splattering him with her blood. Cursing frantically under his breath—any other male might have shouted for his companions, but Vhaeraun's clerics were trained to fight silently—he fought her with darkfire. Hot black flames appeared around his left hand as he slapped it against her head. Her hair instantly ignited, and blazing black flames engulfed her head. Her eyes teared from the agony of a blistered scalp and ears, but she didn't need to see to find her mark. Yanking the cleric close, she twined her spider legs around him. Then she bit.

She expected him to scream as her fangs punctured his soft flesh again and again, driving venom into his body. He did not. He continued fighting her, shouting the words of a prayer of dismissal. It might have worked, had Halisstra been a demon, but she was much more than that. She was the Lady Penitent, higher in stature than any of Lolth's demonic handmaidens, battle-captive and left hand of the dark elf who had become Lolth.

The cleric's struggles weakened. When they ceased, Halisstra yanked off his mask and cast it aside. The male was handsome, with a dimpled jaw and deep red eyes. In another life, he might have been someone she'd have chosen to seduce, but his jaw hung slack and his eyes were glassy. Dark blood—hers—smeared his black clothes and his long white hair.

She dropped him on the ground.

Halisstra waited several moments as the wound in her chest closed. The sting of her scalp eased and was replaced by a prickling sensation: her hair growing back in. When the clench of her flesh knitting itself together at last subsided, she picked up the cooling corpse. Working swiftly, she spun it between her hands, coating it with webbing. Then she stood it upright. The fully grown male was like a child to her, his web-shrouded head barely level with her stomach. She heaved him into the air and hung him from a branch where the others would be sure to find him.

She eyed her handiwork a moment more. Another of her mistress's enemies, dead. Cruel triumph filled her then waned, replaced by sick guilt.

How she hated Lolth.

If only . . .

But that life was gone.

Springing into the branches above, she scuttled away into the night.

Q'arlynd followed Leliana and Rowaan across the open, rocky ground, Flinderspeld trudging dutifully in his master's wake. This was the fourth night they'd spent walking across the High Moor toward the spot where the moon set, but they had yet to reach the shrine. Though the moon was getting slightly thinner each night—waning— and the sparkling points of light that followed it through the sky were dimming, their light still forced Q'arlynd to squint.

The days had been worse, intolerably bright yellow light from a burning orb in the sky. They had stopped to make camp whenever the sun rose, a concession to his "sun-weak eyes." The priestesses had chuckled when Q'arlynd, sheltering under his *piwafwi* and fanning himself, had complained of the heat.

"It's winter," Rowaan had said. "If you think the sun's hot now, just wait until summer."

Winter. Summer. Q'arlynd knew the terms, but until that they'd had little meaning for him. Rowaan had patiently explained to him what "seasons" were, but even that didn't help. She said he would understand, once he'd spent a full year upon the surface.

A full year up here? He found it hard to imagine.

"Leliana," he said, catching her attention. "Forgive my ignorance, but I still don't see any temple."

"You wouldn't," she answered dryly, "not unless you were capable of seeing over many leagues, and through stone."

"Lady?"

Rowaan chuckled. "What she means is there's only one temple: the Promenade. It's in the Underdark. The lesser places of worship are all called shrines."

"I see," Q'arlynd said. He glanced around. "And the shrine we're going to is . . . ?"

Rowaan pointed across the flat ground at a spot up ahead, where the moon was setting against what looked like a row of jagged stalagmites. "There, in the Misty Forest."

Q'arlynd nodded. Those jagged bumps must be the "trees" he'd read about. "How much farther?"

"You asked the same thing last night," Leliana said. "Tonight, it's one night less. Count it on your fingers, if you have to."

Q'arlynd glanced away, pretending to be stung by her rebuke. He sighed. His feet *ached*. The World Above was just too damn big.

Rowaan touched his arm in sympathy. "We should reach

the forest by dawn," she patiently explained. "Two nights more after that."

"Couldn't we just teleport there?"

"No," Leliana answered, her voice firm. "We walk."

"We only prepared one sanctuary," Rowaan explained. "The spot we teleported to in order to escape the lamias."

Q'arlynd frowned. "But that—"

"What?" Leliana snapped.

"Nothing," Q'arlynd murmured.

He'd been about to say that Rowaan's explanation made no sense. It would have been far more prudent to have chosen the shrine itself as the endpoint of the spell. Unless, he'd realized belatedly, you had a stranger tagging along with you. Teleporting a complete stranger directly to a holy shrine—even if that person bore a sword-token of Eilistraee—would be a foolish move indeed. Teleporting him into the middle of nowhere and observing him over the long, tedious slog to the shrine was much more prudent.

He smiled to himself. The females were drow after all. Despite living on the surface, they still possessed some measure of cunning.

He gave Rowaan his most winning smile. "I can teleport as well. I'm quite accomplished at it, in fact. If you'd just describe the shrine in detail, perhaps I could get us there."

"You could do that?" Rowaan's eyebrows raised. "Teleport, with just a description to go on?"

Q'arlynd nodded. "Indeed, Lady." In fact, he had never yet attempted such a thing, but one day, he was certain, it would be within his grasp.

Leliana gave a snort of laughter. "No thanks," she said. "Much as I look forward to one day dancing in Eilistraee's groves, for now I'd prefer to go on living."

Q'arlynd lowered his eyes, a gesture of submission. His mind, however, was mulling over the possibilities the surface afforded. He'd only ever used his teleportation spell over short distances within the confines of Ched Nasad—to escape the iron golem, for example. He was itching to test the spell's limits away from the *Faerzress* that surrounded the ruined city. Attempting to teleport to a destination he'd never seen before would be like a free-fall, exhilarating and terrifying in one.

The priestesses, however, seemed intent on doing things the hard way.

As they trudged along, Q'arlynd realized that Flinderspeld had moved out of his peripheral vision. Out of habit, he dipped into the deep gnome's mind, checking to ensure Flinderspeld wasn't up to anything. Flinderspeld disappointed him. The deep gnome was thinking of his former home, the svirfneblin city of Blingdenstone. Like Ched Nasad, it lay in ruin, destroyed five years ago by the Menzoberranyr. Flinderspeld remembered how that city's orc and goblin slave-soldiers had trampled through his shop, smashing display cases and helping themselves to the gemstones inside. A lifetime's work, scooped greedily into the pockets of those who would never appreciate the intricacies of . . .

Q'arlynd broke contact, not caring to hear any more of Flinderspeld's broodings. He stared at the landscape, instead.

The High Moor wasn't, he noted, entirely featureless. There were landmarks. Not of the type Q'arlynd was used to—rock formations, patches of crysstone, fungal growths and heat vents—but enough for the priestesses to find their way. To the right, for example, was a circular expanse of stone with tufts of blade-shaped vegetation growing up through it. "Grass," Leliana had called the stuff. The circular outcropping was the sixth Q'arlynd had noticed that night. It was the almost-vanished foundation of a ruined tower, but it was the grass that caught his eye. It had grown up through cracks in the stone floor: cracks that followed a peculiar pattern. It reminded him, a little, of the glyph in the Arcane Conservatory's main foyer.

Interesting. He committed the spot to memory, in case he wanted to return later. One never knew what secrets an old ruin might hold.

Leliana noticed him glancing at the ruined tower.

Q'arlynd gave her a bright smile and cocked his head. "Are those circles natural formations?" he asked. "Can they be found everywhere on the surface, or just here?" It was a deliberately foolish question, much like the ones he'd previously pestered the priestesses with: what a forest was, why water fell from the sky, and if the moon and sun always rose and set in the same place, or whether they sometimes reversed their course. He'd known the answers to all of those questions already, of course. It might have been his first time away from the Underdark, but he had read about the World Above and its strange phenomena. Years of dealing with the females of Ched Nasad, however, had taught him caution. "Handsome but dumb" males tended to be forgotten when plots were being hatched. The smart ones became targets. He'd learned that by watching his brothers die one by one.

It was Rowaan who answered him. "They're the bases of ruined towers," she explained. "A city once stood here. Millennia ago, in the time before the Descent—"

Leliana halted abruptly. "Enough," she told Rowaan. She turned to Q'arlynd, irritation plain on her face, and spoke directly to him. "If you want to know where we are, just ask. I'm tired of your oblique questions."

"All right, then," Q'arlynd said. "Where are we?"

"Talthalaran."

The name wasn't one Q'arlynd recognized—though it sounded a little like the formal term for a council of matron mothers. Curiosity warred with the need to continue to feign ignorance. Curiosity won.

"Was Talthalaran . . . the name of an ancient city?" he asked.

"Yes," Rowaan said. "One of the cities of Miyeritar."

"Miyeritar," Q'arlynd whispered, too surprised to purge the awe from his voice.

He stared across the moor with a new appreciation. Millennia ago, that dark elf empire had been scoured clean. It had rained acid, the legends said. Lightning bolts had smashed the cities of Miyeritar to the ground, and the thunderclaps that followed had shattered what remained like invisible hammer blows. Tens of thousands had died, and roaring winds had carried their remains high into the skies, shredding the corpses like rotten cloth. When it was all over, only bare, blood-soaked earth remained.

Such had been the magic the high mages of Aryvandaar had wrought.

Q'arlynd would have given anything to have seen it.

From a safe distance, of course.

Flinderspeld, listening all the while, stood scratching his bald head. "What's Miyeritar?" he asked.

Q'arlynd often permitted such questions from the deep gnome. Since the city's fall, there had been few others he could converse with. He enlightened his slave.

"It's a kingdom that existed at the time of the Crown Wars. Fourteen thousand years ago, during the Third Crown War, it was destroyed by Aryvandaar—a nation of surface elves—in a magical storm of unbelievable proportions. They say—" He broke off suddenly, aware that Leliana was staring at him.

He gave her a wistful shrug. "I'm a wizard. They taught us about Miyeritar at the Conservatory in Ched Nasad."

"But not about ordinary rain?" she scoffed. "It sounds like a strangely lopsided education."

Q'arlynd gave an embarrassed shrug.

"If you studied Miyeritar, then you know that we were all 'surface elves' once," she continued.

Flinderspeld turned to her. "Drow lived on the surface?"

"Dark elves," Leliana told him, "not yet *dhaerrow*. Not yet drow."

"Your point being?" Q'arlynd asked.

"That we came from the surface and must return to it. The drow are not naturally creatures of the Underdark."

Q'arlynd pointed at her eyes. "Then how do you explain darkvision?"

"Adaptation," Leliana. "Our race developed it slowly, over many generations, after being driven below."

"In Ched Nasad, we were taught that darkvision was a gift, bestowed upon us by Lolth during the Descent," Q'arlynd said, "that drow were meant to live in the Underdark."

Leliana folded her arms across her chest. Q'arlynd could tell that, like him, she enjoyed the debate. "Then why do our eyes adapt, over time, to the light of the surface realms?" she countered. "And if darkvision is a gift from Lolth, then why am I—and the other drow who worship Eilistraee, Lolth's chief rival—still capable of seeing in complete darkness?"

"Because Lolth—" Q'arlynd abruptly checked what he'd been about to say, not because he didn't have an argument to counter what Leliana had just said, but because he realized what she was doing. Drawing him out. Probing. Trying to get a sense of whether he truly desired to convert to Eilistraee's faith.

Of course, he had no intention of doing so, unless there was something in it for him.

Flinderspeld had moved closer during the debate. He stood beside Q'arlynd, head cocked. "Lots of races that don't worship Lolth have darkvision," he commented. He held up his gloved fingers and began counting them off. "Svirfneblin, duergar—"

Q'arlynd nearly laughed out loud. Flinderspeld had just provided the perfect distraction. Whirling, he grabbed his slave by the cloak, feigning anger at the deep gnome having taken Leliana's side in the debate. "Keep silent, you!" he ordered, flicking a finger at the gnome.

A bolt of magical energy—a small one, painful rather than harmful—crackled out of his gloved fingertip. It barely touched the skin of Flinderspeld's wide forehead—Q'arlynd wasn't about to damage a valuable slave—but Flinderspeld gave a loud howl of pain. He'd feigned it so many times he was getting good at it. For a moment, Q'arlynd thought his slave had actually been stung by the bolt.

Their act deflected Leliana's attention, but not in the way Q'arlynd had planned. Steel hissed as her sword left its scabbard. Before Q'arlynd could blink, the point of the weapon was at his throat. Leliana's voice was hard as steel.

"Don't do that again. This gnome," she said, pointing down at Flinderspeld, "is under the goddess's protection."

Q'arlynd swallowed. Steel pricked the bulge in his throat as it moved. He gave Leliana his best mournful look, blinked long-lashed eyes, then glanced down at the sword-token that hung on a cord around his neck.

"As am I, surely?" he suggested sweetly.

Leliana removed the blade from his throat. "As are you," she agreed, sheathing her sword. "But remember this: whatever your previous relationship with the deep gnome was below, here under Eilistraee's bright moon, we are all equals. There are no slaves, no matron mothers . . . and no masters." Her eyes narrowed slightly. "Or did Milass'ni neglect to tell you that?"

"Of course not," Q'arlynd said, instantly realizing that Leliana must be talking about the priestess the falling stone had killed. "The instructions she gave were quite clear. It's just that old habits are hard to break." He bowed deeply, holding the submissive posture for longer than was necessary.

When he rose, he saw two things he didn't like. A wary expression in Leliana's eye.

And Flinderspeld, staring thoughtfully at Leliana, his stubby thumb idly rubbing the bulge the slave ring made under his glove.

Thaleste shivered as she climbed the column. She needed both hands to grip the notches in the stone, which had meant sheathing her sword, not that she was very proficient with the weapon, of course. Lady Cavatina had been kind enough to pretend that Thaleste's feeble jab had made a difference during the battle with the aranea, but the novice knew otherwise. Even so, it would have made her feel slightly better to have a weapon in her hand.

She pulled herself through the hole at the top of the column, into the room above. A short passageway led from it to the chamber where Lady Cavatina had fought the spellgaunt. Drawing her sword—and wincing at the loud rasp the blade made as it left the sheath—Thaleste edged along that passage. It was dark and silent. Iljrene and the others had already made a sweep through the rooms and declared them clear. Even so, Thaleste's mouth was dry and her heart pounded. The caverns were never completely free of monsters, despite the constant patrols. Anything could have been lurking in the chamber ahead.

The room, however, turned out to be empty, aside from the purplish smears of blood the spellgaunt had left behind. Its body and web had been burned. All that remained was a charred spot on the floor next to the gaping hole that had been a window.

Thaleste stood, studying the pattern of soot on the walls. She could see that the smoke had billowed upward, then mushroomed out and down again, eventually forcing its way out through the side passages and the hole in the floor. It had also concentrated behind one of the pedestals close to the dais, leaving a faint spiral pattern.

Thaleste smiled. She'd just found what she'd been looking for. Now she was going to be able to prove to the others that being timid had its uses. She'd learned a thing or two, over the years, by creeping through the corridors of her manor. An audience chamber always had at least one secret door that a matron mother could slip away through in times of crisis. *That* was how the aranea and its spellgaunt had slipped past the priestess's defenses, through a back door that none of the priestesses knew existed. Thaleste had found it. No longer would she be pitied as the novice who flinched at shadows and flailed around with a sword. She'd just proven her worth, or rather, she was about to.

The pedestal had to be the key. The bust that stood on it had parted lips and a hollowed-out mouth. Peering into it, Thaleste spotted the mechanism inside. It would, no doubt, be protected by a needle trap. The poison had probably dried to dust long ago, but Thaleste wasn't about to take chances. If the aranea had gone that way, she might have refreshed the supply.

Thaleste drew her dagger and slid its blade into the statue's mouth, triggering the mechanism. The pedestal shifted, rotating on its base. She sheathed her dagger and spun the pedestal farther. A section of wall behind slid open with a loud grinding of stone on stone.

Thaleste silently cheered. She'd done it! She stared into the passage beyond the door, wondering if she should go any farther. She wished she knew the prayer that would have allowed her to report her discovery to Battle-mistress Iljrene immediately, but that spell was beyond her, and what if she was wrong, and the passage led nowhere? That would give the other priestesses even more reason to doubt Thaleste's capabilities. Even if the passage did lead somewhere, calling Iljrene in too soon would only mean that Thaleste's discovery would be overshadowed. Iljrene might not deliberately claim the honor that came from finding the answer to the mystery, but it would accrue to the battle-mistress just the same.

Thaleste squared her shoulders. She was a priestess of Eilistraee. By song and sword, she'd see it through herself.

As soon as she released the pedestal, the door started to slide shut. Thaleste caught the pedestal and stood a moment, wondering if she should prop the door open then decided she'd rather have a wall at her back. If she left the door open, some creature might follow her inside. Besides, the door had a handle on the inside of it, carved into the stone. It obviously could be opened from inside. Releasing the pedestal, she stepped through the door and let it shut behind her.

The passageway extended for quite some distance— north, as far as Thaleste could reckon—sloping gently up then down again. At its highest point, she heard a distant murmur of water. She pressed her ear to the wall then to the floor. The sound came from below. The passage, she guessed, must arch over the Sargauth.

At last the corridor ended in a blank stone wall. Peering closely at it, Thaleste could see a rectangular crack, thin as a hair: another hidden door. To her right was a spiral staircase, carved into the stone, that led downward from that point. Deciding to leave the door for later, she descended the staircase instead, counting the steps as she went. The walls became damp—she must have been level with the river—but still the stairway kept spiraling downward. She looked around as she descended, searching for traces of web that would confirm that the aranea and spellgaunt had come that way. There were none.

Thaleste's foot slipped, and she nearly fell. Looking down, she saw that the steps no longer had square edges. They were rounded, as if from heavy wear. Just around the bend, the staircase ended in a large, open space, a cavern whose floor was utterly smooth, as if an ooze had flowed over it, polishing it clean.

Thaleste stood for several moments, breathing rapidly. What if there *was* an ooze down here? The drow who had built the city above her had worshiped Ghaunadaur. The lonely hole might hold one of his altars. It might even be an entrance to the Pit itself.

Her legs felt weak and wobbly. Her stomach was churning. Every instinct screamed at her to turn and flee back the way she'd come, but giving up would be even worse than never having tried at all.

In a quavering voice, she sang a prayer that would protect her against evil. It helped bolster her courage a little. Then she crept down the last few stairs and peeked into the room.

It was empty, utterly empty. There were no exits, no gaping pits in the floor or holes in the ceiling. The chamber was perhaps ten paces across and more or less round. The walls and ceiling were just as smooth as the floor. It had obviously once been the lair of an ooze, but that creature was long gone. The walls were dry, and the air smelled only of cold stone.

There were, however, several objects scattered across the floor. They were the size and shape of eggs—about sixty of them, by Thaleste's quick estimate. She stepped into the room and squatted down next to one. It turned out to be a polished oval of black obsidian. She whispered a prayer and saw that all of the stones glowed with magic. She had no idea what this signified, but it was certainly worth reporting to Iljrene. She picked up one of the stones and slipped it into the pouch on her belt.

By the time she reached the top of the stairs, she was breathing heavily. In Menzoberranzan, she'd traveled everywhere by drift disc. Even after two years of training she still wasn't used to such exertion, especially in a heavy chain mail tunic. Even so, she all but ran down the corridor, back to the first secret door she'd found. She opened it a crack and peeked out, but the chamber beyond was empty. Stepping out of the passage, she let the door slide shut behind her. She climbed swiftly down the column, and breathlessly hurried back in the direction of the Promenade, keen to report to Battle-mistress Iljrene what she'd just found.

An alarm sounded, just a few paces away. Thaleste started, nearly dropping her sword then realized she'd neglected to sing the hymn that would prevent the magical alarms from sounding. She did so, but the alarm continued to clang.

Something soft and squishy tapped her on the back then pulled away with a soft sucking sound, plucking at the chain mail it had just touched.

Thaleste shrieked and spun. Behind her was a creature from a nightmare, an enormous wormlike *thing* as thick around as a large tree trunk. Eight tentacles waved in front of its face, and its teeth clicked together hungrily. Eyestalks swiveled this way and that as its mouth opened. A foul, rotting-meat stench came from it, together with a dribble of maggots.

A carrion crawler.

Thaleste's hand shook so violently her sword was like a quivering leaf. Backing slowly away, she began a prayer that would strengthen her, but before she could complete it, two tentacles lashed out. Thaleste dodged one, but the other struck her sword hand. The skin felt as if it was on fire. The sensation spread swiftly up her arm, leaving numbness in its wake. Within a heartbeat, it had reached her torso. A heartbeat more, and her face and legs were also affected. She stood, paralyzed, her prayer halted in mid-word. Her breath came in short, fluttering gasps—all her lungs could manage.

Knowing that she was about to be devoured, she tried to bring her hands up to her belt. At the very least, she would spill the stone she'd found from her pouch where a patrol could find it. She strained until tears welled in her eyes, but her arms refused to move.

The carrion crawler advanced, its body undulating, its clawed feet making soft clicking noises on the stone floor. Thaleste watched in horror as the crawler reared above her then descended. Its mouth enveloped her head, and its teeth lanced into her shoulders. The pain was intense. She let out a suffocated gurgle that would have been a scream had her vocal cords not also been paralyzed. The crawler's teeth sawed back and forth, ripping apart Thaleste's chain mail tunic. There was more pain, and blood, flowing down her body in hot streams that soaked her shirt and trousers. Then a sharp pain, deeper than anything she had experienced before, and—

Thaleste blinked. The pain, the stench—all sensation was gone. She drifted on a gray, featureless plain, cradled in soothing song. Moonlight fell gently on her from above. She raised something—arms? No, that wasn't quite it. She could no longer feel her body, but the moonlight understood. The song intensified, the moonlight lifted her toward its source: a swirling dance that filled the air above.

"Eilistraee," she sighed.

The soul of the drow who had once been called Thaleste joined the dance and found peace.

CHAPTER FIVE

Deep in the Underdark below the Misty Forest, the judicator Dhairn stood in a vast cavern whose walls were honeycombed with tunnels that had been bored out centuries ago by a long since vanished purple worm. Above him, webs crisscrossed the ceiling. Cocooned corpses hung from them, dripping putrid liquid onto the floor, and a rancid smell thickened the air. Dozens of faces peered down at Dhairn from the tunnels, faces with ebon-black skin and glowing red eyes. Driders—drow from the waist up, but with the eight-legged lower thoraxes and bulbous abdomens of spiders.

Dhairn himself was a drow—a race the driders would ordinarily attack on sight, but his sudden entrance had given the creatures pause, as had his appearance. His scalp was shaved, save for the circle of hair at the back of his head that was braided into a long strand, the end of which was crusted solid by repeated drippings in blood. His black skin was webbed with lines of glowing white, the hallmark of the deity he served. His eyes had no color, only black dots where the pupils were. Anyone looking closely might have seen the faint yellow lines that formed a web pattern across the white of each eye and noted that his pupils were not truly round but shaped like spiders.

The driders weren't getting that close, however, not after having noted the massive two-handed sword the judicator carried. The hilt of the magical weapon had two guards, each shaped like a spider. One of these had its legs clenched tightly around Dhairn's right fist. He wore no sheath, and he could let go of the weapon with his left hand but never with his right.

Dhairn swept back his cloak with his free hand, revealing red robes and an adamantine breastplate embossed with Selvetarm's holy symbol: a crossed mace and sword, overlaid with a spider. The magical cloak had allowed him to effect an unexpected appearance in the driders' cavern by stepping out of solid stone. As they hissed at him from above, trying to work up the courage to attack, he spoke.

"Spawn of Lolth!" he shouted. "Exiles from Eryndlyn, from Ched Nasad, from Menzoberranzan, by Selvetarm's will, you are to be outcasts no longer! There is a place for you in the ranks of the Selvetargtlin, if you would take it!"

From above him came a rustling and the hiss of whispered speech. One of the driders sprang out of a tunnel and descended toward Dhairn, head-down, on a strand of web. The drider was male, his long, uncombed hair hanging from his scalp like scraps of cobweb. His face was pinched and thin, his eyes narrowed in what looked like a permanent wince. A curved fang protruded from each of his cheeks, its hollow point oozing venom. He turned slowly on the strand of webbing, twisting his head so that he could keep Dhairn in sight.

"You serve Lolth's champion?"

Dhairn's sword swept out, severing the strand. The drider hovered in mid-air a moment too long before falling to the ground, confirming Dhairn's suspicion. The dangling drider had been an illusion. Dhairn followed through with his swing, spinning around to slice through seemingly empty air behind him. His blade bit into something solid. A drider's head flew in one direction, while the suddenly visible body crumpled. Dark blood rushed from the severed neck like wine from a ruptured wineskin. The drider had a glove on one hand that glowed with an intense magical aura. The puddle of blood in which that hand had landed sizzled, disintegrating into nothing.

Dhairn looked up at the remaining driders as his sword drank in the blood that coated its blade. Eyes blinked. Several of the driders drew back into their tunnels. The one Dhairn had just slain had probably been their wizard. A pity, that. His talents would have been useful.

"We are all Lolth's champions," Dhairn told the driders, "drow and drider alike."

"That's not what her priestesses say." The voice was female, probably their leader. Dhairn glanced from hole to hole, trying to spot her.

"We are the damned," she continued. "We failed Lolth and were marked for our weakness. This is Lolth's punishment."

Dhairn spotted her. The female had reared up on her spider legs and held her arms wide. She might have been beautiful once. Her ears were delicately pointed, her eyes slanted to match. Her upper body was shapely above a slender waist. Even the venomous fangs that protruded from her cheeks did little to spoil her appearance, but life as an exile had left her no pride. Her hair was tangled, and her body fouled with the stinking drippings of the corpses the driders loved to eat. Her dark skin was streaked with smudges of rock dust.

"Has it never occurred to you," Dhairn asked, "to wonder why Lolth should have altered your bodies into a semblance of the holiest of creatures? Do you honestly conceive of your half-spider forms as a *punishment*? No, I say it again. You are her champions, as much as Selvetarm is."

He stood, waiting, letting the driders consider what he'd just told them.

Their leader frowned down at him and said, "Lolth's priestesses—"

"Lied to you," Dhairn said in a cold voice, "as Lolth herself orders them to. It is all part of the Spider Queen's plan. Your exile has made you stronger, more cunning. By preying upon the drow, you cull from our ranks the weak, the incapable. You make our race stronger." He paused to let that sink in. "If you had truly fallen from the goddess's favor, then why did she grant you such power? You have been stripped of your House insignia, but you can still levitate. You are no longer drow, but you can still cloak yourselves in darkness and reveal hidden enemies by limning them in magical light. You have powers that Lolth bestows only upon the most favored of her drow children, the ability to recognize your enemies by their auras and to magically spy on them from a safe distance while you plot your ambushes. Lolth has transformed you into the perfect weapon, a creature endowed with a drow's cunning, and a spider's venom and stealth. What you lack is the hand to wield you."

"And you are to be that hand?" the leader asked, a hint of bitterness in her voice.

Dhairn lifted his chin. "Selvetarm is to be that hand," he told her. "I am but his judicator." He lifted his sword. "Come and be welcome in his faith. It is time to reclaim your place among the drow."

It took a moment more, but the leader jumped from her

tunnel and descended on a strand of web. As her spider legs touched the floor of the cavern, other driders followed her lead, some descending on strands, others scuttling down the walls. Soon Dhairn was surrounded by several dozen of the creatures, the majority of them male. None approached within sword range, and all had wary, distrustful expressions, but their eyes also held a cautious hope. They had lost their possessions, their status within their Houses, their ability to carve out their own destinies after their transformation and exile, and something more—the greatest sting of all. They bore the painful stigma of thinking they had been judged by their goddess and found wanting, of thinking that this failure had been branded upon their bodies for all the Underdark to see.

But someone had come to tell them that it was all part of the Spider Queen's plan, that Lolth still carried them close to her dark heart, that there was a place for them in the web of life. And it was not just anyone who told them that, but a powerful cleric of Selvetarm, Lolth's champion, a demigod whose form was similar to their own.

Dhairn could see that the driders ached to believe him, but they needed something more before they would allow themselves to accept his words as truth. Dhairn would give it to them—a bloody victory.

"There are indeed drow who are an abomination in Lolth's eyes," he told them, "drow who have strayed far from the web of life that Lolth intended us to weave, drow who live on the World Above and practice a blasphemous worship. This is to be your task: to be the scourge that either drives these blasphemers back into Lolth's embrace—or that flays their traitorous flesh from their bones. It will be your chance to prove yourselves, a test you will not fail."

He held his sword before him. Its blade was clean, the wizard-drider's blood completely absorbed by its steel. He glanced from one drider face to the next. "Who of you will be the first to join the ranks of the Selvetargtlin?"

The driders hesitated, looking to their leader. She met Dhairn's eye, taking his measure. Then she stepped forward, her spider legs clicking on the stone floor, and kneeled. "Chil'triss, of House Kilsek."

Dhairn nodded. It was probably the first time in decades that she had used her House name.

"Chil'triss of House Kilsek," he repeated, touching the tip of his blade to her cheek. Slowly, he drew the blade down her face, cutting a thin but bloody line diagonally from cheek to jawline. He repeated it, turning the line into an **X**. Two more lines, one horizontal, one vertical, completed the pattern: the radiating support lines of a web. "I welcome you to the ranks of the Selvetargtlin."

When it was done, she smiled through the blood that dribbled down over lips and chin. Her fangs twitched with excitement, and a determined fire had rekindled in her eyes.

"Kneel," she shouted at her people. "Join the swarm."

Dhairn smiled.

Q'arlynd sat some distance from the campfire, cross-legged on the damp forest floor. Well inside the forest, almost at the shrine, there was a chill in the air. The mist that gave the forest its name clung to the ground in patches, leaving a thin sheen of moisture on everything it touched, but at least it was a little less bright under the trees. Their spreading branches filtered out the worst of the moonlight.

He drew his quartz from a pocket of his *piwafwi* and peered through the magical crystal at the surrounding forest. All was as it appeared. There were no hidden watchers lurking in these misty woods. Flinderspeld and the two clerics sat a short distance away, next to a fire, warming themselves. The freshly killed and gutted body of a small woodland creature hung over the flames from a hook, slowly roasting.

Q'arlynd spoke a word and rendered himself invisible. He removed his belt, laid it across his knees by feel, and placed the magical crystal on the inside of the broad strip of leather close by the buckle. Though the rest of the belt remained invisible, the section of it that was immediately under the crystal became visible. On it were words written in tiny glyphs: Q'arlynd's spells. Holding the belt close to his eyes so he could read the script, he moved the crystal slowly across the belt, committing his "spellbook" to memory again.

Halfway through, he paused and looked up. Flinderspeld had been talking with the two priestesses as they waited for their end-of-night meal to cook, but he had gone to lean toward Leliana in a conspiratorial pose, one shoulder twisted slightly forward.

Q'arlynd attempted to listen in on Flinderspeld's thoughts, but the link wouldn't come. His eyes narrowed. The deep gnome was certainly close enough for Q'arlynd's rings to have worked their magic upon him. The priestesses must have done something to block the link. That was something Q'arlynd would have to deal with in future, but for the time being he let them think they had their privacy. He had other means, honed over a lifetime of peering around corners and into locked rooms. He cast a spell that would allow him to observe and listen from a distance.

Flinderspeld had removed his gloves. Leliana held his hand and studied the slave ring on his finger.

". . . remove it," she was saying. "When we reach the shrine, I'll ask Vlashiri to do it. She knows the prayer you need."

Q'arlynd nodded to himself. Such treachery was to be expected, especially of slaves. Nevertheless, it irritated him. The ring on Flinderspeld's finger was the last of Q'arlynd's slave rings. The other four that had formed a set with his master ring had been buried—together with the bodies of the slaves who had worn them—when Ched Nasad collapsed. Q'arlynd would *not* let the last slave ring be taken from him as well.

Leliana dropped Flinderspeld's hand and leaned closer to the other priestess. Her voice dropped to a low whisper that Flinderspeld wouldn't be able to hear but that Q'arlynd's magic conveyed quite nicely.

"I'm going to have a word with this 'master' of his. He's not acting much like a petitioner, if you ask me."

Rowaan looked startled. "But he bears a sword-token," she whispered back.

Leliana looked unimpressed. "So what?" she hissed. "Our tokens have fallen into the wrong hands before. You heard him when I said the name of the priestess who went to Ched Nasad was Milass'ni—he didn't correct me."

Rowaan shrugged. "Some people simply aren't good with names."

"He's not that stupid. He's a wizard, and the academies don't accept dullards."

Flinderspeld had risen to his feet as the priestesses whispered together. He backed out of the circle of firelight slowly, trying not to draw attention to himself. He eased down into a crouch and started to blur . . .

Leliana whirled to face him. "Hold it right there!" She'd drawn her sword, and it was in her fist. Ready.

Q'arlynd scrambled to his feet, one hand darting to his pocket for a spell component.

Flinderspeld halted. He returned to normal again, paler by several shades.

"You're going to answer some questions, too," Leliana told him.

Q'arlynd paused, component in hand. It looked as though Leliana wasn't about to hack his slave in two after all. She just wanted some answers, and if all went well, Flinderspeld would tell her exactly what she hoped to hear. Q'arlynd put the spell component away.

Instead of questioning the deep gnome, however, Leliana did the unexpected. She spun her sword above her head it in a tight circle until it hummed through the air. Then she halted the blade over Flinderspeld's head.

"Tell me how your master came to have Eilistraee's token," she demanded.

Q'arlynd cursed. Leliana had obviously just cast a spell on his slave, and Q'arlynd could guess what its effects would be. As Flinderspeld opened his mouth to answer, Q'arlynd once again tried to slip into his slave's mind. Finally, it worked. Whatever magical shield the priestesses had placed between the two rings had lapsed. Q'arlynd heard Flinderspeld mentally rehearsing the story he'd been coached with before they'd stepped through the portal. Flinderspeld was about to say that he'd seen a priestess of Eilistraee give his master the token, but the words never made it from mind to mouth. The deep gnome instead began to babble something else entirely.

"We found the token in the rubble. My master told me to say—"

Furious, Q'arlynd seized hold of his slave's body. Flinderspeld's jaw snapped shut so quickly his teeth nipped his tongue. Q'arlynd forced the deep gnome's face into a smile, preventing him from wincing at the pain that flared in his tongue.

"To tellanyone . . . that . . . he . . . foundthetoken. The . . . priestess . . . toldhimshe . . . didn't . . . wantanyoneto . . . know . . . she . . . hadcometo . . . Ch-Ch-Ched . . . Nas-Nas . . ."

Q'arlynd frowned. Why was he being so difficult? Even with a truth spell in effect, he should have been able to control Flinderspeld, yet the words staggered out of the deep gnome's mouth one moment, spilled out in a rush the next. All the while, Flinderspeld's mind screamed like a shrieker, desperately fighting Q'arlynd's hold on his body while trying to blurt out the truth.

Rowaan stared at Flinderspeld, her mouth open. Leliana was quicker on the uptake. "The wizard's controlling him," she hissed at her companion. "He must be close by. Find him."

Rowaan touched her pendant, whispering the words of a prayer.

Q'arlynd withdrew from Flinderspeld's mind. The deep gnome continued babbling the rest of his answer to Leliana's question, but Q'arlynd was no longer concerned with what Flinderspeld might be telling the priestesses. The damage had been done, and if Leliana worked her truth-compelling magic on Q'arlynd and learned what he'd done, things would only get worse. The killing of a fellow priestess—even by accident—was something no drow female would forgive.

Q'arlynd's hopes of meeting Qilué had just burned up as quickly as a torch-touched web. It was time to end his little jaunt through the World Above and return to Ched Nasad.

But not without his slave.

Who, strangely enough, stood stock still, instead of backing slowly away as he usually did when trouble reared its head.

Q'arlynd cursed, realizing that Flinderspeld must be magically held. Q'arlynd paused just long enough to fasten his belt around his waist then teleported to the deep gnome's side. A second, quick teleport would—

"There!" Rowaan shouted, pointing straight at him across the crackling fire.

Rowaan's spell had allowed her to spot him, but it didn't matter. Q'arlynd slapped his invisible hand down on his slave's head and spoke the word that would teleport the pair of them to—

Q'arlynd felt his body stiffen. Unbalanced, he toppled

over. He landed heavily on the ground next to Flinderspeld, narrowly missing winding up with his face in the fire. The earthy smell of fallen leaves filled his nostrils.

He heard Rowaan chanting. Suddenly, he could see his nose again. His invisibility had been dispelled.

Leliana rolled him over. She poked his shoulder with the point of her sword, notching a shallow wound in his flesh. If he'd been able to, Q'arlynd would have yelped.

Leliana smiled. "You're wondering what just happened." Indeed he was.

Leliana flipped up the back of Flinderspeld's vest and pointed at something: a glyph, drawn on the inside of it. Q'arlynd didn't recognize the glyph, even though it was written using the drow script. It must have been sacred to Eilistraee.

"Rowaan got the idea from watching you reading your belt," Leliana told him.

Q'arlynd's eyelids were still working, so he gave an involuntary blink of surprise. He barged his way into Flinderspeld's thoughts. The deep gnome was the only one who knew where Q'arlynd kept his travel "spellbook," but Flinderspeld gave the equivalent of a mental head shake. He hadn't told the priestesses.

Q'arlynd decided that Rowaan was more cunning than he'd given her credit for. She must have spied on him, on an earlier occasion, as he'd replenished his magic.

Leliana let the vest fall. "The glyph was triggered by whatever spell you just tried to cast on your former slave," she told Q'arlynd. Her eyes were gleaming, triumphant. She took great pleasure in having outwitted him.

Eilistraee's priestesses, he decided, were no different from any other females. He'd been stupid to let down his guard around them.

"Now you're going to tell us who you really are," Leliana continued, "and why you're so keen on meeting Qilué."

With that, Leliana spun her sword around her head,

repeating the prayer she'd used earlier, casting a truth spell. Inwardly, Q'arlynd smiled. She would no doubt remove the magical hold only from his mouth and leave the rest of his body enspelled, and when she did, a word would suffice. He'd strike both priestesses blind, dispel the magic that held him rigid, and teleport away with Flinderspeld.

Leliana touched his lips, freeing them, then held the sword over his head.

Q'arlynd tried to cast his spell. His mouth, however, refused to cooperate. Concentrate as he might, he couldn't speak the arcane word that would trigger his spell. Instead, he found himself meekly answering Leliana's questions, while the rest of his body remained stiff and uncooperative. He told her about finding the sword-tokens on the priestess's body, about taking the magical boots and rings for himself, about the rock that had struck her dead.

At this, Rowaan gasped then exchanged a pained look with Leliana.

"Where is her body?" Leliana asked.

"In Ched Nasad. I rendered it invisible then left it where it was."

"And her pendant?"

"Taken by Prellyn."

"Who's Prellyn?"

"Weapons mistress of House Teh'Kinrellz, the House I was serving."

She let that go without further explanation. "Where are the other sword-tokens she was carrying?"

"Hidden, together with the boots and rings, except . . ." Q'arlynd tried to choke back the rest but couldn't. "Except for the one that's sewn into the collar of Flinderspeld's new cloak."

Leliana signaled to Rowaan. The other priestess ran her hands along the deep gnome's collar, located the sword-token within then cut the seam, removing it. Q'arlynd was relieved when she didn't search the cloak further. Inside the hem were things he'd prefer to keep.

Q'arlynd continued babbling as Leliana questioned him some more. He confirmed that he was, indeed, a Melarn, and Halisstra's brother, that he had used the portal because he was curious about his sister's fate, that he had no intention of converting to Eilistraee's faith but wanted to meet Qilué so he could offer his services to her as a battle mage.

By the end of it, when Leliana at last touched his lips again, stilling them, he was sweating. The priestess stared down at him, her expression grim. She was thinking, no doubt, about the priestess who had died in Ched Nasad. She obviously intended to execute him, but not swiftly—she wasn't nearly enraged enough. She was probably trying to decide which bits of him to slice off first. She was a female, after all, and drow females delighted in nothing so much as torture.

If Q'arlynd had been capable of it, he would have cupped his hands protectively over his groin. That was usually the spot the blade sliced first. It always, the females agreed, produced the most amusing screams.

Leliana glanced at Rowaan. She said something to her in the drow's silent speech—holding her hand where Q'arlynd couldn't see it. Rowaan glanced briefly down at Q'arlynd then shook her head.

Leliana sheathed her sword and drew a dagger. She bent down and grabbed Q'arlynd's *piwafwi* and lifted him slightly from the ground. Behind her, Flinderspeld leaned forward, struggling to speak. His lips struggled to form a word.

Q'arlynd barely managed to prevent his eyes from widening in surprise. The hold spell Leliana had cast on Flinderspeld was wearing off. The deep gnome's hands twitched slightly as he strained against the spell's ebbing magic. The moment that hold spell ended, Q'arlynd could use the deep gnome as a distraction. He thrust his awareness deep into Flinderspeld's mind, preparing to take it over . . .

And nearly lost his connection, so surprised was he by what he heard. Flinderspeld hoped to plead with Leliana to spare his master's life! Or to grab the priestess's hand, if need be, to prevent her from harming Q'arlynd.

It was inconceivable. Slaves simply didn't do that, especially slaves who had recently been promised their freedom by that very same priestess. Q'arlynd wondered what Flinderspeld thought he could gain through such an action. Something, surely.

Leliana, meanwhile, moved her dagger closer to Q'arlynd's throat. His punishment was about to begin. Q'arlynd wished he could close his eyes. In another instant, the priestesses would carve off something painful. Judging by where the knife was, it would probably be the flesh of his face or throat. He braced himself, mentally whispering a prayer to Lolth. A token effort, really, but the goddess was just capricious enough that she might allow his soul to enter her domain once he was dead.

A horn sounded deep in the woods, a strident blare, loud and long.

Both priestesses were startled. The horn sounded again, a sharp, complex series of notes.

"An attack on the shrine," Rowaan said, her voice tense.

Leliana nodded.

Rowan gestured at Q'arlynd. "What about . . . ?"

"We leave them," Leliana said. She used her dagger to slice the cord around Q'arlynd's neck and let him fall back against the ground. When she stood, the sword-token was in her hand. "Let's move."

She hurried off into the woods.

Rowaan lingered just long enough to glance down at Q'arlynd. "Redemption is still possible," she whispered.

"One day, you might find it in you to—"

"Rowaan!" Leliana shouted from the woods.

Rowaan jumped, then turned and ran after her companion.

A moment later, Flinderspeld began to move. Slowly and stiffly. Q'arlynd knew how he felt. His own body tingled and his joints felt as stiff as a haunch of thawing meat. He stared up at the deep gnome, still not quite believing what he'd overheard in his slave's thoughts.

When Q'arlynd could move again, he used Flinderspeld to lever himself back to his feet. Despite the gnome's small stature, Flinderspeld proved a surprisingly solid anchor.

Leliana hadn't taken Q'arlynd's wand. An oversight, surely.

"What now?" Flinderspeld asked. Belatedly, he added, "Master."

What now indeed, Q'arlynd wondered. Admit defeat, teleport back to the portal, and return to Ched Nasad? He sighed. The prospect of digging through the ruins and groveling to Prellyn for years on end didn't really appeal to him. Nor was there much to be gained by it. If Prellyn had wanted to formally recognize him as her consort and give him a position within her House, she'd have done it long ago. All Q'arlynd would ever be to House Teh'Kinrellz was a fetch and carry boy, one whose talents were wasted on levitating rocks and ferreting out magical trinkets from the heap of rubble that had once been his home. His own House had trained him as a battle wizard, a caster of fireballs and ice storms. He'd wondered, those past three years, if he'd ever get to use those spells again.

Until a few moments ago, he'd thought the answer to that question would be yes. His spells would make him a valuable asset to Qilué. He'd hoped to earn himself a place as her apprentice and learn even more powerful spells, but now there seemed little hope of that.

He paused, suddenly realizing something. Leliana and

Rowaan were the only ones who had heard him admit to killing a priestess, and they wouldn't be able to tell anyone until after the battle they'd just rushed off to was over. If they *died* in that battle, no one else need ever learn Q'arlynd's guilty little secret. He could start afresh—be a "petitioner" once more.

The horn sounded again. Q'arlynd stared into the woods, stroking his chin. Then he smiled. "What now?" he repeated. He pointed in the direction from which the horn blasts were coming. "We're going to join that battle. The priestesses need our help."

Flinderspeld looked uneasy. "But . . ."

Q'arlynd arched an eyebrow. "You want that ring off your finger, don't you?"

Flinderspeld blinked. He started to nod, hesitated, and looked warily up at his master.

Q'arlynd took that as a yes. "Then let's go."

Cavatina strode through the woods, savoring the smell of the forest. It had recently rained, and the scents of earth, fallen leaves, and cedar bark surrounded her. It was good to be back on the surface again, even if the bright face of the sun was hidden by brooding clouds.

She wore a thick, padded tunic under her chain mail, and soft leather boots and gloves. Her long white hair was bound in two braids, tied together behind her back. In addition to her small travel pack, she carried with her everything she needed for the hunt.

Pausing to catch her breath, she rested a hand on the hilt of the singing sword. If it did turn out to be something demonic in nature she was hunting, she was well equipped to deal with it. In addition to the weapon, she carried several other magical items. Hanging beside her magical hunting horn, on its own leather strap, was an iron flask capable of trapping demons. She'd also added a second periapt to the one she habitually wore—a glossy black stone that hung from a silver chain around her neck. If the creature's venom proved so potent that Cavatina wasn't able to utter a prayer in time, the periapt would protect her.

She'd been traveling for six days since her arrival at the shrine. She had left the Velarswood behind and was well into Cormanthor, making her way first north along the River Duathamper then east. Two days ago, she had seen a party of wild elves out hunting and yesterday a patrol of sun elves in their glittering armor—part of the army of Myth Drannor, no doubt—but she had revealed herself to neither. Eilistraee's faithful might have found sanctuary in the Velarswood, but in the greater forest, drow were likely to be attacked on sight. Cavatina had no doubt that she could hold her own, even against a group of attackers, but she was loath to be forced into a situation where she would have to send innocent souls to their gods before their time.

Nor did she seek out the drow of Cormanthor. House Jaelre's members were fervent followers of Vhaeraun, as were those of House Auzkovyn. Blasphemers. They hated Lolth as much as Cavatina did, but she had never subscribed to any of that "enemy of my enemy" nonsense.

Fortunately, there were other ways for her to learn what she needed to know. The Jaelre who had survived the creature's attack and come to the priestesses for aid—himself a petitioner and well on his way to converting to Eilistraee's faith—had given her the starting point, the place where he'd been attacked. From there, she'd followed a scant trail—a strand of web stuck to a tree branch so high overhead she'd had to levitate to find it, spots on the ground where leaves had been disturbed by something heavy landing on them, a broken branch where the creature had passed through the treetops. . . .

Several times the trail had gone cold, and she'd had to turn to the trees for answers. Each time, the creature had turned out to be only a short distance away. In one case, the creature had doubled back on its own trail—almost as if it knew Cavatina was following and *wanted* to be found.

As if it wanted to lead Cavatina into an ambush.

Cavatina smiled. So be it. She'd faced that tactic before. Demons were masters of guile, but Cavatina had decades of experience hunting them. She kept an eye on the ground around her, as well as the branches above, expecting an attack at any moment. None came, however.

Once again, the trail ended.

It was time to ask her guides for assistance. Selecting a massive cedar whose spreading branches touched those of the trees surrounding it, she stripped off a glove and touched her bare palm to the trunk, letting the plain wooden band on her finger make contact with the cracked red bark. She whispered the ring's command word and felt its magic alter her senses. Her blood seemed to slow to a sap-trickle in her ears as they became attuned to the creak of branch against branch, the green-tinged whisper of scale-like leaves, the slow groan of the ever-growing trunk. She felt her vocal chords lengthen and roughen. Tilting back her head, she spoke in a voice that matched the sound of the cedar, a slow, creaking groan.

The tree considered her question. Its upper branches bobbed in the equivalent of a slow nod. It had indeed felt a creature like the one she described scuttle through its branches, but that creature had been moving fast and was long gone.

Cavatina asked a second question of the tree. The cedar considered its answer. It started to sway a negative reply then paused. A shiver ran out through its branches, shaking loose droplets of water that splattered the leaves at Cavatina's feet. The shiver also stirred the branches of the trees next to it and was repeated a moment later by these trees. Cavatina's question was passed on in a leafy whisper, in an ever-widening circle that rippled across the forest canopy. For several moments, there was only silence, as the cedar Cavatina was touching waited for their reply. Then that reply came rustling back. An elm tree reported a cocoonlike sack hanging from it, still sticky—freshly woven. It was hanging in a tree that a creature, exactly like the one Cavatina had described, had just scuttled away from.

"Where?" Cavatina asked, her voice a low drone.

Above her, a branch shifted. Splayed fingers of green pointed.

Cavatina smiled. The wind, praise Eilistraee, was blowing in exactly the right direction. She thanked the cedar then sprang into the air. As she rose through the branches, she drew her sword and prayed. Eilistraee granted her request, rendering her invisible. Slowly, she drifted over the treetops, blown by the wind.

She had to renew her invisibility twice before she spotted an oval of dirty white, twisting slightly in the breeze. The elm from which it hung stood close to an enormous hollow tree trunk—the perfect place for a creature to lay in ambush.

Too perfect.

Cavatina cast a detection spell on the hollow trunk and received the result she'd expected: there was nothing evil inside it. She widened her search, surveying the surrounding forest, turning in a mid-air dance and sweeping her sword around in a circle. Nothing. The air sang a song that was sweet and pure, with no taint of evil.

The creature was gone.

Wait—a faint note of discordance came from the cocoon itself. For a moment, Cavatina wondered if the creature had been even more clever than she'd thought, if it had sealed itself inside one of its own cocoons as a surprise for its stalker, but the aura Cavatina's prayer had detected was weak, almost gone.

She landed beside the cocoon. Whoever was inside it was still alive. Barely. She could see the victim struggling, weakly, inside the sticky strands. Something bulged—an elbow? A faint gasping sounded from inside the tight binding of silk, someone struggling to breathe.

Cavatina flicked her sword, slicing the cocoon open over the spot where a face would be. Her sword point caught on something, yanking it out of the hole. A black mask. It fluttered to the ground and lay still, but it held her attention, much more than the ragged gasps coming from the other side of the hole she'd cut in the cocoon. Something about that scrap of black fabric was *wrong*—something far more disturbing than the fact that it was a holy symbol of a god who was one of Eilistraee's chief enemies.

The mask was somehow *alive*. Cavatina could sense it, screaming at her. Just at the edge of her hearing, like a note that could shatter crystal.

She would deal with it in a moment. For now, there was the victim inside the cocoon. His eyes were still sealed shut by a thick layer of sticky silk, but his mouth was working. His lips were drawn back in agony, revealing a single gold tooth. From between gritted teeth he gasped out a blasphemous prayer, begging the Masked Lord to heal him, to banish poison from his body.

Cavatina reached out and pinched his lips shut before he could complete his prayer. The man inside the cocoon thrashed wildly, but the only effect was a slight swaying of the bundle of sticky silk.

"There will be no prayers to Vhaeraun today," she said, "not while a priestess of Eilistraee holds your lips shut."

A muffled scream of rage came from the pinched lips. Cavatina held them so the corners of the upper lip could lift slightly. The man panted through these tiny holes like a horse that had just galloped a league.

"You're going to die in a few moments," Cavatina told him. "Your lips are already starting to turn gray. You'll be with your god soon enough, but I wonder if you realize that all you've been taught is a lie. Vhaeraun may claim to be working for the overthrow of Lolth, but the truth is that he exists only at her sufferance. The independence that he claims is a lie."

The head of the man inside the cocoon twitched slightly. Back and forth, a shake of the head. He refused to listen, to believe.

"Ellaniath is not a place of refuge, but a prison," Cavatina continued. "Why else would it lie within Colothys, fourth layer of the plane of exile? You who strive to join the god there are as much slaves of the Spider Queen as Vhaeraun is. Of all the Dark Seldarine—Vhaeraun, Kiaransalee, and Selvetarm—only Eilistraee offers any hope of escape from the evil that Lolth spins, or any hope of true reward."

She paused to let him consider that then added, "You don't need to die. Eilistraee can banish the poison from your body, if only you will accept her. Renounce Vhaeraun, and embrace the only god who truly loves the drow race. You have already taken the first step in Eilistraee's dance by climbing up to the surface realms. It's not too late for redemption. If you answer is a truthful yes, I will know it." She loosened his lips, just a little. "Will you embrace Eilistraee?"

His response was a sharp puff of air that sent a dribble of spittle down his chin—the best spit he could manage, under the circumstances.

Cavatina snorted. The answer was exactly what she expected. She'd been going through the motions, giving him the chance that was required by decree. Her obligation to him was at an end. She pinched his lips shut again, watching as they slowly paled. Sweat beaded on his lips, making them slippery, and his struggles became weaker and weaker.

When they at last ceased, Cavatina released the lips.

She stared at the dead man as he twisted slowly inside his cocoon. Her mother would have commented that his was one more soul that might have been redeemed, but that was lost instead. Her mother, however, was dead. And that kind of thinking had killed her.

Cavatina reached down for the mask carefully, not really wanting to touch it. She'd heard rumors of such abominations. Vhaeraun's faithful called the practice soultheft. Someone's soul was trapped in that square of black cloth.

She laid the mask across the blade of her sword and sang a prayer of dispelling. The faint wailing that had been coming from the mask stilled. The scrap of cloth smoothed then hung limp. Cavatina let it slide from her sword then slashed as it fluttered to the ground, slicing the holy symbol neatly in two.

She walked away without looking back at either the scraps of cloth or the corpse in the slowly twisting cocoon.

She continued her hunt.

Long after the Darksong Knight had departed, Halisstra returned to the hollow tree. It was dark by then, but the moon had not yet risen. When it did, the Darksong Knight would be back on Halisstra's trail again. The chase-me game would begin anew.

For the moment, however, there were other things Halisstra had to attend to, as commanded by her mistress. Capricious as always, Lolth had changed her mind. Vhaeraun's clerics were *not* to be killed, especially not the one Halisstra had just dispatched.

Halisstra could see from the footprints on the ground that Eilistraee's warrior-priestess had found the cocooned cleric. A hole had been cut in the cocoon over the dead man's mouth. That hardly surprised Halisstra. Mercy was one of the greatest weaknesses of Eilistraee's faithful. It hadn't done Vhaeraun's cleric any good, however. He was dead.

Then she spotted his holy symbol. It lay on the ground nearby, slashed in two. Halisstra nodded. Perhaps *that* was why Eilistraee's priestess had cut a hole in the cocoon, to retrieve the holy symbol and destroy it. The priestess might not be so merciful, after all.

The thought made Halisstra smile.

She clawed at the cocoon, shredding it. Her claws raked sharp lines across the dead cleric's scalp, torso, arms, and thighs as she ripped the strands of webbing from his body. Blood seeped sluggishly from these wounds. Eventually, the corpse tumbled out onto the ground. Halisstra bent over it, the fangs in her cheeks at first spreading wide then retracting back into the bulges in her jowls that housed them. She would give the cleric another sort of kiss.

His lips were cold and stiff. She pressed hers to them and whispered Lolth's name, forcing a prayer-breath into the dead man's lungs. Then she reared back, watching.

The cleric's eyes fluttered open and he exhaled a ragged breath, one that stank of spiders. For a moment, he stared blankly up at the cloud-dark sky, his pupils slowly dilating. Then he stared at the creature sitting on his chest.

And screamed.

Halisstra sprang off him, laughing, and vanished into the night.

CHAPTER SIX

Qilué brushed a strand of hair away from Nastasia's face. The dead priestess's body showed no signs of putrefaction, despite having lain in a treetop bier, exposed to the elements, for a tenday. The mark of Vhaeraun's assassin could still be seen, an indentation in the neck, left by a stranglecord. Her dark skin was chafed around this wound, and her open, staring eyes were so bloodshot they were more red than white.

The priestess was definitely dead, yet her body was uncorrupted. Even the smell of death was missing. This might have been construed as a sign from Eilistraee—save for the faint discoloration on the lower half of Nastasia's face which Qilué's detection spell had just revealed.

A discoloration in the shape of a mask.

Qilué turned to the four priestesses who had carried Nastasia's body into the Promenade's Hall of Healing. The novices from the shrine at Lake Sember shifted uneasily as Qilué examined the body, particularly at the revelation of a square of darkness shrouding Nastasia's cheeks and chin. Their hands twisted nervously on the leather-wrapped hilts of swords, or fingered the silver holy symbols that hung against their breastplates.

At last, one of them spoke. "Vhaeraun's mark. What does it signify, Lady?"

Qilué's voice was grave. "Nastasia is not dancing with Eilistraee in the sacred groves. Her soul has been stolen—it's trapped inside a Nightshadow's mask. They call it 'soultheft.' "

Eyes widened. "But why, Lady? What does he want with her soul?"

"I don't know." Qilué lied, loath to elaborate. The novices were rattled enough. She didn't want them to panic. The Nightshadows typically used soultheft to revitalize the enchantments on a depleted magical item. In the process, the soul was consumed.

From the look of Nastasia's body, that hadn't happened yet. Her soul was, apparently, still trapped within the mask, her body not yet truly dead, but at any moment, the assassin who had stolen Nastasia's soul might annihilate it.

"You were right to bring her here," Qilué told the priestesses. "We must find the one who did this to her."

"We tried a scrying, immediately after the attack. It didn't reveal—"

"This will."

Lifting her arms, Qilué drew the moon's chill light down into the Hall of Healing. Pale radiance limned her body as she began her dance. Singing a hymn to the goddess, Qilué spun in place, faster and faster until her body became a blur. The moonlight that enveloped her waxed brighter, filling her with radiance. In another moment, she would know the direction of the assassin she sought. That done, she would teleport to another of the shrines and repeat the dance there. The point where the two lines crossed would pinpoint the assassin. Then she could strike.

The sudden, jerking halt of the spell's culmination, however, did not come. Eventually, the glow that surrounded Qilué waned then disappeared. She slowed, lowering her hand.

Her dance had revealed nothing. The assassin had either shielded himself with potent magic, fled to another plane, or died.

Eilistraee might know the answer.

Qilué began a second prayer. Invoking Eilistraee's name, she sent her awareness up into a shaft of moonlight to commune with her goddess. It would be a fleeting link, but it would serve. Radiance filled Qilué's mind as the link was forged.

She asked her first question of the goddess: "Does the person who killed Nastasia live?"

Eilistraee's face—a thing of unearthly beauty that Qilué was unable to look upon without tears—turned slightly, from side to side. The answer, just as Qilué had anticipated, was no.

"Is his mask still with his body?"

The face nodded.

"Is Nastasia's soul still—?"

Wait.

The word startled Qilué. The goddess ordinarily answered a question asked in communion with a simple yes or no. On top of that, Eilistraee's voice sounded strange. The word had been layered with a deeper, rougher tone, one whose reverberations left an ache in Qilué's mind. She could still see Eilistraee's face, but it was more distant than it had been, dimmer than before. It unnerved her, but she did as instructed. She waited.

Another word came: *No.*

The communion ended.

Qilué shivered. What had just happened? Had it been Eilistraee who had answered, or . . . some other goddess? If another deity, why had Eilistraee permitted the intrusion? And what question had just been answered? Had the other deity—if indeed, it *had* been another deity who had spoken—been saying that the assassin did indeed still have his mask, or had the answer been for the question that Qilué had not quite completed?

The four priestesses were staring at her, waiting for answers. Qilué, badly rattled, took a breath to steady herself—and was surprised to smell the odor of decay. She looked down just in time to see the dark shadow that lay across the bottom half of Nastasia's face split down the middle, as if it had been sliced in two. Then it faded.

Hope shone into Qilué, bright as moonlight. She shoved aside the worries about whose voice had answered her.

"Eilistraee be praised!" she said. Something—perhaps the goddess herself—had just broken the soultheft's hold. Qilué immediately laid her hands on the corpse. "Join me!" she cried to the lesser priestesses. "A song to raise the dead."

The other four were startled but swiftly joined Qilué in prayer. Together, their voices washed over the dead woman, calling her soul back to her body. The song ended on Qilué's sustained note, layered by the harmonies of the other four priestesses—and Nastasia's eyes sprang open. She immediately flailed with one arm, as if shoving an attacker away. Her other hand groped for her sword. Then she recognized where she was. She stared up at Qilué, eyes wide.

"Lady," she gasped. She sat up and rubbed her throat, then stared at her own hand, a wondering expression on her face. Her joy at finding herself alive again was obvious, but so too was a hint of sorrow—understandable, in a priestess who for the briefest moment had been dancing at Eilistraee's side. She looked up at Qilué. "You called me back."

Qilué spoke in a gentle voice. "Your soul was stolen, but something caused it to be set free again. All is well now." She paused. "I called you back because we need to know what happened. Tell me what you remember. Everything that followed the assassin's attack."

Nastasia swallowed. Winced. "I was dead."

"And then? Between that time and just now, when you found yourself dancing in Eilistraee's grove?"

Nastasia glanced off into an unseen distance. "Darkness. Nothing."

Inwardly, Qilué sighed. She'd hoped for more.

"And . . ." Nastasia frowned, thinking hard. "There was a voice, the voice of the man who killed me."

The four novices whispered anxiously to each other.

Qilué held up a hand. "Silence." She gently touched Nastasia's shoulder. "Try to remember. What was he saying? Could you make out any words?"

Nastasia closed her eyes. Her frown deepened. She started to shake her head, but then her eyes sprang open in alarm.

"He plans to open a gate." She looked up at Qilué, her face gray with worry. "A gate to Eilistraee's domain, so that Vhaeraun can attack her. He's going to use our souls to fuel it."

"No!" one of the lesser priestesses gasped. She turned to Qilué. "Is it possible, Lady?"

"The Nightshadows are adept at conjuring," Qilué said, "but they would have to send one of their members into Eilistraee's domain in order to open a gate there, and no follower of the Masked Lord can enter Eilistraee's realm without her knowing it."

Nastasia shook her head, eyes wide. "They don't need to enter her domain. The assassin told them they could cast the spell from Toril, from a cavern in the Underdark that lies inside a powerful earth node. He told the other clerics he knew a ritual of high magic that would accomplish this."

"Drow males?" Qilué's lips quirked into a smile. "Casting high magic?"

Even as the others chuckled, reassured, Qilué wondered. If it *was* possible, what then?

Iljrene's spy had turned in a report—something about Vhaeraun's clerics and plans to "open" something. That report had cut off in mid-sentence and Iljrene had been unable to contact her spy since, but he had provided one detail: a name. Malvag. Qilué suspected that Malvag and the assassin who had stolen Nastasia's soul were one and the same.

"Did you overhear any names?" she asked Nastasia.

The priestess closed her eyes, thinking. Then she nodded. "House names," she answered. "Jaelre and Auzkovyn, and another name . . . Jezz. The assassin was angry with him. I think Jezz accused him of worshiping Lolth."

Qilué nodded, then turned to the others. "Whether Vhaeraun's faithful are capable of high magic or not," she continued, "this bodes ill for us."

"But the assassin's dead, isn't he?" one of the priestesses asked. "Isn't that what Eilistraee said?"

"That was her answer," Qilué said.

"Then there's nothing to worry about. That puts an end to the scheme right there."

Qilué gave the priestess a brief nod. She remained troubled, however. Malvag might indeed be dead, but the other clerics were obviously still carrying out his plan. Two nights before, one of Vhaeraun's faithful had been spotted trying to sneak into Eilistraee's temple in the Yuirwood. He had been driven off, but just the past night another attack had come, this time against the shrine in the Gray Forest. It had only been discovered that morning, when the murdered body of a priestess had been found.

As the four priestesses helped their revived companion to her feet, Qilué contacted the high priestess in the Gray Forest with a sending. The answer came a short time later in a whisper only Qilué could hear. It wasn't good news.

The priestess in the Gray Forest also had a square of darkness shrouding her lower face. Her soul, too, had been stolen.

Q'arlynd hurried through the woods, Flinderspeld jogging obediently behind. As they drew closer to the blare of horns, Q'arlynd could hear women shouting as well as the thrum of arrows in flight and the wet, chopping sound of weapons hitting flesh. Above and ahead, he could see dozens of figures hurtling through the treetops. One passed close enough for Q'arlynd to recognize it as a combination of spider and drow.

A drider? On the surface?

The creature spotted Q'arlynd. It hurled a dagger, but the weapon was deflected by Q'arlynd's protective spell and thunked into a nearby tree. The drider shrouded itself in a sphere of darkness as wide as the spreading branches of the tree. Before it could escape, however, Q'arlynd cast a spell, sending a pea-sized gout of fire streaking toward it. Heat bathed his face as it exploded, creating a fireball that filled the magical darkness. A heartbeat later, the blackened corpse of the drider tumbled from the tree, followed by burning branches.

Q'arlynd turned and plucked the drider's dagger from the tree. He handed it to Flinderspeld. "Stay right here. Don't fight unless you're forced to."

The gnome frowned. "I thought you said 'we' would join the battle."

Q'arlynd made a point of looking down at the deep gnome. Flinderspeld was tiny, barely half his height, the size of a child. "You're too valuable to throw away in combat," he told his slave. That said, he spoke the words to a glamor that rendered the deep gnome invisible. He drew his wand and strode toward the sounds of fighting.

The trees screened much of the battle, but it was well illuminated. Balls of silver-white light drifted through the trees, illuminating the scene with the brightness of several full moons, forcing the driders to squint. As he moved through the forest, Q'arlynd counted nearly three dozen of the creatures. The priestesses, many shielded by auras of protective magic, fought with sword and spell, singing as they attacked. Swords flew through the air as if guided by invisible hands, harrying the driders in the treetops.

The driders shifted position constantly, scuttling through the branches overhead and releasing arrows with deadly effect. One struck a priestess in the arm, a grazing wound, but she immediately reeled and fell. Poison. Another priestess rushed to her side and began a prayer, but a second drider dropped suddenly from a tree and landed on her back. As its fangs spread to bite, Q'arlynd blasted it with his wand. Jagged balls of ice smashed into the drider's chest, knocking it away from the priestess. The blows weren't enough to kill the thing, but the priestess finished the job, slashing with her sword in a backhand swing that decapitated the drider. As the head rolled toward Q'arlynd, he noted the pattern of fresh scars on its face which looked almost like a spiderweb. Odd.

The priestess looked to see who had come to her aid. Q'arlynd made a quick hand sign—*ally*—then bowed. The priestess nodded and went back to her healing spell.

Q'arlynd ran off to find more targets—making sure, whenever possible, that a priestess was on hand to observe him fighting. He battled the driders with blasts of ice, no longer caring if he depleted the magic of his wand. If the battle earned him a meeting with the high priestess, it would be worth it. He fought as well with the evocation spells he'd learned at the Conservatory. It felt good to be using his talents again. He blasted the driders with magic missiles or punched holes through them with jagged streaks of lightning. Once, when several priestesses were watching, he used the fur-wrapped rod that was that spell's material component to stitch a lightning bolt through four different targets, delighting in its flashy display of power.

At one point one of the driders—one also with a pattern of scars on its face—attempted to cast an enchantment on him. Q'arlynd had been trained to shield his mind, and he laughed aloud when the drider tried to implant a suggestion that he flee. He pummeled it with a blast from his wand and ran on, searching for Leliana and Rowaan.

He saw someone he thought was Leliana battling two driders, but when he got closer, he realized it was a different priestess entirely. She didn't seem to need his assistance. Q'arlynd watched, fascinated, as she released her sword, which sang as it flew through the air. As the weapon slashed at one of the driders, keeping it busy, she sang a prayer. Her hands swept down, calling a brilliant white light down from the night sky. It slammed into the second drider, knocking it to the ground. In the same instant, her sword stabbed the first drider through the heart. Then it flew back to the priestess's hand.

The streak of light had left Q'arlynd blinking. As his vision cleared, he realized the priestess faced yet another opponent—not a drider, but a drow, a male in armor as black and glossy as obsidian, holding a two-handed sword with an intricate basket hilt. The warrior's skin was covered in a tracery of fine white lines, similar to the scars Q'arlynd had seen on the driders' faces, except that the lines were glowing.

The warrior swung at the priestess, his blade hissing through the air. She dodged it—barely. The warrior whirled, his long white braid whipping through the air as he turned and slashed again. This blow the priestess tried to parry, but the warrior's sword sliced her blade off at the hilt. The priestess threw what remained aside and tried to cast a spell, but even as her lips shaped the first word of her prayer, the enormous black sword slashed straight down, cleaving through her body from head to groin. One half of the body toppled to the ground at once. The other half wavered a moment before falling. As Q'arlynd watched, both halves blackened then crumbled like soot. Soon all that was left was the woman's boots and armor, surrounded by a pool of rapidly blackening blood. This began to bubble, resolving itself into a foul slick of tiny spiders. The warrior dipped the point of his sword into them, and they scuttled up its blade. They disappeared into the steel, as if absorbed.

Q'arlynd realized he was just standing there, staring. Suddenly coming to his senses, he rendered himself invisible a heartbeat before the warrior turned.

The warrior stared in Q'arlynd's direction. He swung his sword in a slow arc until its point was aimed directly at Q'arlynd. The invisibility Q'arlynd had cloaked himself in vanished. He fumbled for his spell components, cursing his shaking hands. He was a *battle mage*, damn it. He'd faced down powerful enemies before. What in the Abyss was it about this warrior that made him so unnerving?

The eyes, Q'arlynd thought. Those pupils looked like spiders crawling around on the warrior's eyeballs. It felt as though they were about to scuttle straight into Q'arlynd's soul.

The warrior smiled.

Just as Q'arlynd finally found the spell components he'd been groping for, a drider called out to the warrior from overhead. "This way!" it shouted. "Another one that's too strong for us."

Shouldering the two-handed sword, the warrior strode

away in the direction the drider had indicated, leaving Q'arlynd behind.

Q'arlynd closed his eyes and shivered. The warrior had *let him go.*

Why?

It took Q'arlynd several moments to regain his composure. When he had, he continued through the forest—less brazenly this time, constantly glancing over his shoulder for any sign of the spider-eyed warrior. He'd almost forgotten that he'd been looking for Leliana when he suddenly spotted her just ahead. She was on her own, surrounded by three driders, all with scarred faces.

He reached into the pocket of his *piwafwi* then hesitated. No one else was around, and it looked as though Leliana would be fighting on her own. He decided to wait and see what happened. If the driders killed her, well and good. It would save him the trouble of doing something that a truth spell might later reveal.

He stepped back behind a tree, out of sight, and settled in to watch, arms folded across his chest.

Even though it was three against one, Leliana put up a good fight, but then a fourth drider pounced on her from above, dropping swiftly out of a cloud of darkness. The priestess smashed it aside with her sword, but one of the other three driders leaped forward and sank its fangs into her thigh, just below the hem of her chain mail. She cried out but didn't immediately fall—possibly she had some magical protection against poison. Then the drider tore its fangs free of her flesh. Blood sprayed from the wound, splashing a tree several paces away. The bite had opened an artery. Leliana crumpled, her face ashen gray.

That was it then. The driders had done the job for Q'arlynd, just as he'd hoped.

Three of the driders levitated away from the body and scurried off into the treetops. The fourth, however, lingered. From behind the tree, Q'arlynd aimed his fur-wrapped rod at the creature and spoke a word, hurling a lightning bolt at it. The drider never saw it coming. The bolt struck the back of its head, blasting it from the creature's body. Spider legs crumpled beneath a smoking corpse.

Q'arlynd thought he heard movement in the woods behind him then. It was difficult to tell, with all of the noise of battle, but a quick glance revealed nothing. He walked toward Leliana, intending to ensure that she was dead. As he stared down at her body, he felt a momentary twinge of an unfamiliar emotion. It was unfortunate, really, that she had to die. Leliana was an attractive female, and he'd enjoyed their verbal sparring matches.

He shook off the feeling. The world was harsh. Leliana had been about to carve Q'arlynd up for the amusement of her goddess. But instead she wouldn't be able to tell the others about the priestess who had died in Ched Nasad. What was done was done.

Or was it? Q'arlynd heard something that sounded like a ragged breath. He glanced down at his feet and saw the priestess's eyelashes flutter. Was Leliana still *alive*?

He readied a spell, one that would finish her off without leaving too much of a mark, but for some reason, he felt a lingering reluctance to do what must be done. Brutally, he shoved this useless sentiment aside and sighted along his finger at Leliana's chest. A faint haze of magical energy danced at his fingertip.

Behind him, he heard someone shouting Leliana's name. Rowaan. She was practically upon him—close enough that she'd witness whatever he did next. That changed things. Adopting a protective pose over Leliana, Q'arlynd sent the magical bolt into the body of the drider he'd already killed. Then he turned and prostrated himself on the ground.

"There were four of them, Mistress, attacking Leliana," he cried. He gestured at the one he'd blasted with his lightning bolt. "I killed one and drove the others off."

Behind him, Leliana's breath rattled raggedly in and out. In moments she would be dead.

Rowaan barely acknowledged him. She fell to her knees at Leliana's side, a stricken expression on her face. Q'arlynd raised his head slightly, watching. His wand was still in his hand, and he shifted position so that it pointed directly at Rowaan. As soon as an opportunity presented itself, he'd blast her with it.

Rowaan ignored him. She lifted her right hand and brushed her lips against the platinum band on her index finger, whispering something. Then she clenched her hand and closed her eyes.

Q'arlynd knew the moment he'd been waiting for had arrived, but curiosity stayed his hand. A moment later, his eyes widened as Rowaan cried out in anguish. He glanced around, expecting to see a drider, but no attackers were visible. By the time he'd returned his attention to Rowaan, she lay on the ground, her face gray and her breathing shallow and ragged. There was a ragged gash in her thigh, a wound identical to the one that had felled the other priestess, and Leliana, amazingly, was sitting up. There wasn't a mark on her. It was as if the drider attack hadn't even happened.

Rowaan gave one final gurgle then died.

Leliana's first action was to glance at Rowaan and cry out. Her second, upon seeing Q'arlynd staring at her, wand in hand, was to raise her sword.

"Mistress, wait!" he shouted. He pointed at the lightning-blasted drider. "I tried to save your life by killing him. Is this the thanks I get?"

She hesitated. She glanced at the dead drider and slowly lowered her sword. She turned to Rowaan and pressed her fingers against the dead priestess's throat in several places, searching for a life pulse without success. Still ignoring Q'arlynd, she raised her own ring to her lips.

Q'arlynd shook his head. He couldn't believe what he

was seeing. Those weren't slave rings, they instead seemed to transfer wounds from one person to the next. Rowaan had *willingly* forfeited her own life to save Leliana, and Leliana was about to attempt the same.

Eilistraee's followers were insane.

Or perhaps there was some other reason for their actions that Q'arlynd didn't know about yet. Perhaps priestesses who died in battle received some boon from their goddess after death. Rowaan might have just snatched that honor from Leliana by dying in her place, and the other priestess wanted to take it back again.

Except that the expression on Leliana's face was not one of anger at having been cheated but of anguish.

Before Q'arlynd could ponder that mystery further, another priestess came rushing through the woods—one of those Q'arlynd had aided earlier. Leliana lowered the hand that wore the ring. Apparently she wanted to continue living, after all.

"Rowaan's been killed!" she cried. "Help her!"

As the priestess set to work, Leliana whirled to face Q'arlynd. "You followed us here. Why?"

"I hoped to prove myself a worthy addition to Eilistraee's forces, Mistress," he said, bowing. He was used to angry females and knew exactly what to say, and his words were no longer constrained by a truth spell. "I thought that by joining the fight, I might atone for . . . that unfortunate accident in Ched Nasad. I arrived as you were battling the four driders. I managed to kill the one you see here, but the other three escaped. Surely, in light of the assistance I've just rendered, you will reconsider your earlier decision to kill me?"

Leliana blinked. "Kill you? What makes you think—"

A low groan interrupted her. The priestess who had just cast the restorative spell sat back and whispered a prayer of thanks to her goddess.

Rowaan was alive again.

Leliana fell to her knees and embraced her. She touched the ring on Rowaan's finger. "That was bravely done, Rowaan."

Rowaan gave a weak shrug. "No need for thanks." She nodded at the woman who had raised her from death. "I knew Chezzara would be along eventually."

"Even so," Leliana said. "Death weakened you. Your magic will never be as strong."

"You would do the same for me, Mother. I know you would."

Q'arlynd's eyes widened slightly at that. He gave a mental nod. He'd already noted the resemblance between the two priestesses, yet he was surprised to hear that they were mother and daughter. Normally, among the drow, that counted for little. "Blood," as the old expression went, "was only a dagger-thrust deep." Mothers, more often than not, outlived their daughters—the slightest hint of treachery was met with brutal retaliation. But Leliana and Rowaan seemed to share something more than a mere House name: one of those rare bonds of genuine affection.

Elsewhere in the woods, swords clashed and a woman cried Eilistraee's name, reminding them that the battle still raged.

"I'm needed," the priestess who had raised Rowaan said. She pointed at Q'arlynd. "And so is he. Whoever he is, he's a formidable fighter, and it's not just driders we're facing. There's a *judicator* fighting alongside them."

Both Leliana and Rowaan startled.

The healer, that dire pronouncement made, turned and hurried away into the woods.

Leliana helped Rowaan sit up then turned to Q'arlynd. She stared at him a long moment then inclined her head. "Thank you."

Q'arlynd bowed. "My pleasure, but before we rejoin the battle, I have one question. What's a judicator?"

"One of Selvetarm's champions," Leliana answered.

"One of his clerics?" Q'arlynd asked. He shuddered at the memory of spider-pupiled eyes.

"More." Leliana's expression grim. "Much more."

Judging by the abrupt way the scream had cut off, another priestess had just found that out.

As the sun rose the next morning, Flinderspeld wandered through the forest, squinting against the harsh glare of the sun. Drider corpses were everywhere—draped over tree branches and splayed on the ground in a litter of shattered legs, blood, and smashed chitin. Strangely, he hadn't seen any dead priestesses, though there was evidence that several had died. Three times, he found a breastplate sliced entirely in two, atop a crumpled pile of chain mail and boots and with a sword lying nearby. It was as if the women who had died wearing the armor had suddenly vanished, leaving their weapons and equipment behind.

Flinderspeld was very, very glad that he hadn't met up with whatever had done that.

He spotted a living priestess a short distance ahead and hurried toward her. Torn links dangled from a slash in her chain mail, and her breastplate was drenched with blood. She stood, sword blade resting on her shoulder, staring down at another pile of empty armor.

"Ah, excuse me," Flinderspeld asked. "I'm looking for the priestess Vlashiri. Leliana told me to seek her out."

The woman looked at him with hollow, exhausted eyes. "You found her."

Flinderspeld couldn't believe his luck. He held up the finger that bore the slave ring. "Leliana said you could remove the curse from this slave ring."

"That's no longer possible."

Flinderspeld blinked. "But Leliana promised. She—"

"Too late for promises," the priestess said. "Vlashiri's . . . gone. There isn't anything left of her to resurrect."

"Oh." Flinderspeld looked down at the empty armor, suddenly realizing that the priestess he was speaking to wasn't Vlashiri, after all. "Is there anyone else who could . . . ?"

The look in the woman's eye silenced him. "Not any more. Not at this shrine, at least." Then she sighed. "I'm sorry. It's just that . . . Try the Promenade, near Waterdeep. That's our main temple. Several of the priestesses there are familiar with curses. Perhaps one of them could help you."

Flinderspeld nodded politely, though he had never heard of the place. Even if this "Waterdeep" was only a league away, he was unlikely to reach it. He'd managed to avoid his master during the frenzy of the past night's drider attack, but with the battle over, sooner or later Q'arlynd would—

As if on cue, he felt his master's awareness slide into his mind, like a dagger into a well-oiled sheath. Flinderspeld turned and saw the wizard walking toward him.

"Ah, Flinderspeld. There you are. I was worried you might have vanished."

Not a good choice of words, Master, Flinderspeld thought back, pointedly nodding at the empty armor.

Q'arlynd paled. Flinderspeld wondered why Vlashiri's empty armor unnerved his master so.

"Vlashiri's dead?" Q'arlynd asked, repeating aloud the information he had just plucked from Flinderspeld's mind. The wizard glanced at the ring on Flinderspeld's hand. "I suppose you'll have to find someone else to remove that ring then, won't you?"

If that's meant to be a joke, it isn't funny.

Q'arlynd wagged a finger at him. "Don't be so bitter, Flinderspeld. This isn't the time for it. I'm about to accept Eilistraee as my patron deity. You're going to be my witness. Come."

Dutifully, Flinderspeld trudged after his master. He had no choice. If he disobeyed, Q'arlynd would take over his body and march him along like a puppet. Flinderspeld had borne that stoically, back in Ched Nasad—as a slave in a drow city, his only chance at survival had been to obey his master, and Q'arlynd, for all his bluster, had never harmed him. After what Flinderspeld had seen the past night, he was starting to question his master's decency. Flinderspeld, invisible, had followed Q'arlynd. He'd seen his master stand idly by while the driders killed Leliana. He'd also noted the flicker of magical energy around Q'arlynd's hands as he stared down at her near-fatal wounds—a flicker that always preceded a deadly magical bolt. Until that moment, Flinderspeld had thought that his master joined the battle to prove himself to the priestesses, but he soon understood that Q'arlynd must have intended to kill Leliana and Rowaan all along.

It was something Flinderspeld should have anticipated. He'd been stupid to think that his master was different from other dark elves.

Q'arlynd led him to a section of the forest that was littered with broken chunks of stone, the ruins of buildings that had fallen long ago. Eventually, they came to an odd-looking structure that must have been a shrine to the drow sword goddess. It consisted of a dozen sword-shaped columns of black obsidian, set point-first into a circular platform of white stone. The hilts of the column-swords were flattened, and supported a circular roof, also of white stone, that had a hole at its center. The shrine looked ancient, its moon-shaped roof weathered until its edges were softly rounded.

Flinderspeld admired the columns as they approached the shrine through the ground-hugging mist. Obsidian was a difficult stone to work with, its brittle edges constantly flaking and splitting. Whoever had carved the rounded contours of those sword hilts was a master, and they'd also known how to use magic. Even after centuries of exposure to the elements, the edges of those swords still looked sharp. There was dried blood on one of them—blood shed, presumably, by driders.

A priestess, still in blood-splattered chain mail and with the fresh scars of magically healed wounds visible against her black skin, waited at the center of the shrine. As Q'arlynd and Flinderspeld approached, she beckoned them to join her. Q'arlynd stepped into the shrine without hesitation. Flinderspeld was more wary. He could sense the haze of magic that surrounded the shrine. It was accompanied by a sound like the high-pitched voices of women distantly singing. Flinderspeld tested the space between two of the sword-columns with a finger, half expecting to encounter some sort of magical barrier. Then, cautiously, he stepped into the shrine.

As the priestess drew her sword, Flinderspeld edged behind his master. He watched warily as she handed the weapon to Q'arlynd, wondering what his own part was to be.

His master "swore on his sword," cutting a nick in his palm as he spoke. Prompted by the priestess, Q'arlynd vowed that he did, indeed, want to honor Eilistraee above all other deities, by joining her faith as a lay worshiper. He promised to use his magic to aid the weak and to battle Eilistraee's enemies, and to obey her priestesses—something that would probably come naturally to Q'arlynd after a lifetime spent in subservience to the women of Ched Nasad. The final oath was a vow to work selflessly to "bring other drow into the light" and treat everyone he met with kindness, until they should prove themselves unworthy of receiving it.

Flinderspeld would believe that when he saw it.

Q'arlynd completed his oath and handed the sword back to the priestess. She bent and offered the blade to Flinderspeld. It took him a moment to realize that he was being asked to join her faith. He glanced, sidelong, at his master. *What do you want me to do?*

Q'arlynd waved a hand dismissively. "That's up to you."

Then, surprisingly, Q'arlynd withdrew from his mind.

It was a test of some sort, but Flinderspeld had no idea how to pass it. Did his master expect him to swear allegiance to the drow goddess? Or to refuse, and make Q'arlynd's "conversion" all the more significant?

The priestess stared down at him. Waiting.

At last, Flinderspeld summoned up the courage to shake his head. Firmly. He had his own patron deity. He wanted no part of any drow religion. "I cannot join your faith," he told the priestess. "I am sworn to Callarduran Smoothhands."

"Very well." The priestess seemed unconcerned by his refusal. She slid the sword back into its sheath and turned to Q'arlynd. "It is done. Welcome to the light, Q'arlynd Melarn. May you serve Eilistraee well."

Q'arlynd bowed. "Would you excuse us, Lady?" His hand gripped Flinderspeld's shoulder. "My friend here is leaving. I'd like a few moments to say good-bye to him."

Flinderspeld's heart beat rapidly as the priestess left the shrine. What did his master not want her to see? It was pointless to call out to the priestess, for Q'arlynd would only clamp down with his mental hold. Instead Flinderspeld obeyed the wizard's mental command, following him into the woods. They walked in silence for several hundred paces before Q'arlynd halted and slid a hand into a pocket of his *piwafwi*—the pocket where he kept his spell components. Flinderspeld's eyes widened.

"Wait!" he told his master. "I won't tell anyone!"

Q'arlynd frowned. "You won't tell anyone *what?*"

Flinderspeld swallowed nervously. "You must have read my mind," he whispered. "You know I was there, watching, when you let those driders kill Leliana."

"Ah. That." Q'arlynd spread his hands. "There were

four of them, and my magic was almost depleted," he said smoothly. "I couldn't possibly have killed them all. I knew another of the priestesses would come along, sooner or later, to revive Leliana, but I wasn't sure if they'd do the same for me. I couldn't run the risk of being killed." The expression of regret he adopted looked genuine, and Flinderspeld wondered if he might have been wrong about what he saw after all.

"Now give me your hand," Q'arlynd ordered.

Flinderspeld did, wondering what was coming next.

Q'arlynd batted the hand aside. "Not that one, fool. Your *left* hand."

When Flinderspeld hesitated, Q'arlynd bent down and grabbed it, then yanked off the glove. The wizard spoke a few words in the drow language then pulled the ring from Flinderspeld's index finger.

The slave ring.

Off.

Flinderspeld gasped. "What are . . . Why did . . . ?"

The wizard flipped the ring into the air, caught it, then tucked it away into a pocket of his *piwafwi*. "I'm one of Eilistraee's faithful, now," he said. "That's what we do. 'Treat everyone with kindness.'"

"But . . ."

Q'arlynd sighed and spread his hands. "All right, so I have an ulterior motive. Consider this: I'm going to remain on the surface, at least for a time, among Eilistraee's priestesses. If I keep you with me, you're certain to stumble across another priestess who can remove curses. The ring was coming off your finger sooner or later—and if a priestess removed it, the ring's magic would be forever negated." He patted the pocket into which he'd slipped the ring. "This way, I hang onto my property, or," he quirked an eyebrow, "part of it, at least."

"I see," Flinderspeld said, and he was starting to.

Q'arlynd liked to pretend he was as cruel and heartless

as any drow, but his actions too often were at odds with his words. It wouldn't have been hard for the wizard to keep Flinderspeld firmly in tow and prevent him from asking the priestesses for help.

Q'arlynd stood with his hands on his hips. "Now I'm going to make sure that you don't tell anyone what you saw."

Flinderspeld blanched. "You're not going to blast me as I walk away, are you?"

Q'arlynd snorted. "Why would I want to kill you? You're valuable property."

"I'm your property no more."

"That's true." Q'arlynd said. He stroked his chin. "What I'm going to do is send you away. Somewhere far from here, ideally—somewhere Eilistraee's priestesses are *not*. You can choose wherever you'd like to go. Just name the place, and I'll teleport you there."

Flinderspeld's jaw dropped. He searched his master's face, looking for some clue as to whether the offer was genuine. "Really?"

Q'arlynd's lips twisted. "Really."

Flinderspeld scratched his bare scalp, thinking. Despite all of the times he'd fantasized about escape, he'd never quite settled that question. "I don't know where I'd like to go," he answered truthfully. "Blingdenstone's destroyed— there's even less left of it than of Ched Nasad. Perhaps one of the lesser svirfneblin settlements—if there's a guild that will have me."

Q'arlynd nodded. "I understand. You have no home, no House. Nothing." He gave an overly harsh laugh, probably intended to sound cruel. "All you have is—"

The wizard halted abruptly and glanced away.

Flinderspeld looked up into his former master's face, suddenly realizing what Q'arlynd was trying to say. The drow wizard had actually grown fond of him over the past three years. They shared a common bond, after all—home and family, destroyed. Q'arlynd was going to miss Flinderspeld.

Perhaps, he thought, they weren't so different after all. Flinderspeld himself had remained hidden while Q'arlynd had battled his way through the woods thick with driders. For a few moments, when he'd lost sight of Q'arlynd, he'd hoped that his master was dead.

Flinderspeld shrugged. "You weren't such a bad master," he told the wizard. "Any other drow would have killed me for my 'insolence' long ago."

Q'arlynd snorted. "Don't remind me of my faults." His voice hardened. "Choose where you want to go. Quickly, before I change my mind and decide to blast you after all."

"All right," Flinderspeld said. "How about Silverymoon? Our city maintained a trading post there."

"Fine."

"Have you ever been to Silverymoon?"

Q'arlynd smiled. "Never."

Flinderspeld didn't like the sound of that. "Then how will you teleport me there? Don't you need to have visited the city yourself?" He wet his lips nervously. "I heard that if a teleportation misses its target, a person could get 'scrambled,' maybe even die."

Q'arlynd reached into the pocket where he'd placed the slave ring. "If you're afraid of a little jump, then perhaps I should rescind my offer."

"No, no!" Flinderspeld said quickly. "I'll go. It just sounds . . . dangerous."

"It is," Q'arlynd said. "That's what makes it so much fun." He pulled out the slave ring and held it out. "I want you to put this on again."

Flinderspeld frowned. Had Q'arlynd been teasing him? Was this all some sort of elaborate joke?

"You only need to wear it for a moment," Q'arlynd said impatiently. "Just long enough for me to observe your thoughts while you visualize a specific location in Silverymoon, one I can teleport to. I need to be able to 'see' it in order to target my spell."

After a moment's hesitation, Flinderspeld held out his hand. "There's a cavern, close to the surface, under the main marketplace. That's where the svirfneblin merchants camp when they visit the city."

"Good." Q'arlynd dropped the ring into Flinderspeld's palm. "Visualize it, in as much detail as you can."

Flinderspeld slipped on the ring and scrunched his eyes shut. He pictured the cavern as he'd last seen it, carefully picturing every rock and cranny. After several moments, the wizard tapped him on the head.

"That's enough," Q'arlynd said. "You can stop now." He removed the ring from Flinderspeld's finger and pocketed it again. He whispered something, and glanced down at Flinderspeld, magic crackling faintly around his fingertips. "Ready?"

Flinderspeld gulped. Nodded. "Good-bye, Q'arlynd, and thanks. If you ever—"

Q'arlynd laughed. "Idiot," he said. "Don't say good-bye yet. I'll be accompanying you."

Q'arlynd's stomach lurched as he found himself plummeting in empty space. Flinderspeld howled in terror as the cavern floor rushed up to meet them. Q'arlynd tightened his hold on the deep gnome's shirt and activated his House insignia, halting their descent just before they hit the floor. He twisted upright and his feet found the floor.

The cavern was just as Flinderspeld had pictured it—a wide space with a leveled floor and a stalactite-studded ceiling. Crates, baskets, pack lizards, and camp gear filled it. The two dozen svirfneblin who were camped there leaped to their feet, shouting in alarm, as Q'arlynd and

Flinderspeld materialized in front of them. One of them threw a dagger, which glanced off the protective shield Q'arlynd had surrounded himself with.

Flinderspeld held up his hands and shouted something in his own language, but the other deep gnomes only glared at him. Q'arlynd was probably making them nervous.

"Go on," he said, giving Flinderspeld a gentle shove forward. "Talk to them. I'm sure they'll come around eventually. They seem friendly enough."

Flinderspeld looked unconvinced.

Q'arlynd saw another of the deep gnomes load then crank a crossbow. He waved to his former slave. "Good luck!" Then he teleported away.

He returned, still laughing, to the forest. Now *that* had been a leap! He hadn't expected the ceiling to be so low. As remembered by Flinderspeld, the cavern had seemed *huge*.

He wondered if he'd ever see the deep gnome again. He hoped the other svirfneblin didn't kill his former slave, even though he realized that that would ensure the deep gnome would never betray him. He told himself there were practical reasons for setting Flinderspeld free. For one thing, if Q'arlynd was subjected to another truth spell, he would be able to honestly say that the deep gnome had gone willingly on his way and come to no harm. And if he ever needed the deep gnome to perform a service for him in the future, Flinderspeld's gratitude at having his life spared could be manipulated into a sense of obligation.

Even so, Q'arlynd was going to miss him.

Q'arlynd shoved the thought aside. It was no time for sentiment. He had to get on with the task at hand—meeting Qilué and winning a place for himself in her House.

CHAPTER SEVEN

Qilué stared down at the tangled links of metal, the pitted remains of a chain mail tunic that had passed through the gut of a crawler. The mystery of the novice's sudden disappearance, it seemed, had been solved. There was no hope of raising Thaleste from the dead. Not even a scrap of bone remained, just a few pieces of chain mail and a misshapen lump of silver that had once been a holy pendant.

"Eilistraee's tears," Qilué murmured. "May they wash her soul clean."

Beside her, Iljrene repeated the blessing.

The temple's battle-mistress was a tiny woman, slender as a wand, with narrow features and highly arched eyebrows. Her voice was high-pitched, almost squeaky—like a child's. Her muscles, however, were whipcord strong, and her skill at arms was renowned. She had been entrusted with the Promenade's defenses and carried one of its cherished relics: one of the singing swords Qilué's companions had carried into battle against Ghaunadaur's avatar. She carried it, always, in the scabbard on her back.

"Why did you summon me?" Qilué asked. "The answer to our mystery seems straightforward enough. A carrion crawler consumed the novice and deposited her remains here."

"That's what the patrol that discovered this thought," Iljrene said, "until they sang a divination. When they saw what else was here, they didn't want to touch it. Try it yourself, and you'll see."

Qilué sang a brief prayer, passing her hand palm-down above the mangled bits of chain mail. An aura appeared around an oval lump that was buried within the mass. It glowed with a flickering purple light that was shot through with a tracery of black lines.

A flick of her finger levitated the object to eye level. She rotated her finger, turning the object around. The lines of magical force shifted back and forth across the face of the purple aura, one moment forming patterns that looked like a spiderweb, the next shaping themselves into something reminiscent of a grossly simplified Dethek rune. The aura, too, kept flickering, shifting back and forth between a benign sky-blue and a dark, evil-tainted purple. Qilué cast a spell that would analyze the dweomer, but pluck as she might at the strands of the Weave, the music the obsidian produced was a cacophony of tangled notes. She could tell that the gem held some sort of conjuration spell, but something blocked her from learning more. It was almost as if the magical item were being held in the hand of a spellcaster whose will was resisting her, though clearly that was not the case.

Qilué let her divination spell end. The magical lines

of force it had revealed vanished. The object once again appeared no more than a polished oval of black obsidian.

"I've never seen anything like it," Iljrene said.

"Nor have I," Qilué said, "though it's clearly a form of gem magic—and many thousands of years old, judging by the ancient form of that rune."

"What word is it?"

"That depends on whether it was scribed by dwarves or gnomes. It's read as *thrawen*, but it could mean either 'throw' or 'twist.'"

Iljrene repeated the words softly. "Do you think it's some sort of trap?"

Qilué slowly shook her head. "I don't think so, or it would have gone off by now, unless it's triggered by touch." Gently, she levitated the stone back to the ground. Then she bent and studied the spot it had risen from, a hollow within the scraps of chain mail. "Has this been shifted?"

"No, Lady."

Qilué pointed. "You see that scrap on the spot where the stone was resting? It looks like a fragment of leather. I'll warrant Thaleste was carrying the stone in her pouch when she died. If so, she probably touched it—without setting off any trap." She straightened. "The question now is, where did the novice pick this up? Her body must have been inside the carrion crawler for some time. She could have found the gem anywhere."

That said, she pulled a soft leather pouch out of one of her pockets and laid it on the ground next to the stone. She nudged the stone into it with a flick of her dagger then drew the strings of the magical pouch shut.

"This isn't far from the spot where the aranea was killed," Iljrene observed. "Do you think the gem might be connected with the Selvetargtlin?"

"That's what I'm hoping Horaldin can tell us."

Eyes closed, the druid Horaldin held his hands over the stone Qilué had just tipped from her pouch. It lay on his workbench, a thick slab of clearstone that had been balanced on the tops of two enormous petrified mushrooms. Living mushrooms sprouted from the walls and ceiling of his quarters. The druid had somehow coaxed them to grow on solid stone.

Horaldin himself was pale as a mushroom, his moon elf skin practically glowing white. His blue-black hair was as tangled as lichen and hung to his waist. One of his slender-fingered hands moved stiffly. The priestesses had healed the mangled ruin the slavers had left it in, but the druid favored it still. Ever since his rescue from Skullport, he'd lived in the Promenade among the faithful. He worshiped the Leaflord still, but served Eilistraee equally faithfully.

After a moment, his eyes sprang open. "Your priestess did indeed touch the gem," he said. "She picked it up from a flat expanse of stone—a floor, by the sound of it, but I can't tell you where, exactly." He spoke softly, barely above a whisper—a habit formed over more than a century of living alone in the woods. "Not too long before the priestess touched it, the stone was handled by a spider-shifter. Before that, a drow with a 'leg' growing from the back of his head—I think the stone means a braid of hair—and a 'shining chest.' A polished breastplate, perhaps."

"A Selvetargtlin?" Qilué asked. Followers of the Spider Queen's champion were known for their single braids.

"Perhaps. The stone makes no such distinctions. Before the drow with the braid handled it, the stone lay under the belly of a large, winged, black creature for what sounds like many centuries. A dragon, I believe. One with a deep wound in its side that never healed. Long, long before that—several millennia, I'm guessing—the stone was shaped by small brown hands. The shaper had a gray beard, and pointed ears. That person smoothed the stone until it was round, and infused it with its magic. Before that, the stone was fractured from a larger piece of rock, quarried, and passed through many different hands before reaching the one who shaped it."

"Small brown hands and a beard," Qilué repeated. "A rock gnome?"

Horaldin inclined his head. "My guess also, Lady."

"What about the rune?" Qilué asked. "What spell does it trigger?"

Horaldin shrugged, spreading his hands. "That, I cannot tell you. The stone itself does not know what magic it contains, but its magic was altered by someone, either the dragon or the drow with the braid, perhaps by both. The stone is uncertain on that point. The threads of magic that wind through the stone—the spiderweb pattern your detection revealed—are linked to the dark elves still. It's tainted by fell magic—either Selvetarm's or Lolth's."

Qilué took a sharp breath. Traces of silver fire danced in her hair.

"Will you destroy it, Lady?" the druid asked.

Qilué considered the question. If she negated the stone's magic, she might never learn the answer to the riddle it posed. The aranea had obviously carried the gemstone into the caverns claimed by the Promenade and hidden it there, only for Thaleste, praise Eilistraee, to stumble upon it.

"I won't be destroying it quite yet," Qilué answered at last. "Not until I've learned what it does."

She levitated the stone back inside her pouch, thankful that whatever fell plans the aranea had been trying to carry out had been thwarted. Whatever the oval of black obsidian was, it could get up to no mischief while inside the magical bag's extradimensional space.

Buoyed by her magical boots, Cavatina floated through the rotting branches, trying to keep an eye both on the murky water below and the trees around her. She'd been fourteen days and nights on the hunt. The moon above had dwindled to a thin sliver, and the twinkling points of light that followed it through the sky were dim as guttering candles. The creature she'd been chasing had left Cormanthor and veered south into the flooded forest. The dead trees that stood in the swamp were fragile with rot, and their branches more often than not broke off in Cavatina's hands as she pulled herself along. Like the creature she hunted, Cavatina left an obvious trail, a path of dangling and broken branches and torn moss.

Yet another branch broke as Cavatina grabbed it, sending her spinning off in a direction she hadn't intended. She twisted, kicking off a tree trunk. The tree gave slightly then groaned to the side, picking up momentum as it tilted. As it fell, it snapped branches off the trees around it with loud cracks then crashed into the swamp below with a tremendous splash. Stinking water flew into the air, splattering Cavatina's armor and clothes.

Cavatina cursed. She couldn't have revealed her location better if she'd tried.

She hung motionless, waiting to see if the creature would double back after hearing the noise. It didn't, but something moved in the swamp below. A shape rose from the water beside the fallen tree. It looked like a mound of rotting vegetation, but it had whiplike "arms" that were twisted bundles of vines and "legs" that were gnarled and blackened roots. It waded away from the felled tree, its humped body twisting this way and that as if it were searching for something. After a few paces, it sank back into the swamp. When the ripples stilled, the only sign of it was a low mound and the vines that made up its arms, untwisted and spreading out over the water's surface like a net.

Cavatina was doubly glad for her magical boots. If she'd waded into the swamp, she would have had to battle her way past those plant-things. That was obviously what the creature she was hunting had intended.

Grabbing another branch, she pulled herself onward, ignoring the mosquitoes that swarmed around her face and arms. She needed both hands to move through the treetops, which meant that the singing sword was sheathed at her hip. Her holy symbol hung from a chain on her belt beside it, ready for spellcasting.

She passed a tree whose trunk was dotted with bright yellow mushrooms. A cloud of spores drifted down from several that had burst after being disturbed. The creature was just ahead.

Cavatina drew her sword and let herself drift to a halt. A fetid breeze stirred the moss that hung from the trees nearby. Through that tattered veil, she could see a faint green glow. It seemed to be coming from a spot on the surface of the swamp.

She whispered a prayer that would protect her from those with evil intent and added a second spell that would enable her to see through magical darkness and other illusions. Then she pulled the stopper out of her iron flask and let it hang from its chain. Sword in hand, she eased her way forward through the branches.

The greenish glow came from a stone platform that lay just under the surface of the water. Ripples spread away from a spot near the center of the platform, as if something had just disturbed the water there. Muck bobbed on the ripples, dappling the glow. The platform was perhaps twenty paces long, an oval whose edges were ringed with broken columns that jutted out of the water like rotten teeth. Steps, also glowing, curved to follow the contours of the platform, leading down from it on all sides into the murk.

All of this Cavatina took in at a glance. The platform

created a gap in the flooded forest, a clear space devoid of trees—and devoid of the creature Cavatina hunted.

"Creature!" she shouted. "Show yourself!"

Mocking laughter drifted out of the dead trees on the other side of the clearing.

The creature was too far away for her to hurl a spell at it. Cavatina needed to flush it out of hiding. She pushed off from a tree and floated into the clearing, sword in hand, deliberately making herself a target.

The attack came swiftly. Darkness blossomed around her, momentarily cutting off the green glow below and the faint light from the sliver of moon above. A heartbeat later, the spell Cavatina had cast asserted itself and she could see again. Just in time, she swung her sword at the creature that hurtled toward her trailing a strand of web. The air filled with song as the weapon swept down.

The creature twisted in mid-leap, faster almost than the eye could follow. The sword struck it, but only a glancing blow against what felt like solid stone. The blow levered Cavatina in one direction, the creature in another. As they sailed away from each other to either side of the magical darkness, Cavatina got her first good look at the thing.

The creature was enormous, just as the House Jaelre male who had survived its attack had said, probably twice Cavatina's height. It looked like a powerfully muscled drow female, but with a hairy bulge emerging from each cheek, just under the eye, and eight legs the diameter of broomsticks jutting from its ribs. It was unclothed, with matted white hair whose ends seemed to stick to its shoulders and back.

"Quarthz'ress!" Cavatina shouted.

The iron flask began to glow. Bright silver light lanced across the magical darkness, striking the creature, but instead of impaling it and drawing it into the flask, the magical beam ricocheted off its glossy black skin like a ray of light glancing off a mirror.

That was it then. The creature was definitely *not* demonic. The flask would have trapped it if it was, or—and this a more disturbing thought—it was some form of demon that was immune to the flask's magic.

The creature landed on a tree trunk at the edge of the clearing. It sprang back at Cavatina, arms held wide as if inviting attack. Cavatina summoned a curtain of whirling blades around herself, but the creature paid them no heed. It sailed through them, laughing maniacally as they struck its body. Most glanced off with sounds like metal hitting stone, but a few slashed deep furrows in the creature's flesh. Then the creature was through the barrier, dripping blood—still very much alive.

It caught Cavatina by the leg and shouted something in harsh, grating words that she didn't recognize, spinning itself past her like a partner in a macabre dance. Cavatina felt a wrench, deep inside her body, as if an invisible hand had reached inside and squeezed her vitals. Intense pain nearly made her black out. Then red light flashed under her chain mail shirt, and the sensation was gone. She felt something as gritty as coarse crumbs of salt against her chest—the red periapt, crumbling, its magic overwhelmed.

She felt a tug on her foot—the creature, yanking off one of her boots. Then the creature sailed out through the barrier of blades, which once again slashed brutally into its body.

Cavatina fell.

The murky water did little to cushion her landing. She crashed down onto the submerged stone platform, scraping the skin of her knees and arms. She scrambled upright, the singing sword still in hand, and braced herself as best she could on the slippery stone. It felt as though she were standing on a thick layer of slime.

The creature crashed into a tree. Dropping Cavatina's boot, it clung to the branches and stared malevolently down at her. The blade barrier had wounded it, carving deep gouges in its stone-hard hide. Blood flowed down its body and dripped from its bare feet into the swamp below.

"Had enough?" Cavatina taunted, her sword held ready.

The creature held out a hand that had been sliced by the blades. Two fingers dangled from it by flaps of skin, dribbling blood. "Why do you hurt me?" it asked in a mournful voice. "I am one of you."

"You're no drow," Cavatina shot back, "and if you once were, you aren't any longer."

Out of the corner of her eye, Cavatina saw a mound of rotting vegetation begin to rise from the swamp: another of the monstrosities she'd spotted earlier. Invoking Eilistraee's name, she hurled a blast of bitter cold at the spot where it lurked, instantly freezing the water around it and holding it in place. A second blast she directed at the plant-creature itself. The water inside its body, frozen, expanding with a force sufficient to split it apart.

All the while, a portion of Cavatina's attention remained focused on the creature she'd been hunting. Its wounds were regenerating even as she watched. This would be a tough fight.

"I *was* drow," the creature continued, flexing its newly repaired fingers. "Now I am the Lady Penitent."

The title meant nothing to Cavatina. "What is it you do penance for?" she asked.

The creature watched as its fingers healed. When they were whole again, it flexed them then lowered its hand. "Everything," it said, "but most of all, my weakness."

"What weakness is that?"

The creature said nothing.

"Come down from the branches," Cavatina suggested. "Let's finish this."

The creature shook its head.

Cavatina knew what the creature was doing: stalling.

Already, Cavatina could feel the effects of the glowing platform. Her legs had started to tremble, and her very bones felt wobbly. The glowing stone's fell magic was affecting her. Even looking at the platform out of the corner of her eye made her feel slightly nauseous. Stepping off it, however, would mean floundering about in deep water that probably concealed more of those rot-creatures. She might be able to drive the monster who gloated down at her away with a spell, giving her time to recover her boot, but Qilué had ordered her to learn as much as she could about it, and a Darksong Knight followed orders. Cavatina whispered a restorative spell. Divine magic flooded into her, negating the effects of the glow.

The creature must have caught the quick look Cavatina had given the glowing green stone and heard her whispered prayer.

"That's right," it taunted. "It's made of sickstone. Appropriate, don't you think, for a temple to Moander?"

Cavatina knew the name well, despite the god's relative obscurity. Moander had been a deity of corruption and decay, a god who had been slain, not very many years ago, by a mere mortal—a bard named Finder. For whatever perverse reasons, Lolth had adopted Moander's name as one of her aliases, possibly to claim his human worshipers.

"Is that why you led me here?" Cavatina asked. "Is this spot now sacred to your goddess?"

"Which goddess is that?" the creature asked. It flicked a hand, sending a spray of tiny spiders into the air. "The Dark Mother, or . . ." she touched forefinger to forefinger and thumb to thumb to form a circle, "her daughter?" Webs flowed from her fingers like pulled taffy as she pulled her hands apart, laughing.

Cavatina's anger rose inside her like a banked fire. "You dare," she whispered.

She hurled her sword, snapping out a prayer as it flew

through the air. Her aim was true. Guided by the goddess's magic, the singing sword plunged into the creature's chest, burying itself nearly hilt-deep. The creature let out a shriek and flailed its spider legs as Cavatina moved her hand through the air, yanking out the sword and preparing for a second thrust.

The creature glared down at Cavatina. "You can't kill me!" it raged. "*Nothing* can kill me. She keeps . . ." It coughed, doubling over, "sending . . . " another cough, one with bloody spittle, "me back."

That said, it sprang from its treetop perch with a leap that sent the dead tree crashing over backward. Cavatina tried to send her sword after it, but the creature was too fast. It scrambled away through the treetops and disappeared from sight.

Cavatina called her sword back into her hand and cast a second restorative spell upon herself. The sickstone on which she stood had once again sapped her strength. Then she waded to the spot where her boot floated. The water rose to her chest before she reached it, and she had an awkward moment of balancing on one foot in the muck while trying to pull the boot on. Foul-smelling water soaked her clothes and slimed her skin. When she at last levitated out of it, the stench clung to her clothing and armor. She cocked each leg, letting the water drain from her boots. Then she set off in pursuit of the creature.

She wouldn't make the same mistake twice—she'd make sure she kept her feet well away from its grasping hands.

The creature was easy to follow. Once again there was a clear trail of broken branches. That trail, however, led in a big circle, back to the ruined temple.

Cavatina kept well out of range of the sickly green glow. To her surprise, the creature did not. It stood on the submerged platform, still hunched over from the wound the singing sword had dealt it—a wound that should have been mortal, but which had already sealed itself shut, leaving only a faint gray scar behind. The creature moved about, as if restless. As Cavatina drew closer, she saw that its movements had a pattern.

"By all that's holy," Cavatina whispered. "It's *dancing*."

The creature spun and splashed, arms raised above its head, spider legs drumming against its chest in time with the dance. Once again, it blasphemed Eilistraee. Its drow hands formed the goddess's sacred circle above its head. Its eyes were closed, and it seemed oblivious to Cavatina's presence. A harsh song came from its lips. Several words were missing, others were roughly abbreviated, as if choked off in mid-syllable. The melody was subtly wrong, like a chord with one note a half-tone off, but even so, Cavatina recognized it.

Eilistraee's sacred Evensong.

Cavatina was outraged. "What are you *doing*?" she shouted.

The creature slowed. Lowered its hands. "Isn't it obvious?"

"You profane our holy song."

"I sing it as I learned it."

Cavatina blinked. "But you're not . . . You *can't* be one of Eilistraee's worshipers."

"I was."

Cavatina gripped her sword so hard her hand hurt. Mute with horror, she shook her head.

"Oh, yes," the creature said, its face lit from below by the sickly green glow. "I once danced in the sacred grove. I rose from the Cave of Rebirth, sang the song, and took up the sword."

Cavatina felt numb with shock. "You . . . were one of the Redeemed? A *priestess?*"

The creature nodded.

"But . . . but how . . ."

"I was weak. Lolth punished me. I was . . . transformed."

Cavatina allowed herself to drift a little lower, but she was careful not to get too close to the sickstone. The glow must have been affecting the creature. Its legs were visibly trembling, sending tiny ripples through the filthy water.

"And now you want to be a drow again?" Cavatina guessed.

The creature gave a bitter laugh. "If only it were that simple."

Cavatina lowered her sword—but only slightly. "Sing with me," she said. "Pray for Eilistraee's aid."

"I can't. Every time I try, my throat fills with spiders and I choke."

"A curse," Cavatina whispered. Part of her wondered if that wasn't a ruse to draw her closer, but the teachings of Eilistraee were clear. Mercy had to be extended to those who pleaded for it, and the creature, in its own unique way, was all but begging. Cavatina reluctantly extended her hand. "Curses can be removed. Let me—"

The creature reared back, water sloshing around its ankles. "Weren't you *listening?*" it howled. "This isn't just a curse, I've been permanently transformed. Nothing— *nothing!*—can redeem me now."

Cavatina's breath caught in her throat. Her eyes suddenly stung. She could feel the cursed priestess's anguish as if it were her own. She suddenly understood why the creature had left a trail for her to follow, why it hadn't simply fled. She wanted Cavatina to end its misery, and—Cavatina stared at the spot where the singing sword had pierced its chest, a spot where not even a scar remained—Cavatina had failed her.

As if hearing her thoughts, the creature looked up. "You're powerful," she said. "I can sense that about you. I thought you might have a spell that could end this, but you're as much of a disappointment as Eilistraee was."

"Don't say that," Cavatina gasped, shocked.

The creature laughed. "Why should I stay my tongue?" it

mocked. "Will Eilistraee *punish* me? She's already punished me enough for my failure. She's abandoned me."

"No, she hasn't," Cavatina said fiercely. "As long as you hold her song in your heart, Eilistraee is with you still."

"No, she isn't," the creature spat back. "Once I was her champion. Now I'm her greatest disappointment. She abandoned me—and Lolth claimed me."

Cavatina stared down at the creature. The face was vaguely familiar, despite its elongated shape and bestial spider fangs. She tried to imagine the creature with hair that wasn't sticky and matted, with a body the size and proportion of a normal drow. It proved impossible.

"Who *are* you?"

"Isn't it obvious?" The creature gestured at the glowing green platform on which it stood. "I, too, once tried to kill a god, but unlike the bard who destroyed Moander, I failed."

Cavatina's eyes widened. "You're . . ."

"I *was* Halisstra Melarn."

Cavatina reeled. "But you were killed! At the very gates of the Demonweb Pits. Qilué saw it in her scrying."

Halisstra shrugged.

Questions tumbled from Cavatina's lips. "How did you survive? Where have you been? What *happened?*"

"I told you, Lolth punished me."

"But surely . . ." Cavatina paused. Shook her head. "It must have been Eilistraee who restored life to you after you were struck down. Why didn't you call upon Eilistraee's aid?"

Another shrug. "By then, I'd already lost my faith."

"You can still be redeemed," Cavatina insisted. "If you just—"

Halisstra gave a bitter laugh. "That's what Seyll said, and look where she wound up."

Cavatina felt a shiver pass through her. "What are you talking about?"

Halisstra stared up at her with eyes hollow as an empty pit. "Seyll sacrificed herself—she let her soul be consigned to oblivion. And for what?" Halisstra's eyes suddenly blazed. "Nothing! I *failed*."

Cavatina spoke softly, as to an injured child. "They asked too much of you. You were a novice priestess, and they asked you to slay a god."

Halisstra shuddered. Weakened by the sickstone, she sank to her knees on the glowing platform. Water rippled across its sickly green glow.

Cavatina extended her hand. "Come away from there. You've suffered enough."

Halisstra gave a heavy sigh. "I *tried* to serve Eilistraee. Even after I knew I'd failed her—after Lolth had her way with me and cast me aside—I tried to redeem myself. The Crescent Blade was broken, but I picked up the pieces and carried them to the temple that Feliane, Uluyara, and I had consecrated when we first entered the Demonweb Pits and laid them down inside it and watched as the sword mended itself together and—"

"What?" Cavatina shook her head. Halisstra was telling her too much, too fast. "Are you saying you created a temple sacred to Eilistraee within the Demonweb Pits?"

Halisstra nodded. There was a light in her eye.

"And that the Crescent Blade—a weapon capable of killing Lolth—still exists?" Cavatina asked.

Halisstra gave a trembling nod. Then a sly smile. "And it's somewhere that Lolth can't touch it. The temple we created is still standing, and the Crescent Blade is inside it."

Cavatina let out a long breath. She held up a hand. "Just a moment." She spoke Qilué's name, and an instant later felt the high priestess link minds with her. In a low whisper, Cavatina sent a message back to the Promenade.

"I found the creature. It's Halisstra Melarn, her body corrupted by Lolth. She said much that you should hear."

The reply was a moment in coming. *Take her to the shrine in the Velarswood. Wait for me there.*

Cavatina nodded. Qilué had sounded worried about something. Distracted. Cavatina wondered what new threat had arisen since she'd left the Promenade.

She extended a hand to the creature that had once been a priestess like herself. "Come," she told Halisstra. "Your chance for redemption may be at hand."

Szorak crept through the darkened forest, muttering to himself behind his mask. He didn't much care for the Lethyr, even though the thick canopy of intertwined branches above screened the moon's harsh light. Despite the magical ring that had turned his skin and clothing the exact color of the shadows he passed through and the boots that enabled him to move in utter silence, stilling even the crack of a dead branch underfoot, he still felt as if he was being watched.

Which he was. The very trees were alive. They whispered the whereabouts of all who entered the forest to its guardians.

Fortunately, his mission that dark night had nothing to do with either trees or druids. It wasn't a druid's soul Szorak was after, but that of a priestess.

As he drew closer to Eilistraee's shrine, the spell he'd cast a few moments before picked up the first of the wards: a dim glow coming from underneath a pile of dead leaves, several paces ahead. Szorak pulled out a rod of black iron and held it at the ready. Then he walked forward. As the ward was triggered, sparkles of frost-white light erupted on his skin, causing him to gasp from their cold. The wand, however, drew the bitter cold down into itself, and after a heartbeat, it was gone.

"Is that the best you can do, ladies?" Szorak muttered.

"I expected something a little more lethal."

He continued forward, the rod held loosely in his hand. The pile of leaves exploded as a sword flew out of it. Szorak was barely able to bring his rod up in time. He smashed it against the sword in a desperate parry. Black iron met shining steel with a loud *clank,* and there was a silent explosion of magical energy. The sword tumbled to the ground, inert.

Szorak took a deep breath. He stared down at the two glyphs engraved in the blade. Both incorporated the word *ogglin*. Enemy. Even a magical disguise wouldn't have fooled them, and Szorak hadn't expected a two-glyph ward. Had he not parried the sword, he might have already been dead.

He chuckled. "That's almost worthy of Vhaeraun, ladies, except that *our* sword thrust would have come from behind."

His detection magic revealed other wards to the right and left. The sword must be one of several placed in a ring around the shrine's perimeter, but that ring had been broken.

Szorak stepped across the neutralized sword. Then he activated the secondary power of his ring, disguising himself. Though he could still feel the soft velvet of his mask against his cheeks and chin, to an observer his face would appear bare, his cheeks smooth and feminine. He would seem taller than he really was, his body more shapely, and his black cloak, shirt, and trousers would instead look like chain mail, covered by a breastplate bearing Eilistraee's moon and sword. The rod in his hand would appear to be a sword. Anyone touching him would instantly perceive that all was not as it seemed, but he fully intended that whoever got close enough for that wouldn't live for more than a heartbeat.

He walked on through the darkened woods. Up ahead, he could hear women singing and see shapes moving through the trees—Eilistraee's faithful, worshiping at their shrine. He veered away from that spot, looking instead for the place where the priestesses made their home. On a hunch, he whispered a prayer that would lead him to the nearest cave.

The cave turned out to be a slit in the hillside, screened by the flow of a stream that tumbled from above. The entrance, however, was protected by magic. Even from a distance, Szorak could feel its power. It produced a high, shrill note that grew in intensity the nearer he got to the cave. Try as he might, he could not get close enough to cancel it with his rod. Forcing himself in that direction made his ears pound until he thought they were going to burst.

He backed away, muttering dark curses. He would have to steal a soul from one of the dancers, instead. "A challenge, Masked Lord?" he muttered. His eyes gleamed. "I accept." He made his way back through the woods.

The shrine turned out to be a natural pillar of black rock, twice the height of a drow, carved with crescent moons. A sword hilt protruded from the top of it. The pillar had been bored through with holes, and the breeze passing through them created a sound like several flutes playing at once. The priestesses danced around the pillar in a loose circle, naked save for the belts that held their hunting horns and the holy symbols that hung around their necks. Each female had a sword which she held at arm's length as she twirled. Blade clashed against blade as the women spun together, then apart again, their swords trailing sparkles of silver light.

The dance might have been beautiful, had it not been a violation of the sacred order. Had Eilistraee not interfered, Vhaeraun might have united all of the darkelves under a single deity millennia ago, but Eilistraee had proved as greedy as Lolth and had stolen the females away from the Masked Lord's worship. She'd taught them to exclude males from her circle, to subjugate and revile them instead.

Vhaeraun's followers had learned a bitter lesson. Females could not be trusted.

Szorak watched long enough to determine that priestesses were joining and leaving the dance at what seemed to be random intervals. Though they danced in a group, there was no discernable pattern to their collective movements. Each female seemed to be following her own path. Satisfied, he altered his magical disguise, giving clothing the appearance of bare flesh. Then, holding his disguised rod like a sword, he danced into their midst.

The women, fooled by his disguise, made room for him. He kept to the fringes, both unwilling and unable to approach the holy pillar. It, like the cave where the women lived, was warded with magic that clenched his belly and made him feel as though he were about to vomit, but the rod in his hand dampened it enough to make it bearable. The excitement he felt at having penetrated their holy dance gave him a sharp thrill. Blood pounded through his body as he danced, leaving him flushed.

Spinning close to one of the dancing priestesses, he moved his rod like a sword. She, in turn, clanked her blade against it. The force of the blow numbed his fingers, but his rod, being metal, gave a convincing *clang,* meanwhile draining the sword of its magic. Quickly, he whispered a prayer.

Before the woman could spin away, he leaned in close to her ear and whispered a harsh command: "Follow."

It was a gamble. If the spell failed, he would have just given himself away as a male, since his voice remained undisguised, but the dice seemed to have rolled in his favor. There was no commotion behind him as he spun out of the dance and strode away into the forest. The priestess he had singled out followed wordlessly, meek as a rothé culled from the herd.

When they were some distance from the dance, he turned to face her. He was glad to see that she was drow and not one of those surface elves who stained their skin black. Killing one of those would be so much less satisfying.

She was still panting from the dance, her breasts rising and falling, her long white hair damp with sweat. She frowned slightly, a hint of confusion in her eyes as she stared at Szorak. Her sword hung loose in her hand.

"What do you want? Why have we left the dance?"

Szorak beckoned to her, leaning forward as if to whisper a confidence in her ear. He had to stand on tiptoe to do it; like most females, she was taller than he.

She leaned closer.

He touched her cheek, whispering the word that would trigger his spell. Dark magic leaped from his fingertips. As her body convulsed, he pressed his lips against hers, sucking her soul into his mask.

But the soultheft spell didn't work. Instead of being slain by his magic, the priestess still lived. She smashed a hand against his chest, shoving him backward. Then she swept her sword through the air in a slash that should have decapitated him, but Szorak's spell had done at least some damage. The priestess staggered as she swung her weapon, and he was able to duck just in time to avoid the blade. Muttering a curse, he sprang inside the arc of her next swing, shaking a weighted strangle cord out of his sleeve. He whipped it around her neck, twisting around behind her and catching it in his other hand. Then he leaped onto her back, wrapping his legs around her waist and levering his upper torso backwards to tighten the cord.

The strangle cord bit into the priestess's neck, preventing her from crying out or casting any spell that required prayer, but she was no fool. She hurled herself backward, smashing Szorak into a tree. The back of his head cracked against rough bark and he lost his grip on one end of the strangle cord. As the priestess wrenched herself away from him, he scrambled to his feet, yanking a poisoned dagger out of a wrist sheath. As he readied it for a throw, the priestess tried to call out, but her voice was still a half-strangled whisper from the cord that had scored a line across her throat. She started to reach for the hunting horn at her belt.

Before she could wrench it free, Szorak threw. His dagger buried itself in her throat. The venom that coated it finished the job his strangle cord had begun. The priestess stiffened, her sword trembling in her hands and her eyes rolling back in her head.

Szorak caught her as she fell. Once more, he pressed his mouth against hers and inhaled—and his mask drank in her soul. He pressed his body against hers, savoring the moment. Even through his clothes, her bare skin felt hot, slippery with sweat from their struggle and slick with blood from the wound in her throat. Fully aroused, Szorak fumbled with his trousers. He would *take* her, he decided fiercely. Just as the priestesses of Menzoberranzan had taken him, so many times when he was just a boy, to satisfy their dark and disgusting needs. Leering behind his mask, he savored the thrill of what he was about to do, mere steps away from Eilistraee's sacred grove. While the song of her oblivious faithful wafted through the trees, he would—

Something slid into his back, penetrating cloth and flesh, something cold and sharp. A sword blade. As pain rushed into the void it had pierced in his body, Szorak twisted his head, a shocked expression on his face. A priestess of Eilistraee loomed above him, her face obscured by the moonlight that haloed her hair in a fierce white blaze. For a moment, he thought he recognized her.

"Seyll?" he gasped.

If it was Seyll, she made no reply. Placing a foot on his back, the priestess yanked the sword free. The blood that

coated it—Szorak's own blood—dribbled from its point
into his blinking eyes.

Eilistraee, spitting in his face.

Then blackness claimed him.

CHAPTER EIGHT

Q'arlynd watched from a distance as Leliana, Rowaan, and the other priestesses who had survived the drider attack stood under the tree and sang, completing their sacred observances for the six who had died at the judicator's hand. Normally, Rowaan had explained, the bodies of the faithful were lashed into a bier high in the treetops, but the judicator's magical attack had left nothing behind of those he had slain. The priestesses had been forced to make do with empty clothing and armor. These they had bundled and lain to rest in the bare branches of the trees to be washed by moonlight—"Eilistraee's tears."

At the moment, however, the night sky was overcast. It wasn't moonlight that fell on the bundles in the treetops but snow. Q'arlynd had read about the stuff in books, but this was the first time he'd experienced it firsthand. It dusted his *piwafwi* like a thick layer of drifting spores—except that these "spores" of frozen water were cold and melted on contact with the skin. They soaked right through his *piwafwi* and into his shirt, making him shiver.

He squinted as the wind blew snow into his eyes. Why he'd lingered to watch the singing, he couldn't say. He was still very much an outsider, despite having spoken the vows that had admitted him to Eilistraee's faith. Males weren't invited to join the sacred dances, nor could they lend their voices to the Evensong. Eilistraee granted magic to her priestesses only, and males could play but a supporting role, just as in Lolth's faith.

Like mother, like daughter, Q'arlynd supposed.

The song ended. The ritual was over. Q'arlynd waved at Rowaan, beckoning her over. She glanced at Leliana, who shrugged, then walked toward him, her boots crunching holes into the ankle-deep snow.

Q'arlynd bowed his head as she approached. "Lady," he said. "May I ask a question?"

"Call me Rowaan. We're all equals, in Eilistraee's eyes."

Hardly, Q'arlynd thought.

"What's your question?"

Q'arlynd took a deep breath. As a boy, he'd once asked this question of one of Lolth's priestesses and gotten a thorough whipping in reply, but he was curious to know what awaited him in the afterlife, having accepted Eilistraee as his patron deity. "What was it like—being dead?"

Rowaan was silent for several moments. "You want to know what awaits you in Eilistraee's domain."

Q'arlynd nodded. "Do you remember much of it?"

Rowaan smiled. "A little. I realized I was dead when I found myself standing, alone, in a place that was featureless and gray: the Fugue Plain. There were others around me—other souls—but I couldn't see or touch them, just *feel* them. Then I heard a voice." She blinked, her eyes shiny with tears. "An indescribably beautiful voice. It was Eilistraee, singing to me. Calling me. A rift opened in the gray, and a shaft of moonlight shone through. I moved toward it, but just as I was about to touch the moonbeam and ascend to the goddess, it was gone. I woke up in the forest, alive. Chezzara had raised me from the dead before I could enter Eilistraee's domain."

She shrugged and gave him a shy smile. "So I really can't tell you what dancing with the goddess is like."

"The shaft of moonlight," Q'arlynd said. "It just appeared?"

Rowaan nodded. "Of course. When Eilistraee sang. It's the gateway to her domain."

"Probably just as well you didn't go there."

"I'm not sure I understand what you mean."

"You might have been attacked and your soul consumed."

Rowaan frowned. "By what?"

Q'arlynd hesitated. "Aren't there usually . . . some sort of creatures your soul has to fight its way past, or some other trial you must endure before passing into the goddess's presence?"

"Why would you think that?"

"Lolth's domain is filled with monsters that consume souls," Q'arlynd explained. "If your soul manages to avoid those, there's still the Pass of the Soulreaver to get through. From what the priestesses teach, it's the equivalent of being flayed alive. Only the toughest and most tenacious survive the passage to eventually stand by Lolth's side. The rest are annihilated." He shrugged. "I expected Eilistraee to at least throw up a wall of swords or something to whittle out the faithful from the dross, to select those who are truly worthy."

Rowaan smiled. "Eilistraee doesn't test her faithful.

We test ourselves. It's what we do here on Toril, before our deaths, that matters."

"What about those who convert to the faith?" Q'arlynd asked. "What if, before they sought redemption, they did things that Eilistraee found abhorrent?"

Rowaan stared at him for several moments. Then she nodded. "Ah. I see. You're worried that Eilistraee won't accept you."

"Actually, I was thinking about Halisstra," he lied.

Rowaan touched his arm, not really listening. "It doesn't matter what you were before your redemption, which deity you worshiped. You belong to Eilistraee now."

His heart nearly skipped a beat at that. Had Halisstra told the priestesses about his earlier, half-hearted "conversion" to Vhaeraun's worship? Q'arlynd opened his mouth, intending to explain that the dalliances of his youth were just that—mere flirtations, the sort of thing any boy might make the mistake of getting caught up in. He paused before speaking, worried that anything he said might bring his more recent conversion into question. If he protested that he hadn't been serious back then, the priestesses might think him less than sincere with them, too—something that would be a mark against him, when he finally got to meet their high priestess.

Rowaan, perhaps sensing his unease, gently touched his arm. "The Spider Queen has no hold upon you any more."

Q'arlynd relaxed as he realized she'd been talking about Lolth, not Vhaeraun.

"I only paid Lolth lip service," he said. "I spoke the words, because her priestesses ordered me to, but I never gave the Spider Queen my heart." He touched his chest as he said that, an earnest expression on his face.

Part of what he said was true. He certainly hadn't made the Spider Queen any promises, let alone claimed her as his patron deity. He'd never seen the point. For the living worshipers of Lolth, there was great reward—power and glory—but only if you were female. Males were told their reward would come after death, but from all Q'arlynd had heard, Lolth handed out only more suffering.

"You've left all that behind in the darkness," Rowaan continued. "You've come up into Eilistraee's light. As long as you've truly taken her song into your heart, you'll dance forever with the goddess."

"Eternal reward," Q'arlynd whispered, adding a touch of reverence to his voice. He needed to appear suitably awed, even though he knew what Rowaan was saying was too good to be true. "But only, surely, for the souls of those who proved themselves worthy of it in life by aiding the goddess in some substantial way."

"No," Rowaan said, her voice firm. "To Eilistraee, struggle and success are the same. It's the intent behind the act that truly counts."

Q'arlynd stroked his chin, mulling that over. If what Rowaan said was true, Eilistraee offered eternal life to anyone who stuck to their vows of aiding the weak and working to convert other drow to the faith. It didn't matter if they actually *succeeded* in achieving those goals, only that they had tried.

It was an astonishing doctrine, one that contradicted everything Q'arlynd had learned in life thus far. From all that he'd observed and been taught, the gods demanded either everything or nothing of their faithful. Vhaeraun, for example, insisted on perfection from his followers. The slightest failure in following the Masked Lord's decree would earn his eternal wrath. Even those who had hitherto been the most devout of his followers could find themselves forever barred from his domain. Lolth, in contrast, reveled in chaos and didn't seem to care what her faithful did. Nor did she take much of a hand in the trials they faced after death, leaving that to the minions of her domain. Souls—from the lowest male lay worshiper to the highest female priestess—succeeded in making the passage across the Demonweb Pits by chance as much as anything.

In contrast, Eilistraee made demands of her followers but showed mercy to them, even when they failed.

Q'arlynd supposed that was a comforting thought to most, but to him the idea of a deity who weighed not just deeds but intentions was more than a little unnerving, and it seemed a little unfair. Vhaeraun's followers, as long as they produced results that were to their god's liking, could harbor whatever rebellious thoughts they liked in their hearts. Lolth's priestesses could do and think *whatever* they wanted, since the rewards their goddess bestowed were so often arbitrary. Eilistraee's faithful, on the other hand, had to always be asking themselves not just if they were doing the right thing but if they were doing it for the right reasons.

Q'arlynd didn't want to have to live up to that. After a lifetime of lying to survive, he wasn't sure himself when he was telling the truth.

Most of the other females had returned to their quarters. Leliana, however, lingered, talking to another priestess who had also remained behind. Q'arlynd could see that Leliana was keeping an eye on her daughter. Despite his avowed conversion, she still didn't trust him. Not fully.

"One other question . . . Is Eilistraee's domain truly a place where the dead are happy?"

Rowaan seemed startled by his question. "Of course. What could bring more joy than slowly becoming one with the goddess herself?"

Q'arlynd lowered his voice. "Then why were you so sad when Leliana died?"

"Because I'd miss her," Rowaan said. She paused a moment then added, "Imagine if someone you loved suddenly disappeared, and you knew it might be many years—perhaps centuries—before you'd see them again.

You'd be terribly sad to see them go. You'd cry, too."

No, I wouldn't, Q'arlynd thought. I didn't, not three years ago, and not now.

"Then why did you use your ring to change places with her?" he asked. "The same would apply. You would be dead, and she would be alive, and it might be many years before you met again."

Rowaan winced. "My mother is a powerful priestess. She can do more to further Eilistraee's cause here on Toril than I can."

She glanced up at the bundles in the trees. "We raise our dead because we must. We're few in number and we can't afford to lose a single one of the faithful from our ranks. That's why the judicator's attack was so devastating. Without a body, we can't resurrect the dead, and there's so much work yet to be done. So many drow haven't yet been brought up into the light. Every one of Eilistraee's faithful is going to be needed in the coming fight." She stared down at Q'arlynd, and for a moment he felt as if a divine being stared into his soul. "Every one."

Q'arlynd shivered.

Behind Rowaan, Leliana ended her conversation with the other priestess and walked toward them. Q'arlynd bowed as she approached.

"What are you two talking about?" Leliana asked.

Rowaan turned, smiling. "He was asking about Eilistraee's domain and what it's like to dance with the goddess."

Leliana cocked an eyebrow and turned to Q'arlynd. "Why? Are you planning on dying some time soon?"

He rose from his bow. "Not if I can help it, Lady. Eilistraee willing, it will be a while yet before I set foot in her domain." He gave them one of his most boyish smiles. "I'm not much of a dancer, you see."

The remark had the desired effect. Rowaan laughed out loud.

Leliana, however, did not.

"I was thinking about my sister, actually," Q'arlynd hurriedly continued. "I wanted to know what happened to her after her death."

Leliana's expression softened. "Don't worry—you'll see her again in Svartalfheim some day." She paused. "If you remain faithful to your vows, that is."

Q'arlynd bowed. "I will, Lady." It was a promise he wasn't likely to keep, but that wouldn't matter until he was dead. As long as he still drew breath, he could always choose a different patron deity, if things didn't work out with Eilistraee's high priestess.

It was time to get moving on that.

He caught Leliana's eye. "You told me a meeting with your high priestess would be possible." He gestured at the bier in the tree. "Now that the funeral rites are over, I was wondering when I might meet Lady Qilué. I understand she's in your chief temple—the Promenade?"

Leliana shook her head. "We can't spare anyone to take you there. Not right now."

"I can teleport, remember?" Q'arlynd reminded her. "I don't need an escort. Just describe this Promenade for me, and I'll make my way there myself."

"No," Leliana said firmly.

"Have you at least told Lady Qilué I'd like to meet with her?"

Leliana threw up her hands. "When would I have had the chance to do that, between battling driders and dealing with our dead?"

"The drider attack was more than a tenday ago," Q'arlynd continued, using the surface dwellers' term for the passage of time. He understood the delay—the priestesses had been busy strengthening their defenses in the aftermath of the attack—but it still irritated him. "When *were* you going to tell Lady Qilué that I'd like to meet with her?"

Leliana folded her arms. "When I'm good and ready—and not a moment before."

Q'arlynd fumed, wishing he had disposed of Leliana when he'd had the chance. Clearly, she'd changed her mind about arranging a meeting with the high priestess, and since she was the one who had taken charge of him, back at the portal, she had the final say over what duties he would have among the faithful—as well as whether he might move on to another shrine or temple. Q'arlynd, however, had higher aspirations than sitting in some mist-choked forest, listening to the females sing. He wanted to be at the heart of things, at the seat of power, which would only be possible if he secured an audience with Qilué. That was how a male succeeded in life, by attaching himself to a powerful female and serving her well.

"It's best for now if you stay here, Q'arlynd," Rowaan said. "The drider attack cut our numbers nearly in half. If the judicator returns, we'll need your spells."

Q'arlynd inclined his head in a show of modesty, inwardly gritting his teeth.

"And if Vhaeraun's assassins show up here—"

"Rowaan!" Leliana snapped, rounding on her daughter. "That's not something lay worshipers need to trouble themselves with."

Q'arlynd blinked. Rowaan had obviously just said something he wasn't meant to hear. It almost sounded as if the priestesses were *expecting* the Nightshadows to strike.

"But Q'arlynd is one of us now," Rowaan protested. "He—"

"Is not a priestess," Leliana said. "He's a powerful wizard, yes, but he's . . ."

She didn't have to finish the sentence. Q'arlynd could do it for her. A male.

He bowed his head, silently acknowledging Leliana's superiority. Whether one worshiped Lolth or Eilistraee, it was all the same. A priestess was a priestess.

Female.

But females, in his experience, often had a weakness for a handsome face, something Q'arlynd might just be able to use to his advantage. He smiled at Rowaan—the seemingly apologetic smile of a male who knew his place in the world but just couldn't help wanting more. She gave the slightest of nods in return.

Rowaan, he was certain, trusted him.

He could use that.

Qilué stared with a mixture of pity and wariness at the creature that squatted before her. Little remained of the drow Halisstra Melarn had once been. Lolth had expanded Halisstra's body to twice its size, enhancing it with wiry muscle and giving her face an elongated, bestial appearance. The spider legs protruding from her ribs and the fangs scissoring out of those bulges on her cheeks made her monstrous indeed, but despite her size and power, Halisstra's eyes hinted that something still remained of the priestess she had once been. Qilué saw a yearning there, a faint spark of hope nearly lost amidst the anguish and rage.

They stood in the forest, Qilué wrapped in protective silver moonfire, Halisstra with a palpable taint surrounding her. Qilué had come armed with a singing sword, silver dagger, and her magical bracer in addition to her spells, but so far there had been no treachery. Halisstra had clearly been claimed by Lolth, but if this was a trap it had yet to be sprung.

Cavatina stood a few steps behind Halisstra, sword in hand. Moonlight glinted off her armor. "Repeat what you told me about the temple," she prompted. "Describe it for Qilué."

Halisstra bared pointed teeth in what Qilué supposed was meant to be a smile. "It stands on top of a tall spire of rock. Feliane, Uluyara, and I shaped it with our prayers from the stone of the Demonweb Pits. It's intact and is sacred ground still. Lolth's creatures cannot enter it."

"Including Halisstra," Cavatina added.

Halisstra bowed her head.

"Yet you were able to place the Crescent Blade inside this temple?" Qilué asked. She wanted to hear this part of the story again to see if there were any inconsistencies.

Halisstra nodded. "From a distance, yes. I tossed the broken pieces of the sword through the doorway. I had thought only to put the pieces somewhere safe, so that the weapon might later be recovered and repaired, but the temple must have worked some kind of magic on the sword. As I watched, blade and hilt slid toward one another and joined. Eilistraee's sacred moonlight filled the temple, and the sword glowed white. The light blinded me for a time. When I could see again, I looked into the temple and saw the sword lying on the floor, reforged."

It seemed strange to Qilué that Lolth had allowed that to happen within her own domain, stranger still that the temple to Eilistraee remained intact. The Spider Queen was known to permit spaces sacred to other deities to exist within her realm—the Demonweb Pits housed portions of the domains of Vhaeraun, Kiaransalee, and Ghaunadaur, after all—but they were deities who had allied with Lolth during her revolt against the Seldarine. Eilistraee was Lolth's enemy. A temple to her within the Demonweb Pits should have been an unbearable burr upon the Spider Queen's throne. Lolth was either suffering the temple to exist for some reason of her own, or—Qilué grimly smiled—she had been weakened by her Silence to the point where Eilistraee might, at long last, vanquish her.

Or Halisstra was lying about the existence of a temple.

"Tell me again how the Crescent Blade came to be broken," Qilué said.

"After Danifae treacherously attacked me, I lay injured for a time. When I regained consciousness—miraculously, still alive—Uluyara and Feliane were dead. Danifae and the draegloth had disappeared. I realized they must have entered the Pass of the Soulreaver and knew I had to follow. I entered the pass and battled the monsters Lolth sent against me. I fought well, but just as I neared the exit, a misplaced thrust wedged my sword in a crack in the rock. When I tried to wrench it free, the blade snapped. I had fought my way through the pass, only to stand at the very doorstep of Lolth's fortress with a broken weapon."

Halisstra paused, her spider fangs quivering. After a moment, she composed herself.

"I still had Seyll's sword," she continued, "so I carried on. I fought Danifae and Quenthel, but in the middle of that battle we were drawn into Lolth's city, to her very throne. Lolth had awakened from her Silence. I tried to fight the goddess herself, but without the Crescent Blade . . ." A shudder ran through her body. "I had no hope. Lolth was too powerful. She forced the three of us to kneel before her. Danifae, she killed and consumed. She was the most worthy, in Lolth's eyes, and the goddess wanted to add her substance to her own. Quenthel she spared and sent back to Arach-Tinilith, where she serves the Spider Queen still. I was deemed unworthy for having renounced my faith to embrace Eilistraee. For this, Lolth said, I would do eternal penance. She seized me and bit me." Halisstra touched the puncture marks on her neck. "Eight times she sank her teeth into my flesh. Then she spun me into a cocoon. When I emerged, I was . . . like this."

Qilué nodded. "What happened then?"

"I made my way out of Lolth's fortress. It was filled with yochlols, but they made no move to stop me. I stumbled away across the plain, back to the Pass of the Soulreaver. I recovered the pieces of the Crescent Blade and entered the pass. This time, nothing attacked me. I made my way to Eilistraee's temple and placed the sword inside."

"Tell her how you escaped from the Demonweb Pits," Cavatina prompted. "It was a very clever tactic."

Qilué shot the Darksong Knight a look. Thus far, Qilué herself had offered neither praise nor criticism of anything Halisstra had said. Qilué wished that she had been able to come more swiftly to the Velarswood. Halisstra had obviously told her story more than once to Cavatina, something that would have allowed Halisstra to smooth out any wrinkles in the tale. Normally, Qilué would have used a spell to tell what parts of the story rang true and which were lies or embroideries, woven onto a slim thread of truth, but whatever hold Lolth had on the tragic creature that Halisstra had become was strong. Even Qilué's magic could not penetrate it.

Qilué wondered what Lolth was trying to hide.

"I escaped by observing Selvetarm," Halisstra continued. "By following him, I learned where one of the portals that leads from Lolth's domain was located. It was guarded by a songspider, a creature whose webs create music that can enslave or even kill. This barrier would have barred my way, had I not been schooled in *bae'queshel*. I used that magic to play the strands of the web like a lyre, plucking it open. The portal led back to this plane, to a place east of Lake Sember."

"Halisstra can show us where it is," Cavatina said, her eyes gleaming, "and lead us to the temple in the Demonweb Pits. The Crescent Blade—"

Qilué held up a hand for silence. She didn't like the look in Halisstra's eye. A former priestess she might be, but her eyes held a gleam as malicious as Lolth's own. Her desire to return to the Demonweb Pits was just a little too strong.

Yet the pain and desperation that Qilué could sense in Halisstra seemed real enough. Part of her, at least, still yearned for a second chance at redemption, but because Halisstra could not die, she would, for all eternity, be in bondage to the Spider Queen, unless the sticky webs with which Lolth held her could somehow be broken.

Qilué suspected that Halisstra was, consciously or not, trying to play both sides of the *sava* board at once. Redemption lay on one side of the board. On the other was the possibility of a reward from the Spider Queen for delivering a priestess of Eilistraee into her hands, except that Lolth was capricious when it came to rewarding mortals for services rendered. The Spider Queen was just as likely to punish as to pardon, as Halisstra was doubtless well aware.

"We can do it, Lady Qilué," Halisstra whispered, "finish what we started. Use the Crescent Blade to kill Lolth." She spread her elongated fingers, looked down at the claws that protruded from their tips. "But she won't die by these hands. Someone else will have to wield the Crescent Blade this time."

Qilué nodded. Eilistraee's faithful would not make the same mistake twice. Three years before, Uluyara's decision to let Halisstra carry the Crescent Blade had proved a disaster, even though the choice had seemed sound at the time. Halisstra had been part of the group that had been seeking Lolth during her Silence. She stood the best chance of infiltrating Quenthel's band and traveling with them to the place where Lolth had secluded herself, but Halisstra had been a novice, not yet fully trusting in her newfound faith. It would be one of Eilistraee's Chosen—Qilué herself—who would carry the battle forward.

If, indeed, the Crescent Blade did still exist.

"Three years ago," Qilué said, "Uluyara came to me and told me what you planned to do. When you entered the Demonweb Pits, I was watching."

That got a reaction. "You were scrying?" Halisstra's spider legs drummed against her chest. Her breathing was fast and light.

Qilué nodded. Deliberately, she added details that Halisstra would recognize. "Could you not feel me, when I shattered the ice that Pharaun used to imprison you? I saw through your eyes when Danifae lifted you by the hair and made you watch as the draegloth tore into Feliane."

Halisstra's eyes narrowed, perhaps in pain at the memory. "You saw Feliane die?" Every muscle of her body was tense.

"Yes."

For several moments, there was strained silence. Qilué waited expectantly for Halisstra to reveal, through some ill chosen word, whatever secret had caused her to tense up. Something had happened after the draegloth killed Feliane—something Halisstra didn't want Qilué to know about—but what?

Halisstra laughed, a wild sound that rippled at the edge of insanity. Qilué thought she heard an undertone of relief in it, but couldn't be certain. "You think I could have done more to save Feliane, but I was weak, nearly dead myself. I could do nothing to stop the draegloth from killing her."

Qilué arched an eyebrow, waiting. Nothing more was forthcoming, however. Qilué at last nodded. "You could do nothing to save her," she agreed.

Halisstra's relief was clearly visible, and perhaps it really was as simple as that. Perhaps Halisstra felt guilty about the deaths of the two priestesses who had accompanied her to the Demonweb Pits, a guilt as painful as any penance Lolth had imposed.

Qilué suddenly wondered if she'd pushed Halisstra too far. She switched to a soothing tone. "A death like Feliane's is disturbing," she said. "It would make anyone question her faith. It's easy enough to think that Eilistraee had abandoned you, but she didn't. It was her magic that revived you, after Danifae's mace shattered your face."

Halisstra cocked her head. "Eilistraee was . . . with me?" she whispered in a dry, strangled voice. "Even when . . ."

Qilué nodded. "She was."

Halisstra's eyes hardened. "If Eilistraee was with me, why did she let Lolth claim me?"

"Strong as Eilistraee is, Lolth is more powerful within her own domain, especially within her fortress," Qilué spread her hands, "but Eilistraee—and I—did not just abandon you. My scrying ended when Danifae struck you down. I assumed you were dead, until Eilistraee hinted otherwise. Whatever happened in the Demonweb Pits after that, Eilistraee will forgive you."

Halisstra stared flatly back at Qilué. There was no conviction in her eyes.

"One last question," Qilué said. "It's been three years since Lolth broke her Silence. What have you been doing all this time?"

Halisstra shifted uncomfortably. "I only escaped the Demonweb Pits a year ago. Since then, I've been . . . busy."

"Doing Lolth's bidding," Qilué suggested.

Halisstra's eyes blazed. "I never attacked *your* priestesses."

Qilué noted the choice of words. "Your" priestesses. A bitter twist to the word.

"It was House Jaelre and House Auzkovyn that I hunted," Halisstra continued. "Vhaeraun's clerics. They're your enemies, as well."

"Those who worship Vhaeraun, yes," Qilué said softly, "but some from those Houses have sought redemption."

"Not all of them," Cavatina interrupted. She nodded at Halisstra. "The last one she killed died unrepentant. I gave him every opportunity to redeem himself before he died, but he refused."

Qilué frowned, not understanding. "You raised one of her victims from the dead?"

The Darksong Knight laughed. "Quite the contrary. He was very much alive, inside her cocoon, when I found him."

"You killed him?"

Cavatina stared back at Qilué, unrepentant. "He deserved to die."

Cavatina seemed disinclined to say more. Rather than pursue the discussion in front of Halisstra, who was listening a little too attentively, Qilué let the matter drop. There were more important matters at hand. The Crescent Blade. If it still existed, the quest that had begun three years ago might continue.

She glanced past Halisstra at Cavatina. The Darksong Knight stood ready, her eyes bright in the moonlight. Cavatina was skilled with a sword and experienced at fighting demons. Aside from Qilué herself, she was the most logical choice to recover the Crescent Blade. If it still existed.

"Priestess?" Qilué asked aloud. "Are you up to the challenge?" At the same time, she used her magic to send Cavatina a silent message. *It will be a trap. In all likelihood the temple no longer exists, and the blade is still lost.*

Cavatina's posture was tense. Eager. *But if it is true? If the sword* can *be recovered?*

"Then you will bring it to me," Qilué said, answering aloud. She kept an eye on Halisstra as she spoke, watching for a reaction. Halisstra gave no sign of disappointment. It didn't seem to matter to her that Qilué herself would not be lured into the Demonweb Pits.

Cavatina's lips parted then closed. Qilué could sense that she had been about to protest, to insist that it should be a Darksong Knight who made the attempt on Lolth, but instead she inclined her head.

"By the song and the sword, we will succeed," she said.

"The drow will be free of the Spider Queen at last."

"By the song and the sword," Qilué murmured. Then she took a deep breath. Halisstra, she thought, was a coin balanced on its edge. Which way would she fall—toward betrayal or aid? The prophecy of three years ago had said it could go either way.

No. The prophecy had said it would go both ways. In the goddess's own words, House Melarn would both aid—and betray. A single coin could only fall on one side or the other.

Was there a second "coin" out there somewhere, waiting to declare itself?

If so, where?

Q'arlynd approached the tree that housed the priest-esses. It was still covered in leaves, despite the recent snowfall. Sustained by ancient magic, its branches sparkled against the night sky with a shimmer of green that reminded Q'arlynd of the faerie fire that had decorated the buildings and roads back home.

The trunk was massive, thick as any of the streets of Ched Nasad had been. Its bark bulged in several places, enormous knots of wood that were called burls. Hollowed into each of these was a room, its entrance a round wooden door. Leading up to the doors were ladders made of individual sticks that floated in mid air. These sticks appeared benign, but glyphs carved into them would activate if anyone of evil intent touched them, instantly making them as sharp as steel. Enemies of Eilistraee who were foolish enough to use a magical ladder would lose their fingers at the very least.

Q'arlynd, however, had an easier means of access at his disposal, his House insignia. With a thought, he activated it and rose into the air to the room that was Rowaan's.

Yellow light shone through the cracks between door and frame. Rowaan might be a dark elf, but she seemed to have forsaken the use of her darkvision. Q'arlynd, still levitating, dispelled the glyph on the door, a simple warding that gave a mental suggestion that dissuaded males from touching the door or its handle. Then he lifted his hand to knock.

He paused, however, without knocking. He'd gone to seduce Rowaan into accompanying him to the Promenade and introducing him to Qilué. He had the perfect story, carefully rehearsed to earn Rowaan's sympathy, the tale of how Halisstra had saved his life after his riding accident. He'd tell her that that had stirred feelings in him he'd never known he possessed, that he'd discovered that he cared for Halisstra. How he even—what was the word for it?—yes, that was it, how he *loved* his sister. He'd follow that up with a plea that if he could just talk to Qilué—briefly, and without interrupting the high priestess's doubtlessly important duties—that maybe he could learn more about the one person who truly mattered to him in the world. Floating on Rowaan's threshold, however, it all seemed too easy—about as exciting as jumping from a table to the floor. He wanted more of a challenge than that.

Above him, he could see Leliana's doorway.

He smiled. Now *that* would be a leap. And being introduced to Qilué by a more powerful priestess certainly wouldn't hurt.

He levitated to her door and dispelled the warding on it as well. Then he knocked, a light, seemingly hesitant tap. As he waited for the door to open, he ran a hand over his hair, smoothing it.

The door opened, revealing a small room that was comfortably dark. Q'arlynd bowed his head. "May I come in?"

Leliana glanced between the wizard and the door. "How did—?"

Q'arlynd waggled his fingers. "Magic."

Leliana's eyes blazed. "You're not permitted here. Only priestesses—"

"I know, but I need to speak to you." He lowered his voice, as if afraid someone might be listening. "It's about the Nightshadows. I have information I think you should hear."

Leliana glanced away, muttering something under her breath. "All right," she said. "Come in."

Q'arlynd pulled himself inside and allowed his levitation to end. The room was furnished with two cushioned stools and an intricately carved table whose legs were joined to the floor. It must have been carved when the burl was hollowed out. Pegs on the wall held Leliana's armor, weapons, and cloak. Wide notches, carved into the walls, were stuffed with baskets, folded clothes and books. Q'arlynd nodded. He wasn't surprised that Leliana read. She had a lively mind. Something else caught his eye, a crescent-shaped harp in an alcove next to the door. He reached out to touch it then lowered his hand, as if suddenly remembering his manners.

"I'm sorry," he said. "I shouldn't touch your things, but it . . . reminds me of my sister." He glanced up at Leliana. "Did you know Halisstra well?"

"I met her only once."

Q'arlynd brushed the strings of the harp with a fingertip. A shiver of notes filled the air. "She was a musician, too. She played the lyre."

"Quit stalling. You came here to tell me something about the Nightshadows. Spit it out."

Q'arlynd raised an eyebrow as he bowed. "As you command . . . Mistress."

"Don't call me that."

"Why not?" Q'arlynd countered. "You were born in the Underdark, weren't you? Menzoberranzan, if I'm not mistaken about your accent. Born into a noble House, no doubt. You certainly have an aristocratic bearing."

Leliana ignored the flattery. She closed the door against the chill wind then folded her arms across her chest. Now that she was no longer wearing her armor, Q'arlynd could appreciate the curve of her breasts and the lean muscles of her folded arms. She was only a little taller than he was—short, for a female.

"Get to the point," she said.

Q'arlynd sighed. "Things really are done differently in the surface realms, aren't they?" he said. "Very well, then. I gather, from our conversation of last night, that you're worried about an attack by Vhaeraun's assassins."

The silence stretched. Leliana neither confirmed nor denied what he'd just said. "Go on."

"The Nightshadows are masters of deception and disguise," Q'arlynd said. He leaned closer, as if about to share a dark secret. "But I know how to spot them."

"So do I," Leliana said sarcastically. "The first clue is that square of black cloth they're so fond of wearing."

Q'arlynd smiled. "That's true, but a Nightshadow can still work his magic, even when his mask is thousands of paces distant." He waved a hand. "But you knew that already, of course. Just as, no doubt, you already know that a Nightshadow's deception spell can mask his alignment, his true faith—even his very thoughts, but what you don't know, I'm willing to wager, is how to counter this deception."

"And you do?"

"Yes."

Leliana's expression was openly skeptical, but she hadn't thrown him out yet. She wanted to hear more.

"Let me explain. Many years ago, back when I was a novice wizard, a . . . " he searched for the right word—it wasn't one the drow frequently used. "A *friend* of mine came to me for help. A Nightshadow. He had a problem he thought my magic could solve."

"What problem was that?"

"He'd been cursed." Q'arlynd walked to the center of the room, deliberately testing her willingness to let him invade her private space. When she made no move to block him, he leaned back against the table, stretching himself out. Showing off his body. He smiled, inwardly, as he saw her eyes linger on it.

"You're familiar with Vhaeraun's avatar?" he asked.

"Not personally—we've never met. Eilistraee willing, I'll never have that pleasure."

Q'arlynd chuckled. "Nor have I, but my friend enlightened me. The Masked Lord's avatar, he said, looks just like a regular drow, except for his eyes. They change color, you see, to reflect his moods. Red when the god is angry, blue when he's pleased, green when—"

"Let me guess—when he's envious."

"When he's puzzled, actually." Q'arlynd waved a hand. "But that's neither blood nor water. What's important to the story is that this Nightshadow had transgressed against his faith. He'd cast an illusion upon himself that made his eyes change color and tried to pass himself off as Vhaeraun's avatar. It was a stupid thing to do, and he paid the price for his temerity. Vhaeraun cursed the Nightshadow so that his eyes would forever betray him. They continued to change color, even after his illusion ended, marking him as a cleric of Vhaeraun, and in Ched Nasad, that wasn't a healthy thing to be."

"So he asked you to remove the curse?"

"Exactly." Q'arlynd sighed. "But that spell, unfortunately for him, was beyond my abilities. I was still just a novice, capable of no more than a few cantrips and simple spells."

Leliana frowned. "Then why did he come to you for help?"

Q'arlynd shrugged and looked away. "He had his reasons."

"Why? Because you were a Nightshadow, too?"

Q'arlynd stared up into her eyes unflinchingly. "No. For a time, I considered becoming a petitioner—my friend took me into his confidence and told me a great deal about the Nightshadows. I even attended one of their secret meetings, but I never did take up the mask."

"So were you able to help your friend?"

Q'arlynd sighed. "In the course of telling him I couldn't help him, it slipped out that I was studying how to render living creatures invisible. He begged me to cast this spell on him, so he could escape the city."

She nodded. "Did he escape?"

Q'arlynd's expression hardened. "No. Instead of invisibility, I cast a spell that rendered him unconscious. Then I handed him over to the matron mother of our House."

That last "slip" had been deliberate. It took less time than he expected for it to sink in. Leliana's eyes widened almost immediately. "You and this 'friend' were blood relatives?"

Q'arlynd nodded. "He was my younger brother." He glanced away, letting the silence stretch for a moment. "I was 'rewarded' for turning him in by being allowed to watch when our mother sacrificed him. She cut his body apart, piece by piece, and offered it up to Lolth. It took . . ." he deliberately let his voice catch. "It took a very long time for him to die."

Leliana looked ill. "You betrayed your own brother."

"I had to. If I helped him, I'd have been marked for sacrifice myself."

"Not if he escaped."

"An invisibility spell wouldn't have helped. It would have worn off long before he escaped the city, and his eyes would have given him away. He'd have revealed who aided him. Lolth's priestesses, just like Eilistraee's, have ways of wringing the truth out of a person."

He sighed. "What I should have done was given Tellik a

swift, clean death, but I wasn't strong enough to do that."
He glanced up at her. "You grew up in the Underdark. You
understand what's necessary. To survive. You must have
. . . done things, things you later regretted."

Leliana's eyes narrowed. "I left all that behind."

"So have I. I've taken Eilistraee's vows. I've come into
the light."

Leliana cocked an eyebrow. "Have you?"

"Yes. That's why I shared this story with you, painful
though it was to relate. I wanted to give you a weapon you
could use against any Nightshadows who try to sneak into
your shrine in disguise." He smiled. "This is what I came
to tell you. If you word a curse carefully, you can create
the same effect, cause a Nightshadow's eyes to mirror his
avatar's. No matter what disguise he's wearing, it will
give him away."

Leliana considered this for several moments. "An interesting story," she said at last.

Q'arlynd felt his face grow warm. "You don't believe
me?" He pointed at her sword. "Then wave that around
and cast your truth spell. Make me repeat my 'story,' and
see if I'm telling the truth."

Leliana's mouth quirked in a smile. "No need," she said.
"Before inviting you in, I said a prayer that would cause
me to hear a ringing sound, whenever you spoke a lie. It's
much more subtle than the truth-compelling spell I used
on you earlier, don't you think?"

Q'arlynd laughed, his anger having evaporated. Leliana
was a drow female to the core. "Nicely done," he said, tip-
ping his head.

"And you," she replied. "You told a heart-wrenching
tale, complete with confessions and self-recriminations
that should have earned my sympathy, and you've offered
a possible method to reveal our enemies."

"The method *will* work," Q'arlynd said. "I've seen it
tested."

"I'm sure you have," Leliana said, "but there's just one small problem. None of us knows how to bestow a curse."

Q'arlynd felt a rush of relief. Things were back on track again. "I realize that," he said solemnly. "Vlashiri's dead, but I overheard one of the priestesses saying that there are others at the Promenade who are familiar with curses. Send me there, and I'll teach them how to word a curse to reveal a Nightshadow in disguise."

Leliana laughed.

"What's so funny?" Q'arlynd asked.

"They know how to *remove* curses, not bestow them. Eilistraee won't permit anything else."

Q'arlynd's had to struggle to keep his emotions from showing. "I see."

Leliana moved to the door. "You're not ready to visit the Promenade yet."

"Meaning you don't trust me."

"Not fully, no." She opened the door, made ready to usher him out. "But I will send a message on your behalf to Qilué, if only to—"

The rest of her words were lost in a metallic crashing noise that came from below. It sounded like swords clanging together, but faster than any mortal hand could wield them. Doors banged open above and below Leliana's room.

"The barrier!" a priestess shouted. "Something's triggered it!"

Leliana sprang for her sword and armor. She shrugged on her chain mail as quickly as someone donning a shirt then ran for the open door. "Come on," she shouted as she rushed past him. "If it's the judicator again, we could use you."

Q'arlynd didn't wait for a second invitation. It was a chance to fight at Leliana's side—to at last prove himself to her. He yanked his wand out of its sheath and followed her to the door. Glancing outside as she hurried down the ladder, he saw magically animated blades whistling by several paces away from the tree, forming a circle around it. He wondered, briefly, why the magical trap hadn't sprung earlier, when he himself had crossed whatever invisible boundary encircled the tree. Perhaps because he was one of the "faithful" now. Shrugging, he cast a protective spell on himself. Then he jumped and activated his House insignia. As he slowly levitated to the ground, other priestesses scrambled past him down the ladders, swords in hand. One of them already stood at the bottom of the tree, spinning in place, her sword held out in front of her.

She stopped abruptly, pointing with her sword. "There!" she shouted. "He went that way."

Another priestess called a bolt of moonlight down from the sky. It lanced down into the woods and illuminated, just for a moment, the figure of a running man with black skin. He staggered as it struck the ground next to him and glanced over his shoulder. Even from a distance, Q'arlynd could see his mask.

"A Nightshadow," he whispered under his breath.

One of the priestesses spoke a word, negating the barrier of blades. As it fell, the other priestesses charged after the assassin, one of them blowing a hunting horn. Leliana ran after them.

"Q'arlynd!" she shouted over her shoulder. "What are you waiting for?"

Q'arlynd hesitated. He'd noticed something she'd missed. Rowaan's door was open, yet he hadn't seen her during the mad scramble to chase the assassin. He levitated to the opening and peered inside.

What he saw didn't surprise him. Rowaan lay on the floor of the room, her eyes bulging, a deep crease in her throat. The assassin must have been strangling her, even as Q'arlynd and Leliana were chatting.

And Q'arlynd had unlocked the door for him.

Leliana would realize that the instant she saw the

dispelled glyph. All of the suspicions she harbored about Q'arlynd would be "confirmed."

That was it then. He'd never get an audience with the high priestess now, except, perhaps, as a prisoner.

He cursed and sheathed his wand. Then he teleported away.

CHAPTER NINE

Qilué was in the Cavern of Song, lending her voice to those of the other priestesses, when Iljrene's urgent message came. *The Nightshadows have struck again. The Misty Forest this time. They've stolen another soul. Her body has just been brought to the Hall of Healing.*

I'll be there at once, Qilué replied. She hurried out of the cavern, gathering up her clothes from the floor as she went.

As she strode down the passageways that led to the Hall of Healing, Qilué's expression was grim. It was the third soul Vhaeraun's assassins had claimed: one from a priestess at the Gray Forest shrine, another from a priestess of the Chondalwood, and the third, from the Misty Forest.

Two other souls that had been stolen had been restored, praise Eilistraee. The soul of Nastasia, the first to fall, had been set free by unknown causes, and the priestess who had been killed at the shrine in the Forest of Lethyr had also been raised from the dead after the assassin who had attacked her was killed. His body had been questioned by a necromancer—an unpleasant, but necessary task. The corpse had revealed that Malvag was alive. The pair had met a day before the attack the Lethyr shrine. The plan to open a gate was indeed going ahead, and when it came to fruition, the souls of Eilistraee's priestesses would be consumed.

Iljrene was waiting for Qilué in the Hall of Healing, beside another priestess Qilué knew well—Leliana. Qilué had taken Leliana's sword-oath more than a century ago, when she had first come up from below.

Leliana turned, a stricken look on her face, as Qilué entered. "Lady Qilué," she said. "It's my daughter Rowaan. The Nightshadows killed her and Chezzara can't raise her from the dead. Her soul . . ."

Qilué touched Leliana's arm. "Let's be certain first." She glanced past Leliana at the alcove where two novice priestesses hastily prepared a bed on which to lay a body. Two other priestesses—both just teleported from the Misty Forest, judging by the snowflakes still melting in their hair—stood by, holding the corners of a damp blanket on which Rowaan's body lay. Even in death, she looked remarkably like her mother.

Qilué moved closer and noted the telltale mark of an assassin's cord around Rowaan's neck. She murmured a prayer of detection, and a distinctive shadow appeared across the lower half of the dead priestess's face.

Leliana moaned.

"Tell me about the attack," Qilué prompted.

"It happened late last night," one of the priestesses holding the blanket answered. "The Nightshadow who did it got away. So did the one who aided him."

Leliana's face twisted with anguish. "It's my fault," she blurted. "I was stupid. I *trusted* him."

Qilué frowned, not quite understanding. "This second Nightshadow—you knew him?"

Leliana nodded. "He posed as a petitioner." A bitter laugh burst from her lips. "He even took the sword-oath, but he betrayed us in the end. He dispelled the glyph on Rowaan's door then kept me talking while the other Nightshadow went into her room and . . ." Her voice faltered, and her eyes strayed to the priestesses who were gently laying her daughter's body on the floor. "Stole her soul."

Leliana tore her eyes away from the body of her daughter. She took a deep breath then spoke again, shaking her head all the while. "I still can't understand it. I questioned him under a truth spell, and he gave his name and the details of his coming to the surface readily enough. He wasn't truly a petitioner—he only sought us out in order to find his sister—but he fought beside us when the judicator attacked, and later, when he took the sword-oath, I thought that perhaps he had—"

"Leliana," Qilué said, cutting the other priestess off in mid-flow with a touch on the arm. "You're getting ahead of yourself. One piece of the story at a time, please. What name did this male give?"

"Q'arlynd Melarn."

Qilué gasped. Moonfire danced on her skin, washing the cavern with light. There was the second coin, dropped at her feet. It had landed, as Eilistraee had foretold, on the side that was betrayal. "Tell me everything about this male—and swiftly, but start at the beginning this time."

Qilué listened as Leliana's tale unfolded, occasionally interrupting with a question. When it was done, she stood in thought for several moments. "It seems odd that he confessed his knowledge of Vhaeraun to you on the very night the Nightshadow struck."

"Q'arlynd *must* be a Nightshadow," Leliana insisted. "He even admitted attending their meetings."

"Did he really?" Qilué said softly. An idea was beginning to take shape. "And now he's promised himself to Eilistraee." She paused. "Perhaps *he's* the one that will aid her."

"Aid who, Lady Qilué?" one of the other priestesses asked.

Qilué, lost in thought, didn't answer. If Q'arlynd was the Melarn who would aid Eilistraee, that meant Halisstra would betray the goddess. Cavatina knew how to take care of herself—she was skilled in hunting demons, and used to trickery—but even so, Qilué worried that she might have sent the Darksong Knight to her death. She steeled herself, telling herself it had to be done. Such sacrifices were necessary, if the drow were to be brought into Eilistraee's light. In the meantime, the new development had to be dealt with.

She stared down at the faint square of black that shrouded Rowaan's face. "Q'arlynd came directly from Ched Nasad, you say?"

Leliana nodded. "Through the portal in the ruins of Hlaungadath."

"Let's hope he tries to return the same way."

Q'arlynd squatted in the tiny patch of shadow cast by the wall, squinting at the portal. An entire night he'd tried to activate it, and nothing had happened. He'd thought it would be a simple matter—a repetition of the phrase that had triggered its magic from the other side back in Ched Nasad, but though he'd read the Draconic characters precisely as written, the space inside the arch remained a blank stone wall. He might as well have knocked on it with his head, for all the good it had done.

In full daylight, the sun beating down overhead, the glare rendered him almost blind. He wondered, for the hundredth time, if he should just give up on the portal and make his way to the closest Underdark city instead. Eryndlyn lay somewhere beneath ancient Miyeritar. Perhaps one of its merchant Houses could use a battle mage to accompany their trading missions. It would be a big step down from his hopes, but it would at least be something.

A sudden noise made him startle. Another lamia? Quickly, he rendered himself invisible. As he rose to his feet, he reached inside his pouch for components for a fire spell. He waited, sulfur-gum in hand, as footsteps approached the doorway to the room in which he stood.

A shadow fell across the floor, a shadow with the outline of a drow. A *naked* drow—and female, too.

Q'arlynd almost laughed. How stupid did the lamias think he was? Still, he had to admire the detail they'd put into their illusion. Those curves were very enticing.

He pulled the quartz crystal from his pouch. With it, he'd be able to see through the lamia's illusions—and pinpoint the creature so that he could incinerate it where it stood. As the shadow lengthened, he activated his insignia and rose into the air, out of the roofless building.

Below him, a drow female appeared to step into the room. Q'arlynd squinted through the crystal at her, expecting to see either the bare stone of the floor below the illusion—or a lamia, underneath a drow-shaped glamor. Instead he saw a female who was tall and beautiful, with silver hair and a proud bearing, like the matron mother of a noble House. She wore a gauzy silver robe that did little to hide the dark curves beneath. A sword hung from a scabbard on her belt, and she wore a bracer on her right forearm that served as a sheath for a dagger. In her left hand, she held a curious looking metal wand with a knob at either end. Eilistraee's holy symbol hung from a chain around her neck. She had a deeply lined face and somber expression, but despite her age she looked as fit as a female in her first century of life. Regardless of the obvious threat she posed—perhaps because of it—he found her intensely attractive. She was, quite simply, the most beautiful woman he'd ever seen.

Q'arlynd lowered his crystal. The priestess was real. She must have been sent to find him, to kill him. He placed a foot atop the ruined wall and gently pushed off, at the same time taking aim with the sulfur-gum.

Without warning, his levitation ended, sending him crashing into the street below. He rose, gasping and spitting blood from a cut lip. As he did, the priestess turned and glanced out into the street. She stared straight at him—*seeing* him. His invisibility must also have ended.

"Q'arlynd?"

He flicked the pinch of sulfur-gum at her and shouted the words of his spell. The tiny ball streaked through the air, igniting in mid-flight. It struck the priestess on the shoulder, immediately expanding into a violent ball of searing fire. Much of it washed back onto Q'arlynd—something it shouldn't have done.

He scrambled to his feet, his hair and skin singed from the blast, furiously blinking away the fiery afterimage that obscured his vision. He expected to see a charred body lying on the ground, but when his vision cleared the priestess was just standing there, completely unscathed. A nimbus of silver fire surrounded her naked body like a second skin, and her hair was one long, sparkling streak of silver. A candle-sized flame flickered at one end of the wand she held, and she raised it to her lips and blew it out.

"That wasn't very nice," she said in a dry voice.

Then she flicked a hand. A silver-white ray flashed from her fingertips to Q'arlynd, striking him in the chest. He touched fingers to the spot where it had struck, but felt no wound. A second flick of the priestess's fingers, and a wall of blades sprang up around Q'arlynd, completely enclosing him. They whizzed in a tight circle around him, giving him no space to move.

"If you try to attack me again," she said, "I'll tighten the ring." She made a squeezing motion with her hand, and the curtain of whirling blades cinched closer.

Q'arlynd, however, had no intention of letting her slice him up. With one word, he could teleport away. He spoke that word—

Nothing happened. He stood in the same spot as before. The magical blades swirled around him, filling the air with a dangerous hum.

"Your spells won't work," the priestess told him. "You're inside a field that negates magic."

"Impossible," Q'arlynd breathed. At the Conservatory, they'd taught that an antimagic field could only be cast by a wizard—on the wizard himself. It wasn't something a priestess hurled at someone else from a distance.

He tried a dispelling, but the whirling blades remained. He tried a second spell, but the magical armor that would have protected him from the blades failed to appear. Not wanting to press his luck—the priestess was watching his every move—he refrained from further spellcasting. His chest was tight with tension.

"Who . . . are you?"

She smiled. "Someone you've been hoping to meet. Lady Qilué Veladorn, high priestess of Eilistraee and Chosen of Mystra."

Q'arlynd's breath caught. He was certain, deep in his gut, that the high priestess was going to kill him. That she hadn't done so already was only because she wanted to question him. His best chance lay in appearing as compliant as possible in the hope that she would show lenience and kill him swiftly. He tried to crouch, in order to prostrate himself on the ground and barely avoided a nasty gash on the forehead. He settled for a partial bow instead.

"Lady Qilué, my profound apologies for attacking you," he said. "Had I known who you were, I never would have dared."

She made no comment, just stood there as the silver sparkle gradually faded from her skin and hair. Q'arlynd kept his eyes firmly on the ground, staring at a patch of sand beside her feet.

"Leliana told me about last night's attack," Qilué said. "She says you made it possible for the Nightshadow to enter Rowaan's room."

Q'arlynd clenched his jaw. His stomach felt cold and hollow. Best to get this over with. He wondered where his soul would wind up once the priestess killed him. Probably in the Demonweb Pits, where Lolth's demonic minions would ensure that he received endless torment for his fall from grace, brief though it had been.

"I did dispel the glyph on her door, it's true," he said slowly, "but not for the reason you think. I simply wanted to talk to Rowaan—to give her some information about the Nightshadows that I thought your priestesses might find useful. I changed my mind and spoke to Leliana instead."

"Why?"

"Leliana's a higher-ranking priestess. I thought she would offer me a greater reward." He spread his hands— and winced, as a blade nicked his finger. "It's as simple as that."

"I believe you."

Q'arlynd glanced up. "You do?" Hope flared in him like a bright flame.

Qilué smiled. She gestured, and the whirling curtain of blades that had surrounded him was gone. "I've come to ask a favor of you," she said. "One favor. You can say yes or no to it of your own accord, but if the answer is yes, I will place a geas on you that compels you to fulfill it. Do you understand?"

Q'arlynd nodded. He did indeed. He'd seen the effects of a geas firsthand long ago. One of Lolth's priestesses had cast it upon a House boy, compelling him to clean her boots each night by licking them with his tongue. Then she'd walked through the filth of the lizard pens. The boy had refused to clean the boots—and had quickly sickened and died, the magic of the geas hollowing him out from within.

His lips parted—he'd been about to flippantly ask what would happen if he said no to her request—then he realized there was really only one answer to her question. "What task must I perform, Lady?"

"You were once a Nightshadow."

"A petitioner, nothing more," he said carefully. "I never wore the mask."

"You attended their meetings." She switched to silent speech. *You know their passwords.*

Ah, so that was what she wanted. A spy. "I know the ones they used in Ched Nasad, decades ago."

Show me one.

He demonstrated one for her: fists drawing apart—as if stretching an assassin's cord—then suddenly flipping upside down, fingers curled, in the sign for a dead spider.

"Do you know what soultheft is?" Qilué asked.

Q'arlynd nodded. He had indeed heard of it. His brother had been stupid enough to boast that he'd one day kill a matron mother and steal her soul—preferably, their own mother. "It's a powerful spell. Done using Vhaeraun's mask, I understand, once the victim is dead."

Qilué moved closer. "Do you think you could pass as a Nightshadow? Could you fool them into thinking you're one of their own?"

He smiled, his eyes still respectfully on the ground. "I believe so, Lady."

Qilué and lifted his chin with a finger. She stared into his eyes. "Will you?"

Q'arlynd was forced to meet her eyes. He saw enormous strength of will there but also something more, something that tempered this strength. He knew, suddenly and with certainty, that she'd meant it when she said she'd let him choose whether to perform this "favor" of hers. She wasn't commanding him. She was *asking* him. A female, asking a male.

He didn't even have to think about his reply. It was his chance to prove himself, to serve not just a powerful priestess but a powerful mage—one who was a Chosen of the goddess of magic. A rush of excitement filled him. If he'd been of a religious mind, he might have whispered a prayer of thanks. To . . . somebody.

"I am yours to command, Lady Qilué."

"A favor," she reminded him, her hand falling away from his face.

Q'arlynd smiled and cocked his head, a playful gesture. He was at ease, on familiar ground. "Of course. A favor. What is it?"

Qilué's expression tightened. "Five nights ago, a Nightshadow attacked our shrine in the Forest of Lethyr. He was attempting to steal the soul of one of our priestesses."

"He did not succeed?"

"No."

The answer had been abrupt. There was more to the story than this, but whatever it was, Qilué wasn't going to tell him.

"There have been other attacks on our priestesses," she continued. "Other soulthefts."

Q'arlynd listened in silence, thinking of Rowaan. He felt a twinge of something. Guilt, he supposed.

"The males committing them are led by a Nightshadow

named Malvag. They plan to use the soul-charged masks to open a gate between Vhaeraun's domain and Eilistraee's, so that Vhaeraun can slay our goddess."

Q'arlynd whistled softly. "Is that possible? The gate, I mean. I'm sure Eilistraee can take care of herself."

"To open such a gate, the Nightshadows would need to work high magic—something that requires complete cooperation between spellcasters and complete faith in one another." Qilué gave a tight smile. "Can you honestly imagine Nightshadows *trusting* each other?"

Q'arlynd chuckled. "Hardly likely."

"Even if they fail to conjure a gate, the attempt will consume the souls of the priestesses who were killed. I don't want that to happen. I want the magic that's binding their souls to the masks dispelled, and the priestesses freed—and that means stopping Malvag."

"You want him killed?"

"If he can be."

The "if" gave Q'arlynd pause, but only for a moment. He could guess what was coming. "You want me to impersonate the Nightshadow who was killed in the Forest of Lethyr."

Qilué nodded. "We know his name: Szorak, of House Auzkovyn. He was one of three Nightshadows who joined Malvag's scheme. He's the only one from House Auzkovyn. The other two were from House Jaelre, and it's doubtful they knew him well. Neither they nor Malvag himself have seen Szorak without his mask. You're about Szorak's height and build, and your eyes are the same color. We won't need to use a glamor on you, and we know much about Szorak, since his sister was one who converted to our faith."

As Qilué said this, a pained expression came to her eyes. There was a story there, but this was not the time to ask about it.

"So far so good," Q'arlynd said, "but if I show up without a soul-charged mask—"

"We will provide a mask," Qilué said. "Not Szorak's, but one that looks just like it. A square of cloth, created by polymorphing a gem—one that contains the body and soul of a priestess who has volunteered to risk herself in this venture."

Q'arlynd stroked his chin nervously. He was being asked to risk just as much. "Won't the Nightshadows be able to tell I'm not one of them?" he asked. "I've sworn myself to Eilistraee—I've taken the sword-oath."

"You spoke the words." She touched fingers to his chest. "But your heart . . ." The fingers lifted. "One day, perhaps, a song will dance there."

Q'arlynd gave a dutiful nod. He'd worry about that later. He had a job to do, and a potential matron to impress.

"Where is Malvag now?"

"We don't know. He's cloaked himself with powerful magic that prevents me from scrying him, but we do know where he and the other Nightshadows will meet on the night of the winter solstice: in a cavern lined with dark-stone crystals. The cavern has no entrance or exit; it's unconnected to anything else in the Underdark. The only way to reach it is to teleport." She smiled. "Fortunately that's something, Leliana tells me, that you claim to be quite adept at."

Q'arlynd allowed himself a modest smile. Qilué had obviously believed Leliana, or she wouldn't have sought him out. "Where is this cavern located?"

"Again, we don't know. We assume that it doesn't lie very deep in the Underdark, and that there's no *faerzress* near it, since teleportation to it is possible. All we have is a description of it, a brief description provided by the corpse."

Q'arlynd's eyebrows raised. "You expect me to teleport there on the strength of a *description?*"

"I realized that this would be impossible, without you having viewed the cavern. That is why I took the additional precaution of having the necromancer animate the body of the dead assassin. He then asked Szorak to 'describe' the cavern a second time—by drawing it."

"Ah," Q'arlynd said. "I see. You want me to study the drawing then try to teleport there."

Qilué gave him a measuring stare. "Can you do it?"

Q'arlynd carefully kept his thoughts from showing on his face. If the sketch had been done by the equivalent of a zombie, with only the shakiest of muscle control and no spirit to guide his hand, it wouldn't be very accurate. The resulting "drawing" would probably be no more than a few crude scratch marks.

He stroked his chin nervously. His stomach felt hollow at the very notion of what Qilué was asking—and he hadn't even jumped yet, but the thought of attempting an "impossible" teleport was tempting simply for the sheer challenge of it. Qilué was hanging upon his answer, every muscle in her body taut. If he pulled this one off, it would *really* impress her. If he managed to stop Malvag and save the souls of a couple of priestesses in the bargain, the rewards would be rich indeed. Qilué was a veritable conduit to Mystra herself. The very thought made him lightheaded.

"I can do it," he said.

Qilué beamed. "Good."

Part of him reveled in that smile. Another part wondered if he'd just signed his own death order. He crushed the second part mercilessly. To advance in life, one had to take chances.

"The geas, then," Qilué said.

Q'arlynd bowed his head.

The high priestess laid cool fingers on his forehead and invoked the names of both Eilistraee—and Mystra. "I command you to perform this service for me," she began. "To locate Malvag, and . . ."

When she finished, Q'arlynd's forehead tingled. A shimmer of silver magic shivered the hairs on his arms erect then was gone.

It was done. The geas had been laid upon him.

Now all he had to do was achieve the near-impossible.

"One favor," Jub whispered as he descended through the cavern on a thread of silk. "One favor I promised Qilué, and *this* is what she asks: to sneak into the lair of a dracolich."

The dracolich in question had already swooped past him once, causing Jub to spin madly on his thread. The undead wyrm was an enormous creature, black as old blood and with wings so broad they brushed the walls on either side of the passage. The monster left the stench of death in its wake and had a deep, unhealed wound in its left flank, yet it lived—after a fashion. Jub was awed by the amount of magic it must have taken for a dragon to transform itself into an undead creature.

Jub had magic, too—the tiny metal box, attached to a leather armband, that he wore above his left elbow. He'd gotten a real bargain on the phylactery from the thaumaturgical shop in Skullport because of its "curse." It didn't polymorph properly—it would only change its wearer into "vermin," but that was just fine with Jub. With it, he could change into pretty much any bug he could think of, big or small. He usually liked to turn into a fly—nobody ever suspected a fly of spying—but Qilué had warned him that that wouldn't be a healthy form to choose this time around. The males he was searching for worshiped Selvetarm, champion of the Queen of Spiders. They were bound to be hundreds of her pets around, wherever they were holed up, so Jub had polymorphed into a spider himself. It was, he reflected with sly grin that set his fangs quivering, the perfect disguise.

The spider body had come in pretty handy so far. It had gotten him past a bunch of traps. It was fist-sized—too light to trigger the spring-spikes or pits. It had also enabled him to scurry into a crack in the wall when a heavy block of stone smashed down. The body had its drawbacks, however. Shooting out strands of web left his ass feeling twitchy, and having three pairs of eyes took a lot of getting used to. All of the colors were flat, and he kept getting mixed up about what was close and what was far away—not to mention distracted by the rush of the walls going past while simultaneously seeing the cavern dwindling away behind him. He didn't know how spiders could stand looking in all directions at once.

Reaching the floor of the cavern, Jub snapped the thread of silk and looked around. Several passages led out of there. They all looked enormous to Jub, but if he'd been walking around in his regular, half-orc, half-drow body, the white bristles on the top of his head would have brushed the ceilings of most of them. That figured . . . Dolblunde had been built by rock gnomes.

He scuttled along the cavern, trying to decide which side passage to explore first. Walking had been tricky at first, but now that he had the hang of having eight legs he could move pretty quickly. He'd covered a fair chunk of the ancient city already. Something was bound to turn up soon, unless Qilué had been wrong about the Selvetargtlin being there, of course. She might have been lied to.

Jub paused at the entrance to one of the passages. A noise issued from it, a clicking sound. It came to him through his feet, which were sensitive to vibrations in the floor. Deciding to check it out, he scuttled into the passage.

His leg hairs quivered more rapidly as he drew closer to the source of the sound, which stopped, then started again, then stopped again. The passage was wide enough for a pair of rock gnomes to have walked through it side by side, its ceiling high and narrow as a knife slash and its floor surfaced with crushed stone. The tunnel wound through the rock like a stream, which it probably had been at one point.

Jub knew he was on the right track when he saw a clump of web on the wall. A spider must have passed that way, maybe one of the Selvetargtlin's pets.

About fifty paces along, Jub spotted a spider clinging to the wall. Hairy and black, it was about the same size as his polymorphed form. It turned as Jub scuttled by, watching him with its multiple eyes. Jub had chosen a spider form with a narrow body and long, graceful legs that would allow him to cover more ground. He hoped that bigger, heavier spider wouldn't see him as prey. He crept past it, ready at a moment's notice to polymorph back into his half-drow form and squish the thing, but the hairy spider ignored him.

The passage opened, up ahead, onto a large cavern filled with humid air. The clicking noise came again, and something moved across the mouth of the tunnel. It looked, strangely enough, like animated black swords walking about on their points. As Jub drew closer, he could see that these "swords" were the legs of an enormous spider, its body big enough to have filled a small room. Its feet, sharp as whetted knives, clicked against the stone floor as it walked. It hung around just outside the passage as if guarding it, its abdomen expanding and contracting as it breathed.

Jub scurried out of the passage, wary of those sharp, stabbing feet. The monster, like its smaller, hairier cousin in the passage behind Jub, ignored him. Good thing, too. All it would have to do was sit on Jub and he'd be dead.

Jub scuttled up a wall, stopping when he was high enough to get a good view.

The cavern was enormous. At the far end was a deep pool of water. Fringing the shore of the pool were dozens of small ruined buildings.

Jub spotted at least a dozen people. Most were drow, easily recognizable, even to his limited eyesight, by their black skin and white hair. They wore robes, but Jub was too far away to tell if they were Selvetargtlin or not. He also spotted several aranea in spider form. He recognized them by their distinctive humpback and the humanoid arms jutting out from just below their chins. Their faces were entirely insectlike, with multiple eyes and gnashing fangs, but they moved with an intelligence and purpose that true spiders lacked.

Jub scurried across the ceiling, toward the city. As he drew closer to the ruins, he could make out details of individual buildings. It looked as though it had once been a marketplace. Each building was fronted with a slab of stone that had probably served as a shop counter. The smashed remains of doors hung from rusted hinges, and the floor was littered with broken pottery, shattered crates, and bones. Most of the skulls that grinned up at Jub were small—rock gnomes—but here and there he spotted the heavy-browed skulls of his full-orc kin. They'd sacked Dolblunde more than six centuries ago, and the city had lain empty since then.

It wasn't empty any more. In addition to the handful of drow and aranea Jub had already spotted, the ruined marketplace was filled with spiders. Jub could see them scurrying around everywhere. Most were about his size, but some of the larger ones were as big as dogs. They'd spun webs in the vacant doorways and shop windows and darted from one chunk of fallen masonry to the next. They paused and stared up at Jub with gleaming, multifaceted eyes as he made his way toward the center of the ruined marketplace.

There, next to the remains of a well, was what at first glance looked like a spider even larger than the sword-legged monster that guarded the entrance. It was motionless, however, and as Jub drew closer he realized it was a statue. The body of a drow lay in front of it, but there was no one else close by.

Jub descended on a strand of web for a better look. Close up, he could see the statue was only partially finished. The most detailed portion was the drow head that perched on top of the spider body.

Qilué had been right. The drow she'd asked Jub to find must be there after all. That statue was of Selvetarm, Lolth's drow-headed spider champion.

The corpse that lay in front of the statue was a drow female. She was sprawled face-down on a block of stone that had been hauled out of a nearby building, by the look of the scuffs on the floor. She was dressed in a long black *piwafwi* embroidered, in red, in a spiderweb pattern. The back of it was stained with dried blood, and more blood crusted the stone she lay on. The smell filled Jub's spider senses, making him twitchy.

He landed on the block of stone next to the corpse. A platinum chain hung around her neck, the medallion on it partially hidden under her shoulder. Jub eased it out with his forelegs. The disk, also platinum, was embossed with the image of a spider—Lolth's holy symbol. On the ground, next to the dead female's dangling hand, was further proof of her status: an adamantine whip handle, topped with what had once been two living snakes. Their heads had been sliced clean off. They lay on the ground next to the whip.

The body presented a puzzle. Those wounds looked like something the sword-footed spider might have done, except that the spider was hanging out by the tunnel entrance and didn't seem inclined to move around much. Jub doubted that a priestess of Lolth—capable of controlling spiders with a thought—would have died like that.

No, those wounds were probably blade thrusts, aimed at the back, just over the vitals, like a rogue's surprise stab, swift and deadly, and without much warning by the look of it. Otherwise, the priestess would have taken a few of her attackers down with her using that whip of hers.

The weirdest thing was that the dead priestess was still lying there. She'd been killed a while ago, judging by the dried blood, but the Selvetargtlin didn't seem to have noticed her yet.

When they did find her, things were going to get hot. Selvetarm was Lolth's champion. His followers would be furious as a swarm of stirges when they found one of the Spider Queen's priestesses murdered. They'd turn the cavern upside down looking for her killer.

Jub's leg hairs suddenly vibrated. It took him a moment to identify the sound as the clash of steel on steel. It came from inside one of the nearby buildings—a windowless, two-story structure that looked as though it might have once been a warehouse. The doorway was invitingly open, its shattered double doors lying on the ground nearby, but Jub wasn't stupid enough to blunder in that way. Instead he scrambled up a wall to the roof. Centuries of dripping water had pitted it, leaving holes in the thin stone just big enough to scuttle through. Jub crawled inside and clung to the ceiling, staring down.

Below him, two Selvetargtlin in blood-red robes danced around each other, one with an adamantine sword in hand, the other with a spiked mace of black iron. Both had long white hair that hung in thick braids that whipped around as they spun, parried, and thrust. Their robes barely moved. As one flipped back, Jub saw it was lined with chain mail. Both males wore steel gauntlets over their hands. A nasty looking blade stuck out of the back of each gauntlet.

The pair fought furiously, sword and mace clanging in a flurry of parried blows. They battled in silence— something that, he'd heard, was unusual for a Selvetargtlin. Selvetarm's priests usually worked themselves up for a fight by shouting out their deity's name. Nor were they using spells against each other. Odd, for a fight that seemed to be in deadly earnest.

The male with the mace feinted—then spun backward, the blade on his gauntlet slicing a line through the other male's robe, exposing the gleaming chain mail that lined it. The second male retaliated by slashing at the first one's neck, torso, and hamstrings—but the first avoided all three swings. He leaped into the air, his lower body twisting sideways. His boots struck the wall and stuck. Running up it like a spider, he crouched, ready to spring, but the Selvetargtlin with the sword was equally quick. He, too, ran up the wall as if it was a horizontal surface. The battle continued until suddenly the sword went spinning to the ground, smashed out of the hands of the male who had been wielding it. The disarmed Selvetargtlin leaped after it, but the male with the mace was just as fast. He landed on the floor a heartbeat after the first and smashed down with an overhand blow that should have left his opponent sprawling and bloody, but though the first had lost his sword, he still had his bladed gauntlets. He twisted and sprang inside the arc of the descending mace, punching both blades into the other male's chest.

The death grunt was loud enough to set Jub's hairs quivering. The mortally wounded Selvetargtlin collapsed on the floor, blood bubbling from his chest as the gauntlet blades yanked free. Shuddering with effort, he twisted his head to the side—an invitation to his opponent, who was at last retrieving his sword, to finish him.

The other drow laughed. "Well fought," he said between gulps of air, sheathing his sword. Then he kneeled and slapped both gauntleted hands down on the other's chest, a palm over each wound, and began to pray. Darkness, threaded with a tracery of white webbing, coalesced around his hands then bled down into the wounds. The threads of white stitched themselves back and forth, sealing the wounds shut, preventing the other from dying.

A moment later, the victor helped the healed Selvetargtlin to his feet. The other male wiped bloody lips with the back of his sleeve then picked up his mace. "You fought well, too," he said, pausing to spit the last of the blood from his mouth. He rubbed the spot where the wounds had been. "I didn't expect that last thrust. Let's hope your chitines prove as competent."

"They already have," the other answered. "They're surprisingly capable of following orders. Of course, it helps that they think those orders come from Lolth herself."

Both males laughed.

Jub's hairs shivered erect. Chitines were four-armed magical creations of the drow. Bred as slaves by wizards centuries ago, they were only three-quarters the height of a male. Abandoned by their creators as unfit, they had escaped, decades ago, to distant reaches of the Underdark, where they lived still. Jub had blundered into one of their web-filled caverns once—luckily for him, just one chitine denned there. He'd killed it but had come away covered in gouges from its hook-lined palms and feet. He'd been lucky to get out alive. The chitines hated the dark elves with an intense, smoldering anger. They attacked all drow on sight—even a half-drow like Jub.

Yet these Selvetargtlin were talking about the chitines as if they were pet lizards.

Lizards that, by the sound of it, were fighting battles for them.

The males were still talking, though in less boisterous voices as their breathing gradually slowed. Wanting to hear more, Jub descended from the ceiling on a thread of silk.

" . . . glad to hear your chitines fought well," the Selvetargtlin with the mace was saying. "What was their target?"

"The Moonwood. They killed eight dark dancers."

Jub jerked to a halt and thought, No wonder Qilué said this job was so important. These guys are attacking Eilistraee's shrines.

"If our underlings do their job too well, we'll bleed them

gray, instead of just drawing them away with our feints," the male with the mace said.

"I hope not. I want a few of them still standing when we jump to the temple, at least sixty-six of the bitches—one for each of us to kill."

Both laughed as they walked toward the door.

"So the chitines didn't suspect anything?" the Selvetargtlin with the mace asked.

"None." The other grinned. "I told them the Spider Queen would reward them with . . ."

The voices faded away as the pair walked out into the street. Jub hung from his thread, slowly spinning in place, waiting for their shouts of alarm. The dead priestess was just outside the door. The two would practically have to step over her on their way outside, but no alarm came. The Selvetargtlin, it seemed, didn't care that a priestess of Lolth had been killed.

Probably, Jub realized, because they'd killed her.

He wondered if he should follow the pair of clerics, but then figured they'd be walking too quickly for him to keep up. He'd heard enough, anyhow. "Temple," they'd said. "*The* temple." They were planning an attack on the Promenade. Sixty-six of them, it seemed—a curiously exact number.

The Promenade wasn't far away—only a few leagues, as the worm burrowed—but its magical protections were rock-solid. Jub wondered how the Selvetargtlin were planning on getting inside. Far as he could see, there was no way they'd be able to.

He turned and scrambled back up the strand of web then out onto the roof. It was time to make his report.

He scuttled back to the tunnel, crossing rooftops where he could, but several times he was forced to scurry along the floor. He had an anxious moment when he reached the exit. The sword-foot spider nearly skewered him, its blade-sharp feet clacking down all around him as he made a dash for it—but then he was in the passage once more.

He hurried along it, back to the empty cavern.

Once there, he ducked into another of the side passages and shifted back into his half-drow form. Qilué had told him to report any discoveries back to her the moment it was possible to do so. She probably didn't expect him to get out of there alive with a dracolich flying around. That pricked his pride, but not so much that he wouldn't do as she'd asked. He owed Qilué. Fourteen years ago, her consort had died while freeing Jub and a bunch of other wretches from a slave ship in Skullport. Instead of blaming the slaves for her consort's death, Qilué had set them free—and invited them back to the Promenade to live. She hadn't even tried to claim the slaves as her own. All she'd demanded, in return for their freedom, was one favor from each of them.

Fourteen years later, Jub was finally going to pay her back.

His clothing and gear had polymorphed with him when he invoked the phylactery's magic, and they were back on his half-drow form. He pulled a slim metal tube from his pocket and uncorked it then carefully tipped out its contents. A feather with a silver shaft fell into his hand, followed by a roll of parchment. He sat, cross-legged, and touched the magical quill to his tongue to prime it. Then he began to write.

His letters were clumsy—simple block letters, like a child would write. If anyone else but Qilué were going to read it, he'd have been embarrassed, but Qilué never made fun of him. She was as beautiful, body and soul, as Jub was ugly.

SELV. CLERICS ATTACKED THE MOON WOOD WITH CHITTENS. BUT IT WAS JUST A FAINT. THEYR GOING TO ATTACK THE PROMENAD, TOO. 66 OF THEM. NOT SURE WHEN.

He paused a moment, thinking, then added:

THEYR IN DOLBLUND, LIKE YOU THOT. I
THINK THEY KILT A LOLTH PREESTIS
THERE.

He paused again. Qilué had told him to write down
every thing he saw and heard, no matter how insignificant
it seemed. So he added:

THEYR GOING TO JUMP ON THE TEMPLE.

His message finished, Jub tapped the magical quill
against the parchment three times. On the third tap, the
words he'd written flowed back into the quill, vanishing
from the page. Jub held the feather close to his mouth
and whispered Qilué's name, then released it. The feather
streaked through the air like an arrow, vanishing in a
sparkle of silver motes.

Jub shifted to a crouching position, hands and knees
on the floor, ready to polymorph again. As he did, he heard
something in the cavern outside, a soft, halting step, as
if someone was shuffling along. As it drew closer to the
tunnel he was hiding in, he activated his phylactery and
scrambled up the wall in spider form. The shuffling—a
vibration he could feel in his legs—stopped at the entrance
to his tunnel. Something peered inside. It was one and a
half times the height of a drow, with a recognizable head,
arms and legs, but its body was entirely covered in a thick
mass of tangled webs. Eight spider eyes stared out of a
face dominated by a gaping mouth and gnashing fangs.
The thing smelled like a combination of spider musk and
rot. Wherever the crude blobs that were its hands and feet
touched stone, they left a clump of clinging web.

The thing stared at Jub for several moments—long
enough to unnerve him. Just when he was certain it had

recognized him as an enemy, it withdrew. It shambled away through the cavern, its feet making sticky, shuffling sounds.

Time to get out of here.

Jub doubled back the way he'd come, climbing the steep walls of the cavern. When he reached its ceiling, his hairs picked up a faint air current emerging from a nearby crack in the rock. The air was flowing into the cavern and was slightly damp. It smelled of melting snow.

The crack was just wide enough for him to squeeze into. It was also a quicker way out—one that didn't lead past all those traps. He scrambled up through it. The climb was a torturous one, and Jub nearly got stuck several times, but the higher he climbed, the better he could smell the wintery scent of the woods above.

The darkness of the shaft was starting to pale to gray when he passed a narrow fissure that opened onto a vast cavern. One glance into it was enough to halt him in his tracks. The floor of the cavern glittered with thousands of gems and coins, strewn about like pebbles on a beach. Half buried in these were statues, books, bejeweled breastplates and helms, silver-chased swords, chalices, and a host of other treasures. It was a sight that Jub had never expected to see in his lifetime—a dragon's horde.

He knew better than to be tempted by it. He turned to go.

Something stirred the hairs on his legs . . . the flapping of massive wings.

A heartbeat later, an enormous head rose to eye level. A massive, slit-pupiled eye, large as a dinner plate and wrinkled as a prune, stared into the hole.

"Not so fast, little orcling," a whisper-dry voice said.

Terrified, Jub tried to scramble away but found himself suddenly unable to move. His heart beat furiously and his rapid breath sent pulses through his abdomen. He screamed at his body to move, but it wouldn't. Terrified—

the dracolich must have seen through his spider disguise and recognized him for what he was—Jub raged at himself. If he'd gone back the way he'd come, instead of trying to take a shortcut, this never would have happened.

The tips of two claws poked into the hole, pinching Jub between them. He gasped as they knifed into his sides. The dracolich plucked him from the hole, and with a harsh whisper, it dispelled the magic of Jub's phylactery, returning Jub to half-drow form. Its breath held the sharp tang of acid.

"I warned you not to trespass up here," the dracolich told him in a voice hoarse as a dying man's. "We had an agreement."

The paralyzation that gripped Jub's body was starting to wear off. "Sorry," he gulped. Hope filled him. The dracolich didn't realize he was a spy—it thought he was one of the Selvetargtlin! "I didn't mean to break it. I thought this was a shortcut to the surface. I didn't know it led to your lair."

As he spoke, Jub desperately tried to activate his phylactery. If he could suddenly turn into a fly, he might be able to buzz away up the shaft and escape. He'd be too tiny for the dracolich to grab. The dracolich, however, seemed to have completely drained the magic from the phylactery.

The undead dracolich hovered, black wings lazily flapping, its massive, wrinkled eyes staring balefully at Jub. "You were warned," it wheezed.

Then it inhaled, filling its lungs. Acid-tinged air seeped out through the chinks between its scales where chest muscle had once been.

Jub steeled himself. This was it. He was going to die. At least he hadn't failed Qilué. Perhaps, when they both met again in Eilistraee's domain, she'd smile at him and thank him. Maybe gently touch his hand and—

The dracolich exhaled. A stream of acid slammed into

Jub's chest, instantly searing a hole through flesh, ribs, and lungs, melting his spine. His upper body flopped backward like a broken doll, acid-seared flesh sloughing from it. There was one brief flash of pain so intense it was blinding.

Then came gray oblivion and a soothing song that swelled through him, washing the anguish away.

CHAPTER TEN

Dhairn stared down at the head Daurgothoth had tossed on the cavern floor. The grisly trophy was deeply pitted with acid, but enough of it remained to show that the intruder had been a half-breed—drow tainted with orc, by the look of the oversized incisors.

"You and I had an agreement," the great black wyrm hissed.

Only its head and neck were visible. Its body was still submerged in the pool that filled one end of the cavern. Foul-smelling water dripped from its emaciated flesh into the water below. A moment before, the pool had been clear, but it had grown murky and stank like rotting garbage. The Selvetargtlin would have to expend magic on purifying it before they could drink from it again.

The dracolich's withered tail swept back and forth through the foul water in obvious agitation. "You agreed that your priests would use only certain parts of the city, and not disturb me."

"He's not one of ours," Dhairn told the dracolich. "He must have been a treasure hunter from the World Above."

Bone scratched against rock as the dracolich flexed its claws against the rocky edge of the pool. "He was climbing up from below. He could only have come from a spot near this cavern."

Dhairn stiffened. "You're certain?"

Leathery muscles creaked as the dracolich nodded. Its skin was dark as soot, its wrinkled eyes like enormous wrinkled balls. "Yes," it hissed. Its acid-tinged breath reeked enough to make Dhairn's eyes water.

Dhairn scowled at the remains of the half-orc head in frustration. The jaw hung by a thread of muscle and the tongue was an acid-eaten stub. The lips were burned away, exposing the teeth. There wasn't enough left of the head to get any intelligible answers out of the corpse. The dracolich had acted rashly. Dhairn would have liked to have learned whether the intruder was alone.

He poked the head with the tip of his sword, rolling it over. "Did the intruder say or do anything before he died? Anything that would lead you to believe he was of a particular faith?"

"He couldn't speak. He'd polymorphed himself into a spider."

Dhairn inhaled sharply. "Lolth." He whispered the name under his breath, the word sharp as a curse.

That didn't bode well. The priestesses of Eryndlyn must have sent out another spy. When that one also failed to return, they would retaliate, but if all went well, the exiled Selvetargtlin that Dhairn led would have a permanent home soon enough, and a powerful new ally once the seals on the Pit were removed.

"Your presence here is drawing unwanted attention," the dracolich observed.

"I agree." Dhairn lifted his sword and rested the heavy blade on his shoulder. "But our forces are ready to strike. I'll send a summons to our knights. As soon as they've loosed their respective companies and assembled here, we'll mount our attack."

The dracolich's eyes glinted. "And my payment for providing the gems and the magic to attune them?"

Dhairn met the undead dracolich's eye with a level stare. "The secrets to the creation of the chitines," he promised, an irresistible lure for Daurgothoth, who had been trying for centuries to magically breed his own unique race of servitors, "and a one-sixth share of all the plunder we wrest from Undermountain over the next six hundred years."

The dracolich gave Dhairn a baleful look. "See to it that you deliver on your promises."

Dhairn bowed, the blade of his sword balanced on his shoulder. "By the strength of Selvetarm's sword arm, we shall."

Cavatina followed Halisstra through the woods. The shrine at Lake Sember was only two days behind them, but they had come to a region of Cormanthor that few trod. The elm and birch trees gradually thinned, giving way to towering black oaks with trunks as twisted as a wizard's tower. Thorn trees grew thickly between them, their long, sharp spines tearing at Cavatina's cloak. Halisstra shouldered her way through the undergrowth, the thorns snapping like glass against her tough skin.

Cavatina's breath fogged in the chill air. So late in the year, the days were short and frost sparkled on the ground from sunrise to sunset, but under the twisted oaks, the ground was bare, black and soft, as if something had melted it from below. Instead of the clean tang of impending snow, Cavatina smelled a sickly-sweet odor, like rotting flesh. As the ground began to descend sharply, she realized where Halisstra was leading her.

"The Darkwatch," she breathed.

Her mother had told stories of the place. Millennia ago, in an age before Myth Drannor was founded, the surface elves had imprisoned an ancient evil there—according to some, the god Moander. The taint lingered still. To venture into the Darkwatch was to court madness, a madness that unleashed unspeakable violence, the kind that would set sister against sister. Cavatina could feel it nibbling at her awareness even then. She hacked at a thorny branch, barely containing the urge to slash and slash until the tree was a splintered ruin.

Halisstra grinned back over her shoulder. "Scared?"

Cavatina gritted her teeth. "I'm a Darksong Knight. We don't scare that easily."

Halisstra nodded.

Cavatina wiped sweat from her forehead with the back of her sleeve. She didn't trust Halisstra, despite what Qilué had said. Just before Cavatina had set out, the high priestess had told her of the prophecy she'd received three years before about the Melarn. One from that House would aid Eilistraee—but another would betray her. As was foretold, two Melarn had shown up at a time of great need: Halisstra and one of her brothers. Which one would betray the goddess was still an open question, but if it was Halisstra, Cavatina would be ready for it. Forewarned was forearmed.

She'd attributed her uneasiness at first to that warning, but she soon realized its cause must have been the Darkwatch itself. Why did the valley unnerve her so? She had slain yochlol in the deepest regions of the Lightdrinker, a chasm whose magic had prevented her from seeing farther than the tip of her outstretched sword, and she'd once battled a chaos beast on the lip of Throrgar, where shrieking winds had nearly torn her from the cliff's edge, but there was something about the Darkwatch—something that ate its way into her resolution like dry rot into wood.

A dry branch cracked behind her. Cavatina whirled, singing sword at the ready.

A dog stood watching her—a hunting hound. It was thin, ribs standing out sharply against its sides. One flank was matted with dried blood. The hound must have been injured by whatever game animal it had been tracking. It whined softly, eyes pleading.

Cavatina hesitated then decided it posed no threat. The animal was in need of healing, something Eilistraee could provide.

Halisstra had halted at the same time as Cavatina. She loomed over the Darksong Knight, her spider legs twitching. "Kill it," she hissed.

The dog let out a low groan.

"No," Cavatina said. Halisstra was obviously spooking the dog. "By Eilistraee's mercy, I'll heal—"

The dog launched itself at Cavatina. Teeth snapped at her outstretched hand with a fury that made her gasp. She yanked her hand back and backed away, singing a prayer that should have soothed the beast, but instead of calming, the dog only became more savage in its attacks. Cavatina batted it away with the flat of her sword, but still it came at her, snarling.

Behind her, Cavatina heard Halisstra laughing, high and shrill. The sound worried at something in Cavatina—something brittle as a dried twig. Her restraint snapped, and she found herself returning the dog's fury blow for blow, slashing at it again and again with her sword. Rather than singing in a sweet voice, the magical weapon keened. Blood splattered her arm and face, and soon she found herself on her knees, the sword in both hands, hacking at the fallen dog with furious swings that slammed her blade deep into the ground. Screaming with rage, she pounded the ruined body again, and again, and again . . .

A distant corner of her mind saw what she was doing and was sickened. The dog was a mutilated mess of splintered bone and pulverized, bloody flesh. With a wrench that she felt through her entire body, she at last halted her attack. Panting, trembling, she climbed to her feet.

Halisstra moved closer, sniffing at the bloody corpse. A low chuckle burst from her misshapen mouth. "Eilistraee's mercy . . . " she muttered.

"Get away from it!" Cavatina shouted. "And shut up. Shut . . . *up!*" She flailed with her sword. A harsh note pealed from it.

Halisstra scampered back.

Cavatina closed her eyes and whispered a fierce prayer: "Eilistraee, help me. Protect me from this madness." A moment later, the last vestiges of the rage ebbed. She opened her eyes again and took a deep, steadying breath— and winced, as the stench of blood filled her lungs. She turned her back on what she'd just done and spoke to Halisstra. "How much farther to the portal?"

Halisstra cocked her head, as if listening to something Cavatina couldn't hear. "Not far." She pointed at a rocky outcrop farther down in the canyon. A stunted black oak grew on top of it. "It's under that tree."

Cavatina grimly nodded. "Let's go."

They walked some distance farther, descending into the valley filled with stunted trees whose limbs seemed to claw at the sky above. As they drew closer to the outcrop, Cavatina could see that it was a jumble of square-cut masonry, the edges of the blocks worn down by the elements. Tufts of blade-stiff grass grew from crevices in the rock, and the tree atop the pile had a trunk so contorted it might have been twisted by a giant's hand. Several large roots spread down over the pile of stones below like black fingers. As Cavatina walked around the rocks, she counted eight such roots—a number she was certain was no coincidence.

Halisstra clambered up onto the pile, which stood about twice Cavatina's height. The bottom of the trunk was slightly raised, as if poised on its roots like a hunting spider about to spring. There was enough clearance between trunk and stones for even the monstrous Halisstra to have crawled through on hands and knees without touching the tree above.

"In here," she said, hunkering down beside it and gesturing at the space beneath the tree.

Cavatina climbed warily up to where Halisstra waited. If it was indeed a portal to Lolth's domain, Cavatina would have it sealed once the expedition was over. For the time being, she cast a spell that would allow others of her faith to find it. If she didn't return from her quest, someone else could deal with it later.

She heard a faint, high-pitched sound like the wind whistling through taut-strung wire. It was an eerie wail, one that made Cavatina's skin crawl. "The songspider?" she asked.

Halisstra nodded. "She must have repaired her web."

Cavatina squatted beside Halisstra and peered between the roots. She could see faint lines of violet against the darkness—brief shimmers of hair-thin light that were there one moment, gone the next.

"Silence it," she ordered.

Halisstra ducked her head—the best nod she could manage, with those thickly corded neck muscles—and reached into the hollow under the tree. Her fingers plucked at the strands of violet light. As she worked, a low, rasping sound came from her throat: a song. When it was done, Halisstra pulled her hands back. Her long, dark fingers were sticky with violet threads. The sound that had been coming from inside the hollow had stopped.

"It's done," she said. "The way is clear."

"Good," Cavatina said. "You first."

Halisstra bowed her head. "Mistress."

The look she gave Cavatina made it clear she under-stood that the Darksong Knight didn't fully trust her. She turned and scrabbled her way into the space beneath the tree and stood, the upper half of her body vanishing from sight. One foot stepped up, then the other—and she was gone.

Cavatina took a deep breath. She had fought demons on the doorsteps of the Abyss as they emerged from portals, but she had never traveled to the outer planes herself. She fairly tingled with the thrill of it, even though it was not truly a hunt but a recovery mission. She cast a spell that would allow her to resist the negative energies of the Demonweb Pits then followed, singing sword in hand. As her body penetrated the spot occupied on the Prime Material Plane by the tree, the smell of moldy sap filled her nostrils. An instant later, her head forced its way through strands of web, snapping them with vibrations she could feel but could not hear. A thin film of stickiness covered her hair, shoulders, and clothes—strands of the songspider web. She climbed up, as Halisstra had done—and suddenly was standing somewhere else.

The first thing she did was search for the spider whose web they had just broken, but it was nowhere to be seen. A divination spell revealed nothing.

"Where's the songspider?" she asked.

Halisstra shrugged. "Gone." She pointed at something that lay a few paces away that looked like a bundle of old sticks. "I think her children ate her."

Cavatina nodded as she recognized the dried husk as the remains of a spider. She'd expected a living foe. The passage had been easy. Too easy.

She looked around. The Demonweb Pits looked nothing

like she'd expected. She'd always envisioned them as a vast cavern filled with steel-strong webs, upon which Lolth's iron fortress crept like a spider. Instead the portal had delivered them to a blasted plain of barren, purple-gray rock, under a sky that was utterly black, save for a cluster of eight blood red stars that glared down like the eyes of a watchful spider. Hanging down from the sky on strands of web—so far overhead that they appeared little more than dots—were off-white balls. Every now and then, one of them burst, releasing the ghostly gray form of a drow—a soul, freshly dead. The souls were caught by the wind, which blew steadily in one direction, toward a distant line of cliffs.

The plain was as uneven as a pox-scarred face, cratered with depressions and gouged with deep chasms. Everywhere Cavatina looked, there were webs. They drifted on the wind and snagged on her clothes and hair. Feeling something tickle her bare knee, she glanced down. The ground was covered in tiny red spiders, each no larger than a grain of rice. They swarmed up onto her boots. She whispered a prayer. Under its compulsion, the tiny spiders leaped from her boots and scurried away into cracks in the rock.

"Where is the temple?" she asked in a low voice. The cluster of red "stars" overhead made her wary of raising her voice.

Halisstra pointed at a spot, perhaps a league away, where dozens of what looked like flat-topped spires of stone protruded from the ground. "On top of one of those."

Cavatina squinted at the distant objects. "What are they?"

"The petrified legs of giant spiders."

Cavatina frowned. "*That's* what you built Eilistraee's temple on top of?"

Halisstra gave a lopsided grin. "It offered the best vantage point, easier to defend than anywhere else." She gestured with a misshapen hand. "Come."

Halisstra scuttled away across the wasteland toward the spires. The Darksong Knight activated the magic of her boots then followed, not wanting to let Halisstra get out of sight. Cavatina levitated and descended, levitated and descended, in a series of long, graceful strides. Each time a boot touched ground, it slipped slightly as it squished the tiny spiders that swarmed there. Certain that Lolth would react to this defilement of her domain any instant, Cavatina kept a watchful eye for whatever the Spider Queen would hurl at her, but there were no attacks. No spiders descended from the skies, no darkfire boiled up from the ground below, no madness-inducing peals of laughter echoed across the landscape. It was as if the domain itself held its breath, waiting to see what Halisstra and Cavatina would do.

It was certainly the Demonweb Pits, but one vital element was missing: Lolth's fortress. Said to be shaped like an enormous iron spider, it should have been ceaselessly patrolling her realm, yet Cavatina could neither see nor hear it. Was the Demonweb Pits so vast that Lolth's fortress was beyond the horizon? It was a question Cavatina could not answer. She knew only one thing. Wherever Lolth's fortress might be, she was glad it wasn't on top of them.

As she descended from yet another floating leap, her eyes were drawn to a web-choked crevice in the ground where something stirred. This gave her the warning she needed to spring to the side as a cluster of spider-things burst from the crevice and swarmed toward her. She recognized them at once: chwidenchas, creatures made from the magically altered bodies of drow who had displeased Lolth. Each of the four creatures was the size of a small horse, composed entirely of bristly black legs tipped with claws as sharp as daggers. Additional barbs lined the inside of each leg, turning it into the equivalent of a saw blade. Once a chwidencha landed on its chosen prey, those barbs would hook fast in a grapple. The only way to avoid being crushed when the creature squeezed was by tearing free—something that would carve jagged wounds into the victim's flesh.

Cavatina had escaped the chwidenchas by levitating, but Halisstra wasn't so fortunate. Attracted by the vibrations of her footfalls, the spider-things veered toward her. Halisstra whirled and blasted one of them with a web, suffocating it under a thick coating of sticky silk, but then the other three were on her. Legs rose and fell, the claws stabbing down. Most skittered harmlessly off Halisstra's stone-tough skin, but a few of the jabs sank home. In an instant, Halisstra's body was coated in blood.

Halisstra stood and fought them. If it was a ploy on her part to gain Cavatina's sympathy, it was a dangerous one.

Cavatina landed, stamping her feet to draw the chwidenchas' attention. Two of them broke off their attack on Halisstra and scurried toward her. Cavatina sprang into the air, lifting her hunting horn up to her lips. She blew a strident note straight down at them. As the waves of sound struck the chwidenchas, they halted and curled into tight balls. A moment later, they sprang open again. Cavatina hesitated then blew the horn a second time. Once again, the two spider-things shuddered to a halt then opened more slowly. Visibly staggering, they scuttled around in circles, at least half of their legs dragging uselessly behind them.

Even in their weakened state, fighting the chwidenchas with a sword would be futile. The fist-sized "heads" of the spider-things were buried deep at the center of the creature. The legs would have to be hacked off, one by one, in order to do the creature any real damage, and the legs could regenerate.

Still floating above the wounded spider-things, Cavatina pressed her lips to the horn a third time, knowing that she might be inviting disaster. The magical horn was meant to be blown only once each day. Unleashing its energies more than that could trigger an explosion that could knock her senseless at the very least or snap her neck at worst, but Cavatina had not been invited into the ranks of the Darksong Knights by being unwilling to take chances. Anyone who fought demons for a living had to be bold.

She blew—and a third wave of sound shuddered through the chwidenchas, pulverizing them. They collapsed, twitched once or twice, and died.

Halisstra, meanwhile, was still battling the chwidencha that had attacked her. She knocked it away with a sweep of one powerfully muscled arm, but as soon as it stopped rolling it sprang at her again. It landed on her back, knocking her to the ground. Its legs sawed against her body, scrabbling for a hold.

Halisstra was not so easily beaten. She rose, wrenching the creature over her head to the front of her body—a move that tore deep gouges in her shoulders. She sank her fangs into one of the chwidencha's legs. The chwidencha tried to push itself free, but Halisstra's own spider legs held it fast, crushing it against her chest. She bit it again and again, working her way in toward its center, where the legs joined—and at last a deep shudder ran through the chwidencha and its legs fell limp.

Cavatina drifted to the ground beside Halisstra. "Bravely done."

Halisstra, eyes gleaming, hurled the lifeless chwidencha aside.

Cavatina moved closer, her hand raised. "Those wounds. Shall I try to heal—"

"No." Halisstra's voice was harsh as she flinched away. "Lolth's pact will heal me."

Cavatina lowered her hand. She walked to the chwidencha that was bound by the web and levered it onto its back with her sword, exposing the throbbing ball of flesh that was the thing's head. She skewered it with the point of her sword. The weapon sang in a joyful tone as the chwidencha died.

"Hard to believe these were once drow," Cavatina said as she pulled her sword free.

Halisstra's head came up.

"Created by Lolth, just as you were." Cavatina moved to the second chwidencha, levered it over, and thrust again, ensuring that it was dead. "Each leg was a person who angered Lolth in some way. They were transformed by fell magic and bound together to create a creature that knows only pain and hatred." She moved to the third, flipped it, and drove her sword home. "We do them a favor by killing them. Among the legs might be some whose 'crime' against the Spider Queen was to contemplate the worship of some other deity, perhaps even Eilistraee. Some of the souls we free may go on to dance with the goddess in her domain." She turned to face Halisstra. "Which proves that there's always hope, no matter how grim things seem."

Halisstra either missed the point or deliberately ignored it. "You've hunted chwidencha before."

Cavatina nodded. "Among other things." She nodded at Halisstra's wounds. Already they were closing over. "Are you able to continue?"

"Yes."

They continued toward the spires of rock and soon were among them. Cavatina could see that they were, indeed, petrified legs, most of them snapped clean and flat at the second joint, their clawed tips fused with the stone of the ground below. Each was as big around as a house. She tried to imagine the spiders whose legs they once had been, and shuddered. Such creatures could only have been spawned in the Abyss.

Most of the spires of rock were thick with spiderwebs that fluttered like torn flags from the bristles protruding from their sides. One spire, however, was clear of webs. Nearly two hundred paces tall, it was twisted in a way that reminded Cavatina of the tree that had served as the portal. Halisstra stopped in front of it and patted the black stone.

"This one," she said, craning her neck up. "The temple's on top."

"Show me."

Halisstra climbed, her bare hands and feet sticking to the rock like those of a spider. Cavatina sprang into the air, levitating beside her. As she neared the top, she saw a structure perched on top of the flat expanse of stone. It was a simple box of a building little bigger than a shed: four square walls, a roof, and a single arched doorway in which fluttered a tattered blanket that served as an improvised door. The walls were deeply pitted, as if from acid, but one section of stone above the arch was untouched. On it was a crude carving of a sword atop a circle that represented the full moon—Eilistraee's symbol. Seeing it, Cavatina felt a comforting warmth. That much of Halisstra's story, at least, had been true. Together with Feliane and Uluyara she *had* raised a temple to Eilistraee, shaping it by magic out of stone—in the heart of the Demonweb Pits.

Cavatina landed in front of the building and sang a song of praise. As she finished the divination spell, the symbol on the building began to glow. The temple was still consecrated—though dark streaks of evil were worming their way into its stone walls.

Halisstra had not yet clambered onto the top of the spire. She hung at its edge, wincing and turning her head away from the building, as if it pained her to look at it.

Cavatina gestured at the temple. "The Crescent Blade is inside?"

Halisstra nodded. Her matted hair, stuck to her shoulders, did not move. "On the floor."

Cavatina moved to the entrance and used her sword to move the fluttering blanket aside. She could see something that glinted inside the temple against the back wall—a sword with a curved blade. The blanket fell, and the wind caught it, blowing it to the back of the room. It landed on the curved sword, covering it.

Cavatina glanced up, making sure nothing was lurking on the inside ceiling, then back at where Halisstra clung to the top of the spire, only her head and shoulders visible above the edge. The fangs that protruded from Halisstra's cheeks were twitching. Her eyes were wide with anticipation and her drow mouth hung open slightly, panting. Her whispered hiss came to Cavatina on the wind: "Yes."

One eye still on Halisstra, Cavatina eased into the room. The temple was small, barely four paces across. Its interior had an odd feeling about it, sacred and calm, yet balanced on the edge of turmoil. Cavatina felt as though she were walking across a pane of clearstone waiting for it to crack.

She flicked away the blanket with the tip of her sword and stared down at the weapon that lay on the floor. Words had been inlaid in silver along its curved blade. They were in the language of the drow and thus easily read. A portion of one word was missing, at a spot where the upper and lower halves of the blade had been fused back together. The silver in that spot had melted away. The script read:

> *Be your heart filled with light*
> *and your cause be true,*
> *I shall n— fail you.*

A divination spell showed that the sword still held its magic. Cavatina stared down at it in awe.

"The Crescent Blade," she whispered.

Forged centuries ago from "moon metal," it had a blade so keen it could cut through stone or even metal. It was a weapon said to be capable of severing the neck of any creature—even a god.

Cavatina sheathed her singing sword and reached down for the Crescent Blade. As her hand closed around the leather-wrapped hilt, she felt a rush of power surge up her arm. Holding the weapon in both hands, she spun like a sword dancer, savoring the perfect balance of the blade. With it, she would be the penultimate hunter. Her foes would fall like wheat before a scythe. "Eilistraee!" she cried. Still spinning, she threw back her head and laughed.

A loud hissing sound brought her to her senses. Halting abruptly, she peered outside the temple and saw splatters of rain hitting the stone. Where they landed, the stone began to bubble. Foul-smelling steam rose and pock marks formed.

Acidic rain.

Halisstra stared up at the sky, rain streaming down her face and soaking her matted hair. If the acid stung her bare skin, she showed no sign. "A storm is coming," she said. She glanced down. "We need shelter."

Cavatina gestured at the temple. "Eilistraee will shield us."

Halisstra shook her head. "Not me." She glanced down again then sprang away from the edge of the cliff, out into space.

Cavatina rushed to the exit, but the acidic rain blowing in through the open doorway drove her back. She sang a prayer of protection and forced her way against the wind to the edge of the spire of rock. She stared down but saw no sign of her guide.

"Halisstra!" she called, but her voice was snatched away by the rising wind.

Acidic rain bounced away from her skin, hair and clothes without touching them, repelled by her spell. Its magic would protect her—but only for a time. She needed to get back under shelter herself, but as she turned back toward the temple, she heard a sharp crack. A large split appeared in its front wall, beside the arch. Rain streamed off the roof in rivulets, eroding the crack further. Even as Cavatina watched, it widened. Then, with a terrific groaning sound, the structure gave way. The roof fell in, and the walls crumbled. Soon all that remained was a shapeless blob, atop which rested a single, jagged chunk of solid stone, bearing Eilistraee's symbol.

The temple was no more. It had stood only as long as it needed to, by the grace of Eilistraee. With the Crescent Blade recovered, Cavatina was on her own.

She ran to the edge of the cliff and leaped, letting her boots carry her gently downward. As she descended, she contacted Halisstra with a spell. *When the storm is over, meet me at the portal,* she sent.

Halisstra's reply came a moment later. A thin, drawn-out wail. *I can't! Lolth calls.*

Cavatina repeated her spell. *I can help you resist her. Tell me where you are.*

She felt Halisstra's mind brush hers, but there was no reply, just a low, half-mad gurgle of laughter.

Something came hurtling up at her from the base of the spire: two creatures that glowed with a faint, greenish-yellow light, legs trailing behind them. Cavatina recognized them in an instant. They were myrlochar—"soul spiders"—deadly foes capable of stealing a victim's life essence and adding it to their own, and they could levitate just as skillfully as Cavatina could.

She halted in mid-descent and hurled a spell down at them. Two brilliant white shafts of Eilistraee's holy moonlight flashed down, each striking one of the myrlochars and instantly charring it to a flaming husk. They tumbled, legs snapping off as they fell, and landed with twin thuds on the ground below.

Cavatina almost laughed. Was that the best Lolth could

send against her? She renewed the spell that prevented the acidic rain from harming her and landed beside the still-smoking husks of the soul spiders.

As if in answer to her silent challenge, the weather changed. The rain stopped and small, hard balls of stone began to fall from the sky. As they tapped off Cavatina's metal armor, she saw that they were tiny spiders. She tried to grind one underfoot, but it was like a pebble under the sole of her boot. She realized they must be petrified, like the spire of rock behind her.

More petrified spiders fell, larger ones. Soon they were the size of grapes, then eggs. They pelted down in a bruising hail. Cavatina sang a prayer, creating a shield-shaped disk of energy above her head. Most of the spider-hail bounced off it, careening away to either side, but some of the missiles came through and struck her head and shoulders.

Just ahead was a wide crack in another of the spires of rock—a natural cavern. Cavatina ran into it, escaping the hail. She skidded to a halt as she saw that the cavern was already occupied. A drow female, bloody and bruised, lay against one wall. When she stirred, Cavatina recognized her as Uluyara, one of the priestesses who had accompanied Halisstra into the Demonweb Pits. She was alive, but just barely.

"Behind . . . you!" Uluyara croaked, staring past Cavatina at something outside in the storm.

Cavatina was half-turning when the singing sword blasted away the veil the false drow had used to cloud her mind. She whirled, the Crescent Blade still in her hand, and found herself facing a yochlol instead of Uluyara. The demon had assumed its natural form, a shapeless heap of reeking flesh, and it towered above her. A single red eye glared out at her from the center of eight writhing tentacles. The limbs lashed forward, at least half of them scoring hits on Cavatina's arms, shoulders, and chest.

They inflicted only minor wounds, but their tugs threw Cavatina off balance. She lashed out with the Crescent Blade and managed to strike one of the tentacles, cutting clean through it. The severed appendage struck a wall and flopped to the ground, leaking gore.

The yochlol screeched, and all was in darkness. Cavatina countered it with a prayer that would enable her to see again and slashed with the Crescent Blade, trying to find her foe, but her blade swept through empty space. The yochlol had either recognized her as a Darksong Knight and teleported away or . . .

As Cavatina's spell pierced the magical darkness, she saw a roiling cloud of yellowish vapor. The yochlol had assumed gaseous form. The stench punched into Cavatina's stomach like a greasy fist. Fighting the urge to double over and vomit, she sang a healing word. The nausea passed, but the demon changed form again, assuming the shape of a large spider. It leaped toward her, fangs distended to bite.

Cavatina met it in mid-leap with an overhand swing. The yochlol had no neck to sever—in spider form its head and thorax were fused—but the Crescent Blade did its job. The blade struck the creature at the midpoint of its cluster of eyes, slicing cleanly through cephalothorax and abdomen, cutting each in two. Hot, stinking ooze splattered Cavatina from forehead to feet as the two halves of the body sailed past on either side, landing behind her.

She blinked and spat the foul taste out of her mouth. Demon blood dribbled down the blade onto her hand and dripped onto the floor. "That's some sword," she said softly, hefting the Crescent Blade appreciatively.

Who are you?

Cavatina blinked. Was that a voice she'd just heard? Another yochlol, announcing its presence? She whirled in place, the Crescent Blade ready in her hand. The spell that had allowed her to see through the yochlol's magical darkness was still in effect and showed nothing out of the ordinary. She was alone in the cavern.

Alone with the Crescent Blade.

You're not the one.

Cavatina stared at the weapon. "Is . . ." She paused, feeling foolish. "Is that you talking, sword?" She'd heard of weapons with an intelligence of their own but had never owned one.

The sword—if indeed it was the sword that had spoken—made no reply.

Cavatina heard something stirring deeper in the cavern and suspected it was another yochlol. The place might well have been home to an entire brood of demons. Though she'd like nothing better than to slay them, one by one, Qilué's orders had been strict. Cavatina was to recover the Crescent Blade from the Demonweb Pits and return with it promptly, not linger in Lolth's domain, where it might be damaged or lost. There would be demons aplenty to kill, another day.

Cavatina glanced outside. The hail of spiders had stopped. She stepped out of the cavern, still holding the Crescent Blade. The singing sword would have been a better weapon to be carrying if she encountered more yochlol, but practicality took precedence. The Crescent Blade was too curved to fit in her scabbard. She had to carry it.

She headed back toward the portal, once again using her magical boots to cross the ground in long, graceful leaps. As she did, she peered between the spires of rock, trying to see where Halisstra had gone. She also attempted to send a message to Halisstra, but the sending met with silence. Perhaps Halisstra had already used the portal to return to the Prime Material Plane. Once she was through it, a sending wouldn't necessarily reach her.

Even if Halisstra hadn't reached the portal yet, Cavatina was certain the former priestess could take care of herself. Halisstra had survived, by her own account, for two years in Lolth's domain. She was as adapted to survive there as any demon—her immunity to the acidic rain had proved that.

As Cavatina passed the last of the spires, she saw something in the distance that sent a chill through her: a spider so enormous that she could make out the details of it, even from so far away. Its body was crowned with a drow head, and it reared back on six of its eight legs. The two front legs held weapons that glinted a dull red in the ruddy starlight, a straight steel sword and a thicker knob-headed mace.

By his weapons alone, Cavatina would have recognized him. It was Selvetarm himself, champion of Lolth, and no mere avatar—not at home in the Demonweb Pits—but the demigod himself.

Cavatina whispered a fervent prayer as she drifted to the ground. Her heart pounding furiously, she stood, utterly motionless, as Selvetarm turned. It took all of her willpower not to cringe as the demigod's gaze swept over her. Would Eilistraee hide her from sight? Could she, from a demigod in his own domain? Selvetarm had the power to see the invisible—and would immediately spot Cavatina if he so much as suspected anyone was there. She only started breathing again when the head turned away once more.

Her relief at not being spotted drained away as she realized where Selvetarm was standing almost exactly on the spot where the portal was, and he wasn't moving.

Cavatina had been feeling certain she could defeat anything Lolth could toss at her, but suddenly things had become complicated. To escape the Demonweb Pits, she was going to have to fight her way past a demigod.

You can do it.

Cavatina blinked. Had that been the sword talking—or her own pride?

Her grip tightened on the Crescent Blade. She could do it. The weapon in her hands had been forged for exactly that purpose, to kill deities.

Yes, the sword whispered.

Cavatina smiled grimly and thought, what a hunt this is going to be!

If she succeeded in killing Selvetarm, her name would be praised forevermore from the Promenade to the smallest shrine.

And a demigod's head would be her trophy.

CHAPTER ELEVEN

Malvag waited impatiently in the cavern. It was difficult to keep from pacing back and forth, though his surroundings helped. It was peaceful there. Dark. Separate. Silent. The only sounds were the *thud-thud, thud-thud* of his heart and the soft exhalations of his breath. The darkstone crystals that lined the walls created a void of utter blackness around him, drinking in even the darkfire that danced like a shadow across the skin of his right hand, yet the shadows weren't quite enough to calm him.

It was the night of the winter solstice—the longest night of the year—and midnight was rapidly approaching. The moment he'd been waiting for was almost at hand. In just a little while, Urz, Valdar, and Szorak would arrive with their soul-impregnated masks, and the conjuration could begin.

At midnight, according to the astrologers, Toril's shadow would fall fully across the moon, completely eclipsing it. The darkest hour of the longest night of the year would begin with Eilistraee's holiest of symbols completely enshrouded in shadow.

Malvag stared down at a drift disc, no larger than a dinner plate, that floated in the air before him at waist level. On it was a treasure he'd spent the better part of a century searching for, a prayer scroll from ancient Ilythiir. It was made of silver foil, tarnished to a mottled black and crumbling at the edges after ten thousand years of lying in the blasted ruins of an ancient temple. Delicate as a dried leaf, it had deep creases from being crushed flat by the tumbled masonry that had helped to preserve it, yet the words that had been written on it in Old Espruar by the high clerics of vanished Ilythiir could still be discerned.

Malvag moved his index finger above them, silently reading with the aid of the darkfire. When the time came, he and whichever of the Nightshadows had been successful in their soulthefts would read them aloud, activating the scroll's magic.

Malvag savored the irony of what was to come. The scroll had been intended to open a gate between Lolth's domain and Arvandor, so the Spider Queen could mount a second attack on the Seldarine. It had never been used, however—probably because it had been created in the final years of the Fourth Crown War, just before the *ssri Tel'Quessir* had been transformed into drow and driven below.

Instead it would be used by Lolth's enemies to make their god stronger. After killing Eilistraee, Vhaeraun would secretly assume that goddess's portfolio and add her worshipers to his ranks. All of the drow in the Night Above—male and female—would come under one god.

Strengthened by their worship, Vhaeraun would mount an attack on Lolth herself, and the reign of the Spider Queen would, at long last, be at an end.

The thought sent a thrill through Malvag.

It was tempered by the memory of the demonic creature that had first bound him then revived him. He shuddered. When the demon-thing had attacked him, he'd assumed it had been sent by Lolth, but after it had revived him, he hadn't been so sure. He'd later decided that it must be a thing of Selvetarm, but the Selvetargtlin had denied that, which left him wondering if the creature was Lolth's after all. The Spider Queen could certainly want Malvag to live so that his work could continue and Eilistraee be killed, no doubt about that, but the thought of Lolth meddling in what should have been purely Vhaeraun's vengeance made Malvag uneasy.

He pushed the thought aside. He couldn't allow himself to be distracted, not when so much rested on his shoulders. He would need all of his concentration to invoke the scroll's powers.

He closed his eyes and inhaled deeply, drinking in the invisible energies that rippled back and forth in the enclosed space. The cavern couldn't sustain life for long. The air already smelled slightly stale. For one night, at least, it would suffice, and that one night was all that mattered.

A whisper of air announced the arrival of another cleric. Malvag turned and saw Urz, his red eyes glittering above his mask. The other cleric's posture was eager and his close-cropped hair stood on end, as if a shiver had just passed through him. He wore a single, wide-bladed dagger at his hip and a homespun black shirt and trousers with frayed cuffs and worn knees. He looked more like a laborer than an assassin, but that natural camouflage served him well. Urz had won Vhaeraun's favor many times over with his bold attacks on Lolth's clergy.

"Dark deeds," Malvag murmured.

Urz inclined his head, paying Malvag the respect due a higher ranking cleric.

"Were you successful?" Malvag asked.

Urz touched his mask then gave the sign for a job completed. "She put up a good fight, though," he said, "broke two of my ribs and nearly cut off my hand." He turned his right hand over, showing Malvag the fresh gray scar across his wrist just below the older burn mark. Then he waggled his fingers. "Good as new now, praise Vhaeraun, but I had to stab her, sop up the soul and get away quick. The Gray Forest was like an overturned beehive after all the noise she made."

Malvag barely listened to the details. Urz had arrived and his mask held a soul. That was all that mattered.

The Jaelre strode toward the drift disc, his hard-soled boots crunching across the crystal-studded floor. "I'm the first one here?"

"As always. I knew I could count on you."

The two males clasped arms—a form of greeting used by the surface elves. Urz's grip was tight and rough on Malvag's forearms, but Malvag returned it in equal measure before letting go.

Urz's eyes crinkled above his mask. "And the others?"

As if in answer, Valdar appeared in the cavern. The slender-boned male landed with a cat's grace on the crystals, a bloody dagger in one hand. He nodded to the others, pulled a lace-trimmed cloth out of a pocket of his *piwafwi*, and wiped the blade. His pink eyes held a glint of amusement.

"Sorry to be late. I had a little unfinished business to attend to. It's finished, now."

That said, he slid his dagger into a wrist-sheath. He wore a wrist-crossbow on his other arm, and the ties of his *piwafwi* were stiff from the ends of a strangle cord. He moved with a grace that would have put a tavern dancer to shame, picking his way with silent footfalls over the crystals on the floor. He took up a position that put him equidistant from both males, close enough that he could step inside the range of a crossbow but far enough apart that he could dance away from a drawn blade.

Malvag's eyes narrowed slightly. Valdar didn't quite trust the others yet, nor did Malvag fully trust *him*, but mutual trust was essential for the ritual to work.

Valdar cocked his head to the side, silently reading the scroll. Urz stood with his arms folded across his chest, staring across the cavern, waiting placidly. Malvag tapped a foot impatiently as the night lengthened. Midnight approached—the deadline Malvag had set for the others' return—and still Szorak didn't appear. Malvag started to wonder if something had happened to him. Four clerics—and four souls—would make the ritual that much more certain and would ensure that the gate opened, but it looked as though Szorak had failed them. Or perhaps—a darker thought that Malvag allowed to alight in his mind only briefly—it had been Szorak's blood on Valdar's blade. Fewer to reap the rewards.

Malvag shrugged off that thought. As long as the three could work together, it didn't matter.

"It's nearly midnight," he told the others. "We must begin."

He turned the drift disc so that the scroll faced him, and indicated where the others should stand, Urz on his right, Valdar on his left. Urz moved readily into the indicated spot, and Valdar eased in sideways.

"I will commune with Vhaeraun," he told them. "At my signal, we'll begin to read. It's important that each of you not get ahead of the others or lag behind. We—"

A startled shout filled the cavern. A drow male appeared in mid-air, arms and legs flailing as he fell. He'd materialized about a dozen paces above the cavern floor, and only just managed to check his fall in time. Levitating, he twisted awkwardly in place, his feet scrabbling against the bumpy crystal floor. Then he stood, smoothing his clothes.

"Szorak!" Urz called. "You're just in time. We were about to begin without you."

"My apologies," the newcomer said from behind his mask. "I must have miscalculated the teleport. I forgot how big this place is." He glanced around then nodded to himself. "Perfect for tonight's dark deeds."

Malvag frowned. Szorak seemed . . . different, somehow. It took Malvag a moment to put a dagger point on it. The voice. It was lower, huskier, and at the same time somehow tight with tension. And Szorak's body language was off. He leaned slightly forward, a posture that caused the lower half of his mask to hang away from his lips and chin, as if he was loath to touch it.

As if overhearing Malvag's thoughts, Szorak reached under his mask and rubbed his throat. "The bitch managed to cast a spell," he said, "one that transferred her injuries to me." He gave a croaking laugh. "I nearly wound up strangling myself."

Urz chuckled.

"Clumsy," Valdar breathed under his mask.

Malvag frowned. "I've never heard of such a spell."

"Nor had I." Szorak shrugged. "It must be something new the priestesses have come up with." His hand dropped away from his throat. "But I trapped a soul, nonetheless."

It was an odd turn of phrase. Trapped a soul. Not "stole." Something was wrong. Malvag didn't want to sow mistrust—Valdar was already twitchy enough—but he had a growing suspicion that "Szorak" was not who he claimed to be. He moved his hand at his side, where only Szorak could see it. *I know who you are.*

Szorak stiffened. For a space of several heartbeats, there was silence. Then he exhaled. "You know my secret," he said. "You know about my sister. It's true. Seyll was a priestess of Eilistraee, but I assure you, Malvag, that I am not."

Valdar gave a dark chuckle. "Not a priestess?" His eyes ranged up and down Szorak's body. "That's pretty clear."

Szorak gave Valdar a level look. "If you think I've disguised myself, cast a divination that pierces glamors." He gestured at his body. "What you see is what I am."

Urz glanced back and forth between Szorak and Malvag. One hand was raised, fingers twitching slightly, as if ready to cast a spell. He was clearly only waiting for Malvag's command to strike. "His sister's a priestess?"

"A dead priestess," Szorak said. He chuckled. "Killed years ago by a priestess of Lolth who was masquerading as a petitioner, but I assure you that I'm no spider kisser." He spread his arms. "Go ahead. Inspect me."

Malvag took him up on the offer and whispered two prayers in quick succession. They revealed that the mask did indeed contain a trapped soul—one that glowed with the irritating silver sheen of good. Szorak's own aura, in contrast, was a dull brown.

Malvag relaxed. He'd been wrong. It *was* Szorak. He'd very nearly let his suspicions ruin everything. He touched Urz's arm.

"No need for that," he told the other cleric. Then he turned back to Szorak. "Take your place," he instructed. "We've already wasted too much time. We should begin."

Szorak moved toward the drift disc. He hesitated for a moment then stood next to Urz.

Malvag gestured, and the drift disc moved to a position where all could read it. His previous darkfire spell had ended some time ago, so he whispered the prayer again, causing the flames that only those with darkvision could detect to dance once more about his fingertips.

"When I lower my finger to the page," he instructed, "begin to read."

That said, he enshrouded his head in magical darkness, stilled his breathing, and made the sign of the mask. He prayed, his fingers signing in time with his words. "Masked Lord, God of Night, Shadow of my Soul. Hear me on this, the longest of nights. Your Nightshadows stand ready to open a gate to Eilistraee's domain. Masked Lord, are you ready? Should we proceed?"

The communion came, as it always did, on softly creeping feet. One moment there was nothing, then came a whisper from behind, as faint as breath. Malvag felt a presence slip softly into his awareness. He sensed, rather than truly saw, a pair of eyes peering over his shoulder. The eyes were black, flecked with silver. They matched the weapons that swished through Malvag's awareness in streaks of utter black and gleaming silver—the long sword Night Shadow and the short sword Silverflash. A cloak swirled as the god spun, leaving streaks of starlight. Vhaeraun took several moments to answer—his eyes kept darting about—but at last the word came, cutting the air like a hissing blade.

"Yes."

Malvag smiled. A thrill raced through him. The hairs on his arms shivered erect as he opened his eyes, dispelled the magical darkness, and started to lower his finger to the scroll. He heard the clerics on either side of him take a breath as they prepared to read aloud.

But from his right came an intensely bright flash of light. An explosive boom filled the cavern as a jagged lightning bolt erupted from Urz's chest and forked toward Malvag and Valdar. It slammed into Malvag's own chest, sending waves of pain crackling through his body and filling his nostrils with the stench of seared flesh. As both he and Valdar reeled, gasping, Szorak ripped off Urz's mask. He slapped Urz on the back with his other hand and shouted. As the mask fluttered away, Urz went rigid and toppled to the floor with a loud crash. Szorak danced back, shaking a wand out of his sleeve and catching it deftly in his hand.

"Traitor!" Malvag gasped.

Szorak pointed the wand at the scroll. Raging with fury, Malvag threw himself at Szorak. His fist closed around the wand even as it went off. Chunks of ice blasted into the floor, sending shards of crystals flying.

"Faer'ghinn!" Malvag croaked through cracked and bleeding lips.

The wand became an inert stick.

Something whizzed past Malvag's ear—a bolt from Valdar's wrist-crossbow. It glanced off Szorak's shoulder, deflected by an invisible barrier. So close had it come to striking Malvag that a terrible thought flashed through his mind. Was Valdar in league with Szorak? Were the pair of them trying to steal the scroll? No, that blast of ice from the wand would have destroyed it.

The traitor's fingers flicked, and a tiny object leaped out of one of his pockets and into them. It was a chunk of amber, studded with silver dots. A spell component, Malvag realized, even as another bolt of lightning streaked toward him. It punched into Malvag's chest, blasting him off his feet. Something sharp ground into his back and he dully realized they were the points of crystals. He'd landed on his back on the cavern floor.

Dazzled though his eyes were, he caught glimpses of what came next. Valdar fired another crossbow bolt, which struck home, punching into the wizard's shoulder. The wizard staggered but managed to hurl a spell back at Valdar. A hollow column of fire sprang up around the cleric, trapping him inside it. Instantly, Valdar's hair and clothing ignited. The roaring flames closed inward, then Valdar vanished. He reappeared behind the wizard, the flames extinguished, and drew his dagger in a cat-quick motion. Even as the wizard realized his danger and began to turn—sluggishly, the bolt's poison at last taking effect—Valdar slammed his dagger into him.

The wizard's eyes flew open wide. He sagged to the ground, gasping, a ball of gum Arabic falling from his limp fingers. Valdar slit the wizard's throat, finishing the job. Dark blood sprayed from the wound, splattering the crystal floor.

Valdar stepped back and murmured a prayer. A heartbeat later, his flesh mended. His clothing, however, remained charred.

Malvag staggered to his feet. One wary eye on the dead wizard, he hurried to the drift disc. The scroll, praise Vhaeraun, was undamaged.

The same could not be said of Urz. Malvag kneeled beside the other cleric and touched a hand to his neck. Urz's body felt cold and hard.

He'd been turned to stone.

Malvag felt the blood drain from his face as he realized the implications. Had Urz merely died, Malvag could have raised him from the dead. But there was only one thing that would allow the night's work to continue—a miracle.

"Masked Lord, hear me," Malvag said, forcing the tremble from his voice as he prayed, trying to shove his anger aside so he could concentrate on the words of the prayer. He'd only heard it spoken once, and it was well above his abilities, but he had to try. If he didn't, all would be lost. "Send your dark energies into my hands, that they might perform a miracle. Aid me in restoring your fallen servant's flesh to its natural state."

Malvag waited expectantly, his palms on Urz's stone-cold chest. Valdar stood behind him, watching, wiping his dagger clean on a charred corner of his shirt.

"It's not working," he observed.

Malvag's anger flared. "Shut up," he hissed.

The other cleric raised his dagger, inspecting the hollow point that held the poison, then shoved it home in its sheath. "My apologies."

Malvag tried again. He put both hands upon Urz's chest and pleaded with Vhaeraun to turn Urz's body back to living, breathing flesh.

Nothing happened.

Vhaeraun watched. Malvag could feel the god's presence just over his shoulder. He whispered yet another prayer, one that would allow him to touch the god's omniscience.

"I need him," he pleaded. "Why won't you help me?"

The answer was a whisper only Malvag could hear. *You lack the skill.*

Malvag rocked back on his heels, stunned. That was it then. It was over. With only two of them remaining, the scroll couldn't be used. Malvag would have to wait fifty-seven years before the conditions would be right again—an eclipse wouldn't occur at midnight of the winter solstice until then.

"Abyss take him!" he howled. Rising to his feet, he strode toward the traitor and gave his body a savage kick. Then he turned away, his hands balled into fists.

As Malvag raged in silence, Valdar kneeled beside the traitor's body and removed the mask, revealing a male with a nose that canted to one side: a break, long since healed. He fingered the mask, spoke a prayer of detection, then nodded to himself.

"What are you doing?" Malvag snarled.

Valdar nodded at the body. "Looking for something that will tell us who he really was." He pointed at the mask. "That's no holy symbol, even though it does seem to hold a trapped soul." He tilted his head, musing aloud. "Is he one of Lolth's minions, perhaps?"

"What does it matter?" Malvag screamed. "He's ruined everything. Without Urz, we can't proceed. High magic requires a minimum of three clerics, working together, to cast it."

Valdar shrugged. He continued searching the body. His sleeves quickly became dark with blood. He pulled two rings out of a blood-wet shirt pocket and held them on the palm of one hand, poking at them with a fingertip. "Do we need three clerics to open the gate?" he asked slowly. "Or three *spellcasters?*"

"What does it matter?" Malvag paced back and forth, trying to contain his fury. Unlike Valdar, he hadn't bothered to heal his wounds yet. His skin still felt hot and tight where the lightning bolts had struck his chest. It hurt to breathe.

Valdar jingled the rings together on his palm. "These are master and slave rings," he said. He pointed at the body. "And he's a wizard. If it's three *spellcasters* that are needed to conjure the gate, we can force him to participate." He jingled the rings again. "With these."

Malvag halted abruptly and whirled in place. His eyes met Valdar's. "Slave rings," he whispered.

Valdar's eyes crinkled in a smile. "Yes."

Malvag glanced at the drift disc where the prayer scroll waited. What Valdar was suggesting would be extremely difficult. Malvag would have to control the wizard's mouth while speaking the words of the prayer himself at the same time, but perhaps it could be done. He'd read the spell in silence enough times that he could have recited it aloud from rote.

"Raise him from the dead," he told Valdar. "The instant the gate is open, and Vhaeraun passes through it, we'll kill the infiltrator. Permanently, this time."

Qilué grasped the edges of her scrying font, staring down with intense concentration into the holy water that filled it. The wide alabaster bowl glowed like a harvest moon from the light that filled the room in which it stood—the silver fire that poured off Qilué's body like light from a torch. Qilué was barely aware of Jasmir, the moon elf priestess standing behind her. The scenes unfolding in the holy water that served as her window on the world beyond were deeply disturbing.

"Send another six priestesses and two score warriors to the Chondalwood," Qilué commanded.

The pale-skinned Jasmir whispered a sending, relaying the command. She was fully dressed for battle in leather armor whose spiral patterns matched the tattoos on her forearms. Her long white hair was in two braids, tightly bound into a bun at the back of her neck.

Qilué stared into the scrying bowl, tense with anticipation. It was focused on the shrine in the Chondalwood, far to the southeast. There Eilistraee's priestesses fought a bloody battle against driders who had boiled up out of the Underdark without warning—just as they had in the Misty Forest last month. Even as Qilué watched, a drider knocked a priestess to the ground with a web and landed on her back, opening its spider fangs wide to bite.

Qilué stabbed a finger down into the water and sang a note that was strident and shrill. The drider shook his head, disoriented. As it did, a sword came dancing through the air, slashing the monster nearly in half. A priestess ran into view behind it, and the sword returned to her hand. She kneeled on the snow-covered ground beside the first and tore away the webs, freeing her companion.

Qilué didn't wait to see the rest. She shifted the scrying's focus to a frozen pool of water not far from the shrine itself. A moment later, its icy cap exploded upward as a priestess burst out of the shallow pool from below, sword in hand, the first of the reinforcements Qilué had just ordered to the Chondalwood.

Qilué shifted the scrying rapidly from one location to the next, checking the other shrines. From the Moonwood to the Shaar, more than half of Eilistraee's holdings were under attack. Priestesses, backed up by lay worshipers, fought pitched battles at the Dancing Dell, in the Velarswood, the Gray Forest, the Yuirwood, the Forest of Shadows. Each battle involved creatures of the Underdark not normally found on the surface: driders, fighting with webs, poison, and spells; neogi—creatures that looked like spiders with wormlike necks and tiny heads filled with needle-like teeth—using their magic to dominate those who fought them, turning Eilistraee's faithful against each other; and chitines, fighting with four weapons at once, one in each spindly hand. Through it all, spellgaunts dashed here and there, gobbling up magic. Their presence alone hinted at the authors of the highly coordinated attacks—the Selvetargtlin, yet none of Selvetarm's clerics could be seen.

Where were they?

"A dozen priestesses and a score of warriors to the Gray Forest," Qilué ordered.

Jasmir dutifully repeated the order. She closed her eyes a moment, listening, then relayed the reply. "Iljrene can only send nine priestesses. That's the last of them, unless you want to start sending the Protectors."

Qilué shook her head. "Keep the Protectors here," she ordered. "We'll need them if the Promenade is attacked." And that it would be attacked, she was certain. It was too glaring an omission, but when? And from which direction? Two Protectors, each armed with a singing sword, stood guard at every possible entrance, including the portals. Qilué scried each of those pairs of priestesses in turn, but all was quiet.

She frowned. Should she really hold her best fighters back? A singing sword would certainly help tip the balance in any of the battles she'd just observed.

A faint tapping sounded at the room's only door. Qilué looked up as Jasmir hurried to answer it. Iljrene would have used a sending to contact her, and a lay worshiper had no business here, not now. Before Qilué could caution Jasmir, the priestess opened the door.

A feather zipped inside the room and fell at Qilué's feet. Its silver spine was bent nearly double and its vanes were split and fouled with spiderwebs and dust, but Qilué recognized it at once as the magical token she'd given Jub. She'd been wondering where the spy had gotten to, and by the looks of the webs sticking to the quill, he'd had some bad luck.

Turning from her font, she bent and picked up the quill. She straightened the spine then touched the nib to the floor. She spoke the command word and watched as the quill slowly and laboriously scratched out its message in glowing silver letters on the dark stone floor.

SELV. CLERICS ATTACKED THE MOON WOOD WITH CHITTENS. BUT IT WAS JUST A FAINT.

Yes, Qilué thought. She'd guessed that already. The attacks took place after the moon had risen, ensuring that the Moonspring could be used to send reinforcements.

THEYR GOING TO ATTACK THE PROMENAD, TOO. 66 OF THEM. NOT SURE WHEN.

She nodded. Just as she'd suspected. But why sixty-six? And why hadn't the attack come yet?

THEYR IN DOLBLUND, LIKE YOU THOT. I THINK THEY KILT A LOLTH PREESTIS THERE.

Qilué knew who her enemies were. Most likely the exiles, the renegade Selvetargtlin who were tossed out of Eryndlyn for "blaspheming" by worshiping Selvetarm in his own right instead of as a servant of Lolth.

The quill was still scratching out its message. THEYR GOING TO JUMP ON THE TEMPLE, it wrote. Then it fell to the floor.

Qilué stared down at the quill a moment more, as if willing it to continue, but the message was at an end. And it hadn't told her much. The feint Jub warned of was already in progress, and though Qilué had been forced to send troops to reinforce the shrines, she'd held back her Protectors—two dozen of her best warriors—to maintain the Promenade's defenses. The Protectors would be outnumbered three to one if sixty-six Selvetargtlin did attack, but each Protector was armed with a singing sword and powerful spells. Whatever direction the Selvetargtlin chose to attack from, they would be forced to fight their way in through a choke point that would allow Eilistraee's faithful to concentrate their spells. One or two Selvetargtlin might be able to battle their way inside the temple, but they wouldn't last long.

Qilué turned her attention back to the scrying bowl. Shifting her awareness, she concentrated on Jub. For the past few days, her attempts to scry him had been blocked by something. She'd assumed that to be Daurgothoth's doing. The undead black dragon didn't appreciate anyone peering into his lair, but as the marketplace of the abandoned city came into focus, she began to wonder. Why, suddenly, was she able to scry the dracolich's lair? Had some protection suddenly fallen—or been removed?

The water in the bowl rippled then stilled. Qilué looked down on a severed head. Jub's. It lay next to a foul-looking pool. What remained of the head was deeply pitted by acid.

"Eilistraee have mercy," Qilué whispered.

Jasmir peered over her shoulder. "Who was it?"

"A lay worshiper. One who deserved better than that." There was no time to mourn Jub's loss. Later, when the crisis was at an end, she would send a priestess to recover what was left of Jub so that he could be resurrected.

She pulled her focus back, noting the vast, empty cavern. The Selvetargtlin seemed to have abandoned it, but where were they?

"Send a warning to each pair of Protectors," she ordered. "An attack by the Selvetargtlin is imminent."

"Lady, I have already told Iljrene about the warning," Jasmir said, nodding down at the message on the floor. Her leaf-green eyes gleamed in anticipation of the battle to come. One slender hand rested on the hilt of her sword. Ready. "Iljrene is relaying it to the Protectors even as we speak." She glanced down at the floor, her brow furrowed. " 'Jump on the temple,' " she repeated. "Does that mean the attack will come from above?"

Qilué shook her head, only half listening. The tide had finally turned in the Moonwood. The priestesses there were beating the chitines back. The battle in the Gray Forest was the same. The extra priestesses Qilué had sent had managed to drive the neogi off, and in the Shaar . . .

Something moved against her hip. Her bag bulged and thrashed, as if an animal were trapped inside it and was trying to claw its way out. Qilué swore and tore the bag from her belt, tossing it to the ground. She started to sing a spell, but before she could complete it, a knife blade pierced the bag from within. The bag suddenly ruptured in a tremendous explosion of magical energy that sent the water in the font sloshing back and forth.

Her ears still ringing from the blast, Qilué stared down at the spot where the magical bag had lain. The gem it had held was gone. No, not gone. Qilué kneeled and touched what felt like sharp-edged but sticky grit—the crumbled remains of the gem. Her fingers came away dotted with tiny flecks of blood.

All at once, she understood what form of conjuration magic the gem had contained. It had been the focus of a teleportation spell. Whichever Selvetargtlin it had been attuned to had teleported into Qilué's magical pouch, realized something was wrong, and tried to cut his way free. Piercing the bag from within had ruptured the extradimensional space it enfolded—with disastrous results. The

Selvetargtlin was as good as disintegrated.

This was the jump Jub had warned her about. And the cleric who'd teleported into her pouch wasn't the only one making it. Sixty-five others would have made similar jumps. To other gems, like the one Thaleste had found. Gems that must have been somewhere close to the spot where Thaleste and Cavatina had encountered the aranea—the Selvetargtlin who had carried the gems inside the Promenade and died to protect that secret.

"Lady Qilué," Jasmir asked, her voice tight with worry. "What is it?"

Qilué didn't bother to answer. She whirled and grasped the sides of her scrying bowl. Images flashed through the holy water one after another: the caverns south of the Sargauth River, and the rooms in the ceiling above them. Nothing. All were empty.

"Where?" she said, her voice tight. "Where?"

Jasmir tensed. Her lips parted to frame a question. Closed again.

Qilué shifted her attention to the Promenade itself. She made a sweep of the Hall of Healing, the priestess's cavern, the main living quarters, the garrison and armory, the Cavern of Song and the Moonspring. Nothing. Nothing.

All empty. No Selvetargtlin.

Where were they? One of the connecting corridors, perhaps?

As a corridor near the river came into view, Qilué saw what she'd been dreading. Selvetargtlin dropped into that corridor through a hole in the ceiling and fanning out into adjoining passages like an erupting hill of termites. Half a dozen of them, led by a judicator, had already reached the Cavern of Song. As Qilué watched, horrified, they toppled the statue, revealing the hidden staircase that led to the Pit of Ghaunadaur and disappeared down it. The Selvetargtlin immediately behind the judicator carried an iron rod, its perfectly spherical head so dark that looking at it was like staring down the deepest well. Qilué recognized it at once as a rod of cancellation, its disjunctive magic capable of snuffing out even the most powerful of magic, including the seals on Ghaunadaur's Pit.

Silver fire flared around Qilué as she used her magic to shout a warning to all of the Protectors at once.

The Selvetargtlin have breached the southern corridors of the Promenade. All Protectors converge there at once! Iljrene, to me, at the Mound.

Jasmir gasped. She, too, had heard the warning. Metal rasped as she drew her sword from its scabbard.

"Ready, Lady!" she cried.

Qilué touched the other priestess's shoulder. "I need you here. Continue scrying. Direct the Protectors to where they're most needed."

Jasmir's shoulders slumped, but only for a moment. "Yes, Lady," she said briskly, turning her attention to the font.

Qilué meanwhile sang a prayer that would send her to Eilistraee's mound.

As Jasmir and the scrying room vanished from sight, Qilué wondered who would arrive at the Mound first. She and Iljrene—or the judicator and his Selvetargtlin.

Still invisible, Cavatina bounded with long, graceful strides toward the spot where Selvetarm stood. As she moved into position, she squinted to protect her eyes from the strands of web that blew on the breeze. They turned invisible as they stuck to her, but she could feel them fluttering like streamers behind her as she loped toward the spot where the demigod stood. She didn't waste time trying to circle around behind Selvetarm. The demigod, even though his eyes were in the front of his drow head, could see in all directions at once, like a spider.

She had cast every protective spell on herself that she could, but offensive prayers would be useless. A mortal might succumb to her spells but never a demigod. With his vast powers, Selvetarm would instantly negate anything she threw at him. Worse yet, his fighting prowess was without equal. Selvetarm would see through any feint she might try, would read the slightest shift of her posture or grip and anticipate any thrust long before it came. His own moves would be impossibly swift and smooth, and no wonder. He had been birthed, after all, by Zandilar the Dancer, an elf deity equal in grace to Eilistraee herself.

Cavatina was certain she would get only one swing. All she could do was trust in the power of the Crescent Blade and in the strength of her own sword arm.

She should have been terrified as she made her way toward the hulking demigod. She wasn't. Instead, a thrill of anticipation shivered through her. This was it—the penultimate hunt. She had devoted her life to that moment, honing her body until it was a weapon. Her senses were keen, her muscles taut. Even if she died, it would be glorious.

"Eilistraee," she breathed. "Help me strike true."

The words were mouthed only. No sound came from her lips. Her voice was muffled, like her footsteps, by the magical silence she had cloaked herself in, but it gave her satisfaction to speak. Cavatina wanted to believe that Eilistraee was watching, listening. "Dark Maiden," she continued as she drew closer to the god—she was only a few paces away, and Selvetarm loomed over her, his head a black blot, haloed by the eight blood-red stars, "I do this for you."

And for yourself.

The whisper from the sword momentarily distracted her. She missed her footing and her boot splashed down into a pool of stagnant water. No sound came from the resulting splash, but when Cavatina looked behind her,

264 • Lisa Smedman

she saw ripples spreading across the surface of the pond and tiny spiders scurrying away from the lapping water. If Selvetarm glanced down, he would see it.

The demigod's attention, however, was firmly fixed on the distant horizon.

Cavatina landed beside one of his legs, next to a claw that had been driven into solid rock as if the ground were putty. Gripping the Crescent Blade in both sweating palms, she squatted then launched herself into the air. As she rose to the level of the god's bulbous body, the arc of her jump carrying her over the bent leg and past the point where abdomen and cephalothorax met, she saw movement out of the corner of her eye. She glanced in the direction in which Selvetarm stared and saw a pyramid of metal, red starlight glinting off the eight legs that held it aloft.

Lolth's fortress. And it was headed their way.

Something else scuttled across the ground, between the fortress and the spot where Selvetarm stood. Cavatina at first thought it was a spider, but then realized it was a drow, scurrying along on hands and feet. As the drow rose and broke into an upright run, Cavatina recognized the eight legs that drummed against the ribcage like restless fingers. Halisstra. She pointed at Selvetarm and shouted.

"There!" she cried, her voice wild and cracking. "There!"

Halisstra had just proved herself a traitor, but no matter. Even as she shouted, Cavatina's feet touched down on the demigod's shoulder. She landed between black, bristling hairs, feet braced in a position that put her at right angles to the neck. The Crescent Blade was already above Cavatina's head, raised for a killing blow. The blade swept down, screaming as it descended.

Die, Selvetarm!

Selvetarm's head twisted around. His body shifted, throwing Cavatina off balance. She tried to correct her swing as she staggered backward, but it was no use. The Crescent Blade slashed into Selvetarm's face, instead of his neck. It bit deep, turning his mouth into a bloody grimace and sending a tooth flying, but the wound healed in an instant.

Glaring with eyes that each had eight blood-red points for pupils, the demigod shouted a single word.

The word was unclean, twisted, foul, woven from the fell energies of the Demonweb Pits, and sticky as old sin. It slammed into Cavatina, sending her tumbling from the god's shoulder. She hurtled toward the ground, blinded, deafened, paralyzed. The Crescent Blade fell from her numbed fingers, and an instant later she slammed into the ground face-first. Her cheek cracked against rock with a force that sent stars exploding through her head, and her breastplate caved in like tin punched by a fist. Pain flared in her chest: broken ribs. Blood dribbled from her split lips. A fresh, sharp pain erupted in her back as something splattered onto it: acid dripping from the mace in Selvetarm's hand. Cavatina couldn't move, couldn't see, couldn't hear, but she could feel the ground below her tremble as the demigod's massive claws punched into it. Selvetarm was turning. She could feel him looming over her, staring down at her. His presence was a blot of evil, his shadow a pall that nearly suffocated her. A lesser, more rhythmic tremble in the ground was the iron fortress, drawing nearer.

Lolth, coming to gloat at what her Champion had just done.

Eilistraee, Cavatina pleaded silently, wishing she had the strength to speak the words aloud. *Save me*. Her fingers twitched slightly as she struggled against the paralysis that gripped her, tried to grope for the Crescent Blade. Spiders scuttled across her hand, a mocking tickle on her skin. *Send me . . . a miracle*.

A finger prodded her in the side. A muffled voice, speaking urgent words, came from above—Halisstra, also coming to gloat, taking a closer look at what her betrayal had wrought.

Her vision dimly returning, Cavatina could see the blurry figure of Halisstra, who gingerly lifted the Crescent Blade. She held the hilt between finger and thumb, as if picking up a disgusting piece of offal.

"Abyss take you," Cavatina groaned, finding her voice at last.

Above her, Selvetarm gave a booming laugh. "It already has," he hissed.

Then he lowered his head to deliver the killing bite.

CHAPTER TWELVE

So this is it, Q'arlynd thought.

He floated in a featureless gray void that was neither hot nor cold, damp nor dry, soft nor hard. It just . . . was. Endless. Eternal. Still.

"I'm dead."

The sound of his own voice startled him. So did something that materialized, suddenly, under his feet. Ground. Gray as the void he'd been floating in, and smooth as glass, it neither gave under his feet nor resisted them. Like the void, it just . . . was. Something to stand on.

He could sense his arms and hands, even though he couldn't see or feel them. He moved them against himself, trying to touch his body. They passed through where it should have been. It was like trying to grasp smoke, except that his hands, too, were made of smoke, gray smoke, without a ripple or an end point.

His body was gone. He *was* dead.

Panic nibbled at the corners of his mind like a ravenous mouse. If he allowed it to, it would consume his awareness, what little of him there was. He steeled himself, forcing himself to remain calm. He was dead, but he still *was*. His soul continued.

His mind, such as it was, held the logical facts that explained his situation. His soul, like those of all who died, had entered the Fugue Plain. He could see it starting to take shape around him. There: a distant horizon, a line of gray on gray. And there: the jagged spires of the City of Judgment. Restless forms—mere dots, from a vast distance—surrounded its soaring walls. Demons herded the shapeless gray forms before them, driving unclaimed souls into the city where they would be consumed.

Other presences hovered closer to Q'arlynd—the souls of others who, like him, had just died.

"Can you hear me?" he asked as one drifted by.

It made no reply, just sighed past him, leaving a sheen of tears in its wake.

Q'arlynd realized then that he was slowly drifting toward the city. The thought sent a chill through him, colder than any he had ever experienced. He looked wildly around for the moonbeam that Rowaan had described, listened intently for a scrap of song.

Nothing.

"Eilistraee!" he called. "Aren't you going to claim me? I took the sword oath. I'm one of yours, now. You're my patron deity!"

No reply.

Something prickled where Q'arlynd's forehead should have been. If he'd still had a body, he would have sworn it was nervous sweat. He drifted more rapidly toward the city, and already it was half again as close as it had been.

"Eilistraee!" he screamed.

Nothing.

The city walls drew nearer. He could make out individual demons, scourges in hand, arms raising and snapping forward as they drove the dead. Souls wailed as they streamed in through the gates of the City of Judgment.

Q'arlynd shuddered—a ripple that passed through him like an icy wind. Panic once again crowded in at his awareness. He looked wildly around for the servant of a deity—any deity—to claim him.

"Mystra?" he pleaded, desperately hoping that Qilué's other deity might have taken notice of him, even though he hadn't pledged himself to her.

Nothing.

The walls had drawn close enough that he could see the individual stones in them writhing against one another. Each stone a soul trapped for all eternity.

A demon turned to stare at him. It crooked a cracked red finger, beckoning him closer.

"Lolth?" Q'arlynd croaked, desperate. "Anyone?"

Come.

Q'arlynd whirled. He saw nothing, but the voice came again. A male voice.

Return. To the land of the living. Will you return?

He recognized the voice: Malvag's. Probably the last person he wanted to call him back from the dead, but anything was better than—

"*Yes!*" Q'arlynd screamed.

The Fugue Plain disappeared.

His body returned.

He lay on his back on a sharp, lumpy surface, his arms underneath him. His fingers were tightly pinched. It felt as though they'd been lashed together with wire. His throat ached and there was a faint taste of blood in his mouth. He spat.

Then he saw the two Nightshadows staring down at

him, framed by the crystal-lined cavern, and realized where he was and what had just happened. He tried to hurl himself erect but only managed to flop over on his side.

"Y—"

His mouth froze. He was aware of a second presence inside his skull, the mind of the Nightshadow closest to him—Malvag, the cleric he had nearly killed with lightning bolts. Malvag's eyes gleamed as he stared mercilessly down at Q'arlynd. The Nightshadow shook his head slightly and raised a warning finger. Q'arlynd's master ring was on it. Malvag spoke directly to him, mind to mind.

No spells, slave.

Get out! Q'arlynd raged. The second ring must have been on one of his own fingers under the wire that bound them. *Get out of my mind!*

Malvag's eyes crinkled in a mirthless smile. *Get up.*

When Q'arlynd hesitated, Malvag's awareness shoved its rough way into his torso and legs. Q'arlynd found himself drawing his legs up against his body. He rolled onto his stomach, rose to his knees, and finally lurched to his feet. He swayed and nearly fell before Malvag found his balance. All the while, Q'arlynd raged. He was a *Melarn*, damn it. His House might be gone, but he was still of noble birth. Never—*never*—a slave.

He might as well have been shouting against a howling wind. Malvag's laughter reverberated through his mind, overpowering Q'arlynd's inner voice.

This, Q'arlynd realized suddenly, is what Flinderspeld must have felt like.

But Flinderspeld was a deep gnome, a race that was used to such indignities and bore them stoically. Q'arlynd was a *drow*. He was forced to suffer Malvag's torments for the time being, but dark anger smoldered in his heart. The Nightshadow was going to pay for every moment. Pay dearly.

I doubt it, Malvag said.

Q'arlynd fell silent, not wanting to give the other male any further satisfaction.

Malvag walked him over to the drift disc that held the prayer scroll, and made him stand there, rigid. The second Nightshadow—the slender one—cocked an eyebrow and watched Q'arlynd, his eyes bright with fascination.

"Welcome back," he said. "I guess, since you're here, Eilistraee had no use for you." He laughed. "But we do."

Malvag pointed at the body of the Nightshadow Q'arlynd had turned to stone and spoke to the other male. "Get his mask."

Q'arlynd tried to swallow but couldn't. They knew. Everything. That he was Eilistraee's—or would have been, if only the goddess had bothered to claim him, yet they'd brought him back from the dead. Something he'd *agreed* to. What had he been thinking?

Malvag must have been listening, but he made no comment.

Hands appeared from behind Q'arlynd, holding the dead man's mask. It was tied into place around Q'arlynd's face. Unlike the polymorphed gem, which had prickled Q'arlynd's skin with a heat like raw pepper, this mask felt smooth as silk, but it was restless, shivering, afraid.

Valdar moved back around where Q'arlynd could see it. A smirk was in his eye. He pointed at the mask. "One of your friends from the Misty Forest. Go on—kiss her good-bye."

Q'arlynd blinked—a concession Malvag allowed him. That was *Rowaan's* soul in there. Q'arlynd felt a momentary twinge of guilt. He pushed it aside. Rowaan had been pleasant to him, but she'd been soft, he told himself. Weak. Gullible. If she'd fought harder against the assassin. . . .

It was her own fault—but even so, Q'arlynd felt terrible.

The mask grew even colder against his face. A shudder passed through it. Then it stilled. It felt . . . calm, somehow. Resigned.

That was odd.

As Valdar took his place beside Malvag, the higher-ranking cleric raised his right hand. Darkfire burst into flaming life across Malvag's skin. "We will begin."

Malvag and Valdar bowed their heads, eyes firmly fixed on the prayer scroll. Q'arlynd's head, too, was wrenched down. As Malvag's darkfire-limned finger descended toward the scroll, Q'arlynd could feel the cleric peering out through his eyes. His mouth opened. He drew breath and began to read.

Q'arlynd listened as his mouth, under Malvag's control, spoke the words of the prayer scroll in time with the other two males. As they read it aloud, each word on the silver sheet flared bright then faded, that portion of the scroll crumbling in its wake. Streaks of silver spiraled up and off the page to circle above their heads. Slowly, the circle grew. It widened, and wisps of something gray and flowing, like vapor, streamed out of their masks. The souls, Q'arlynd realized. They were fueling the magic the clerics were weaving. The crystals in the cavern hummed softly, throbbing in time with the words the three males spoke.

As the spell slowly unfolded, Q'arlynd's apprehension gave way to a growing sense of wonder. Malvag's presence was a brutal fist inside his mind, but Q'arlynd could sense Valdar's awareness as well. Both men were excited, tense with anticipation. They were doing it! Working high magic. No drow had ever done it before, not since the time of the *ssri Tel'Quessir*, the original dark elves.

Their voices droned on.

Yes, Malvag whispered into Q'arlynd's mind. *Together. We can. Do it.*

Together, Q'arlynd whispered back. He saw it all, the brotherhood that was possible. His link with the two males next to him was as real as the connection between skin, muscle, and bone. Separate, the three were dead matter. Together, they moved, breathed and lived—and worked magic. Q'arlynd could see the Weave itself, could glimpse the hitherto invisible connections that linked the drow one to another. All his life, he'd been yearning for something like that, a bond, a true bond. He had thought he'd find it in his Ched Nasad once Halisstra was on the throne. He'd planned to forge it link by link by seeking out loyal Melarn who would work together to build and sustain their noble House, but he had come to see the futility of that dream. Only someone who had experienced the linking of minds, the oneness that was high magic, could understand what the word "bond" truly meant. Q'arlynd understood Malvag—understood what had driven the other male's nearly century-long quest to find that scroll. And Valdar, a male Q'arlynd had only just met—a male who had slashed open Q'arlynd's throat, just a short time ago—was like a brother to him. Valdar had grown up in Menzoberranzan, under the lash of Lolth's priestesses, before House Jaelre fled that city, but he had lived to be master of his own destiny.

Master.

Q'arlynd could no longer feel his fingers—the wire wrapped around them was that tight—but he no longer cared. He managed to glance off to the side to meet Malvag's eye. The Nightshadow inclined his head in the slightest of acknowledging nods, his own eyes still locked on the scroll.

Vhaeraun, Malvag managed, while somehow still reading the scroll himself and forcing Q'arlynd's mouth to do the same. The other male's self-control was amazing. *Vhaeraun offers power. Seize it.*

For just an instant, Qilué's face flashed through Q'arlynd's mind. The geas she'd cast on him took hold, and a near-crippling pain lanced through him, but a heartbeat later it was gone, that strand of the Weave slashed like a flimsy ribbon by Vhaeraun's sword. Q'arlynd saw eyes hanging in the air before him, eyes that were blue with delight.

Malvag and Valdar paused, drawing breath. Q'arlynd did the same. Together they watched as the three souls that had been swirling within the circle, like smoke, were suddenly sucked into its center in a flash of white light. That surprised Malvag—through his connection with the other male, Q'arlynd could sense it. Malvag had expected the souls to simply vanish, consumed by the gate, but then again, Malvag thought with a mental shrug, perhaps that was the way the spell was supposed to unfold.

They were almost done, and very little of the scroll remained. The link between Q'arlynd and the other two males was so strong that he could feel his heart beating in unison with theirs. The crystals, too, pulsed in time.

Ready? Malvag signed.

Valdar nodded.

So did Q'arlynd.

Q'arlynd started as he realized that Malvag had relinquished his hold, and Q'arlynd's body was his own again. His surprise deepened as he realized the Nightshadow was giving him a choice. Q'arlynd could ruin the spell then and there by the simple act of shutting his mouth, or he could continue reading the scroll.

A choice. Something Qilué had offered him in name only. She'd been all too quick to back up that "choice" with a geas.

The gate loomed over Q'arlynd's head, large enough, and clear enough, that he could see a dark forest within it one moment, a bleak and rocky pit the next. Eilistraee's domain, and Vhaeraun's, almost connected. Only two lines of the scroll remained.

Q'arlynd locked his eyes on it and continued to read, his voice in perfect cadence with the two Nightshadows.

"The bridge between realms is Woven," he intoned. "The crossing is complete."

As they completed the conjuration, the gate, fully

formed, opened. Their masks flew from their faces and fluttered into it. A figure sprang through in their wake and vanished into the woods of Eilistraee's domain: Vhaeraun, swords in hand, eyes gleaming gold above his black mask.

Hungry for Eilistraee's blood.

Qilué landed in the cavern that was all that remained of the former temple of Ghaunadaur and looked around. The cavern was empty. The floor was a jagged field of rubble that had tumbled from the walls and ceiling to seal the deep pit into which Ghaunadaur's avatar had been driven. Smaller fragments of stone hung above the floor, suspended by magic to form a mosaic-like statue of Eilistraee—the seal that capped the pit. The statue was posed as if dancing, balanced with the toes of one foot touching the floor and the other leg extended, arms sweeping up and out. Almost imperceptibly, the mosaic-statue's pose was changing as the magic that animated the chips of stone went through a cycle that began anew with each full moon.

With a thought, Qilué shifted her awareness, enabling herself to see magic. The statue's aura was a pure, sweet silver. The seal was untouched.

An instant later, Iljrene materialized beside her. The tiny battle-mistress was fully armored, a singing sword in her hand. Her doll-like face was set in a frown of determination as she took up a position beside Qilué. She held a hand to one delicately pointed ear and listened. "Here they come."

Qilué, intent upon her prayer, merely nodded. She pointed a finger at the cavern's only intact entrance, the foot of the staircase that twisted down from above. The sound of running footsteps echoed down it.

Jasmir, Qilué sent. *Have any of our priestesses entered the staircase that leads to the Pit?*

None, came the confident reply.

Qilué smiled. Silver fire danced in her hair and on her skin. Focusing it within her hand, she let it build to a ravening white flame. The silver fire roared, filling the cavern with a sudden, brilliant light. As the first of the Selvetargtlin burst into the room, Qilué hurled it at him. A streak of silver shot toward the base of the stairs, rippling the rubble floor below it as it went. It smashed into Selvetarm's cleric, burning away his scarlet robe and turning the chain link lining below it red-hot. Qilué expected him to collapse, incinerated, but the Selvetarm kept coming, his flesh burning from his bones even as he ran. He charged the two priestesses, screaming his god's name and hurling a spell. Three of the stones that made up the floor between Qilué and Iljrene grew in the blink of an eye, becoming monstrous spiders that loomed over the two priestesses.

Spiders of stone.

He collapsed, dead.

Iljrene was busy with a prayer of her own as a second Selvetargtlin burst into the cavern, also screaming his deity's name. Singing loudly, her magical sword whistling over her head in whirling counterpoint, Iljrene flicked her hand in his direction then squeezed. The second cleric's eyes widened, and he took a staggering step, another—and his body collapsed into a bloody ball of mangled flesh pierced by protruding splinters of bone. Carried forward by the aborted charge, what remained of the cleric fell to the ground, a wet, bloody ball inside a suddenly loose robe.

It had been a brutal spell, but there was no time for Qilué to mourn yet another drow soul forever beyond redemption. The stone spiders were on them, even as four more Selvetargtlin came running into the room screaming their god's name. The second of the four held a black rod in his hand—the rod capable of breaking the seal on the Pit.

The judicator who had been leading them was nowhere to be seen.

The stone spiders were quite large—their backs level with Qilué's head—but they were a distraction only. The one closest to Qilué clamped its fangs onto her shoulder, piercing her flesh and driving in venom, but Mystra's silver fire instantly purged the poison from Qilué's body and sealed the wound. With a flick of her fingers—never once taking her eyes off the clerics who were charging toward her—Qilué touched the creature and spoke an arcane word, instantly slaying it. She stepped out from beneath the spider as it toppled over, letting it crash to the floor behind her. A snap of her fingers summoned her singing sword to her hand. She swept it over her head and listened to its gleeful song.

Iljrene, meanwhile, had dealt equally swiftly with the other two spiders. Her song of prayer caused them to soften then sag. They melted away into mud that seeped into the rubble on the floor. The battle-mistress stepped forward beside Qilué, braced as her superior was to meet the four clerics who rushed toward them.

One of the Selvetargtlin chanted a prayer that caused his body to sprout dozens of blades, turning him into a living weapon as he ran. Another shouted a garbled prayer at Iljrene, but the battle-mistress whirled her sword around her head, and the magical confusion was dispelled.

Yet another of the Selvetargtlin shouted a prayer that caused a cloud of utter darkness, shot through with crackling white spiderwebs, to envelop Qilué. Flames raced along them as the web ignited. Qilué felt a brief flash of heat on her skin—heat that was absorbed by the scepter that hung from her belt. Silver fire flared around her and exploded, snuffing out the fire storm.

Then the clerics were on them, and they were fighting

hand to hand. Iljrene squared off with the cleric whose body was studded with blades. Qilué fought two of the others, swiftly dispatching one with a thrust that caught him in the throat and trading a flurry of blows with the other. All the while, she kept an eye on the cleric who held the rod—the only one who had not yet closed in battle. When he drew back his arm, she realized he was going to hurl it at the statue in an attempt to disrupt the seal—an act of desperation, surely, since the throw was a long one and might miss. Parrying the cleric who slashed savagely at her with his sword while screaming Selvetarm's name, Qilué waited for the throw. When the rod passed above her, Qilué would release Mystra's silver fire in yet another form—one that would temporarily disrupt the Weave, preventing the rod from functioning. The cleric whipped his hand over his head, threw . . .

Before Qilué could release Mystra's fire, the rod had passed her—so quickly that Qilué could not even bring her head up to watch the black streak that it became. The cleric who threw the rod also moved in a streak, across the room to a spot beside Iljrene. His sword somehow wound up in her stomach, its bloody point protruding from her back. The battle-mistress gasped, stricken with surprise and shock.

Qilué realized what had just happened. The Selvetargtlin had temporarily halted time.

The metal rod should have landed with a clatter behind Qilué, but she'd heard nothing. She whirled and saw a fifth Selvetargtlin—the missing judicator—standing next to the statue. The rod was in his right hand, which was still raised from catching it. His head was shaved except for a braid at the back of his head that whipped around as he whirled to smash the rod against the statue.

"No!" Qilué cried.

Silver fire flashed throughout the cavern, momentarily blinding even her. She heard a smash as the metal rod struck the statue then a pattering sound: chips of stone, flying away. As her vision cleared, she saw, to her relief, that the magic of the seal held. Though a gaping hole had been smashed in the middle of the statue, nearly cutting it in two, it refused to collapse. The void-black ball at the head of the mace had vanished, temporarily snuffed out by Qilué's silver fire.

The judicator snarled. The lines of glowing white that criss-crossed his skin in a web pattern flared as he cast the depleted rod to one side.

Iljrene, meanwhile, sagged away from the cleric who had just stabbed her. The other two closed in, swords raised to deliver killing blows. Qilué turned away from the judicator to hurl silver fire at them. The roaring, swirling cone of silver-white caught all three clerics, sending them reeling with robes and hair smoking. One immediately collapsed, dead. The battle-mistress, too, was caught by the edge of the blast, but it simply spun her around like a wind-blown leaf, leaving her unharmed.

Gasping her thanks, Iljrene slapped a hand over her wound and croaked out a prayer, healing herself.

Dealing with the other three clerics had given the judicator time to close with Qilué. His enormous two-handed sword swept down, and she barely had time to raise her own weapon to parry it. The singing sword wailed in a minor key as the judicator's weapon crashed against it, smashing it to one side. The judicator followed with a hilt-punch that sent Qilué staggering back. Her face burned where the spider-shaped guard of the judicator's weapon had struck.

She danced back, hurling herself out of range of his next blow. There was no time to cast a spell, no time to worry about Iljrene, who had plunged back into battle with the other two clerics, her sword singing furiously as she swung, parried, and swung. The judicator pressed Qilué with a flurry of blows, his eyes with their spider-shaped pupils glaring at her.

"Tonight," he announced in a funereal voice, "you all die, and Eilistraee with you."

Qilué fought back grimly, wondering if the Selvetargtlin were in league with Malvag. The fact that their attack had come on the night the Nightshadows planned to work their magic wasn't lost on her. Selvetarm was, after all, Vhaeraun's bastard child.

The judicator's sword whistled uncomfortably close to Qilué's face, reminding her of more immediate concerns. She returned with a slash that glanced off the judicator's breastplate, scoring a groove in the adamantine across the holy symbol that was embossed there. Her opponent paid the blow no heed. Unlike the other two clerics, who kept shouting their god's name, the judicator fought in silence, and not only with that massive sword. As his blade met Qilué's and they strained against each other, face to face, his mouth parted, revealing fangs. He bit her hand then whirled away, the blood-clotted end of his braid smacking her in the face for good measure.

Qilué, thanks to Mystra, was immune to poison. At her whisper, the punctures in her hand healed. Out of the corner of her eye, she saw Iljrene cut the legs out from under one of the Selvetargtlin she fought, then sweep her sword around, bloody and still singing, in an upward arc that caught the other just above the ear, slicing off the top of his head.

Qilué whispered a prayer of thanks. The seal held, the six lesser Selvetargtlin were down—only the judicator remained. He was outnumbered two to one, but the rod, she saw, was no longer disrupted. Its round head had reformed, a black blot against the floor where it lay. Thankfully, it was at least half a dozen paces from the statue.

She pressed home her attack, driving the judicator before her until his back was against the statue. Iljrene angled in from his left, her own sword singing a deadly counterpoint. Letting the battle-mistress take the initiative, Qilué stepped back, intending to cast a spell, but the judicator was unbelievably quick. His weapon flashed up, then down, catching Iljrene at the point where shoulder and neck met. It cleaved through her tiny body in an instant, cutting her torso in half from neck to hip. Blood rushed from the two halves as the pieces fell and sprayed into the judicator's face, momentarily blinding him.

Qilué screamed and hurled spellfire at him, hoping to kill him before he blinked the blood clear, but though the silver-white blaze made the judicator reel back, he remained on his feet. As the two halves of Iljrene's body crumbled in on themselves, reduced in an instant to a boiling mass of black spiders, he touched the point of his sword to it. The mass bulged upward, questing for the blade, then sizzled, dissolving into it. He held it there, his spider-pupiled eyes stared at Qilué. A challenge.

Furious, she hurled herself at him, knocking his sword away from the heap of tiny spiders. The sight of Iljrene, her steadfast companion and battle-mistress, reduced to a profane mass of spiders, rattled her badly. She swung wildly at the judicator, fury boiling out of her in waves of silver fire.

It was her undoing. The judicator's sword swept down, slicing off her right arm at the elbow. Qilué reeled back, nearly fainting from the pain. Her singing sword clattered to the floor with a wail, then fell mute. Qilué stumbled over a loose chunk of stone and nearly fell. Her left hand tightly clasped the stump of her right arm, and blood sprayed through clenched fingers.

"Eilistraee!" she gasped. "Heal me."

She felt flesh knit together under her fingertips, saw the spray of blood stop as the arm began to regenerate.

The judicator, however, gave her no quarter. He rushed Qilué, his terrible sword raised for a killing blow, and Qilué had nothing to parry it with. She could escape with just a word, but that would mean abandoning the Pit and its seal, and the rod was once again fully active.

"Mystra!" Qilué cried, desperately calling forth spellfire.

The judicator's sword swept down, even as moon-white fire blazed through the cavern.

Selvetarm loomed above Cavatina. Another dollop of acid dripped from his mace and landed with a bubbling hiss on the stone next to her, splattering and burning her skin. The god's mouth was enormous—wide as a doorway. Hot, foul-smelling breath washed over her as his fangs clamped hold of her torso. She gasped as she was lifted from the ground, the spiderwebs that had accumulated on her body hanging from her like limp hair. Dangling upside down from Selvetarm's fangs—which had yet to puncture her breastplate and deliver a final, poisoned bite—she saw the blur that was the traitor Halisstra sway through her field of view.

Halisstra waved one of her twisted, elongated arms. Behind her, a black dot that was the iron fortress of Lolth thundered toward them on its eight metal legs, its feet clashing like gongs against the ground.

Halisstra shouted something. Garbled words, to Cavatina's ears, which still rang from the unholy word Selvetarm had used to fell her. Cavatina could see more clearly. That flash of silver was the Crescent Blade, being waved overhead by a triumphant Halisstra, a creature that had only pretended to be seeking redemption, a demonic thing of Lolth.

Halisstra shouted something. It sounded like the word "slay."

Cavatina nearly laughed. Selvetarm needed no urging. In another moment his fangs would clamp down on her, and poison would be driven into her paralyzed body.

Selvetarm's fangs continued to squeeze Cavatina's chest, preventing her from drawing breath. Strangely, they had yet to pierce her armor. A miracle, that—but not exactly the one she'd pleaded with her goddess for. Even magically enhanced armor would only hold back the fangs of a demigod for so long.

Halisstra waved the sword over her head, still shouting—but at the same time looking nervously over her shoulder at the approaching fortress.

"Slay it!"

Selvetarm shifted his grip, still trying to bear down on Cavatina with his fangs. He'd yet to raise his head fully; Cavatina swung back and forth, just over Halisstra's head.

Cavatina realized what Halisstra was shouting. Not "slay," but "take." She held the sword by its point, blood dripping from her hand where she gripped the blade, offering the hilt to Cavatina.

Realizing that, Cavatina nearly cried. With an effort that took every bit of her will, she forced a numb arm to move. Leaden fingers spread. As she swung past Halisstra, she seized the hilt of the sword.

Selvetarm straightened, and Cavatina nearly dropped the sword. Slowly, with intense concentration, she forced her other hand to also close around the hilt. She closed her eyes, whispering a prayer with numbed lips . . .

And she could move again.

Selvetarm's eyes widened.

Now! the sword howled.

Twisting in Selvetarm's grip, she bent the upper half of her body forward, toward the god's head. At the same time, she swung the Crescent Blade.

"Eilistraee!" she screamed. "Do not fail me!"

The Crescent Blade flashed toward Selvetarm's neck, glinting red in the eerie light of the eight stars clustered above.

Selvetarm's eyes widened.

The breeze that blew incessantly across the Demonweb Pits stilled.

Spiders halted in mid-scurry as the blade bit into flesh—and cut clean through it, in a spray of dark blood.

The neck was severed.

The head fell, at last releasing Cavatina.

"Eilistraee be praised!" Cavatina cried, exultant. "Selvetarm is dead!"

She twisted in mid-air, halting her fall with her magical boots. The demigod's head slammed into the ground and shattered into bloody pieces, his body belatedly crumpling to a heap beside it. Cavatina threw back her head and laughed, tears streaming from her eyes. She'd done it! Slain Selvetarm.

Killed a demigod.

It felt incredible—a greater thrill than any she'd ever experienced. She raised the Crescent Blade above her head, triumph surging through her. For just an instant, her body flared with the moon-bright white of Eilistraee's holy moonfire. On the ground below, spiders scurried away in terror, seeking shadows.

This, Cavatina exulted wildly, must be what Qilué feels each time she calls on Mystra's silver fire.

It was incredible. Indescribable. Glorious.

Yes, the sword whispered. *This is what it feels like to be a god.*

The words startled Cavatina, brought her back to the here and now, reminding her that she was in the Demonweb Pits. Lolth's domain. She saw the Spider Queen's fortress hurtling toward her at an impossible speed, hastened to fury by the flare of moonlight that was Eilistraee's sign.

Cavatina gripped the Crescent Blade firmly then decided against testing her luck a second time. Killing one deity had taken a miracle. Trying to kill a second would be demanding too much, especially if that god was Lolth, fully cognizant of what had just happened and protected within her fortress of iron.

Cavatina looked around. Halisstra was nowhere to be seen. Had she already escaped through the portal? Cavatina hoped so. She realized now that she'd been wrong about Halisstra. Even someone twisted into an evil caricature of her former self could, it seemed, be redeemed.

"Halisstra!" Cavatina shouted. The wind was rising, and spiderwebs snagged at the edges of her open mouth.

There was no reply.

Lolth's fortress drew nearer. Halisstra or no, Cavatina had to leave.

Shaking her head at the sheer wonder of what she'd just done, she sprinted for the portal and leaped into it.

Dhairn cried out in triumph as he brought his blade down in a killing blow. The light pouring from the priestess was blinding him, but he would cleave her in two, even with his eyes closed.

"Selvetarm!" he shouted.

Victory was his! The Promenade was his!

The blade struck the priestess's forehead—and crumbled in his hands. Instead of solid steel, Dhairn held nothing but a blade-thin line of spiders. The creatures scattered as though they'd burst from an egg sac when they met the priestess's forehead and showered like black soot onto her shoulders. Dhairn gaped at them then flexed a right hand that was empty for the first time in more than a century. He raised it, staring at it in disbelief. His sword? *Gone?*

"Selvetarm?" he whispered.

He felt nothing. Only . . . emptiness.

The priestess bent, scooping up her weapon with her off hand. Dhairn ducked instinctively as silver flashed within a hair's breadth of his face. He danced backward, weaving to avoid her sword. Something had happened to his weapon, something inexplicable, but he still had his spells. He raised a hand to cast one—and blinked in surprise at his skin, which had turned a clear, solid black.

The white lines—Selvetarm's holy web—were gone.

The priestess's sword flashed down. Too late, he jerked his hand back. The blade bit into it midway between the fingers, splitting the hand lengthwise. He howled in anguish—then turned the howl into a shout. "Selvetarm!" he cried, trying to summon up the battle fury that would carry him past the pain, but the cry rang hollow in his ears.

He would not faint from the pain. He could not. Forcing his body into a spin, he whirled, whipping the priestess's face with his braid. At the same time he furiously whispered a prayer. He thrust his wounded hand out, reaching for Selvetarm, but no healing came.

Worried, he tried another spell—one that would cover his body in venomous blades, turning it into a living weapon. Ducking and weaving all the while to avoid the priestess's furious but not quite coordinated slashes, he cried his deity's name.

"Selvetarm!" he shouted. "Make me your weapon!"

Nothing happened. The demigod refused to answer.

Nervous sweat prickled Dhairn's skin. Something had happened. Something terrible. Had Selvetarm turned his back on Dhairn and his followers—abandoned those who sought to worship Selvetarm as a deity unto himself? Had *Lolth* ordered her Champion to do it?

What . . . was . . . *wrong?*

Utterly unnerved by the sudden absence of his deity, Dhairn backed away from the high priestess, who pursued him with fury in her eyes. Behind him, he heard another of Eilistraee's priestesses hurrying down the stairs, shouting something about the Selvetargtlin being defeated.

He only realized how close to the exit he was when her blade skewered his back. He stared, uncomprehending, at the sword point that had mysteriously emerged from his chest. As the cavern began to vanish into a gray mist, he croaked out one final plea.

"Selvetarm," he gasped through lips suddenly gone ice-cold. "I commend . . . my soul . . . to . . . "

But the demigod was no longer there to claim it.

CHAPTER THIRTEEN

Malvag reeled as the gate closed with a thunderclap that rattled the crystals in the cavern. It was several moments before the ringing in his ears subsided. When it did, he turned to Valdar and Q'arlynd, his body quivering with excitement. "Vhaeraun be praised! We did it!"

The slender Valdar wove back and forth where he stood, exhausted. Q'arlynd looked equally drained, his face an ashen gray. Both males nodded weakly.

The wizard turned and lifted his bound hands. "If you wouldn't mind. . . . "

Malvag hesitated—but only for a heartbeat. Old habits. In the moment of communion their spellcasting had provided, he'd glimpsed Q'arlynd's soul. The wizard wasn't going to turn on him.

Malvag stepped forward and untwisted the wire, releasing the wizard's hands. Then, for good measure, he slipped the slave ring off Q'arlynd's finger and took the master ring off his own. He tucked both rings into a pocket of the wizard's *piwafwi*.

Q'arlynd's fingers were gray and puffy, with deep indentations from the wires. He rubbed them stiffly together, wincing.

"I can't feel them," he said. He extended his hands slightly. "Could you—"

"Of course."

Malvag took the wizard's hands in his own and whispered a prayer. He felt the rush of power that was the Masked Lord's reply course through him as the fingers healed. When he released Q'arlynd's hands, silver-white motes danced upon the wizard's dark skin.

Malvag jerked his hands away. What *was* that?

Valdar stared at the wizard's hands. "Moonfire," he gasped.

The wizard, sensing the knife-edge in Valdar's tone, held his hands perfectly still as the sparkles slowly faded.

"If this *is* moonfire, it's not my doing," he said. "I'm a wizard, not a cleric."

Valdar stood just to Malvag's left, tense as a cocked wristbow. He glanced sidelong at Malvag. One hand was behind his back, where the wizard wouldn't see it.

Has he turned back to Eilistraee? Should we kill him?

Malvag took a deep breath. By Vhaeraun's holy mask, was it really going to unravel so quickly? "No," he said aloud. He turned. "You touched his mind, Valdar, and you know he's no traitor. He's one of us, now."

"There's a simple explanation for what just happened, Valdar," the wizard added. "We just opened a gate to Eilistraee's domain. There's certain to be lingering effects from that."

Valdar relaxed. Slightly.

The wizard smiled and spread his hands. "What's more, I could easily have teleported away just now—which would be the logical thing for me to do, if I *was* a traitor—but I'm still here with you." He shook his head, an exasperated expression on his face. "We just cast *high magic*. Drow, casting high magic, perhaps for the first time. Do you honestly think I'd turn my back on that kind of power?"

Malvag answered, before Valdar could, "Of course not."

Abruptly, the wizard turned and strode to where Urz lay. He touched the fallen Nightshadow and spoke a word. "There. I've just turned Urz back to flesh and blood. He is, however, unconscious. Looks like he took a nasty hit on the head when he fell—but I'm sure your healing magic can deal with it." His lips quirked slightly. "Just be sure, when he wakes up again, to let him know I'm on your side. No hard feelings, I hope."

Malvag nodded at Urz's body. "Do it," he told Valdar.

The pink-eyed drow cocked an eyebrow. "Very well." He kneeled beside Urz, put a hand to the dead male's chest, and began a prayer. His other hand was raised to his mouth, hiding it.

Malvag, watching, reflected on how odd it was to see a fellow cleric casting magic bare-faced. He resisted the urge to cover his own mouth with a hand. Even in the company of other clerics, going without a mask felt like being naked.

A low groan came from Urz's lips as Valdar completed his prayer. Urz stirred—and his body was limned in a haze of silver-white light. Valdar reeled.

"More moonfire! The wizard *is* doing it!" He raised his wrist-crossbow.

"Valdar, stop!" Malvag shouted.

The crossbow thrummed. The wizard jumped back but not quickly enough. The bolt sliced a bright red line through the flesh of his cheek. He returned Valdar's attack with a flick of his fingers, sending a bolt of magical energy back at the slender male. Valdar grunted as it bored into his chest and began a prayer, one that would summon enough darkfire to incinerate the wizard on the spot.

"Stop it!" Malvag cried. "Both of you. There's got to be another explanation!"

Urz sat up, holding his head. The silver-white glow had faded from his skin.

Darkfire raced from Valdar's hand across the cavern, but instead of burning the wizard, it swirled harmlessly around him. Within the dark flames were flecks of white. More moonfire. Valdar gaped at his hand, a shocked look on his face.

"How did he . . . ?"

Malvag stared at Q'arlynd and Valdar, worried. That *was* moonfire, *within* the darkfire—something that should have been impossible. And it hadn't just appeared when the spell had struck Q'arlynd, it had come straight out of Valdar's hand at the same time the darkfire did. Had opening a gate to Eilistraee's domain somehow corrupted their magic?

The wizard had halted in mid-casting, magical energy crackling between his extended fingers. His lips parted, as if he were about to say something. Then he seemed to think better of it. Slowly, the magic faded from his hand.

Urz gave a howl of anguish, startling all three of them. "He's dead," he cried. Eyes closed, mouth a grimace, he pounded with his hands against the crystal floor until his hands were bloody. "He's . . . *dead!*"

"Who's dead, you idiot?" Valdar snapped.

Malvag, however, didn't have to ask. A chill slid into his gut like an ice-cold blade. He said a hurried prayer, seeking communion with his god.

"Vhaeraun?" he whispered, his mouth dry. "Are you there?"

Valdar stared at him, tense.

Urz continued to wail and beat the floor. "Dead!"

The answer came to Malvag at last, a strangely double-timbered voice, as if a male and female were speaking at once.

"I . . . am . . . here," it said, the voices blending into one by the final word.

Malvag felt his face pale. His legs no longer seemed willing to support him. He sagged, felt the points of crystals jab into his knees as the enormity of what he'd just done came down on his shoulders like a collapsing tunnel. That was Eilistraee who'd just spoken, not Vhaeraun. Instead of the Masked Lord absorbing her power into himself, the opposite had happened. Eilistraee was posing as Vhaeraun and answering his clerics' prayers, tainting them with moonfire, and there was only one way she could have done that.

By killing Vhaeraun.

Malvag tried to convey that to Valdar, but all that would come out was a dry croak. "Eilistraee . . . No use . . . Vhaeraun is . . . gone. We can't . . ." He gestured weakly at Q'arlynd. They could hurl all the spells they liked at the wizard, but he was under Eilistraee's protection—even if he didn't know it himself.

Valdar glanced at the still-howling Urz, then back at Malvag. "No!" he raged. The slender cleric summoned darkfire to his hand a second time—darkfire tainted with moonfire—then hurled it. Not at the cleric, as Malvag had expected, but at Malvag himself.

It sloughed off Malvag, just as it had the wizard. As the dark glare of it died down, Malvag noticed that Q'arlynd was gone. He must have teleported away. So had Valdar, it seemed, after hurling the darkfire. The cavern was empty save for Urz, who, by the sound of his hoarse cries, had been driven mad by the loss of his patron deity.

Everything Malvag had worked for was in ruin. The bond, strong as adamantine, that had allowed drow to cast high magic was broken. Not that it mattered anymore.

"It's true," Malvag said, answering a Valdar who was already gone. "Vhaeraun's dead. We helped Eilistraee kill him. I was a fool to think she wouldn't prevail within her own domain." He lowered his face into his hands—a mask that no longer held any power. Then his hands fell away. One brushed against the dagger that was sheathed at his hip.

Slowly, he drew it. He stared at the poison-coated blade for several long moments. There was no longer any god to claim his soul when it entered the Fugue Plain, but that suited Malvag just fine. The torments of the demons would be nothing compared to what he felt at that moment, and if Eilistraee tried to claim him, he'd spit in her face.

Touching the blade to his arm, he drew it across his wrist.

Q'arlynd staggered through the Promenade looking for a priestess, the mask that had been his disguise clenched in one hand. He was in the cavern where the lay worshipers lived—buildings reared up around him on either side—but the passageways between them were empty. Where *was* everyone? His face throbbed and his limbs felt leaden: the wristbow bolt's poison doing its work. He wasn't going to last much longer without a healing spell, but if he died there, Qilué would surely see to it that he was restored to life. She'd have to, in order to learn what had just happened.

Unless, of course, she simply had a necromancer speak with his corpse.

No, Q'arlynd thought. Qilué wouldn't do that. She'd want details—descriptive nuances the stagnant mind of a corpse couldn't provide, and even if she used a truth spell on him, Q'arlynd had the perfect excuse for his actions.

He slipped a finger into his pocket, touching the master-

and-slave rings. He could honestly say that he'd been *forced* to open the gate despite the geas, that he'd had no choice in the matter. Well, not until the end—but the high priestess didn't need to know that. If Q'arlynd chose his words carefully, she never would.

He slipped on something and scrabbled at the stone wall next to him for support. Looking down, he saw a smear of blood on the cavern floor. Someone had been hurt there. Badly hurt. Pushing himself away from the wall, he staggered on, still searching for a priestess. Where had they all gotten to?

Qilué would be angry, of course, when she learned that three priestess' souls had been consumed by the spell, but Q'arlynd had managed to bring back the "mask" that held the body and soul of the fourth priestess. That had to count for something, and opening the gate had all worked out for the best in the end. Vhaeraun was dead. If Q'arlynd chose his words carefully, perhaps the high priestess might reward him yet, and what a reward it would be. Qilué was, after all, a Chosen of Mystra. She must know spells that would rival high magic. If he could become her cons . . . her . . .

His mind stumbled. He couldn't find the word, nor could he see very well. The edges of his vision blurred and his stomach felt as if he'd swallowed hot coals. He tripped over something. A body. Looking down, he saw a blood-red robe and braided white hair. For one terrifying moment, he thought it was the judicator who had confronted him in the woods. Then he realized it was another Selvetargtlin. A very dead Selvetargtlin.

A pace or two away lay a scatter of bodies: males and females of various races, their bodies hacked to pieces. Lay worshipers from the temple. Kneeling beside them was a priestess. Q'arlynd fell to his knees beside her, shook her shoulder.

"Lady," he gasped. "Help me. Poison . . ."

The priestess fell over on her side, revealing a chest soaked in blood. She, too, was dead. Q'arlynd fumbled at the pendant that hung around her neck: the goddess's holy dagger. If he prayed, then maybe, just maybe . . .

He gasped as a hand touched his shoulder. He tried to turn but only managed to fall over onto his side next to the bodies. He stared up from the cold stone floor at a terrifying sight: an armored female, hair and body shrouded in sticky webs, holding in one hand a sword that fairly hummed with latent magic. One of Lolth's priestesses, he was certain. Weakly, he laughed. Of all the stupid luck. . . .

The female laid her sword on the ground as she knelt beside him. Cold metal touched Q'arlynd's cheek—a silver dagger. Why slit his throat? That was too quick, too clean for one of Lolth's priestesses. A prolonged flaying with a whip of fangs was more their style. Q'arlynd tried not to grimace as the pain roiling in his gut intensified. He wouldn't give her the pleasure of seeing how much he was already suffering.

"Eilistraee," he whispered, half-heartedly. As if the goddess would answer him.

"Eilistraee," the female above him repeated. "Heal him. Drive the poison from his body."

The pain was gone.

Q'arlynd sat up. He touched a hand to his healed cheek and shivered. He'd been within a heartbeat or two of death, but he was healthy again. Strong. He saw that it was a priestess of Eilistraee who had come to his aid, but not one he recognized. He stood, and bowed his thanks.

"Lady. To whom do I owe my rescue?"

"Cavatina Xarann," she said. "Darksong Knight."

Q'arlynd got a good look at her weapon as she picked it up again. The sword looked ancient and had a script running down its curved blade. Q'arlynd moved his fingers behind his back and pretended to cough, hiding a one-word divination. The blade's aura—visible only to him—nearly made him wince. That weapon was power-ful. An artifact. With a start, he realized it must be the Crescent Blade.

The priestess glanced around. "What happened here?"

Q'arlynd shrugged. "I know as little as you do. I only just teleported here."

Coal-red eyes bored into his. "Only a priestess can do that."

Q'arlynd waved a hand, trying to appear nonchalant. "I know, I know—the wards and all that. Qilué herself taught me the song that would bypass them."

She lifted her sword slightly, a subtle threat. "Sing it now."

Q'arlynd did.

The Crescent Blade lowered. "It seems you are what you say. My apologies. I didn't ask your name. What is it?"

He bowed a second time. "Q'arlynd Melarn."

The priestess's eyes widened. No doubt she too had known his sister.

"I have to go," Q'arlynd said in an apologetic voice. "Urgent tidings to report. I must find Qilué." He lifted the mask. "I have to return this to her."

"Wait." Cavatina's voice cracked like a whip. Her hand gripped his shoulder tightly, and it fairly stank of spider. She stared off into the distance for a moment, then back at him, a hint of surprise in her expression. "It seems Qilué *is* expecting you. She's on her way here now."

Her brief touch had left strands of web on his *piwafwi*. Q'arlynd brushed them from his shoulder.

Cavatina smiled, and wiped away some of the web that clung to her own narrow face. She still kept an eye on him, but she'd relaxed slightly after talking to Qilué. "The offal of the Demonweb Pits," she said, pride in her voice. She grinned. "But I'd gladly wade through the stuff a second time, if the reward were the same."

She expected him to ask the question. He obliged her. "What reward?"

Her eyes glittered as she hefted the Crescent Blade. "I killed a deity today."

She waited, obviously expecting awe. She was proud. As vain as any matron mother. Q'arlynd couldn't resist.

"So did I," he said with a smile.

Cavatina listened as Halisstra's brother made his report. It was an incredible tale, if it could be believed. Three drow males, working high magic? Opening a gate that bridged the realms of Vhaeraun and Eilistraee?

She waited impatiently, anxious to make her own report. The wizard's tale was incredible and almost certainly untrue. It was woven, through and through, with boastfulness masquerading as modesty. He was acting as if he expected some sort of reward from Qilué. The high priestess, however, either missed his cues—or ignored them.

Which was just fine with Cavatina. She didn't like Q'arlynd. He was too deliberately self-depreciating in that smarmy way that males fresh out of the Underdark had.

She stood slightly behind Q'arlynd, where he wouldn't see her silent communication to Qilué: *Remember the prophecy. His sister proved herself loyal. This must be the Melarn who will betray us.*

Qilué gave her a brief glance. *Q'arlynd's betrayal is already past*, she sent back, communicating mind to mind. *I expected as much from him. He will be redeemed yet.*

The wizard was still talking. "It would appear, Lady Qilué, that Eilistraee has triumphed over the Masked Lord. Moments after the gate closed again, the magic of his clerics became corrupted. The spells they tried to cast were laced through and through with Eilistraee's moonfire. Upon seeing that and realizing it must be significant, I came back immediately to make my report." He held up the mask. "And to return this to you."

Q'arlynd looked at the high priestess expectantly, but Qilué merely nodded and took the mask from the wizard's hand. Her expression remained noncommittal.

The wizard's shoulders slumped slightly. Then they straightened again. "Lady," he said, bowing once more. "I must say that it gives me great joy that, despite my blunders—despite being *killed* and later *enslaved*—I was still able to serve Eilistraee." He bowed again and added, "and to serve you."

The silence stretched.

A short distance away, lay worshipers cleared away the dead. The bodies of the faithful were gently laid onto blankets and carried away, but the corpse of the Selvetargtlin was left where it lay. Later, it would be burned.

Qilué touched the wizard's shoulder, bidding him to rise. Aloud, she said, "Go to the Hall of Healing, Q'arlynd. Someone is waiting there for you."

The wizard hid his disappointment well. He gave Qilué a puzzled look. "Who, Lady?"

"Rowaan."

The wizard's eyes widened. "But . . . her soul . . ."

"Flew straight to Eilistraee's domain, with those of the other two priestesses, as the gate opened. By the grace of our goddess, it was not consumed."

Halisstra's brother gave a relieved sigh. Perhaps he wasn't as unfeeling as he seemed, or perhaps he was just a good liar.

"Lady," he exclaimed. "I can't tell you how glad I am to hear that." He bowed again then hurried away.

Cavatina watched Q'arlynd make his way out of the cavern then turned to Qilué. "What a tale that one told!"

The high priestess nodded. "It's true. If not every word, at least in its essence."

That made Cavatina blink. "It is? Vhaeraun's really dead?"

Another nod. "I expected that Q'arlynd might fail in the task I assigned him, despite the geas I placed on him. Shortly after I sent him on his way, I entered communion with Eilistraee and warned her that Vhaeraun was poised to enter Svartalfheim. The goddess was prepared. Vhaeraun might be a master of stealth, but when the advantage of surprise was taken away from him, Eilistraee's prowess with the sword prevailed."

Cavatina let out a long, slow breath. "So it is true. Two deities, dead. In one day." She gave a fierce grin, unable to contain her pride. "And one of them by my hand."

Qilué glanced at the Crescent Blade. "Your sword served you well."

A voice whispered into Cavatina's mind from the sword. *Dead*, it chuckled. *By my blade.*

Cavatina bristled. It had been her victory. The sword was just . . . a sword. Not only was she irritated at it, but also at Qilué's almost blasé response to the news. Chosen of Mystra Qilué might be, but surely she would acknowledge that Cavatina had just slain a *demigod*. Instead the high priestess just seemed . . . weary.

"You already knew that Selvetarm was dead?" Cavatina asked.

Qilué gestured at the dead cleric who lay a few steps away. "The Selvetargtlin nearly prevailed. They came within a blade's edge of taking the Promenade then all at once, their prayers failed them."

Cavatina noted Qilué's bloodstained armor and her freshly healed scars, one of which completely encircled her right arm. It *had* been a close thing. That realization sent a chill through Cavatina, one that tempered the thrill of her triumph.

"Make your report," Qilué said. "Tell me everything that happened." She clapped a hand on Cavatina's web-shrouded shoulder. "And . . . well done. I owe you my life."

That was better. Taking a deep breath, Cavatina related her tale, ending with her escape from the Demonweb Pits.

"I'm worried about Halisstra," she concluded. "There was no sign of her on the other side of the portal. I would have returned to the Demonweb Pits to search for her, but I didn't want to run the risk of the Crescent Blade falling into Lolth's hands. I came here instead, as quickly as I could."

"You did the right thing," Qilué answered. "I'll scry for Halisstra. We'll find her."

The conviction in the high priestess's voice reassured Cavatina, who felt terrible about leaving Halisstra behind. Not only had the former priestess redeemed herself, she'd tipped the balance between victory and defeat. Halisstra deserved better than to fall into Lolth's hands.

"If Halisstra is still within the Demonweb Pits, I'd like to lead the mission to rescue her," Cavatina said.

"Of course." Qilué pointed at the Crescent Blade. "But that will remain here, in the Promenade, where I can keep an eye on it. Until the time comes to challenge Lolth herself, it will be safer in my keeping."

Yes, the blade whispered. It quivered, slightly, leaning toward the high priestess.

Cavatina realized that Qilué was holding out her hand, but she didn't want to give up the sword, not just then. The Crescent Blade felt so right in her grip. Her fingers seemed loath to uncurl from it.

She glanced down at the singing sword sheathed at her hip, a holy weapon of the Promenade. It was a magical weapon, yet it seemed like a novice's wooden practice sword in comparison to the Crescent Blade—in comparison to a weapon forged for slaying deities.

A sudden realization came to her then. No matter what she hunted next—no matter how powerful a demon she faced—the kill would be anticlimactic. The knowledge filled her with great sorrow.

Gently, Qilué pried Cavatina's fingers from the hilt of the Crescent Blade.

Cavatina at last let go. Strangely, her feelings were mixed. Parting with the weapon was, in some small way, a relief—and a disappointment. It would be Qilué wielding the Crescent Blade when the time came to take Lolth's life. Cavatina told herself that the high priestess was the logical choice—a Chosen of Eilistraee—but the thought made Cavatina's entire body ache. Just for a moment, she understood the envy that unredeemed females could feel for one another. For just an instant, she *hated* Qilué.

She stuffed the emotion down, smothering it, and asked, "What now?"

The high priestess glanced wearily around. Her eye settled on two lay worshipers—a drow female and a human male—who were removing the dead. They bowed in acknowledgement before lifting a body onto a blanket and carrying it away.

"We raise our dead and rebuild our defenses," Qilué answered. "The Promenade must be protected, and we must maintain our vigilance against the enemies that remain: Ghaunadaur and Kiaransalee." She cradled the Crescent Blade against her chest. "And we must prepare for the ultimate battle against Lolth."

Again, Cavatina felt a stab of jealousy. She stared down at the dead Selvetargtlin. "With their god dead, I suppose the Selvetargtlin will turn to Lolth—but what of the Nightshadows?"

"Eilistraee has stolen Vhaeraun's portfolio. His clerics draw their power from her, now—though," and Qilué smiled, "it may take some of them a while to realize it. When they do, they'll be ripe for redemption and ready to be drawn into the dance. Our priestesses have a lot of work ahead of them."

Cavatina gave the high priestess a sharp glance. "*Nightshadows* will join our ranks?"

Qilué nodded. "They already have, albeit unwittingly." She stared across the cavern, as if trying to see into the future. "There is a lot to be worked out yet."

Cavatina shook her head. If ever there was an understatement, that was it. The thought of clerics of Vhaeraun defiling Eilistraee's holy shrines with their black masks and evil deeds—especially after all that had just happened —made her flesh crawl.

"I don't like it," Cavatina said. Blunt, as usual, but it had to be said. "The Nightshadows are cowards and thieves and traitors, slinking about like—"

"People change. Even Lolth's vassals have been redeemed, including, it would seem, the Lady Penitent."

"What if they refuse redemption? What if they reject Eilistraee and choose *Lolth* instead? What you've done may have just made our enemy stronger."

Qilué's eyes blazed. "What I've done was necessary and inevitable."

"Even so, it worries me," Cavatina continued. "I'm sure I don't need to remind you, Lady Qilué, of the sacred teachings. Just as Selvetarm was corrupted after he destroyed Zanassu and assumed the Spider Demon's divine power, so might our worshipers be, if we accept Vhaeraun's clerics into our ranks." She paused, suddenly realizing the ramifications. "So might Eilistraee be, if Vhaeraun's evil seeps into her—"

"Enough!" Qilué's voice was sharp. "It is done. Eilistraee has slain Vhaeraun. There is no going back from that now." Her eyes bored into Cavatina's. "Do you really think, Darksong Knight, that I had not considered this before sending Q'arlynd on his mission?"

Cavatina hung her head. "Of course not, Lady." But secretly she wondered. She didn't know Qilué well, but according to reputation, the high priestess wasn't one to display anger. Cavatina's blunt words must have disturbed her. Deeply.

Then again, Cavatina realized, perhaps Qilué had been offered no choice. The high priestess must have realized what a gamble Q'arlynd's mission had been and known that it would likely fail. Without Qilué's warning, Vhaeraun might have surprised Eilistraee, even killed her. Cavatina tried to imagine Eilistraee's holy light, corrupted with creeping tendrils of shadow—to imagine herself, slowly corrupted—and shuddered.

"For now," Qilué said, "I would like you to keep secret everything Q'arlynd just told us. I would prefer the Nightshadows to think that Vhaeraun's destruction was entirely of our own devising. Remember, good will come of this. The Nightshadows will be brought into the light. Willingly or not, the *drow* will be brought into the light."

Cavatina bowed her head. "Praise Eilistraee," she murmured.

Her heart, however, remained shadowed with doubt.

As Q'arlynd walked away he ground his teeth at the high priestess's lack of response. He'd expected gratitude from Qilué, even praise, but she hadn't thrown him so much as the smallest scrap. Instead she'd listened to his report as if it bored her then dismissed him like a commoner. Obviously, whatever boastful report the Darksong Knight was making was more important to the high priestess.

He walked slowly, concentrating on his spell and not bothering to keep up with the two lay worshipers he was supposed to be following. He had no interest, really, in talking to Rowaan. He'd rather listen in on Cavatina and Qilué.

He walked through the temple, pretending to be on an

important errand and found himself on a bridge above the river. By then, he was already almost at the limit of the spell's range. No matter, he thought. The report the high priestess hadn't wanted him to overhear was astonishing, but it was true—the death of the demigod Selvetarm, at Cavatina's hand. Still, it was of little more than passing interest to Q'arlynd. He'd learned everything he needed to . . .

Just a moment. What was that the Darksong Knight had just said? Had she really just uttered the name, "Halisstra"?

He jerked to a halt, listening intently.

She had.

Q'arlynd stood, utterly still, oblivious to the rush of the river below.

Halisstra. Alive.

She had been with the Darksong Knight in the Demonweb Pits when Selvetarm was slain. She'd come to Cavatina's aid when all seemed lost, but then Halisstra herself was lost, perhaps left behind in the Demonweb Pits. But—Qilué promised—Halisstra would be found again.

Elation surged through Q'arlynd. There, at last, was something he knew his way around, something he could work with. With Halisstra alive, House Melarn could be reforged. Halisstra would be its matron mother and Q'arlynd, her oh-so-obedient brother, would be the true power behind the throne. When the time was right, the pair of them would return to Ched Nasad and claim their rightful place as its ruling House. They would rebuild the city to its former glory. They would . . .

Q'arlynd's imaginings slammed back to earth again as he realized what he'd been overlooking. Halisstra was one of Eilistraee's faithful. If Q'arlynd did manage to talk her into returning to Ched Nasad, she'd probably insist on trying to "redeem" everyone she met. She'd last about as long as fungus wine in the tankard of a thirsty orc. Then Q'arlynd would be on his own once more—and in an even worse position than before. He'd wind up reviled. Hunted. Maybe even dead.

He ended his spell. He'd heard enough.

He stood, drumming his fingers on the rail of the bridge and thought, What now?

A pair of lay worshipers hurried across the bridge, carrying a body toward the temple. Q'arlynd pressed himself against the rail, letting them pass. In the distance, faintly, he could hear the voices that emanated from the Cavern of Song; they rose and fell in rhythmic waves. The song was sweet, seductive—but it didn't call to Q'arlynd. Not any more.

From below came the sound of rushing water. One hand on the smooth rail of the bridge, Q'arlynd contemplated the cold, dark river that came from some distant place, briefly intersected Eilistraee's temple, then moved on.

Perhaps it was time for him to move on, too, but where? And to what?

He sighed, wishing the brief bond he'd experienced with Malvag and Valdar in the darkstone cavern had lasted just a little longer, but it was gone—dead as Vhaeraun, thanks to Eilistraee.

Q'arlynd shook his head, still not able to believe it—a bond like that, forged with clerics of Vhaeraun, the most mistrustful, backstabbing males on all of Toril. Who would have ever thought . . .

A realization came to Q'arlynd then, sudden as a bolt of darkfire. If such a bond could be forged with *Nightshadows*, then surely it could also be created among wizards. Perhaps Q'arlynd could build his own power base around a cabal of like-minded males. He knew where he was most likely to recruit them—in Sshamath, a city ruled by a conclave of wizards rather than by a council of matron mothers—by *male* wizards, rather than female priestesses.

Excited, he pondered the possibilities. During his brief link with Malvag's mind, he'd learned that the ruined temple the Nightshadow had found, far to the south, had held only the one scroll. That ruin was a dead end, but other artifacts from the time of the Crown Wars might also have survived in other locations. It would simply be a matter of finding them. Q'arlynd already had an idea where he might start—in the ruins of Talthalaran, in ancient Miyeritar. More specifically, within that ruined tower he'd spotted while hiking across the High Moor with Leliana and Rowaan, the tower whose floor pattern had reminded him of the Arcane Conservatory in Ched Nasad.

The tower had been a wizards' school. He was certain of it.

For the first time in many years, a smile crinkled Q'arlynd's eyes. He didn't *need* Halisstra. Or House Melarn. He'd find his own road to power—one that wouldn't force him to walk in the shadow of a female.

He climbed onto the rail of the bridge then stepped off into space. A heartbeat before he struck the cold, dark surface of the river, he teleported away.

CODA

The dice fell to the *sava* board and bounced once, twice, then came to rest in the shadow of Lolth's Mother piece. Eilistraee leaned forward, her long white hair brushing the board as she strained to see which numbers were upright. Her lips parted as she read the numerals and a song of joy, pure and radiant as moonlight, burst from the swords that floated at her hips.

"Double ones!" she cried.

Lolth had been reclining on her dark throne, certain the die roll would fail, but she hurled herself forward. "No!" she hissed. "It can't be!" Tiny red spiders spilled from her lips and fell shuddering to the board.

Even as Lolth railed, the dice began to alter. Where once they had been black obsidian with a mere speck of moonlight at their heart, they became moonstone. The side that had been inscribed with a symbol for the numeral one—a multi-legged spider—bore the smooth circle of Eilistraee's moon. Deep within the translucent octahedrons, something black wriggled, struggling to be free: a tiny black spider.

Eilistraee basked in the moonlight that shone down through the branches above her head. "One throw," she cried, "and it came up in my favor, despite the odds." Her perfect lips quirked in a smile. "The impossible is possible, it seems. Corellon might forgive your betrayal yet, Mother."

Lolth's red eyes smoldered with fury. The hand that gripped the side of her throne tightened until it turned ashen gray. Beside her, Selvetarm hunkered down on his eight hairy legs, ready to rend Eilistraee at her command. His drow head twisted back and forth, and his sword and mace fairly quivered in his hands. His fangs were spread wide, dripping poison onto the board. A drop of it splattered the head of Lolth's Mother piece and dribbled down its obsidian-dark contours.

Lolth shot her champion a foul look. "Apologize!"

Selvetarm returned her glare for several moments in stony silence. At last words wrenched themselves out of his mouth, a dark mutter, barely audible. "Forgive me."

Eilistraee watched the exchange with a serenity born of certainty. She would win the game, or at least the current play. "A sacrifice," she said. "I claim it now." She moved her Priestess piece to the spot on the board Lolth had just left bare—the spot where Selvetarm's drider-shaped Warrior piece had stood before Lolth picked it up.

"Priestess takes Warrior," Eilistraee announced, nodding at the piece in Lolth's hand.

Lolth hissed. Rage as she might, she was bound by her oath.

Ao himself was watching.

The Spider Queen's fingers tightened around the Warrior piece. One of its spider legs cracked. As it did, Selvetarm stumbled and clutched at Lolth's throne. His drow head swiveled toward Lolth, eyes wide with loathing—and with fear.

"No," he shouted.

Two more of the piece's legs splintered. Two more of Selvetarm's legs gave way.

"I am your *Champion,*" the god roared, brandishing his weapons. "You can't—"

"I must." Lolth's eyes were as cold as extinguished coals. "And I will. Gladly. You are no champion of mine—*traitor.*"

A push of her thumb, and the neck of the piece snapped. The head fell.

Selvetarm gave a strangled gurgle as his own neck broke. His head fell with a heavy thud to the middle of the *sava* board, rattling the pieces. Several fell over then vanished.

Lolth dropped the broken Warrior piece to the floor, next to the corpse of her former Champion. She flicked away a piece of leg that clung to her web-sticky hand. A second gesture levitated Selvetarm's head from the board. The blood had drained from it and been subsumed into the World Tree. Selvetarm's face was slack and gray, his mouth drooling open.

"A trophy for your victory?" Lolth asked her daughter, her voice flat and emotionless.

Eilistraee shook her head, her lips tight. "How far you have fallen, Weaver. He was your grandchild."

Anger rekindled in Lolth's eyes at the use of her former title. She tossed Selvetarm's head behind her and settled back onto her throne. "You also have fallen, *daughter,*" she said in a soft voice. "You also, and it's my move."

Eilistraee nodded. The game would continue.

Continue, until only one player remained.

Casually, as if she cared nothing for what had just

happened, Lolth pushed a piece forward then eased into a reclining position once more. She used a Slave piece, shoved into a vulnerable position, where it was certain to be taken.

Eilistraee wasn't about to fall for that a second time. She studied the board carefully, wondering which of her hundreds of thousands of pieces to move next. The Priestess that had just forced Selvetarm's sacrifice? From where it stood, it could easily take out any of a dozen of Lolth's Slaves. No, she decided. That piece was too powerful to waste on any of those moves. She would save it for later.

She looked around for the Wizard that had taken Lolth's Slave a moment before, but that piece seemed to have temporarily removed itself from the board.

It would be back, Eilistraee was certain, but on which side?

No matter, there were thousands of other pieces equally as powerful.

Swords humming contentedly at her hips, Eilistraee studied the *sava* board, lost in contemplation. Her next move should be something unexpected, something devious enough to take Lolth completely off guard, an attack from behind—from the shadows.

As Eilistraee pondered, one of her hands strayed to a piece at the side of the board, the Slave her Wizard had captured—the Slave that was not a slave, nor even a cleric, but something more.

Vhaeraun. Her brother.

She sighed—a sound that was picked up by the swords at her hips and turned into a mournful dirge. As sigh turned into song, something fluttered against her face.

A square of black, so thin as to be almost invisible.

Vhaeraun's mask.

R.A. SALVATORE

The New York Times best-selling author and one of
fantasy's most powerful voices.

DRIZZT DO'URDEN

The renegade dark elf who's captured the imagination of a generation.

THE LEGEND OF DRIZZT

Updated editions of the FORGOTTEN REALMS classics finally in
their proper chronological order.

BOOK I
HOMELAND
Now available in paperback!

BOOK II
EXILE
Now available in paperback!

BOOK III
SOJOURN
Now available in paperback!

BOOK IV
THE CRYSTAL SHARD
Now available in paperback!

BOOK V
STREAMS OF SILVER
Coming in paperback, May 2007

BOOK VI
THE HALFLING'S GEM
Coming in paperback, August 2007

BOOK VII
THE LEGACY
Coming in paperback, April 2008

BOOK VIII
STARLESS NIGHT
Now available in deluxe
hardcover edition!

BOOK IX
SIEGE OF DARKNESS
Now available in deluxe
hardcover edition!

BOOK X
PASSAGE TO DAWN
Deluxe hardcover, March 2007

BOOK XI
THE SILENT BLADE
Deluxe hardcover, June 2007

BOOK XII
THE SPINE OF THE WORLD
Deluxe hardcover, December 2007

BOOK XIII
SEA OF SWORDS
Deluxe hardcover, March 2008

MARGARET WEIS
&
TRACY HICKMAN

The co-creators of the DRAGONLANCE® world return to the
epic tale that introduced Krynn to a generation of fans!

THE LOST CHRONICLES

VOLUME ONE
DRAGONS OF THE DWARVEN DEPTHS

As Tanis and Flint bargain for refuge in Thorbardin, Raistlin
and Caramon go to Neraka to search for one of the spellbooks of
Fistandantilus. The refugees in Thorbardin are trapped when the
draconian army marches, and Flint undertakes a quest to find the
Hammer of Kharas to free them all, while Sturm becomes a key of a
different sort.

VOLUME TWO
DRAGONS OF THE HIGHLORD SKIES

Dragon Highlord Ariakas assigns the recovery of the dragon orb taken to
Ice Wall to Kitiara Uth-Matar, who is rising up the ranks of both the dark
forces and of Ariakas's esteem. Finding the orb proves easy, but getting
it from Laurana proves more difficult. Difficult enough to attract the
attention of Lord Soth.

July 2007

VOLUME THREE
DRAGONS OF THE HOURGLASS MAGE

The wizard Raistlin Majere takes the black robes and travels to the
capital city of the evil empire, Neraka, to serve the Queen of Darkness.

July 2008

WELCOME TO THE

WORLD

Created by Keith Baker and developed by Bill Slavicsek and James Wyatt, EBERRON® is the latest setting designed for the DUNGEONS & DRAGONS® Roleplaying game, novels, comic books, and electronic games.

ANCIENT, WIDESPREAD MAGIC

Magic pervades the EBERRON world. Artificers create wonders of engineering and architecture. Wizards and sorcerers use their spells in war and peace. Magic also leaves its mark—the coveted dragonmark—on members of a gifted aristocracy. Some use their gifts to rule wisely and well, but too many rule with ruthless greed, seeking only to expand their own dominance.

INTRIGUE AND MYSTERY

A land ravaged by generations of war. Enemy nations that fought each other to a standstill over countless, bloody battlefields now turn to subtler methods of conflict. While nations scheme and merchants bicker, priceless secrets from the past lie buried and lost in the devastation, waiting to be tracked down by intrepid scholars and rediscovered by audacious adventurers.

SWASHBUCKLING ADVENTURE

The EBERRON setting is no place for the timid. Courage, strength, and quick thinking are needed to survive and prosper in this land of peril and high adventure.